The world can't get enough of J.D. Robb

'Whether she writes as J.D. Robb or under
her own name, I love Nora Roberts. She is a woman
who **just doesn't know how to tell a bad story** ... an
authentic page turner, with Eve Dallas – tough
as nails and still sexy as hell ...'
Stephen King

'J.D. Robb's novels are **can't-miss pleasures**'
Harlan Coben

'Gut-searing **emotional drama**'
David Baldacci

'Anchored by **terrific characters, sudden twists** that
spin the whole narrative on a dime, and a
thrills-to-chills ratio that will raise hairs of even
the most jaded reader, the J.D. Robb books are the
epitome of **great popular fiction**'
Dennis Lehane

'This is **sheer entertainment**, a souped-up version of
Agatha Christie for the new millennium'
Guardian

'Truly fine entertainment ... sure
to leave you **hungering for more**'
Publishers Weekly

J.D. ROBB

DEVOTED IN DEATH

piatkus

PIATKUS

First published in the United States in 2015 by G.P. Putnam's Sons,
a division of Penguin Group (USA) Inc.
First published in Great Britain in 2015 by Piatkus
This paperback edition published in 2016 by Piatkus

1 3 5 7 9 10 8 6 4 2

A CIP catalogue record for this book
is available from the British Library.

ISBN 978-0-349-40371-7

Printed and bound by CPI Group (UK) Ltd, Croydon, CR0 4YY

Papers used by Piatkus are from well-managed forests
and other responsible sources.

MIX
Paper from
responsible sources
FSC® C104740

Piatkus
An imprint of
Little, Brown Book Group
Carmelite House
50 Victoria Embankment
London EC4Y 0DZ

An Hachette UK Company
www.hachette.co.uk

www.piatkus.co.uk

Some dire misfortune to portend,
No enemy can match a friend.

JONATHAN SWIFT

But Evil saith to Good: My brother . . .

ALGERNON CHARLES SWINBURNE

1

The first kill was an accident. Mostly.

All they wanted was a nice car – it didn't even have to be fancy – because their piece of shit truck shuddered, wheezed, then let out a death rattle just after they'd crossed over into Arkansas from Oklahoma.

It was Ella-Loo's idea how to go about acquiring a new ride. She'd always had ideas, and dreams along with them, and since meeting Darryl she'd come to believe those dreams would come true.

She'd been working in a cowboy bar in Dry Creek, a place many who lived there considered the armpit of Oklahoma as it sat on a curve of a desolate spit of land where the Panhandle cornered into Texas. None of her dreams had come true; and, in fact, the man she'd been with – that son of a whore Cody Bates – had given her a black eye and split her lip open before he'd left her flat on the ground in front of the very bar she now worked.

She knew she was made for better things than serving up beer and rotgut whiskey to cowboys and the hard-eyed women who dogged them. She was made for better than pulling in extra giving blow jobs or quick bangs in the bathroom stall or the cab of a pickup to men with beer breath and no ambitions beyond the next ride.

The better walked into Rope 'N Ride one fateful night in the person of Darryl Roy James. She knew, the minute she laid eyes on him.

He was the one. What had been missing. What she needed to complete all she was and could be.

Later she would tell him how when he came through the fake saloon doors, light – red-gold as a sunset – had glowed around him. His bright hair had shimmered with it, and his eyes – blue and clear as lake water on a postcard – had glowed.

And she knew all she needed to know.

He wasn't like the others, nothing like the barn-smelling, ass-grabbing sort that frequented the Rope 'N Ride.

He had *something*.

After a brief, intense mating dance, after he'd all but nailed her to the stall door in the bathroom, then again against the wall outside the break door, he'd told her the same.

One look, he'd said. Like, no sooner looked than loved. That was from a book. From Shakespeare. Darryl had read some Shakespeare – Slick Willy, he called him – while getting his high school diploma courtesy of juvenile detention in Denton County, Texas, where he'd run off to find his fortune at sixteen.

He'd walked out of juvie at eighteen, into a job at his mother's boyfriend's garage. Darryl had a way with engines as some had a way with horses. Barlow, who nagged Darryl to distraction, said if he spent as much effort on the job as he did dreaming about being somewhere else, he'd be a rich man.

But Darryl had never seen the point in working himself to death when there were so many other ways to get what he wanted. And taking it from somebody else was the best way he knew.

Still, since he didn't want to go back to jail, he stuck it out for the lifetime of nearly three years.

Then he'd gotten what he wanted by stealing the $6,800 under-the-table cash Barlow kept hidden under the false bottom of a drawer in his office.

Which showed what a dumbass Barlow was.

Then he'd helped himself to some equipment, some parts, busted open the display case on Barlow's prized bowie knife – figuring he could sell it along the way.

He'd packed up while his mother was at work waiting tables as she always had for piss-poor pay and worse tips. He pocketed $3,200 from the pouch she kept in her flour tin – it rounded him up to $10,000.

As he considered himself a good son, he'd left her the remaining $646 with a note that read:

Thanks, Ma. Love, Darryl

He'd loaded up the truck he boosted from the garage, and said *adi*-fucking-*os* to Lonesome, Oklahoma.

He walked into the Rope 'N Ride, and Ella-Loo's life, on his twenty-first birthday.

That was fate, they determined, as they were a gift to each other.

Within twenty-four hours she and the duffel bag holding all her worldly possessions were loaded in the truck with him.

They drove fast, spent lavishly, stole when the mood struck, and fucked like a pair of rabid minks at every opportunity.

By the time Darryl was arrested in Tulsa for trying to pocket an engagement ring for his soul mate, they'd blown through nearly every dollar they had between them.

He got four years – as he'd had the bowie knife on him – and this time in the Oklahoma State Pen.

Ella-Loo waited for him. She took a job at another bar, made extra with bjs – though she wouldn't, even for good money, allow any other penetration.

She was a one-man woman.

As devoted as a priest at Sunday Mass, she visited Darryl every week, and, in fact, conceived a child on a conjugal visit.

Darryl read more Shakespeare and honed his mechanical skills. He learned more about engines, learned how to build bombs, learned more complex ins and outs of computers and electronics.

He got himself an education he might've put to good use on the outside.

She named the baby Darra, after her Darryl, and drove her back to Elk City where Ella-Loo presented the infant to Darra's grandma.

Though she could hardly stand to be away from Darryl so long, she gave it ten days. Long enough for her mother to fall in love with the baby, and for her stepfather to relax his guard.

Knowing her mother would never allow her stepfather to set the cops on her, she took her great-grandmother's silver – it would've come to her one day anyway – left the baby, and drove back to McAlester for the next visiting day.

Maybe, when they were ready to settle down, she and Darryl would go back for their daughter. But like Darryl said, they were star-crossed lovers, and had to live and love every minute to the full.

A baby didn't fit in with that.

He got out in three and a half years, due to good behavior, and she was waiting for him wearing a tight white dress and red high heels.

They barely made it to the by-the-month room before the dress was on the floor and the shoes were in the air.

As they both agreed they wanted McAlester in the truck's rearview, they spent only that night eating, drinking – the sparkling wine Ella-Loo had copped from the bar where she would no longer work or give bjs – and having sex.

She wanted to go east, clear to the Atlantic Ocean. She wanted big city lights and noise and everything that wasn't Oklahoma.

New York City, she told Darryl, was their destiny, as it was the only town big and bright enough to hold them.

So when Darryl's truck coughed and wheezed, he used his skill – and parts he stripped off another he found in a parking lot – got it running pretty smooth again. He headed east with the radio blaring and Ella-Loo curled against his side like an appendage.

Even with his skill, the old truck couldn't handle the miles or the speed, and died like a dog.

And Ella-Loo had her idea.

Darryl managed to baby and jury-rig the truck enough to limp it off the main road while she consulted the in-dash computer. It seemed to her they might have some luck on a little stretch along Highway 12, some ways south of Bentonville.

She dug out that white dress and those red heels, reddened her lips and, bending from the waist, finger-combed her long blond hair.

She was hoping for a man – a lone man – as she had no doubt a man would stop for her. The dress sat snug on her curves, rode high on her thighs, and when she flipped her hair up again, it tumbled like a siren's.

She laughed, and shooed Darryl back when he tried to grab at her.

'You just wait, baby, you just wait. And stay out of sight now. A man comes along, he's going to stop to help me out for sure.'

'He's gonna want to do more than that. Holy Jesus, Ella-Loo, you're sexy as black lace panties. I got a boner so big it's killing me just looking at you.'

'That's the idea. If a woman comes along, she might stop, might not. A couple of men will, a couple of women might. Mix it up, it's back to maybe. But sooner or later, baby.'

She ran her finger over his mouth, gave him a grind, crotch to crotch, that made him moan before she nudged him away.

'More of that later, honey. It's not full dark yet. People are more inclined to stop to help before it gets dark. Go on back in that brush there. I've got to look helpless, and I won't when I've got myself a strong, handsome man beside me.'

She'd chosen the spot well – maybe too well as the sun dipped lower without a single vehicle passing going either way.

'I maybe could get it running again,' Darryl called out. 'Enough to get to a motel or a town, just boost something there.'

'This is going to work, Darryl.' She had her mind set on it. 'We just have to – I see a car coming. When he stops, give me some time to play it up. Then you come out, baby, and take care of it. You'll take care of it, won't you, Darryl?'

'You know I will.'

She stood beside the car, hands clasped together as if in prayer, big blue eyes wide with what she hoped came off as a little hope, a little fear.

She loved playacting.

And she felt her excitement rise as the car – and a fine one, too – slowed. The man lowered the window, angled across the seat. 'Having some trouble?'

'Oh, yes, sir, I surely am.' Older, she noted, maybe right around fifty, so he'd be easy for Darryl to knock out, tie up, and drag off into the brush. 'It just up and died on me. I tried getting hold of my brother – it's his truck – but my 'link must be broken, or maybe I forgot to pay the service fee. I'm always forgetting something.'

'You didn't forget to fuel up, did you?' he asked.

'Oh, no, sir. That is, my brother, Henry, had it topped right off. That's Henry Beam (the name of her US history teacher back in high school) from Fayetteville? Maybe you know him – it seems everybody knows Henry.'

'I'm afraid I don't. I'm not from around here. Let me pull up in front of you, and I'll take a look.'

'Thank you so much. I just didn't know what I was going to do. It's getting dark, too.'

He pulled up. His car was a shiny silver, and though she'd have liked red – just like her shoes – she wouldn't complain. She fluttered around when he told her to unlock the hood, so he reached into the truck, released the latch himself.

He had a nice wrist unit, she noted, silver and shiny like the car. She wanted Darryl to have it.

'I don't know much about trucks,' he began, 'so if it's not an easy fix, I can take you into Bentonville. You can use my 'link to get in touch with your brother.'

'That's so nice of you. I was afraid somebody maybe not so nice would stop, and I didn't know what to do.' She glanced toward the brush, kept up a chatter to mask the rustling Darryl made as he came out. 'My ma's going to be worrying soon if I'm not back, so if you're going to Bentonville, that would be just fine. She'll thank you herself for bringing me home.'

'I thought you said Fayetteville.'

'What? Oh, Henry,' she began.

Something must have shown in her eyes or he heard the quiet step of Darryl's boot, as he reared back, turned just as Darryl raised the tire iron. It struck the man on the shoulder.

And he leaped at Darryl like a demon from hell.

It happened so fast – the flying fists, the animal grunts and snarls. Thinking only of Darryl, Ella-Loo snatched up the tire iron that had spun out of his hand, tried to get a solid grip.

She swung, striking the now raging Good Samaritan hard across the back, realized her mistake when it didn't stop him. The next time, she aimed for the legs.

One of them buckled – she clearly heard a crack. Even hurt he managed to swing around, backhand her. Before she could steady herself, try for the other leg, Darryl went crazy.

'Put your hands on my woman, I'll kill you!'

He pummelled, fists flying, eyes wild, teeth bared. She barely had time to scramble clear before the man, unbalanced on his bad leg, face bloody, fell back.

His head struck the front bumper of the truck, bounced off, then slapped against the pavement. Before she gave it a thought, she jumped in, smashed the tire iron across his face. Two hard blows.

He lay still now, eyes wide in his ruined face. Blood began to seep and pool under his head.

Ella-Loo's breath puffed like a steam engine, whooshing out as her body quivered. 'Is he . . . is he dead?'

'Shit, Ella-Loo, shit.' Staring down, Darryl pulled a bandanna out of his back pocket to mop at the sweat and blood on his face. 'He looks dead to me.'

'We killed him.'

'Didn't do it on purpose. Shit, Ella-Loo. He hit you right in the face. I can't allow that. I can't let anybody hurt my girl.'

'I didn't want him to get up and hit you again, either. So I . . . You got to get him off the road. Get him back behind all that brush, Darryl, and quick before somebody else comes. And you take his wallet, his wrist unit. Take anything he's got on him. Hurry.'

She found a rag in the truck, wiped down the tire iron, then tossed it into the backseat of their new car.

'Take his clothes, too, baby.'

'What?'

10

'Take everything. You never know, but hurry!'

She began hauling their things from the bed of the truck to the car. 'Just put everything in the back, and we'll sort through it later.'

Her heart hammered; her hands shook. But she moved fast and sure.

'We need to get everything of ours out of the truck, baby, and I guess we need to wipe the steering wheel and so on. Anything we think we've touched. I'll do that.'

She did the best she could, then finished with Darryl's help as they didn't have much to transfer from truck to car. In ten minutes Darryl was behind the wheel with Ella-Loo beside him.

'Don't go over the speed limit now. We're just going to put some distance between us and that man and the truck.'

She held on, a mile, five, ten. At twenty-five, she broke.

'Pull off, pull off! See that road there? God Almighty, pull off, Darryl, go back in the trees there.'

'Are you gonna be sick, honey?'

'I can still smell his blood. It's on you. It's on me, too.'

'It's all right, now. It's gonna be all right, now.' He pulled off, bumped his way through some trees, stopped. 'Honey.'

'Did you see his face? His eyes staring at us, but not seeing us? And the blood coming out of his mouth. Of his ears.'

She turned to him, her face lit like the sun, her eyes huge, full of wonder and want. 'We killed somebody. Together.'

They fell on each other. For them, sex was always hot,

hard and heady, but now, with the smell of fresh blood, with the *knowing*, it turned feral until her screams, his shouts echoed in the car.

When they were done, when sweat fused their flesh together like glue and the white dress was tattered, stained with blood as red as her heels, she smiled at him.

'Next time, I don't want to do it so fast. We're going to take some time with the next one.'

'I love you, Ella-Loo.'

'I love you, Darryl. Nobody's ever loved like we do. We're going to have everything we want, do anything we want, from right here all the way to New York City.'

The first kill, mostly an accident, took place on a hot night in August. By the time they arrived in New York, in mid-January, their tally was up to twenty-nine.

With her first look at New York, Ella-Loo had the same reaction she'd had with her first look at Darryl.

She knew they were made for each other.

An ice-pick wind stabbed down the litter-strewn alley, slicing at exposed flesh, hissing and snarling as it hacked its way from Madison Street through the tunnel formed by graffiti-laced buildings of crumbling red brick or pitted concrete.

The few lights that worked cast purple shadows along with sickly yellow glows so the pools and splashes of them bloomed bitter, like a bruise.

The lowest of low-level street whores – licensed or not – might take a john into one of the narrow niches hoping for shelter from the worst of the cold and wind while business was conducted. A junkie desperate enough for a fix might follow an illegals dealer into those bruising shadows.

Anyone else thinking to shortcut through might as well wear a flashing sign offering themselves up to muggers, rapists and worse.

None of those options applied to Dorian Kuper as he'd met his unfortunate fate elsewhere before his body had been wrapped in plastic and dumped, much like the wind- and vermin-tattered bags of garbage beside a broken recycler.

The vicious wind wouldn't trouble Dorian any longer. Its toothy knives cut keenly enough, so Lieutenant Eve Dallas gave into necessity and yanked on the ski cap with its embarrassing snowflake. But she drew the line at the fuzzy gloves – both given to her on a cold December day by the dreamy-eyed Dennis Mira.

She thought, fleetingly, that twenty-four hours earlier she'd been basking, mostly naked, on the sun-washed sand of her husband's private island with Roarke, also mostly naked, beside her.

However she'd begun 2061, she was back in New York now, and so was death.

She was a murder cop, so while others slept in the blustery dark still an hour shy of dawn, she crouched over a body, hands bare but for sealant, brown eyes flat and narrowed.

'Killed the hell out of you, didn't he, Dorian?'

'He's got an Upper West Side address, Dallas.' Detective Peabody, wrapped in a pink coat, her feet toasty in fuzzy-topped pink boots, and her face all but buried in the many swirls of a multicolored scarf, relayed the data from her PPC to her partner.

'Age, thirty-eight, single, no cohab. He's with the Metropolitan Opera company. First cellist.'

'What's a cellist from the Upper West Side doing dead in Mechanics Alley? Wasn't killed here. Plenty of blood on the tarp, on him, smeared from surface to surface. Ligature marks, wrists and ankles, and some of the bruising, the lacerations from struggling look at least a day old. Maybe more. Morris will confirm.'

'A lot of cuts, punctures, burn marks, bruising.' Peabody, her eyes a deeper, darker brown than Eve's, scanned the body. 'A lot of them superficial. But then . . .'

'Yeah, a lot of them not. Bound, gagged – the corners of his mouth are cut and abraded – tortured for hours. Maybe a day or more before it stopped being fun. And then . . . the slice across the gut, that ended him. But it would have taken time for him to bleed out. Some painful time.'

Taking out her gauges, she established time of death. 'The painful time ended at twenty-two-twenty last night.'

'Dallas, there's a missing persons on him. Just filed this morning. His mother filed it. Ah . . . okay. He didn't show for work night before last, didn't answer his 'link, missed his class – he's teaching one at Juilliard – yesterday afternoon, and was a no-show for last night's performance.'

'So about two days. Contact whoever caught the missing person, get a full report. We'll notify next of kin.'

Hunkered back on her heels, Eve studied the face of the dead. His ID shot had shown an attractive man with deep green, flirtatious eyes and long, rich blond hair. A face sharp at the cheeks, full at the lips.

His killer had hacked at the hair, leaving thin tufts and ugly little wounds, burned small circles in his cheeks, like blackened dimples. Spiderwebs of red shattered the whites of his eyes. But the killer had focused most of his energy and creativity on the body. She thought Morris, the chief medical examiner, would find multiple broken bones and damaged organs.

'Some of these burns are small and precise,' she noted. 'Probably used a tool. But see on the back of the hands here? Bigger, not precise. Somebody put out cigarettes, herbals, joints, whatever, on the vic's hands. Cellist. A cello's that violin type thing, right?'

'Well, it's ... ' Peabody made a large shape in the air with her hands, then mimed sawing across it with a bow.

'Yeah, a big, fat violin. You need your hands to play one of those. Burned the hands, broke four of his fingers, right hand, crushed the left hand – heavy object. Maybe personal. Hacking off the hair, that reads personal. Dumping him naked could read personal.'

Eve lifted one of the hands, used her light to do a cursory exam of the nails. 'I don't see any skin under here, and nothing that looks like defensive wounds.' She shifted to the head, lifting carefully, feeling the skull. 'Big knot back here.'

'He has a fight – verbal, I mean,' Peabody began. 'With someone he knew, turns his back, and they give him a good bash. They're pissed off enough to bind him, gag him, torture him.'

'This isn't pissed off.' Eve shook her head, finally straightened up. The wind snatched at her long, leather coat, sent it billowing, snapping around her legs. 'It isn't patient and intricate like— Remember The Groom?'

'I'm not likely to forget. Ever.'

'He made a science out of torture. It was his work. This looks more like play.'

'"Play"?'

'Pissed off usually whales right in. Pissed off would go for the face more, especially if there's a personal connection.'

But here, she thought, the face was the least of it, as if the killer had wanted to keep it fairly unharmed.

So they could see the victim? So he remained recognizable?

'Pissed off doesn't torture like this for a couple days,' she added. 'Pissed off and crazy, maybe. But again, I'd expect to see more physical contact – more from fists or saps. Some damage to the genitals, but again, not as much as I'd expect if it was a pissed-off friend or lover.

'But we'll look at that.'

Shifting, Eve looked down the alley toward Madison, turned, looked north toward Henry.

'The killer had to have transpo, and likely pulled up on Madison. The dump site's close to Madison. The vic's – what was it – five-ten, and one-fifty-five. We'll have the sweepers determine if the plastic with the body was dragged down the alley, but it doesn't look like it. Hard to be certain in this light, but dragged or carried, the killer had some muscle. Or help. We'll see if the canvass turns up anything.'

She looked up, scanned dark windows. 'Middle of the night, middle of the winter. Cold as a bitch's tit.'

'It's "witch's."'

'Why? Doesn't matter,' Eve said quickly. 'Neither way makes sense. If somebody's a witch, why do they put up with cold tits? I'm a bitch, and twenty-four hours ago, my tits were plenty warm.'

'Was it wonderful? Your vacation?'

'It didn't suck.'

Blue skies, blue water, white sand and Roarke. No, it hadn't sucked.

And now it was done.

'Let's call in the sweepers, the morgue, and get a couple of uniforms back here on the body.' She checked her wrist unit. 'We'll go by the vic's residence first. There's no point waking his mother up at this hour to tell her he's dead.'

Eve tugged the silly cap farther over her frozen ears,

17

bobbled her light. As she leaned over to retrieve it, her gaze flicked toward the body where the end of the beam arrowed.

'Wait. Is that ... Peabody, microgoggles.'

'You see something?'

'I'll see if I see something better with the microgoggles.'

She was kneeling beside the body now, drawing the left arm farther out.

'Fuck me, I almost missed this.'

'Missed what?' After she pulled the microgoggles from Eve's field kit, Peabody pushed them at her, tried to angle to see what Eve's light beamed on.

'It's a heart. So much blood and bruising, I might've missed it. Morris would have caught it once the vic was on his table, but in this light, I didn't see it.'

'I don't see it now.'

'Just under the armpit.' Leaning closer, goggles in place, Eve bookended it with her fingers, top to bottom, then side to side. 'About an inch high and wide. Precise as a high-dollar tattoo. Initials inside. *E* over *D*.'

'*D* for *Dorian*.'

'Could be.' And it sure as hell shifted some angles. 'Maybe a pissed-off lover or wannabe or used-to-be lover after all. Ante- or postmortem?' she wondered. 'A signature or a statement? This part's precise. The killer took some time and care carving this in.'

'McQueen carved numbers in his vics,' Peabody remembered, 'so the cops would know how many he'd done.

Maybe this is *E*'s signature, and *E* picks the vic and develops some sick, delusional relationship. And since sick, delusional relationships never end well, the killer bashes, ties up, gags, tortures, kills, then carves in the heart – killer over vic inside it.'

Eve nodded – a good theory. Solid and logical. 'It could play.'

'Maybe this isn't E's first sick, delusional relationship.'

'That could play, too.' Eve rose, pulled off the goggles. 'We'll run the elements through IRCCA, look for like crimes. Right now, let's go check out the vic's place. Maybe we'll find out who he knew whose name starts with *E*.'

'His mother lives in the same building,' Peabody said as Eve signaled to one of the uniforms at the mouth of the alley.

'Well, that saves us time. We'll go through his place, then do the notification.'

'She's with the orchestra, too. She plays a baby cello.'

'They have babies?'

'It was, like, a joke. She's first violin. So, ha ha, baby cello.'

'Assume I laughed. Lives in the same building, works the same job – basically. She probably knows anybody with the initial *E* he knew. And how he got along at work, with lovers.'

Eve turned away, had a short conversation with the uniform.

With the scene secured, and no witness – so far – to interview as the body had been discovered by beat droids, she climbed into her car. And with unspeakable relief, ordered the heat on full.

With even more unspeakable relief, she pulled off the snowflake hat.

'Aw. It looks cute on you.'

'If I wanted to look cute, I wouldn't be a cop.' She forked her fingers through her short, shaggy brown hair. 'Address, Peabody.'

'West Seventy-first between Amsterdam and Columbus.'

'A long way from where he ended up.' Needles pricked along her fingers as they thawed out.

One of the things she'd figured out how to operate in the fully loaded, purposely nondescript vehicle her husband had designed for her was coffee from the onboard Auto-Chef.

And right that minute, she thought she might kill for real coffee.

'Computer, engage AutoChef,' Eve began.

'Yippee!'

'Shut up, Peabody, or you won't get any.'

AutoChef engaged. What would you like, Dallas, Lieutenant Eve?

'One coffee black, one coffee regular, both in go-cups.'

One moment, please. Is front-seat delivery desired?

20

'Yeah, yeah, yeah, that's desired.'

'I didn't know it did that,' Peabody piped up. 'I thought it was just backseat – Whoa!'

Order complete, the computer announced as two go-cups slid out from under the dash.

'That is totally iced.'

'It better not be iced.' Eve snagged the go-cup with the black top, leaving the cream-colored top for Peabody.

It was hot and strong and perfect.

'I love this ride,' Peabody stated, cuddling her coffee.

'Don't get used to the coffee service. Maybe the next time it's shy of five a.m., minus three with a windchill of you don't fucking want to know, we'll do it again. Otherwise, forget it.'

Peabody only smiled, took the first glorious sip. 'I love this ride,' she repeated.

2

Eve concluded playing a big, fat violin paid pretty well. Dorian Kuper had lived in a two-level apartment in a meticulously rehabbed building – one that had survived the Urban Wars. It stood, bright white brick and long sheets of glass gleaming, in a tony area of the Upper West Side.

When the doorman, wearing a classic black topcoat over his livery, greeted her by rank instead of snooty insults on the bland appearance of the DLE she drove, she knew Roarke owned the building. Obviously Doorman Frank had gotten the memo.

'How can I help you today, Lieutenant?'

'We need access to Dorian Kuper's apartment.'

His round, almost cherubic face fell. 'I was afraid of that. Please, come inside, out of the wind. I heard Mr Kuper was missing. I guess you found him, and I guess it's not good.'

She stepped inside, into warmth and white marble veined with gray, into the strangely spicy scent of whatever the masses of bold flowers cast off from their silver urn on the central table.

'We found him. It's not good,' she confirmed.

'This will crush Ms McKensie. His mother. They were really tight. He was a nice guy, Lieutenant, I just want to say. Always had a word, you know?'

'Do you know anyone who didn't think he was such a nice guy?'

'Not right off, I'm sorry. He had a lot of friends. They'd come over for parties, for music.'

'Girlfriends, boyfriends?'

Frank shifted on his feet.

'Anything you can tell us,' Peabody said, adding a light touch to his arm. 'Anything may help us find who killed him.'

'I get it, but it's hard to talk about a resident's personal life. I'd say Mr Kuper had both, and nothing really serious.'

'All right. Has anyone been around in the past couple weeks, asking about him?' Eve asked. 'Any former friend make any trouble?'

'Not that I know of. And when you're on the door, you usually know.'

'Okay, Frank, thanks. I need you to clear us up to his place.'

'Sixth floor. Apartment six hundred. That's the main entrance. I'll clear the first elevator. I need to get clearance to get his pass key and code. It'll take a minute.'

'I've got a master. We'll get in.'

With a nod, Frank walked over to a blank granite counter,

tapped and brought up a screen. 'Lobby droid's in the back. I don't activate her this early. It's usually quiet, so what's the point? You're clear, Lieutenant.'

He cleared his throat as Eve and Peabody stepped to the elevator. 'Ah, does his mom know?'

'We'll speak to her after we see his apartment. Like you said, it's early. No reason to wake her up with this kind of news.'

'It's going to crush her. They doted on each other, you know?'

Though she didn't know what it was to have a mother dote on her, or to dote back, Eve nodded before she stepped into the elevator.

Ascending to sixth floor, the computer announced as they started to rise, proving Frank as efficient as any droid.

'Nice guy, lots of friends, loved his mother, bisexual.' Eve considered. 'Not a bad rundown from a doorman in a couple minutes.'

'He looked sad,' Peabody commented. 'When the doorman looks sad, you know you're going to be dealing with a lot of sad in an investigation.'

'If you want happy, don't be a murder cop. Or a cop period,' Eve decided.

The elevator opened to a wide hallway carpeted in dignified gray with the classy touch of artwork arranged on the walls. Curved tables holding slim, clear vases of white flowers ranged between apartment doors.

Six hundred took the west corner farthest from the elevator. Prime real estate in a prime building. Yeah, Eve thought, playing the big, fat violin brought in the bucks.

'Full security,' she noted, engaging her recorder. 'Cam, palm plate, double police locks.'

She bypassed all with her master, opened the right side of the double entrance doors. Lights that had been off went automatically to a soft ten percent illumination.

'Convenient,' she said, 'but not enough. Lights on full,' she ordered.

'Wow.' Peabody's eyes widened as the light strengthened. 'It's totally uptown.'

Classy old-world, was Eve's sense. The sort of deal Roarke preferred. Rich, deep colors, sink-in sofas and chairs. High backs, graceful curves. Dark, gleaming wood, the glint of silver and crystal. Flowers in vases that looked old and precious, candles in slender holders.

Art ran to landscapes, cityscapes, seascapes.

'Let's take this floor first, see if he kept an office down here. We'll want a look at his computers, his house 'link.'

Eve moved left, Peabody right.

When Eve opened double pocket doors, she found the unrestricted space created one large L. Living area, dining area, kitchen.

A serious sort of kitchen, she concluded, with a massive cooktop and oven in addition to double AutoChefs, miles of counter done in pale gold with tiny glinting flecks. Like beach sand, she thought as she walked through, opened cabinet doors, drawers at random.

A lot of serious kitchen tools, precisely organized.

Tucked inside a large, fully stocked pantry, she found a house droid created to depict a pleasant-faced, middle-aged woman of short stature and sturdy build. The droid wore a gray uniform and white apron, and the dead-eyed expression of a droid at rest.

'Got a droid here!' Eve called out, and began to examine it for its manual operating switch.

'There's a powder room, a totally mag music room,' Peabody began as she came in. 'Piano, cello, double bass, three violins, flutes, piccolos. It'll open up just like this area. High-class party central. Here.'

She moved around Eve, reached under the steel-gray bun at the base of the droid's neck and did whatever needed to be done to activate.

The dead blue eyes became full of life and merriment. The slack mouth curved up in a cheerful smile.

'And what is it I can be doing for you this fine morning?'

The plank-thick Irish brogue would have made Roarke – whose own Irish was like a hint of music gliding through words – laugh or wince. Eve just lifted her eyebrows, and her badge.

The merry eyes scanned the badge, processed, confirmed. 'And what, Lieutenant ma'am, would the local *gardi* be wanting with the likes of me?'

'Dallas. Lieutenant Dallas. Detective Peabody. At what time were you last activated?'

'I'll be pleased to answer that, and any other questions you might have once I've cleared the matter with my Dorian. That scamp would still be abed at this hour if you hadn't come 'round.'

'"Scamp"?'

'He's a lively one, he is. Works hard, plays the same. If he's been waked so early, he'll be wanting his coffee. I'm happy to serve you as well.'

'He won't be wanting his coffee. Dorian Kuper is dead.'

Something resembling shock came and went in the droid's eyes. 'I can't process that information. Please repeat.'

Once again Peabody moved in. 'Could we have your name?'

'I'm Maeve.'

'Maeve, we regret to inform you Dorian was killed last night. We're very sorry for your loss.'

'But, he's young and healthy.' Grief, and anyone would have sworn sincere, clouded the voice, the eyes. 'Killed? An accident?'

'He was murdered. Let's move out here,' Eve demanded. 'There's no point standing in a closet.'

'No one would do him harm. I think there's a mistake of some sort, begging your pardon.'

'There's no mistake,' Eve began. 'His identification's been verified and confirmed.'

The droid moved to the counter, sat on one of the stools. 'Why are humans so fragile?'

'It's a mystery. When did you last interact with Dorian?'

'One moment, please.' The eyes went blank for a moment, then filled with apparent distress. 'Ah God, ah God. My records show it's been sixty-two hours and eighteen minutes since my Dorian deactivated me. Has he been dead so long?'

'No. No one has activated you until now?'

'No.'

Eve wondered why the officer on the missing persons hadn't activated and questioned the house droid – then remembered the report had only just been filed.

'Was Dorian alone when he deactivated you?'

'He was, aye. He was going out to the rehearsal hall, he said, before the evening's performance. It's *Giselle* they're doing right now. He said not to wait up for him – he liked to joke with me – and that he'd wake me himself in the morning as it might be late on both counts. He thought to have a late supper with friends. He often did so.'

'You could give us a full list of his friends, of people who've been on his guest list here for parties.'

'I could certainly. I could generate that for you, print it as well if that would help you. Or I can interface with any computer and create a disc.'

'Intimate friends, too,' Eve said.

'My Dorian had a large and lively group of friends, of

28

all manner. He enjoyed having parties and musicales here, or quiet evenings with just a few, or the one of the moment.'

Like a doorman, Eve thought, a house droid could be informative. 'Anyone get pissed when they were no longer the one of the moment?'

'I never heard of it, and sure I would have. He talked to me, my Dorian, and would have said if he'd been troubled by a difficult ending. For those intimate friendships, as you say, he tended toward those who wanted as he did, of the moment. He wasn't ready to settle down. His music came first, always. When he worked, Lieutenant, he worked.'

The droid actually let out a little sigh.

'Many's the hour I've passed doing my duties here and listening to him play. He was writing an opera himself, and worked on that as well when time allowed and the mood was on him.'

'Okay.'

'I'll miss him.' When Eve raised her eyebrows again, the droid shook her head. 'It's not as you would understand, not a human emotion. But his mother had me made to resemble, in all possible ways, the Maeve who was nanny to him as a boy, and who loved him dearly. As he loved her.'

Weird, Eve thought, but there were plenty of the flesh-and-blood variety who couldn't muster the sincerity of Maeve the house droid.

'Then I'm sorry.'

'His mother. I can be of comfort and help to her, should she wish it. Sure they were devoted to each other.'

'We'll ask her. If you could provide that list, both hard copy and disc, it would be very helpful. My partner and I need to go through the apartment.'

'I'm glad to be of any help. Can you tell me, Lieutenant Dallas, why humans kill humans? It doesn't process.'

'It never will,' Eve said.

Eve gave Peabody the computers and 'links, took the master bedroom on the second floor.

She found his goodies drawer as she thought of it, fully stocked with sex aids, toys, protection. That showed her he'd been adventurous and open in that area of his life. The scarcity of drugs – all she found legal – indicated he'd been in good health.

Plenty of high-end skin and body care, grooming tools, so he'd taken care with his appearance. And his extensive closet showed a range of styles – formal to grunge – that said he'd had a flexible sense of fashion.

She found the small wall safe in the closet, and found herself pleased when – in probably triple (at best) the time it would have taken Roarke, who'd been teaching her – she got it open.

Some cash, she noted, his passport, a small collection of wrist units, cuff links, nothing out of the ordinary, nothing over-the-top.

He kept a small office on the second floor, but it didn't take long for her to discover he did only the absolutely necessary work there. He paid his bills promptly, kept an up-to-date calendar, for rehearsals, performances, travel, social engagements.

She found nothing of particular interest in either of the two guest suites, only a continued reflection of the victim's taste and style, and apparently his droid's exceptional skill for maintaining cleanliness and order.

'I've got the list from Maeve, and a copy on disc. It's a long list,' Peabody added as Eve came back down to the main level. 'And I deactivated her. She requested it, and said she'd be available for Ms McKensie, whatever she needed or wanted.'

'We'll let her know.' Eve glanced at her wrist unit. 'Now's as good a time as any. Nothing upstairs that rang. Comps, 'links?'

'Lots of communication. Conversations with friends, arrangements to meet up, orders out for party supplies, wine. I tagged for EDD, but I didn't come across any threats, arguments, anything that seemed hinky, like someone trying to track him. Work stuff, too.'

'Work?' Eve repeated as they lowered the lights, went out into the hall. 'He's got an office upstairs, does bill paying and so on there.'

'No, music work. He has a comp in the music room. I thought it was a closet at first, but it's a small work area. He's got music on there, compositions he's working on, and recordings he must listen to. No other business or communication on it. Music only.'

'Okay.' Eve fixed a police seal to the door. 'You might as well have EDD pick up the electronics, go through them.' She didn't think any of the geeks in the Electronic Detectives Division would find anything relevant, but it paid to be thorough.

'Send a query to the officer who caught the missing persons. Give him or her the status, take anything he's got, which at this stage is likely nothing.'

'Got it.'

'It's 508 for the mother, right?' Eve got in the elevator, requested the fifth floor while Peabody sent the email. 'Anything back from IRCCA?'

'It's early, and we only sent it about an hour ago. They're always a little backed up. You're thinking he wasn't the first?'

'Why does somebody torture, for what looks like about forty-eight hours, and kill a cellist? Maybe it was personal. Maybe one of those of-the-moment types wasn't as happy to keep it that way as the droid says. Maybe some other big, fat violin player wanted that first chair. Maybe the vic knew something about something or someone that somebody else wanted to know. Lots of angles yet. And one of them is he wasn't the first. The heart's bugging me. How many *E*'s on the list?'

'Can't say right off, but I saw an Ethan, an Elizabeth, an

32

Edgar, an Ellysa at a quick glance. Since there's a couple hundred names on there, we'll probably find a few more than that.'

They walked out on five, where Mina McKensie had the unit closest to the elevator. Same security, Eve noted, and pressed the buzzer.

In short order the light on the security cam blinked to green.

'Good morning. May I help you?'

The voice was rich and fruity and British.

'Lieutenant Dallas, Officer Peabody.' She held up her badge for the scanner. 'We need to speak with Mina McKensie.'

'Yes, of course.'

Locks disengaged; the door opened.

Another droid, Eve thought, this one created to mimic a distinguished gentleman with a shock of dark hair silvering at the temples. He wore butler black.

'Please come in. Ms McKensie hasn't yet come down. I'll inform her you're here.'

He escorted them into the living area where the vic's mother had gone more contemporary than her son. Still classy, Eve mused, but sleeker, slicker, more primary colors, bolder art.

'If you'd wait here. Please sit and be comfortable. May I provide you with any refreshment?'

'No, thanks. Just Mina McKensie.'

'Of course.'

He moved to the curve of stairs and walked up.

She'd know, Eve thought. She'd know as soon as the droid said the cops were downstairs. There'd be a desperate glimmer of hope, but she'd know.

Eve caught the movement, looked up. Mina hadn't dressed as yet, and wore a full-length cream-colored robe, silk and fluid. On her face – an arresting face of sultry eyes against golden skin – Eve saw the hope fighting to overcome the grief.

Her hands whitened at the knuckle on the rail as she came quickly down.

'Dorian. Please, say it quickly. Say it fast.'

'Ms McKensie, we regret to inform you your son was killed.'

She held up both hands as if she could shove the words away, lowered as carefully as an invalid into a chair of lipstick red.

'You're sure it's Dorian. You're absolutely sure?'

'Yes, we're sure. We're sorry for your loss.'

'"Loss"? That's such a small word, isn't it? Most of what you lose, you can replace again. Like a key card or an earring. You just get another. But . . . '

She rocked herself, gently, gently, while tears swam and shimmered. 'I knew. I knew. I knew. When he missed the performance. He would never miss a performance. But I thought, No, it's just . . . anything else. Anything else. But he didn't answer his 'link, and I begged him to just let me know he was all right. He would never cause me to worry. He would never do that. They said, the police, that we had to wait to file a report. Why, why?'

Peabody sat, leaned toward her. 'A lot of people, adults, sometimes take a day or two, just need that space.'

'Dorian isn't like that.'

'I understand, Ms McKensie.'

'Would it have made a difference?' A rawness in the question, just short of accusation. 'If you'd looked sooner, would it have—'

'I don't think so.' In her gentle way, Peabody took her hand. 'I don't think so, I'm sorry. Can I get you some water, Ms McKensie?'

'I need . . . ' She closed her eyes, and two tears slid through. 'Jarvis, I need a brandy, please.'

'Of course, madam, right away.'

'I need a brandy,' Mina repeated, opening her eyes again. 'And I need just a moment. Then I need you to tell me what happened to Dorian. I need you to tell me that, and to tell me where he is so I can go see him. I need to see my son.'

'We'll arrange that, Ms McKensie.'

She took the brandy from the droid, brought it to her lips for a long, slow sip. 'I won't fall apart. That's for a private moment. I won't fall apart,' she repeated, but her voice shook, and the tears slid down her face. 'Tell me what happened to my son.'

'Ms McKensie, is there anyone I can contact to come and be with you?'

'I don't need anyone. I need to know.'

'Ms McKensie.' Eve stepped in, sat on the slick silver table, trained her eyes on the brimming ones. 'What I have to tell you is hard. It's very hard. If there's someone you trust, you depend on, you might want that person to come and stay with you after I tell you. We spoke to your son's house droid. Do you want us to activate her, bring her down?'

'Maeve.' Another tear spilled, but she drew in, shook her head. 'No, not Maeve, not yet. Ethan. Ethan Chamberlin. My conductor. My lover. I asked him not to stay last night, but . . .

'Jarvis, please contact Mr Chamberlin and—'

'It might be better if I spoke with him.' Peabody rose.

'Jarvis, give the officer the information.'

'We'll take this in the next room.' Peabody gestured to the droid to lead her out.

'I won't fall apart,' Mina repeated. 'I'm very strong. I raised Dorian on my own after his father died. Dorian was only six. I raised him on my own, and built a career. I'm very strong. Tell me.'

'His body was found in Mechanics Alley. Do you know that area?'

'I'm not sure.'

'It's downtown. It's Lower East Side. Do you know any reason he might have been in that area?'

'No. No. He has friends downtown. In the Village, in Tribeca, SoHo. Dorian made friends easily. I want to know how he died.'

'The medical examiner will determine that.'

'You know. It's what you do, isn't it? You know what happened to him. I'm his mother, and I need to know.'

'Ms McKensie, the ME has to determine cause of death. I can tell you that from our on-site evaluation, it appears he'd been restrained. He suffered multiple injuries.'

Very carefully Mina took another sip of brandy. 'They restrained him so they could hurt him? So he couldn't stop them from hurting him.'

Yes, she was a strong woman, Eve concluded. And far from stupid.

'It appears to be the case, but the ME will have to examine Dorian. I'm very sorry. Do you know of anyone who would do something like this to your son? Someone with a grudge, a former lover, a competitor?'

'No.' Mina pressed her fingers between her eyebrows, took a slow breath. 'No, I don't. I'm not just dismissing what you asked, but he was well-liked.'

'He taught at Juilliard. Maybe a student he reprimanded.'

'None that I know. He liked teaching. He didn't need to teach for financial reasons. He gave that time because he enjoyed nurturing new talent. It excited him to help a student come along. No one who knew him could have done this. No one who knew him could have hurt him this way, taken his life.'

'You were close.' She kept her eyes on Mina's as Peabody came back in.

'Yes. Very.'

'Then I'm going to ask you, do you know anyone who'd want to hurt you by hurting your son? The same question from a different angle, Ms McKensie. Someone with a grudge, a former lover, a competitor?'

'Oh God.' Her hands trembled as she set the snifter aside, so she gripped them together in her lap. 'Kill Dorian to hurt me? I don't know anyone who's capable of such a terrible thing. There are people who don't particularly like me, or people I've had disagreements with. Even serious ones. But I swear to you, no one I know would hurt Dorian. Even people who didn't particularly like me liked him. The idea, even the thought that someone would hurt him because of me—'

'Ms McKensie, we have to ask. We have to look at every possibility.' Peabody sat again. 'Mr Chamberlin is on his way.'

'Thank you.'

'Did your son mention anyone bothering him? He'd have fans, right?' Eve suggested. 'People who follow the opera, who enjoyed his work?'

'Yes — I mean, yes, he had many who enjoyed his work, who might attend performances, and wait to speak with him or have him sign a program.'

'Sometimes a fan can cross a line, can develop a fictional relationship, and become angry when the object of that interest doesn't reciprocate.'

Mina folded her hands again as if to keep them still,

nodded. 'Yes, I understand, and Dorian had followers, yes, of course. He's young and very attractive and talented. He'd play at clubs now and again, especially off season. Not opera, of course. Jazz, blues. Dorian can play a number of instruments. Some would hear he'd be at a certain club and go to see him. Or wait by the stage door after a performance. There's no one I can . . . Wait.'

She sat straight up. 'There was a girl he spoke of in the last few weeks. What did he call her?' Mina closed her eyes a moment. 'Earnest Tina.'

'Earnestina? Do you have a last name?'

'No, no, *Earnest* – as in she was earnest. Overly so. He had a drink with her once, which tells me she's attractive. And he said she spent most of the hour dissecting Wagner and Mozart and so on. Not a musician, not that, she was composing. That's it. Composing an opera, and very, very earnest. He said she'd come to whatever club, somewhere he'd jammed, a few days after he'd had a drink with her, and was very displeased he wasted his time and talent on what she considered lesser music. He laughed about it, but she'd been angry.'

'"Tina",' Eve repeated. 'No last name?'

'I'm sorry. He never said. It was just an anecdote over coffee one morning. He might have mentioned her to a friend in more detail.'

'We'll look into it,' Eve said as the buzzer sounded.

Peabody rose, gestured the droid back. 'I've got it.'

'I don't want to see anyone but Ethan. I don't want to—'

39

'Don't worry,' Eve assured her.

'I need to see my son, Lieutenant. I'm sorry, I can't remember your name. I can't quite remember.'

'Dallas. I'm going to arrange it. I'm going to go see him myself when I leave here, and I'll arrange it. Dr Morris is looking after him. I promise you he'll be well taken care of.'

'Mina.' The man who rushed in was dashing, dramatic in looks. Tall, imposingly so, and whippet lean. Like the droid, he had a generous mane of hair gone silver at the temples, and eyes of dark and piercing brown under arched black brows.

Ignoring Eve he dropped to his knees by Mina's chair, drew her into a hard embrace.

'Dorian. It's Dorian. It's—'

Though she'd kept her word, hadn't fallen apart, she broke now on one keening wail.

3

On the street, Eve surrendered to the wind and dug the silly hat out of her pocket.

'She held up longer than I thought she would,' Peabody commented.

'That's an iron spine. We'll check in with Morris now, then start hitting friends, coworkers. I want to talk to Chamberlin. The conductor guy's the in-charge guy, so, yeah, we need a conversation.'

She got behind the wheel, sat a moment with an eye on the side mirror to judge traffic. 'Earnest Tina.'

'He had a sense of humor,' Peabody said. 'He probably told somebody else about her, and we can get the names of the clubs he liked to play in.'

'She's a possibility.' Eve took her shot, zipped out, left a blast of horns in her wake. 'She's writing an opera — do people still do that? I thought all the people who wrote operas have been dead for centuries.'

'There was that thrash opera a couple years ago — *Noise*. I sampled the disc, but it gave me a headache. I think people still write the regular ones.'

'Well, she's writing one, and with a name like Earnest Tina it won't be thrash. She wants to pick Kuper's brain about dead opera-writer types. Maybe she wants him to use his influence to get hers produced. His mother's sleeping with the in-charge guy, another potential leg up there. But he's not serious enough by her standards, goes around playing at dingy clubs. Disrespectful to her and the opera.'

It seemed seriously out of orbit as motive, but . . .

'People kill people for all sorts of screwy reasons,' Eve concluded.

'The torture?'

'We have to meet this Earnest Tina, figure out just how screwy she is. Let's do a run on Ethan Chamberlin. He's got the initial. Maybe he couldn't get what he wants from the mother with the son so tight in there.'

'Or maybe he really wanted to do the son instead of the mother.'

'Now you're thinking.'

'I bet you've been to the opera,' Peabody said as she started the run on her PPC.

'Twice. Then I drew the line. I'd go again when they finished building the ice palace in hell.'

'I think I'd like it – I mean to at least go. The costumes, the music, the drama, and everybody all dressed up and sparkly.'

'You can't understand anything anybody's saying, then they all die. We get plenty of that on the job.'

'But if they're doing all that in Italian – I'd want to go to an Italian opera, I think – then it's romantic.'

'I don't get how dying's romantic.'

'Well, like Romeo and Juliet—'

'Double teenage suicide. Yeah, that makes my heart melt.'

Sulking a little, Peabody continued the run. 'It's romantic tragedy.'

'That's one of those oxygons.'

'Moron.'

Eve turned her head, aimed steely eyes. 'Repeat that.'

'I meant *oxymoron*. It's oxy*moron* not *gon*. Sir.'

'Either way.' Eve added a shrug.

'Moving right along,' Peabody said quickly. 'Chamberlin, Ethan, age sixty-two. Divorced, twice, one offspring, daughter, thirty, resides in London. He's been the in-charge guy for eleven years, and was in-charge guy for the London Symphony Orchestra prior. Resides … huh, just two blocks south of the vic and his mother. Few bumps here and there. Destruction of personal property – busted up a viola – paid the damages. Same deal for throwing a piccolo out of the window and threatening to throw the piccolo player after the instrument. Assault, charges dropped. Another assault, suspended sentence with mandatory anger management.'

'Violence. Temper.' Eve shook her head. 'That's a run of a

flash temper. This murder doesn't read that way. But we'll talk to him. Pull out the *E* names – just first for now – start quick runs. Can you do a geographical, so we have the most efficient route for interviews?'

'Totally can do. His mom seemed really sure nobody who knew him could do this.'

'His mother loved him, and figured everybody else did, too. At least one person didn't, whether they knew him or not. So we check it out.'

A thin snow started to spit out of grumpy gray skies. Which meant, Eve knew, that at least fifty percent of the drivers currently on the road would lose a minimum of one-third of their intelligence quotient, any skill they'd previously held at operating a vehicle thereby turning what had been the standard annoying traffic into mayhem.

She bulled her way south, determined to beat the onset of insanity.

The minute she stepped into the morgue, she yanked the cap off her head, stuffed it in her pocket.

The white tunnel echoed with their footsteps – the post-holiday, frozen-tundra lull, Eve thought. It wouldn't last.

She caught Peabody eyeing the vending machine that offered hot drinks.

'You know everything in that thing is crap.'

'Yeah, but it's snowing a little, and when it starts to snow I start thinking hot chocolate. Even though the strange brown liquid that machine pees out doesn't bear much of a resemblance. Why can't law-enforcement facilities get decent vending?'

'Because then we'd all be snuggled up with hot chocolate instead of doing the job.'

She pushed open the door to Morris's domain.

She recognized opera – not which one, but identified the soaring tragedy in the voices, the mournful blend of instruments as some opera or other.

Morris stood over Dorian Kuper. A clear cape protected the chief ME's plum-colored suit, and the fascinating high-planed face was unframed as he'd tied back his black hair in one of his complicated braids, twined it with silver cord.

Blood smeared his sealed hands. Kuper's chest lay open from the *Y* incision.

'*Giselle*,' Morris said, glancing up as if seeing the music. 'I was going to see it next week.'

'You're into opera?'

'Some.' He stepped away to wash the blood and sealant from his hands. 'I knew him.'

'The vic?' Eve's thoughts shifted from Morris's eclectic taste in music, zeroed in on connection. 'Kuper? You knew Dorian Kuper?'

'Yes. He was a brilliant musician. Truly brilliant – not just his ability, which was striking, but his affinity. I'm sorry to have him in my house this way.'

'You were friends?'

45

'Very casually. He sometimes came into After Midnight – a blues club we both enjoyed. We jammed a number of times. Had a drink, talked music.'

Saxophone, Eve thought. Morris played a hell of a saxophone. 'I'm sorry.'

'As am I. I took Amaryllis to a party at his apartment, just a few weeks before she was killed. It's strange, isn't it, how things link together?'

She saw the grief come over him, fresh after so many months, for the woman he'd loved.

He turned, reached into his friggie for a tube of Pepsi, the orange fizzy he knew Peabody preferred and a ginger ale for himself. He passed out the tubes, cracked his own.

'A drink to old friends,' he said.

'What can you tell me about him?'

'Personally? He had a large and eclectic group of friends if the party – and the various people who'd come with him to the clubs – is an accurate gauge. He and his mother adored each other – it showed. I've seen him with men and with women – in a romantic sense. That showed, too. He could play anything. You could hand him an instrument and he'd bring joy or tears from it.'

Morris drank, looked back at the body – the work to be done.

'I didn't know him well, but I liked him.'

'Do you know of anyone named Tina in connection with him?'

'As I said, he had a large and ... Tina?' Morris let out a quick laugh. 'Earnest Tina.'

'That's the one. You know her?'

'No, not at all. She came in one night – oh, before the holidays. Closer to the beginning of December, I think. I couldn't settle one night, and took my sax, went into the club. He was there already, as were some others we both knew. She came in – a brunette, yes, an attractive brunette, took a table, looked very disapproving. He went over, talked to her for a short time. I thought, Lover's quarrel, as she appeared very angry.'

He paused, took another drink as he narrowed his eyes. 'Let me think back. He ... Dorian put a hand over hers, as if to pat it, and she snatched it away. I can't tell you what was said, but she did most of the talking, then – somewhat dramatically – stormed out. I do recall her parting shot: "I'll never forgive you. Never." With tears in her eyes.

'Someone teased him when he came up to play again, about his angry girlfriend, and he said, No, not a girlfriend, not a friend. Earnest Tina, he said, and he didn't go for too much earnest. Pissed because she thinks I'm slumming – that's what he said, and laughed, and said, Let's jam one for Earnest Tina.'

'No last name.'

'No.'

'Can you describe her?'

'Yes, I'm sure I can.'

'Well enough for Yancy?' she asked, referring to the police artist.

'I can certainly try if it helps in any way. The *E* in the heart. *E* and *D* inside the heart the killer carved in him.'

'There's that. I don't know if someone who takes themselves that seriously would use the initial from a sarcastic nickname, but maybe. I want to talk to her, so if Yancy can get a sketch close enough for us to run through facial recognition, we'd pin her down.'

'I'll contact him myself, make arrangements.'

'Appreciate it.'

'All right.' Morris drew in air, turned back to the body. 'That helped, oddly enough. Now, let's talk about what was done to him.'

He picked up microgoggles for himself and Eve, understanding Peabody would happily skip the more up close and personal, and began.

'The blow on the back of the head, heavy, blunt object, from the shape of the wound, my conclusion is a wrench. A pipe wrench.'

'Plumber's tool.'

'Yes, and easy to come by. This is the oldest injury. I haven't finalized my reconstruction, but . . .' He ordered the image on screen, watched with Eve as the computer-generated figure of the victim was struck from behind by another.

'It reads the blow came from above and behind.'

'Driving down,' Eve noted, 'from over the attacker's head.

So, yeah, yeah, the vic was bent or leaning over when struck. To pick something up, reach for something, tie his damn shoe, but angled down, exposed. He wasn't killed in the alley.'

'From the crime scene images you sent, I agree.'

'Attacked, then transported somewhere so the killer could take some time with him. Attacked, put in a vehicle. Logically, attacked at or near the vehicle, dragged in. The first strike would have put the vic out, right?'

'Rendered unconscious, yes.'

'So, easy to restrain him.'

'Duct tape. I believe the lab will concur,' Morris told her. 'Gummy residue in the wounds, wrists, ankles.'

'But not the mouth.'

'The wounds at the corners of the mouth were caused by rubbing and struggling against a strong, thin cord. Some silicone residue on the teeth and tongue.'

'Ball gag.'

'That's my conclusion, yes.'

'Humiliation, sexual overtones. Was he raped?'

'There's no evidence of sexual activity of any kind.'

'Okay.' Her hands slid into her pockets as she let the image play through her mind. 'So he's knocked out, restrained. He'd still be able to make sounds with that sort of gag, but nothing intelligible. But the killer would hear him try to scream or beg.'

'I have to believe Dorian would have done both. I've sent

for a tox report, so we'll see if any drugs were administered. I didn't find any signs of stunner marks, pressure syringe.'

'Tranq him, he feels less. Where's the fun in that?' She caught herself. 'Sorry, Morris.'

'No need, thinking like the killer leads to finding him. The burn marks. I concur with your on-site. Some were caused by a cigarette, others by a tool. These, for instance.'

He fit on the goggles, as did Eve, and both leaned over the body. 'Lower torso, abdomen, genitals, precise, from a narrow flame.'

'Hand torch. And the limbs, the hands. Those are wider, not precise, grinding out a smoke of some kind. The bruises here, along the rib cage. Not from fists.'

'More likely a sap. Used on the bottom of the feet as well. You see many of the cuts are shallow. Punctures, slices. At least two different blades used.'

'Punctures I'm looking at? Ice pick, or something similar.'

'And the slices, a jagged-edge blade, not smooth like the punctures.'

'Had himself a toolbox.'

'The more superficial wounds came first, along with the burns. Some are approximately two days old.'

'Just getting started. Don't want him dead. Want the fear, the pain, the helplessness.'

'His fingers were broken over the two-day period, not all at once. And the right hand, these bones were crushed. The left were snapped.'

'Stomped on the right, or pounded with a tool, or dropped a heavy weight.'

'The second is my conclusion. A hammer, striking here, along the top ridge of the knuckles, repeatedly, and with force. Left hand first, right within the last twenty-four hours. The deeper cuts and punctures, also within the last twenty-four.'

'Increasing in severity over that twenty-four, working up to the kill.'

'Yes, but, Dallas, the killer treated some of the wounds.'

'What? How?'

'There were traces of what I'm sure the lab will identify as NuSkin or one of its derivatives. Some of the more severe wounds were treated to stop the blood flow, then opened again. And more than once, until the mortal slice along the abdomen.'

'It would take him a while to bleed out from that.'

'Even with the other injuries, the trauma, at least an hour. More likely two before the loss of blood would have taken him under, taken him away from the pain. Death would have taken longer still, but that, at least, would come gently.'

'Does he watch, does he record? The Groom recorded everything, his grand experiment. But this . . . it doesn't feel as organized, as sickly scientific. Humiliate, torture, terrorize.'

She pulled the goggles off, took a hit from her tube of Pepsi, wandered as she tried to visualize.

'Organized enough to have a plan, to have tools, to have

transportation and a place to work. But snapping the fingers of one hand, pulverizing the other, stubbing out a smoke on the limbs, hands, feet, using the tool on the torso and genitals. The sap. Ice pick, jagged blade. Naked. Ball gag. Is it a psychotic grab bag or ... The heart? When did the killer carve the heart?'

'Postmortem, and that with a thin, smooth blade. Very precise, again.'

'Because it's the signature. It's pride or maybe ... Maybe the *D* isn't for Dorian. He didn't matter. His pain, yes, the fun of torturing him, having him splayed out for entertainment, but who he was, his name? What if that didn't matter a damn? If his mother's right, no one who knew him could have done this to him. If no one who knew him did, his name meant nothing. But *D* and *E*, they're important.'

'Carving the heart in him,' Morris murmured, 'like lovers carve a heart and their initials into a tree.'

'Two of them?' Peabody hissed out a breath. 'A couple?'

'It's a theory. And it's Mira territory. I need to run this by her, but it's an interesting theory. They strip him, use a ball gag – a SMB tool, they strip him, burn his balls. But no sexual assault or activity? Because they have each other for that.'

'If this is valid, it would make what they did to him—'

'Foreplay,' Eve finished when Morris couldn't.

Morris laid a hand on the shoulder of his dead friend. 'I never ask, and shouldn't now. But find them.'

No, he never asked, Eve thought. And she shouldn't answer as she felt compelled to. 'I will. You can bank on it.'

'He's sad again.' Peabody waited until they were outside. 'The vic made him think of Coltraine, so he's sad again.'

'He'll get through it.' But Eve considered calling the priest, remembering Morris had found both comfort and friendship with Chale López. 'We work the case, we get it done, and he'll get through it faster.'

'Do you want me to see if I can schedule a meeting with Mira?'

'Yeah. We're going into Central first. I want to get the book and board going, stew on this couple theory a little. Tell her I'll send her a report.'

'Got it. You think this was random – I mean the choice of vic.'

'Can't say. Right now we don't even know where he was attacked, where he was snatched. We need to talk to friends and associates,' she continued as she drove through thickening snowfall. 'Stick with the E's first – we don't throw out one theory for another. But start contacting them and arranging for them to come to us at Central. That way if Mira has a window, I can slip through it.'

Peabody fell silent and into work, then paused, frowned out the window at the snow. 'I think it was a couple.'

'Because you think I think it was?'

'That made me see the maybe, but my first reaction was

53

no. Just no, that's too sick. Then – I'm going to say it before you do – we've seen sicker. A lot sicker. But it was the classic romance symbol of the heart that made me say no, then made me see the yes. They signed him – or one did for the other – not like a piece of art, but in a symbol of their twisted idea of love.'

Eve waited a beat. 'Why does that piss you off?'

'Because I believe in symbols of love, goddamn it. There's this big-ass tree back home. My dad carved his and Mom's initials in it before any of us were born. And when we started coming along he built this circular bench all the way around it – gave it plenty of space between to grow more. And it has. It was so they could sit there, watching us play, and looking out over the gardens. And when each of us got to be about six, he helped us each build our own birdhouse, so there's all these birdhouses hanging in the limbs, and wind chimes my mother made, and . . . It's special, it's really special, and it started when he carved that heart and their initials inside it. And . . . '

'Don't blubber, Peabody,' Eve warned, hearing it coming.

'I'm not going to blubber. It's just that when we went there for Christmas my parents took us both out there, to the tree, and my dad handed McNab his knife, and told him he should carve our initials in the tree. Because they know I love him, and he loves me, and they believe it's the real, long-haul thing. It meant so much to me, just so much, because the tree, it's special. It matters. Symbols matter, and they shouldn't be used like this. That's all.'

Eve said nothing until she'd pulled into the garage at Central, parked in her spot. 'People defile and despoil what's good and pure and special every single fucking day. We see it, we know it, we deal with it.'

'I know, but—'

'Shut up. You think about this. When some sick fuck uses what's good and pure and special in his sick-fuck way, it just makes the symbol stronger and more important. It doesn't lessen it one damn bit, unless you let it.'

Because she had blubbered a little, Peabody scrubbed her hands over her face. 'You're right. You're so completely right. I just let it get to me.'

'It was nice,' Eve said as they got out of the car. 'What your parents did, it was nice.'

She glanced over at the quick click of heels, saw Mira cutting toward the elevator from her own space.

Eve thought the color of the coat that skimmed to the knees of Dr Charlotte Mira's excellent legs might be called aquamarine. The heels were certainly emerald as was the hint of the dress under the coat. A sassy beret of rich sapphire blue perched on her smooth bob of mink-colored hair. She carried a purse of the same color as the beret and a shoulder-strap briefcase of supple bronze leather.

'Well, good morning. Are you just coming in, or ... Peabody, are you all right?'

Instinctively, Peabody scrubbed at her face again. 'Oh yeah. I just had a moment, that's all. And I just tagged your admin to see if you could squeeze Dallas in for a consult.'

'So you're just getting in, but not just coming on.' Mira turned her quiet blue eyes to Eve. 'I'm actually not due in for another twenty minutes. I left early as I wasn't sure how traffic would be once the snow started. I can come up with you to your office now, if you have the time.'

'I'll make it.'

When she could grab time with the department's top shrink and profiler, she grabbed it.

'A new case? You've just gotten back from holiday.'

'We got back yesterday afternoon. We caught the case about four this morning when a beat droid found the body.'

Seeing no point in wasting time, Eve started the rundown as they got on the elevator.

'Dennis and I went to the Met with friends, saw *Giselle* just last weekend. Your victim must have been playing.' Mira shifted as the elevator shuddered to a stop on nearly every floor and more cops piled on. 'Held and tortured for two days. Sexual component?'

'None that shows. The killer used a precise flame – probably a hand torch – to inflict small burns on the genitals.'

Every male cop on the crowded car shifted, and Eve imagined cop balls shrinking up in sympathy and defense.

'No mutilation?'

'Not your standard. Broken bones, burns, cuts, bruises.

Primarily torso, abdomen, limbs, broken and crushed fingers. Hacked his hair off, left insulting little tufts of it. He had a lot of thick, shiny hair.'

'Humiliation. But the face, nearly unmarked, no mutilation of the genitals. It doesn't feel personal.'

'Somebody takes a torch to my balls, I'm taking it personal,' one of the cops said. Mira smiled at him.

'Burns heal, Officer, given the time. Personal would be slicing them up or off.'

'Acid.' Eve spoke casually. 'I caught one once where the girlfriend got pissed, and when the guy was crashed on Zoner, poured acid on his balls.'

Grateful when the elevator stopped on Homicide level, Eve pushed her way through cops, did her best to make a hole for Mira and Peabody.

'Everyone with balls on that car is going to check his own, first chance,' she said, and made Mira laugh.

'I think that's an accurate analysis.'

When they turned into Homicide, Eve saw Detective Baxter start to stand up, as if he'd been watching for her. But he settled back again.

'Hey, Dr Mira. Looking good.'

'As do you, Detective. Always.' Mira glanced toward the corner where they'd had the perfectly pathetic holiday tree. And where Eve, Baxter and nearly every cop currently in the room had come far too close to death on the last day of 2060.

'I'll miss your very eclectic and inclusive holiday decorations,' she said. 'Maybe you can do something for Valentine's Day.'

'Not ever.' Eve said it definitely in case anybody got some weird ideas. 'Peabody, start arranging the interviews. Dr Mira, why don't you go into my office? I'm right behind you.' But she crossed to Baxter first.

'Something hot?'

'No, nothing hot, boss.' He shrugged shoulders that filled out a smart, perfectly cut suit. 'Just something I wanted to touch base with you on when you get a minute.'

'After I talk to Mira.' She looked across the room, studied Jenkinson's tie. Today's had white snowflakes swirling against a blue so bold and lively Eve thought it might have a pulse.

'That's never going to stop, is it?'

Baxter grinned, shook his head. 'It's now a Homicide Division tradition. Reineke told me Jenkinson's found a street vendor who'll sell them to him at a discount when he buys five at a go.'

'God help us all,' Eve muttered, and walked away to join Mira.

4

In Eve's office with its single skinny window, Mira sat in the ass-biting visitor's chair – as close to its edge as she could manage without tipping over.

'Let me get this set up, then you can take the desk chair.' Eve frowned at the ugly, miserable excuse for a chair she'd had since she'd had the office. 'I guess I should probably requisition a new visitor's chair.'

'Which you haven't done before because you'd prefer not to have visitors in here.'

'It's getting hard to keep them out. I didn't mean you.'

Understanding perfectly, Mira pulled off her beret, fluffed her rich brown hair. 'Not today at any rate.'

'You want some of that tea? I've got some.'

'Actually, at this time of the day I wouldn't mind some of your superior coffee.'

Eve walked to the AutoChef – every bit as ancient as the chair – programmed two coffees. 'I want to get the board up. It'll be easier to show you.' With the coffee at her elbow, Eve sat at the desk to get it started. After interfacing her recorder, she ordered the crime scene shots she wanted.

'I'll have a report written up, and a copy of Morris's findings within the hour,' she began. 'Next of kin – vic's mother – has been notified and interviewed. Other than the vic's doorman, we haven't talked to anyone else. Peabody and I went through his residence, tagged electronics for EDD, but there's nothing in there to indicate he had trouble. The picture coming through,' she continued as she transferred images to her board, 'is of a successful, talented man who had a wide group of friends. That included Morris, as a kind of acquaintance.'

'Morris knew the victim?'

'The vic routinely dropped into jazz and blues clubs, jammed with other musicians. He had a range of musical talent and interests.'

'As does Morris,' Mira said with a nod.

'Quick aside. It hit him kind of hard – reminded him of Coltraine. You could see it. I thought about calling the priest – López. They hit it off.'

Mira nodded again. 'It's a good thought. I'd give him a day or two, see if he reaches out himself, or feels the need. You're a very good judge, a good friend. You'll know.'

'Okay.' It helped, and bought her time before she moved on the idea of poking into Morris's personal business. She'd give it a day or two.

'Morris's impressions of him jibe with the mother's

interview,' Eve continued, more comfortable with the business of death. 'Nice guy, talented guy, friendly, who enjoyed intimate relationships with both sexes on, reputedly, a casual basis. No enemies, no particular lover, very social, very dedicated to his craft.'

Rising, Eve pointed to her chair. She preferred standing in any case. 'We haven't established when he was taken, or if he went willingly. As the blow to the back of the head was the first strike, it's more likely he was attacked and taken, then held for two days. Tortured.'

Though Mira rose, she didn't take Eve's chair but stood beside her, studying the board. 'Burns, lacerations, contusions. Bones crushed and broken.'

'Increasing in severity. Lesser ones are older. Three kinds of sharps is Morris's opinion. An ice pick or something similar, a jagged–edged blade and a smooth blade. The burns are from both cigarettes and a flame tool – one capable of pinpoint, precise flame. The vic was restrained with duct tape, or a similar product, but gagged with a ball gag.'

'Most usually a sexual tool.'

'No sign of sexual assault or activity. And you can see the wounds on the genitals are less severe than those on the torso and limbs.'

'The same with his face, but the hair was shorn and hacked off – crudely. And the body was naked. Those are humiliation, and the hair would be more personal. But the lack of mutilation, face and genitals is more impersonal.'

61

'And this.' Eve tapped the photo of the carved heart and initials.

'*D* for Dorian. *E* for the killer.' Mira frowned. 'Very personal, even romantic. It's very precisely done, isn't it? But . . .'

'Yeah, but.'

'I would expect to see more attention paid to the genitals, the face. I would expect some sort of sexual component. If this was a jilted or unhappy lover, or a delusional fan who craved and imagined a relationship, I would expect to see that reflected in his wounds.'

'Yeah. And what we see is an escalation – humiliation, pain, fear, blood – and Morris said some of the wounds were treated.'

'Ah.' Mira nodded. 'To keep it from ending too soon. The slice across the abdomen was the final?'

'Yeah, that's the kill shot, and would have taken some time to take the vic under, for him to bleed out.'

'We'll need more data on the victim, a better sense of him and those around him. But if this was random – not personal – it's very possible you have a team.'

That clicked, just clicked for her. 'Romantically, sexually linked, initials *D* and *E*, who get off on torture and murder.'

'I need more data,' Mira began, 'but if the victim was specifically targeted, you'd look for someone who wanted to humiliate and terrorize, while having complete control. If Dorian Kuper was chosen randomly, and this is where I lean with the current data, you would still look for a sadist, one who uses both the symbolic sadism of cutting off the hair, as well as the infliction of pain while the victim is bound and helpless.'

'The heart changes it. The signature changes it,' Eve insisted.

'Perhaps. If this is a couple then it's highly likely they are sexual sadists who use this humiliation, this control, this infliction of pain as sexual stimulus – which they use for each other rather than the victim. There's no piquerism,' she murmured. 'No stabbing of the breasts, the buttocks, no mutilation of genitals, no rape. The variance in wounds, in tools ...'

She broke off and, as Eve often did, circled around the board, the office. 'Most usually you'd expect a dominant and a submissive. One to inflict the pain, one to watch. Or one to order the submission to inflict the pain. But, at this preliminary stage, it may be they are a true couple, a team of equal power and authority.'

'It has to be planned out – not impulse. Had to have the place – private place to torture this vic for two days. The transportation, the tools.'

'Predatory psychopath – or psychopaths – who plan, even rehearse. Sadists who enjoy and are stimulated by inflicting pain. Lust murder perhaps. The death and dying he or they cause brings intense pleasure. The heart symbolizes love, unity. They believe themselves in love, and the victim is a gift to each other.'

'I don't know if Kuper's the first – we're running like

crimes – but he won't be the last. Predators have to hunt. Sadists need victims. And lovers, if we're dealing with that, need that sexual rush.'

'Agreed. It is possible that, while the heart is a signature, a symbol, the killer romanticizes his kill, the victim. It may be a single predator, lacking the sexual drive and component. A romantic. I'm sorry I can't be more definitive.'

'No, I've got clear avenues to pursue. And we'll have more data once we pull in friends, coworkers. We'll know more when we get something from IRCCA. I'll send you a report once I have enough to put together. Thanks for the time.'

'Paid in full by the coffee.' She handed Eve the empty cup, then smiled. 'You look well rested. I can't say that often.'

'I had days to do pretty much nothing but lie around.'

'You earned it. None of us will forget how we spent the last day of the year anytime soon. Keep me in the loop,' she added, with another glance at the board before she left. 'I very much want to profile this one.'

Alone, Eve sat to write up her preliminary report, to start the murder book, to refine the board. She added Morris's report when it came through, then glanced up when she heard the clomp of Peabody's fuzzy-topped boots.

'I've got the first of the interviews coming in,' she reported. 'I staggered them by thirty minutes. I was able to pull in Chamberlin. He talked the vic's mother into taking a tranq, and activated Maeve the droid to stay with her. He's pretty anxious to talk to you, so I put him first.'

'Good. Always good to talk to the top guy. Now if they'd just send me – Finally,' she said when her computer signaled incoming. 'IRCCA results. Computer, on screen.'

Peabody edged in as the data began to scroll.

'Holy shit, Dallas, that's a lot of like crimes.'

'Computer, remove any closed cases. Remove any result that includes sexual assault, mutilation or rape.'

Leaning back, Eve lifted her eyebrows. 'That takes it down. Computer, highlight all results with the element of a heart carved or burned into the body.'

Those brows lowered and knit when twenty highlighted.

'Results with the initials *D* and *E* carved or burned into the body.'

'I repeat, Dallas. Holy shit.'

'Twenty,' Eve stated. 'Twenty from Tennessee to New Jersey. Males, females, an assortment of races, ages. No specific type. First one's last September. It averages about one a week, but . . . '

'Some gaps,' Peabody commented. 'A couple weeks between some, or ten days, then see how it escalates in Ohio, Pennsylvania to two a week, then it drops off again.'

'Because there's more than twenty.'

'More?'

'A predator like this? Once they get a taste they need more, and like a junkie they start to need faster. Destroyed some of the bodies?' Eve speculated. 'Concealed them, buried them? Maybe tried something different so it doesn't pop here, but it's more likely they concealed, destroyed. Killed a few nobody's looking for. A vagrant, an itinerant worker, a sidewalk sleeper.'

'The *D* doesn't apply to the vic after all.'

'No. *E* and *D*, just a couple of crazy kids in love. Computer, display route pattern by victim, chronologically.'

Working . . .

'The first one here,' Eve began while the computer analyzed, 'in September, in Nashville. Female, early twenties, missing for fifty-six hours. Found dead in an unoccupied home by the real-estate agent and a potential buyer.'

'I bet that dropped the asking price.'

'Ha. She'd been dead for about twenty-eight hours. Didn't spend as long with her. No unidentified prints or DNA at the crime scene.

'She wasn't their first.'

Task complete, the computer announced.

'Display on screen.' Eve watched the route form, point by point, death by death.

'Some winding around,' Peabody noted, 'but pretty much heading northeast.'

'A couple short detours.' Maybe taking in some points of interest, Eve speculated, maybe visiting friends. 'You might have to take a quick side trip for your fun. Is New York the destination, or just another point on the route?'

Insufficient data to reach conclusion.

'I wasn't asking you. Computer, copy all data to my home unit, to Detective Peabody's home and office unit. Peabody, start contacting primary investigators on these cases – and find out if the FBI's nosed in, and if so, get the agent in charge.'

'I'll start on that. Chamberlin's going to be here any minute.'

'I'll take him. Did you book a room?'

'You've got Interview A, for six hours if you want it.'

She only nodded. 'Dorian Kuper didn't know his killer. He was just next in line. But maybe we'll find out something. I'll start the interviews. You get the data. Let me know when you've got all you can get. Have Chamberlin put in Interview A if he comes in before I'm out. I need five minutes. Shit. Ten.'

She banged out a report to Mira – she'd report to her commander as soon as she could, but wanted Mira to have the new data. Before she'd finished, she heard a brisk clip coming her way.

Not Peabody, she thought, lighter step, better shoes.

Baxter.

And when she glanced over, mildly annoyed, Baxter stepped into her doorway.

'Got a few minutes?'

'I'm a little pressed here.' She finished the report as she spoke, sent it.

'Yeah, I see that.' He glanced at her board, her screen. 'Fuck me. The same?'

'I haven't had a chance to run probability, but I'm going to say it's high. I've got somebody coming into interview, Baxter, make it fast.'

'It can wait.'

If she didn't make time for her men, she might be a good investigator, but she'd be a lousy boss.

'Spill it. I've got a few.'

'It's just ... Trueheart's going in for the detective's exam in a couple days.'

'Yeah. I've got it marked. Is there a problem?'

'No. Maybe. No.'

Eve sat back. Baxter stood with his hands in his pockets, jiggling whatever was in them. It wasn't his usual style. She waited.

'I pushed him, you know. I really leaned on him to apply – and I nudged at you to clear it.'

'I didn't clear it because you nudged me.'

'So he's ready?'

'Have you got any reason to think otherwise?'

'No. I mean he's sweating it some. You have to sweat it some. He's been studying. I've been grilling him.'

The jiggling stopped, started up again. Eve let it play out.

'He's got good instincts, LT, and a hell of a work ethic. He's a damn good cop. He's still got some green on him, but he's never going to lose all of it. It's part of what makes him the kind of damn good cop he is. It's just – I really pushed him to try for detective.'

'Do you think, if he didn't feel ready, he'd try for it just to make you happy?'

Baxter opened his mouth, then blew out a breath. 'No. He doesn't push that easy, not anymore. It's me. Jesus, boss, it's me. I haven't had a decent night sleep since – well, since we all nearly blew up. I figured it was because we all nearly blew up, but it's not. Hell, you get used to nearly buying it somehow or another on the job. I don't want to let the kid down.'

'Then relax, you haven't. I wondered when I hooked him to you how it would go. He needed some of the dew wiped off. And you wiped it off without taking away what makes him. You've trained him, Baxter, and you helped make him a damn good cop. If he doesn't make detective this time, all it means is he's not ready for it. If he does, and it's more likely, I figure you're going to ask me to assign him as your partner. And that's what I'll do, but I'm also going to tell you if, at some point, you want to train another, I'll put that through. You're better at it than I thought you'd be.'

'Okay. Okay. Appreciate it. You know, I wasn't this tied up when I went for my own detective's shield.'

'Because you were cocksure of yourself. Are you on anything hot?'

'No. We had an open and closed first thing this morning. I thought we'd review a few open and unsolveds, keep his brain turned on sharp.'

'I may have something else that would do that. Go ahead and start a review. If this turns out how it looks, I've got plenty to keep his brain sharp. Now beat it.'

'Beating it.'

'Baxter? If somebody's not a damn good cop, they don't stay in my division.'

He nodded, relaxed a bit. 'Thanks, LT.'

As he walked away, she took another minute to sit, to study the board, to think of Dorian Kuper.

Then she pushed away from her desk and started out. Peabody turned into the bull pen as Eve turned out.

'Good timing. I just put Chamberlin in Interview A. He's in pretty rough shape himself, Dallas.'

'I might get more out of him that way. Mira's got the data now. You should write up a report for Whitney. And don't say *Me?* in that stupid tone,' Eve warned. 'You know how to write a damn report, and it'll save me the time. Contact all the primaries you can manage, and we'll go over that when I'm done with the interviews. If you need any help, tap Baxter and Trueheart. They're clear, just reviewing some open and unsolveds.'

'Ellysa Tesh – violin – should be here in thirty.'

'I'll take her after Chamberlin. Let's keep it moving.'

She found Chamberlin sitting in Interview A, his hands

folded on the scarred table. Exhausted eyes shifted from his hands to Eve's face.

'I need to get back to Mina as soon as possible.'

'I won't keep you long. I'm going to record this interview. Record on,' she ordered. 'Dallas, Lieutenant Eve in interview with Chamberlin, Ethan. Mr Chamberlin, I'm going to advise you of your rights. This is procedure.'

'It wouldn't be the first time.'

Eve read off the Revised Miranda.

'I understand, and I don't want some damn lawyer. Am I a suspect?'

'Right now we're gathering information. I think you can help us with that. You worked with Dorian, and are, I believe, in a relationship with his mother.'

'Mina and I have been in a committed, monogamous relationship for a number of years.'

'You don't live together.'

'We both enjoy our separate spaces. Dorian ... Dorian was the world to her. It's a cliché, I'm aware, but it's the truth that he was like a son to me. If we had disagreements they were always over the music. He has – had – such tremendous talent. With such talent comes opinions.'

He nearly smiled; it nearly reached his eyes. 'Now and again those opinions proved better than mine. Not often, but now and again.'

'You've got a temper, Mr Chamberlin.'

'That's right. I've paid my share of fines, done the anger

71

management bullshit. Screw it.' He flicked that away with a dramatic sweep of his hand. 'It's my passion and temper that make me great. It's my passion and temper that make every musician I work with perform brilliantly. Because I demand it.'

'And if they're not brilliant enough, you break their piccolo.'

'I've been known to.' He shrugged it off. 'If someone doesn't perform brilliantly, they don't deserve to be in my orchestra.'

As she'd said essentially the same to Baxter about her cops, Eve could find no fault there. 'Did you ever bust up Dorian's cello?'

'Dorian was always brilliant. The world's lesser for the loss of him. Lieutenant . . .'

He gripped his hands together again until the knuckles went white. 'Please don't allow Mina to see him until he's . . . She told me he'd been tortured, and if there are physical signs—' He broke off, looked away for a moment. 'Please don't let her see him until he's been made . . . I don't want what was done to him to be her last memory of him. I know exceptional makeup artists.'

'You can trust Dr Morris – the medical examiner – on this.'

'I don't know this Morris.'

'I do. You can trust him.'

His gaze arrowed back, pinned hers. 'If Dorian isn't – if he doesn't look as he should, I'll hold this Morris, and you, responsible.'

'Understood. Accepted.'

'Do you really think I could have done what was done to him. Torture?'

'No,' Eve said easily, watched Chamberlin blink in surprise. 'But it's early in the investigative process. You tell me who could have done this to him.'

'I don't know.' The admission had him fisting his hands on the table. 'I know a great many of his friends and acquaintances. I know every member of my orchestra. And I don't know.'

'He was, by your own words, always brilliant, and thought of like a son by the conductor. That could easily foster jealousy, resentment, rage.'

Chamberlin shook his head. 'He'd work with anyone who might be having difficulty. He'd come in early, or stay late. He lived for music and for people. Is there competition, conflict, drama, in the orchestra? If not, there's no passion, and without passion there can't be brilliance. But I know my orchestra, and no one in it would have done this.'

He leaned forward. 'What was done to him? Will you tell me? What did they want from him? If they'd wanted money, he'd have given it to them! What did this maniac want from Dorian?'

His pain, Eve thought. His blood. His death. But she only

said, 'It's early in the investigation. I can promise you Dorian has all my attention, and we're actively pursing all angles.'

'That's double-talk.'

'It's truth, and all I can give you. When did you last see Dorian?'

'Two nights ago – three come tonight. At the perform-ance. Mina and I had a late supper afterward with some friends. When we realized the next day he hadn't come home, we weren't alarmed, but we were when he missed his call for the next night's performance. He had never – would never. I explained all this to the detective when we reported him missing.'

'Tell me now.'

'We asked if anyone had seen him. Theo Barron, oboe, said he and a couple others were going to meet Dorian at this club downtown. After Midnight. He often went there to jam, to unwind. But he hadn't shown up. Theo thought he'd probably just ended up with someone. Drinks, sex. Dorian had a varied sex life. Theo had tried his 'link, left a couple messages, but didn't think much of it. But then he still didn't answer, and he hadn't come home at all.'

'Why didn't they go down together? This Theo and Dorian?'

'Theo was in a flirtation with one of the altos in the opera company, and he wanted to wait until she'd changed as he'd convinced her to go with him. Theo said Dorian went on ahead.'

'How would he get downtown, generally?'

'A cab. He'd have taken a cab.'

'Okay.' She made a note. 'What do you know about Earnestina?'

'Ah.' Chamberlin let out a half laugh. 'Pompous little twit. She interviewed me and some of the others – both orchestra and stage – for a paper she claimed to be writing. *Earnest* was a kind word. Pompous, as I said, overbearing, extreme. Dorian was kind to her, likely considered sleeping with her, but she caused a scene at that club he enjoyed. I don't know the details as I wasn't there, but she annoyed him. He would never have gone anywhere with her after that.'

'Do you have her full name?'

'Tina R. Denton. I remember it as she insisted on the full name – including initial.' He sat back, pressed his fingers to his eyes briefly. 'Lieutenant, she was like a mosquito. A woman who buzzed around until you wanted to give her a good slap, but wasn't capable of doing more than making you itch a little.'

'Every angle,' Eve reminded him. 'Go back to Dorian's mother now. When Dr Morris has him ready, you'll be contacted. If you think of anything else, any detail, I want to hear it.'

As she escorted him out, she saw a woman – early thirties, long blond hair yanked back in a tail, exposing a lovely face, a face splotchy from tears, and deep blue eyes swollen and red-rimmed.

She said, 'Maestro,' in a voice that broke.

Chamberlin turned to her and, when she hesitated, held out his arms.

'Maestro,' she said again, flung herself at him to press her face into his chest. 'Is it a terrible dream? Can you tell me it's a terrible dream?'

'No. He's gone, Ellysa.'

'How?' She reared back, grief and fury warring on her face. 'No one will tell us how, no one will tell us why.'

'I will. Ellysa Tesh?'

'Yes. Who are you?'

'Lieutenant Dallas. We'll talk in here.'

'Do you want me to stay with you?' Chamberlin asked.

'It's best if I speak with Ms Tesh alone. In here,' Eve repeated, and opened the door to Interview A.

'I'll be all right. Mina?'

'I'm going to her now.'

'Should I come? When I can? Should we come?'

'Not now. Let me see, and perhaps tomorrow.' He laid his lips on her brow. 'Perhaps tomorrow.'

Once she'd taken Ellysa in, reengaged the recorder, read off the Revised Miranda, Ellysa pushed her hands in the air as if shoving all that aside.

'I don't care about my rights or your recording. What happened to Dorian?'

'You're here to answer questions. Let's start with that. When did you last see or speak with Dorian?'

'At the performance, the night he went missing. What happened to—'

'Where did you go after the performance?'

'Oh for God's sake. I went with Theo and Hanna and Samuel. We cabbed downtown to a club. After Midnight. Dorian went ahead of us, but he wasn't there. I wanted to go with him, but . . . I got hung up.'

'Hung up?'

'My mother. She lives in Austin, and she tagged me up right after the performance. My sister got engaged. My mother was so excited, and I got hung talking with her, and didn't catch up to Dorian in time to tell him I'd go with him. If I had . . . If I had.'

Her eyes filled again, tears shimmering on the edge. 'We must have been close to an hour behind him. Hanna had to change out of her costume, and take off her stage makeup. At least thirty or forty minutes behind him, I don't know. But he wasn't there, and Stewie said he hadn't come in.'

'Stewie?'

'The bartender. We're regulars – Dorian most of all, but a lot of us go down to listen to music, or to play, to relax. He wasn't there,' she murmured. 'I thought – we thought – he'd run into someone and decided to go somewhere else. Theo tried to tag him, but it went to v-mail. He didn't come the next night. He's never missed a performance. That's when everyone started to worry. We couldn't find him, but the police said we had to wait before Mina could file a missing persons. If you'd started to look sooner—'

'It wouldn't have mattered,' Eve finished. 'Did he know you were in love with him?'

Ellysa pressed her lips together, shook her head as her eyes welled yet again. 'No. I was careful he didn't see it. He'd have been kind, and kindness would have crushed me. We slept together now and then, but I knew for him it was sex and friendship. Affection. I liked to think one day, when he was ready, he'd see. He'd see I'd loved him since the first time . . . Three years, two months, five days. That's when I joined the company. That's the first time I saw him, the first time I heard him play. That's how long I've been in love with him.

'Please. *Please* tell me what happened to him. You know. Tell me what happened to Dorian.'

'Who do you know who'd want to hurt him?'

'No one. No one,' she repeated. 'Some people have the ability to walk lightly through the world and still leave a deep impression. That's Dorian. I know who you are. I knew when your partner contacted me. I've read the book, I've seen the vid. I watch screen. I know you investigate murders. Was it a mugging?'

'No.' It would come out, Eve thought, soon enough. 'The current line of investigation indicates he was abducted, held for two days in a currently unknown location where he was tortured and killed.'

'Tor— What do you mean?' Her face froze; her color

drained so that for a moment she seemed carved in ice. 'What does that mean?'

'Whoever held him against his will hurt him. Do you know anyone who had that kind of grudge against him? Do you know if Dorian had information someone would want enough to give him pain in order to get it? Did he owe money, did he have secrets?'

'No.' The word choked out of her, then she shook her head furiously. 'No, no, no. He had secrets, I imagine, as anyone does. He didn't owe anyone money, not that I know of, and he didn't gamble particularly, he didn't do illegals. He didn't do the sorts of things that put you into debt. Two days? Oh God, two days? All that time, hurting him.'

She shoved up from the table, crossing her arms, hugging herself as she circled the small room. 'Two days. God. God. No, no, no. No one who knew him could have done that.'

She spun back to Eve, eyes ravaged. 'You're married. The book, the vid, and what I've seen on screen – it makes it clear you're in love with your husband.'

'My life's irrelevant.'

'It *isn't*! You know what it is to love someone, to know them, because to really love, all the way in, you have to know. I know Dorian. No one we know could have done this. Someone else. Some sick, twisted, sadistic bastard. Can you give me a hand, can you spare a few dollars, can you show me how to get to Seventh Avenue – that's all it would take. He'd help. Dorian would help. He took a cab.'

She pressed her hands to her face. 'What time, what time? It couldn't have been much past eleven-thirty. He'd have gone right out front, hailed a cab. You find out. You need to find out if he got in a cab or whoever did this, if they took him right from Lincoln Center. Or if he got downtown, and they took him from there. You need to—'

'I'll do my job, Ms Tesh, I promise you.'

'You didn't know him.'

'That doesn't matter. He's mine now, and he'll get my best.'

'Are you as good as they made out you are in the book, in the vid?'

'He'll get my best,' Eve repeated.

5

Eve walked back to the bull pen and Peabody's desk.

'Give me what you've got. We're going to switch off.'

'FBI's in it. The agent in charge is Carl Zweck. They're following up a lead in Branson, Missouri, but have already connected with the primary in Pleasant Acres, New Jersey, on the murder last week. I just finished talking to her,' Peabody continued. 'Detective Francine Lupine. They're small town, Dallas, and don't have a lot of resources or experience with serials. She's looking for all the help she can get.

'Transferring notes to your computer right now. I reached out to the two primaries in Pennsylvania. Working my way back. FBI's profiled a team, the romantic angle, just where we're leaning.'

'Suspects? Descriptions?'

'They got nothing.' Peabody lifted her hands. 'I'm wading through reams of reports and federal doublespeak, but it comes down to not so much. It looks like the unsubs switch vehicles here and there, and the ones recovered – in the cases where the owner was a vic – are wiped clean. Dozens of interviews over the past couple months, and conflicting reports, as you'd expect. A man and a woman, two males, various races, age ranges. The probability run is higher on the hetero couple, and the profile is giving an age range of twenty-five to thirty-five.'

Which was, Eve agreed, not so much.

'I'll work with this. The interviews here indicate the vic left after the performance, with plans to go downtown to After Midnight. Several friends were to join him. Earnestina is Tina R. Denton. She's not going to play into this, but we'll follow up.'

A follow-up wasn't wasting time, Eve thought, even when it felt like it.

'The most likely now is Kuper caught a cab, went downtown, and they grabbed him. Random choice, wrong place, wrong time. You're looking for insight from the remaining interviews, and corroboration on the timeline and movements on the night the vic went missing. And if I'm wrong, any sense he was stalked or threatened prior.'

'You're not going to be wrong. Everything I've got here says these two breeze into a town, a community, choose a vic, have their fun and move on. Identified areas so far are usually remote areas or, in more urban areas, an abandoned building. Two or three days, they're done. They could already be done here, Dallas, and gone. That's the pattern.'

'We follow through. Look at the route, Peabody. They

were aiming for New York. This is where they wanted to be. Let's find out why.'

In her office, she reviewed Peabody's notes, and set up a second board. For once as she arranged the data on previous victims, she wished for bigger office space.

It took some doing, but she tracked the cab. Her vic had hailed one on Broadway, and taken it downtown where – at his request – the cab dropped him at the corner of Perry and Seventh – a few blocks shy of the club.

Why? Eve wondered. Nice night?

She did a quick back check on the weather, nodded.

'Nice night,' she murmured. 'Take a little walk, stretch your legs, get some air. You know the neighborhood. How'd they mark you?'

She sat again, put her boots on the desk, shut her eyes.

The female, she thought – because she believed the probability of a hetero couple – use the female to lure him.

Excuse me? Try flirty but flustered, just a little helpless. Certainly harmless. *Could you help me? I'm lost.*

Yeah, maybe, maybe just that simple.

Or the ploy Dahmer used – that classic had proven to do the job in all the decades following.

Lone woman struggling to lift something heavy into the back of a vehicle.

Can I give you a hand?

Oh, golly. Would you mind? I just can't quite get it up there.

83

Vic does the good deed, and the male comes up behind, bashes him. They drag him into the back of the vehicle – van or all-terrain – one jumps in with him to restrain, the other gets behind the wheel.

She opened her eyes again, studied the board.

Can't hold him in the vehicle for two days. Got a hole somewhere, got a place. How'd they get it? Downtown, highest probability. It's where they took him, it's where they dumped him.

She ran the route, the drive time from Perry to Mechanics Alley. Highlighted the sector on her map.

Possible kill location, she thought. Somewhere in that sector.

Abandoned building? Nothing stayed empty for long, she thought. Junkies, sidewalk sleepers, squatters, somebody moved in.

She did a search, found six potentials, arranged for uniforms to check them out.

Then she picked up where Peabody had left off, began to reach out to other cops with other victims.

Mid-afternoon, and looking a little hollow-eyed, Peabody came in, dropped a vending bag on Eve's desk.

'What is that?'

'It a Vegalicious Pocket – it's new. And, well, I'd call it Vegaterrible, but it fills the hole. Can I get coffee, my post-holiday-workout-daily butt is seriously dragging.'

Eve just wagged a thumb at the AutoChef, and filled

Peabody in on the victim's movements, the notes from other primaries.

'The one in Woodsbury, Ohio, is keeping it front and center. It's the first murder in his town for over a decade, and he's taking it personal. He may be a good resource as we progress, and – Jesus Christ.'

Eve managed – barely – to swallow the bite she'd taken out of the vending pocket, then grabbed Peabody's coffee regular, gulped. 'Oh, and nearly as bad. Who deliberately makes anything that tastes like that?'

'Maybe there are more sadists out there than we can possibly imagine.'

'Crap. Crap. I don't even want to think about what's in there, and now it's inside me. Along with coffee murdered by milk and sugar. And now I'm hungry.'

Eve dumped the offensive pocket in the recycler where it belonged. 'I wasn't hungry, and now I am. Damn it.'

She went to the AutoChef, programmed a vitamin smoothie.

And was shocked when that's exactly what she got.

It has worked for Feeney, she thought, bitterly, disguising his real coffee for a spinach smoothie in his office machine. But did she get the candy bar she'd disguised in there?

No, she did not.

'Goddamn Candy Thief. I should've known he'd steal me blind while I was on leave.'

'You have candy in there? What kind of—'

'Not anymore.' In disgust, Eve went back to her desk, yanked out a drawer. 'Bastard leaves the dumbass power bars, takes the really good chocolate.'

'Chocolate!'

'Gone.' In penance for her own failure, Eve took a glug from the smoothie – which could have been worse – unwrapped the power bar.

'On the map,' she said. 'It's logical to assume they hit him between Perry and Christopher. Tag-teamed him, disabled, got him in the vehicle, restrained. Most probable hole would be this sector. I've got uniforms checking out abandoned buildings.'

'I'm not getting anything new or salient in the interviews. Theo Barron and Samuel Deeks came in on their own, so I went ahead and talked to them.'

'Part of the After Midnight group.'

'Right. Theo cried the whole time, kept saying if he hadn't tried to score with the singer – Hanna – he'd have been with Dorian, and Dorian would still be alive.'

'He's right about that.' When Peabody's tired eyes widened, Eve waved her off. 'It doesn't make him guilty or responsible or at fault, it's just fact. These two wouldn't have tried for a couple of guys at once. They take singles – that we know of.'

'You still think there's more.'

'It's not fact, yet. But it's logical. Some gaps on the route. Now, maybe they were in a hurry to get from one point to another, or maybe they just didn't find anybody who did it for them, but the most logical conclusion is they killed somebody in these gaps. It hasn't been connected, or the body hasn't been found. But here . . . ' With the power bar she gestured to the New York map. 'This is promising. We'll check it out.'

'I scheduled this break time, but we've got more coming in for interviews.'

'Are Baxter and Trueheart still in the bull pen?'

'Yeah, they haven't caught anything.'

'Fill them in,' Eve ordered. 'They'll take over the interviews while we're in the field. Give me five to update Mira, send an update to Whitney.'

She tried for an actual conversation with Mira, but was told in no uncertain terms by Mira's dragon of an admin the doctor was in meetings. So Eve settled for hammering out a quick update, copying both Mira and her commander.

Because it was there, she drank down the rest of the smoothie, then grabbed her coat.

'You set?' she asked Baxter, with a nod to Trueheart as she hit the bull pen.

'We've got it.'

She paused a moment, shifted back to Trueheart's young, earnest face. 'Are you set otherwise, Officer?'

'I . . . yes, sir.'

'She means the detective's exam, my young apprentice.'

'Yes, sir. I'm prepared for it.'

'Stay that way. Peabody, with me.'

Eve swung on her coat as she headed to the glides and, remembering the vicious cold of the morning, pulled out the scarf Peabody had knitted her.

'The FBI are looking at Tennessee as the first,' she began. 'I don't buy that. It was too organized, too clean. Wouldn't the first be sloppier, maybe even impulsive? How did they come to figure out killing – torturing and killing – was their deal?'

'Maybe somebody they knew the first time.' As they rode down, Peabody wound her mile-long scarf into some sort of complex and artistic looping knot around her neck. 'Somebody they – or one of them anyway – was pissed at, or wanted something from.'

'More possible,' Eve agreed. 'How did they team up? How long have they been together? And the first, add in possible defense or accident, another crime gone south. But somewhere in there, they found their romance.'

When they were close enough to keep it short, she switched from glide to elevator. 'Are they from New York and coming home – or again one of them – or are they from out west, and looking for some fun in the big city? Not enough to see them yet. We don't have enough to see them yet. But they're not picking on the type of victim. It's not just random, it also reads opportunity. The one prior to ours, a woman in her seventies, most likely taken from the parking lot of a small outdoor mall where she worked – out of range of the security cameras, then dumped two days later into a ravine six miles away. And we've got a twenty-year-old male who went missing from a rest-stop area in Pennsylvania, dumped two days later off the highway heading northeast.'

She got out, headed for her car. 'Always a single vic, always alone, and what looks like opportunity rather than specific targets. The body dump some distance from kill zone, or most usually. Which means their hole is more likely Lower West than near the Mechanics Alley dump site.'

She got behind the wheel, backed out. 'If Kuper hadn't gotten out on Perry, if he'd had the cab take him all the way to the club, he'd probably be playing his cello and someone else would be dead.'

'They could still be heading north,' Peabody commented. 'They've never hit anything as big or as urban as New York.'

'Exactly why it strikes as a destination.'

And look at them all, Eve thought as she drove. Millions of possible victims.

The LCs, the beggars, the unwary tourists, the executive hurrying to make a late meeting, his mind on business, the shopkeeper, shutting down for the night, the stripper heading home in the predawn dark.

Pick and choose, Eve thought, and the variety was endless.

She parked on Perry, thought about the neighborhood.

'Do me a favor. Contact Charles or Louise, they live pretty damn close, and Louise, especially, would come and go at odd hours and alone.' Doctors and cops, Eve thought, kept no hours. They kept all hours.

'I already did, after I saw the map.'

'Good thinking. The cab dropped him here. Perry and Greenwich. Three blocks to Christopher, and another block and a half on Christopher to the club. Somewhere on these four and a half blocks, they hit him.'

She began to walk, scanning, considering, trying to see it.

'He knows the area, comes down here a lot. It was cold, but clear. No wind to speak of, nothing spitting out of the sky. A nice frosty night for a brisk walk, clear out the opera, maybe, pull in the jazz.'

'It wouldn't take more than five minutes to walk it,' Peabody pointed out.

'That's all they needed.' She stopped. 'Here. Look at that brownstone. Nobody cleared the snow off the walkway or the steps. All the privacy screens are down. What do you want to bet whoever lives there is away? Business trip, vacation.'

'Do you think they used this place? But like you said, the walk, the steps. If they took him in there, there'd be signs someone walked through the snow.'

'I don't think they took him in there, I think they took him here. Park in front of this place. Yeah, other houses around, but no one directly. And it's going on midnight, a cold, clear night in a settled neighborhood. I bet a lot of the lights were off in the neighboring houses. They have to take him fast, and quiet. Distract him with the female, the male moves in – that's got to be it. Disable, restrain, transport. Let's knock on doors.'

They tried the nearest neighbor, another dignified brownstone with a square of front courtyard that set it back from the sidewalk. They got the nanny, and after she electronically scanned their ID, eyeballed them herself, she admitted them as far as the front foyer.

'The kids are having their afternoon snack. If Justin knows there's a cop around, he'll get hyper. He loves cops vids and games. Is there a problem?'

'Nothing here. Just a few questions. The people next door? Are they away?'

'The Minnickers, yes.' The nanny, all five feet of her sniffed. 'Don't tell me somebody broke in there. They got enough security for the White House. Not what you call friendly people, either. Pretty snooty, not like my people. And *that* woman. She came over here getting all up in my face last summer because my little Rosie picked one of her flowers. It was coming right through the pickets, out to the sidewalk. What harm did it do for Rosie to have it? But what did my lady do, my lady has *class*. She had the florist take *that* woman a big arrangement. And didn't even get a thanks for it. That's what kind of people they are over there.'

She folded her arms at her chest with a distinctive *hmmph*. 'I bet they got in trouble, didn't they, out in Hawaii? That's where they are, right up till March is what I heard.'

'I couldn't say. Are you live-in?'

'Nope. Eight to four most days. What's this about?'

'Have you noticed a strange vehicle around the neighborhood in the last few days? Maybe just driving by too often, or parked next door.'

'I can't say I have, no, sorry.' She stopped, head angled, eyes narrowed. 'They're starting to get into it back there. I've got to get back to them. You could try Mr Havers, on the other side of *that* house. He works nights a lot – at home. They're nice people.'

They found Havers at home and willing to talk.

He was a bulky man in his middle fifties, by Eve's gauge, and with an absent look in light brown eyes.

'Not last night,' he muttered. 'Not the night before. Night before that. Okay, okay, I'd've been working. I write horror novels, and right now it starts rolling for me about ten at night.'

'Drew Henry Havers?' Peabody asked.

'That's right.'

'You've scared the bejesus out of me for years.'

His plain, pale face lit up like a runway. 'Best compliment ever. Thanks.'

'Where do you work?' Eve asked.

'Oh. Upstairs. I have a studio facing the street so I don't disturb my wife and the kids. Bedrooms face the back. A vehicle you say, a strange vehicle. I get caught up in the work, don't notice much outside it. But . . . ' He scratched his head, rubbed his eyes. 'I was pacing around the studio, trying to figure out if the psychotic demon should disembowel the character or if flaying was more appropriate given the build-up. I did see someone parked in front of the house next door. Very unfriendly people over there – away now. But I didn't think anything of it, I'm afraid. Didn't even remember they were away. I might've thought, huh, the un-neighbors – that's what we call them – must've bought a new ride. But they were away.'

'What kind of vehicle?'

'Ah . . . I barely registered it. Dark, yes, it wasn't white or cream, but a dark color. Not a car,' he considered, 'bigger. Maybe one of those burly all-terrains. Or a van. Maybe a van.'

'Did you see anyone around it?'

'I barely glanced out the window, just as I was pacing around. I do think I saw someone. I can't tell you if it was a man or a woman. Bundled up. I think they had a chair. I must be imagining that, mixing it up. Why would anyone stand out on the street with an armchair? I'm very likely mixing it up, I'm sorry.'

'What was this person doing with the chair?'

'I can't say – there probably wasn't a chair. My wife is always saying I live in my head more than out of it. I get the impression they were putting it in the back of the van, or maybe they'd taken it out.'

'Do you remember the time, the time you saw this?'

'I have no idea. It would've been after ten, when it started rolling. Probably well after ten, as I'd written right up to the kill. And it would've been before two, when I stopped and went to bed – well before two as I decided on the disemboweling, and wrote right through to the sacrificial rite before I tapped out.

'I wish I could be of more help. I appreciate all you do – the police. I especially appreciate police who read my books.'

'We appreciate the time, Mr Havers,' Eve told him. 'If you remember anything else, please contact us. Peabody, give Mr Havers one of your cards.'

They knocked on a few more doors, but got nothing to match Havers.

'He's responsible for most of my nightmares,' Peabody said as they got back into the car.

'Why would you read something that gives you nightmares?' Life and the job, Eve thought, gave her plenty of her own.

'I don't know. Irresistible. He's really good. Mostly I like stories that have happy endings – and his do. I mean good overcomes evil – after a lot of blood, terror, death. Sort of like us,' Peabody concluded. 'Maybe that's why.'

'Dark colored A-T or van. He was leaning van. It's not much, but more than we had. And the woman with the chair.'

'He didn't say woman.'

'It's going to be the woman. The woman trying to get the chair into the back of the vehicle.'

'Classic ploy,' Peabody added.

'Because it often works. Kuper comes along, sees her struggling, steps over to offer a hand.'

Just as she'd seen it, Eve thought. It had been the most logical because it was the most true.

'It all works, including the timing. Let's hit the club since we're here.'

After Midnight was a moody little place with a scatter of patrons, and an ancient piano player noodling the keys as a woman with the face and body of a siren swayed and sang about love gone the wrong way around.

She could see Morris here, clearly see him adding the mournful song of his sax. And with the picture formed in the last hours, she could see Dorian Kuper, adding those down-low notes of the cello.

An intimate place, she thought, with tables crowded together and huddled close to the stage. A single bar and the man who tended it, and the lighting dim and faintly blue.

She talked to the bartender, the lone waitress, the old man and the young siren. She got fresh grief and shock, but no new information.

'They really liked him,' Peabody commented when they walked from the blue warmth to the gray cold.

'He seemed to have that effect on most people. What did we learn?'

'Well, that he went there at least three or four times a month, and they liked him.'

'That, and his killers never went in there. It's small, it's intimate, and while they get people who just go in, a tourist who's heard of it, they mostly have regulars. A couple who'd been in there around the time the vic went missing, they'd be noticed. And that leads more weight to random. Wrong place, wrong time.'

'Okay, yeah. Yeah, I see that. Everybody remembered Earnestina – in detail.'

'And speaking of.' Eve checked the time. 'I'm going to drop you back at Central. Any progress Baxter and Trueheart have made, I want to know. Check in with EDD in case they found something on the vic's electronics we missed. Unless something else pops, go home after that. I'll go by and talk to Earnestina on my way home – both her work and residence are on the way. She doesn't play in, but we'll cross her off anyway.'

'She should be home. I checked her schedule.' Peabody climbed in the car. 'Her last class should have ended about a half hour ago. Even if she hangs around the school for whatever, she should be home by the time you get uptown. You might want to check there first. Traffic's going to be a bitch.'

6

Traffic was a bitch, but, then again, Eve thought, so was she. She shoved, bullied and smashed her way uptown. In her own way, she enjoyed snarling at a lumbering maxibus or thinking bitter thoughts about the driver of a single-passenger Mini who wove through the narrow spaces between vehicles like a needle and thread.

She could sneer at the ad blimps cheerfully blasting out news about NEW SPRING LINES! at the fricking SkyMall when the temperature hovered at twenty-eight degrees Fahrenheit.

In the time it took her to travel north, she updated her notes, reviewed Trueheart's on three interviews conducted and contacted Juilliard.

Tina R. Denton had indeed left for the day.

She found the building easily enough – a whitewashed row house she could see had been converted into four units.

Finding parking was another matter. She considered double-parking, but recalling her own traffic fight couldn't justify it. Some of the drivers and passengers out there were innocents.

But when she spotted a space on the other side of the

street, she had no compunction against hitting the sirens, boosting into vertical and crossing over above car roofs to drop into the opening.

The blast of horns didn't bother her in the least.

She walked down to the corner, crossed over, walked up, and with a glance at the numbers on the doors, pushed the buzzer on Earnestina's apartment.

'What do you want?'

At the impatient voice, Eve held up her badge for scanning. 'Lieutenant Dallas, NYPSD. I need to speak with Tina R. Denton.'

'This isn't a convenient time. I'm working.'

'Hey, me too. If this isn't convenient we'll arrange to have you brought down to Central in the morning for questioning.'

'You can't make me do that!'

Eve just smiled. 'Watch me.'

There was an angry hiss, then the clunk of locks being disengaged.

Earnestina showed more flatteringly in her ID shot. In person, at the moment, her brown hair was scraped back from her long, edging toward horsey, face. She hadn't bothered with facial enhancement, but obviously had enhancements of another sort.

Eve could smell the Zoner, could see its effects in the just-going-glassy look of her pale and narrow blue eyes.

'This is harassment.'

'File a complaint. Then I won't feel obliged to ignore the illegals I can smell — along with the faint haze of Zoner smoke that's not yet dissipated. Or you can let me in, we'll have a conversation, then we can both go about our business.'

'A person is entitled to do as she likes in her own home.'

'No, a person isn't entitled to engage in illegal activities, anywhere.' Feet planted, Eve met those just-getting-high eyes with cool contempt. 'You want to push this one, Ms Denton?'

'Oh, come in, then. Believe me, I've made a note of your name and badge number.'

'And I've made a note you're uncooperative.'

The living area in the apartment showed a tendency for compulsive neatness. Nothing out of place, and a minimalist style that included no personal photos, no flowers or plants. A single sofa in dark gray faced a wall screen. A single chair in the same tone angled under a floor lamp.

Earnestina — as Eve would forever think of her — didn't suggest they sit down, and Eve didn't ask.

'You were acquainted with Dorian Kuper, and in fact, had an argument with him at a club called After Midnight.'

'I knew Dorian, yes. I heard today he'd been killed. That's a great loss for opera, but has nothing else to do with me.'

'You were pretty angry with him.'

'Disgusted is a more accurate term, that a man of his considerable talents would waste them on the lowbrow.'

'He won't be doing that anymore.'

'Nor will he transport those who value true music with his skills and comprehension.'

'Let's move on to whereabouts. Where were you Sunday night between eleven p.m. and one a.m.'

'I was here, and would have been in bed by eleven.'

'Alone?'

'My personal life is none—'

'Alone?' Eve repeated, her tone hard as brick.

'Yes, alone. I attended an afternoon musicale, and was home by six. I had a meal, and worked until ten. You can't possibly believe I had anything to do with Dorian's death.'

'Last night, between ten p.m. and one a.m.'

'I attended a rehearsal of *La Bohème*, at Juilliard. I was there from seven until after ten. Two colleagues and I went for a drink afterward to discuss areas that required improvement or change. We met until a little after midnight, then we shared a cab, and I came home.'

'Names.'

'You're insulting.'

'Yeah, add that to your notes. Names.'

She reeled them off, chin jutted high. 'I want you to leave now.'

'Heading that way. Do you own a vehicle?'

'I do not. I live in a city with excellent mass transit, and my work is a five-minute walk from my residence.'

More to needle the woman than anything else, Eve

threw out one more. 'Have you ever been to Nashville, Tennessee?'

'Certainly not, why would I? That's the land of *Opry*, isn't it?' She said the word as if it was the vilest expletive. 'For that reason alone, I will never step foot anywhere in the state.'

'I'm sure they'll manage without you. Thanks for your time.'

'If you harass me again, I'll have a lawyer.'

'The only way I'll come back is if you lied to me about any of this. If that turns out to be the case, you'll need a lawyer.'

And now, Eve thought as she stepped out into what felt like beautifully fresh air – and Earnestina slammed the door behind her – she needed a drink.

At least the traffic fight comprised a much shorter distance, and she drove through the gates of home not long after the sky went to indigo and the streetlights spread pools of white.

The deeper silhouette of the house that Roarke built, the house that had become hers, rose and spread castle-like with its fanciful turrets and towers. Lights glowed in too many windows to count.

She wanted home more than she wanted that drink. Home, where she would find peace, space, time to clear her head. A place to set up fresh for murder.

She left her car out front, pushed her way through the wind that had decided to kick up its heels again, and went in the front door.

She knew he'd be there, the skeletal build in funereal black with the pudge of a cat at his feet.

Summerset, Roarke's majordomo, raised his eyebrows. 'A completed first day back with no apparent injury or damage. How long can it last?'

'It could end right now if I decide to kick that stick you're so fond of any farther up your ass.'

'And the day wouldn't be complete without such an observation.'

She tossed her coat over the newel post because it was handy – and because it annoyed him. And with the cat now rubbing a feline welcome at her leg, started up the stairs.

Stopped.

'I bet you're a big fan of the opera. That would be right up your alley.'

'I enjoy many of the arts, including opera. I've heard Dorian Kuper play, at the Met, at After Midnight, and other venues. I heard of his death shortly ago. To lose someone who's young and so vibrantly talented is tragic.'

'All murder's tragic.'

'And some felt more keenly than others. He's in your hands now? The report didn't name the primary.'

'He's mine now,' Eve said and continued upstairs.

She went straight for the bedroom and the locator.

'Where is Roarke?'

Roarke is not in residence at this time.

Not home yet, she thought, and remembered to check her 'link. Sure enough, she found a text from him.

Lieutenant, I hope your day's going well. She stripped off her jacket as she listened to his voice, to the Irish whispering through it. I've a need to make an unscheduled trip to Detroit, but it shouldn't take long. I'll be home by half-seven if not before. Until then, take care of my cop.

That gave her some time, she thought. She could get her board set up in her office here, start reviewing notes and reports.

Or, she considered while Galahad wound through her legs like a furry snake, she could clear her head first.

She sat, removed her boots, rubbed the cat who jumped up beside her. Then she changed into workout gear.

When she started for the elevator the cat sat, stared at the opening doors with his suspicious bicolored eyes.

'I'm not a big fan of the moving box, either, but . . . I'll be back,' she said as the door closed.

She hadn't had time, not really, to fully appreciate Roarke's Christmas gift as the dojo had been completed while they were away.

Now she stepped out into it and took one long, relaxed breath.

The floors, soft gold, gleamed. The space boasted its own little garden where white flowers fanned over the stones of a quietly bubbling water feature in the far corner. Sliding panels concealed a small kitchen area, fully stocked with bottles of spring water and energy drinks.

Coffee was banned, which didn't seem right in any world, but she'd had to accept the edict.

More panels opened to a dressing area fully stocked with white towels, with mats, with gis of black or white. And the door within would lead to the shower, and through that she could access the gym if that space was more to her taste.

He'd even thought of art – but, then, the man thought of everything. Serene gardens, arching cherry blossoms, green hills misted with morning.

The space spoke of peace and discipline, and simplicity.

And was a fully operational holoroom.

The gift had been twofold. The dojo, and Master Lu. When time allowed she could go to the master for instruction, or schedule a session in her own dojo.

And when it didn't, she could call him up holographically.

She did so now, eager for a good, strong workout with a master of martial arts.

His image shimmered on in the center of the room. He wore his hair in a long queue, and a plain black gi over his sinewy body.

He clasped one hand over the other, bowed. 'Lieutenant Dallas.'

'Master Lu. Thank you for this honor.'

'I am pleased to have a worthy student.'

'I only have thirty minutes, but—'

'Then we must make each count.'

'Your flying spin kick is, well, almost unbelievable. I've never been able to get that height, or that form. If—'

'You are very kind. This will come. For this our first lesson, you will learn to breathe.'

'To . . . "breathe".'

'Breath is the beginning of all. Breath,' he said as he approached her, 'then breath and movement. Hands.'

He took her hands, pressed one palm to her belly, the other to her heart with his dark eyes locked on hers. 'Breath is life. You are not the pebble washed to shore by the wave, but the fish that swims in the wave. Breathe in to fill, to draw in the light. Slow,' he told her, 'with awareness. Breathe out to empty. And pause, hold in that space between. Now in to fill.'

She breathed.

When she took the elevator back up, she had to admit her brain had cleared out. Who knew there were so many ways to breathe?

When the elevator opened to the bedroom, and Roarke stood there unbuttoning his shirt, well, she lost her breath.

His hair fell nearly to his shoulders, a black silk frame for a face created to steal the breath, to weaken the knees, to capture the heart. It had done all to her, and more.

There were times like this when he looked at her, just looked, and those perfectly sculpted lips curved, those eyes – wilder, bluer than any sea – lit with what she knew was love, it wasn't just more. It was all.

'A session with Master Lu?'

'Yeah.' She stepped in so the door could close behind her. 'I've been learning how to breathe. I thought I already knew, being alive and all, but apparently not. Did you know you can breathe into your toes? I think I did it. It sounds like bullshit, but I think I breathed into my toes.'

He laughed and, putting his hands on her hips, drew her to him. 'You were the fish, not the pebble. I reviewed the first couple of lessons.' His hands slid around her waist. 'Here's what I missed today.' He pulled back, kissed her – slow and deep, like breathing. 'I got used to being able to do that at any time of the day or night.'

'Back to reality. Detroit?'

'Just a few bolts that needed tightening, and my hand on the spanner – *wrench*,' he corrected. 'And you, I hear, a murder already?'

'They probably had a few while I was gone, too.'

'Undoubtedly. Dorian Kuper, the cellist.'

'Did you know him?'

With a shake of his head, Roarke stepped back, took off his shirt. 'By reputation only, and I've heard him play. How was he killed? The reports were very thin – deliberately so, I assume.'

'He was tortured for two days before they – and it was they – sliced open his belly and let him bleed out.'

Roarke pulled on a gray sweater, and made Eve wonder why the color had looked so dull and stiff in Earnestina's apartment, and was so rich and soft over Roarke's torso.

'Back to reality, indeed,' Roarke murmured. '"They"? You've identified his killers?'

'Not yet, but there are two, and he wasn't their first. He was a long way from their first.'

'It sounds as if we should have a glass of wine, a meal, and you should tell me.'

'I could use a glass of wine. Sexual sadists,' she began as they walked out of the bedroom together. 'With a twist.'

She ran it through for him as she would for another cop. He might've winced at the comparison, but he could – and did – think like a cop.

While she arranged her board, he put a meal together. Which meant she wouldn't get pizza, but compromises had to be made. It was in the marriage rules. He certainly made them, she thought, just by having the meal in her office at the little table with murder and death on full display.

'You believe New York was their destination.'

'Long-term, can't say, but you've only got to look at the map, see their kill spots. It's not an arrow from point to point, but any time they veered off, then shifted right back – north and east.'

She took the wine he offered, gestured with it to the map. 'Detours, that's how it looks to me. Maybe you need fuel for your vehicle, for yourselves, or there's some attraction, or someone you know, so you jog off a few miles.'

'But come back,' he said, nodding, 'to that same direction. What do they take from their victims?'

See, she thought. Cop thinking. 'Cash and jewelry if there is any. A vehicle, or in some cases parts from a vehicle. Most – not all – of their known victims run in the high-risk area. LCs, the homeless, but they target others. Often remote areas. A woman in her seventies living alone. They used her residence as their torture/kill zone, took her easy-to-transport valuables. A guy in his twenties heading home on the back roads, late – from a bar. They used some vacant cabin for him.'

'And no trace?'

'They wipe it clean – maybe they seal up, maybe the forensics have been sloppy.' Too many to know, she thought, too many to pick over, step-by-step. 'I can't say for certain. But at least one of them's organized enough to be careful. They haven't found all the kill zones. The killers don't leave the body where they work as a rule. They use dump sites, and generally a fair distance off. And plastic tarps.'

'So, someone might think they've had a break-in, but without the blood, the gore, not report a possible murder.'

'Exactly. And by the time they've put some of it together, the crime scene's been thoroughly compromised. Lucky,' she mused. 'Some of it's just luck. Organized, careful, but lucky.'

'Come eat.' He took her hand, drew her over to the table.

The square white plates held a line of pork medallions drizzled with some sort of sauce, a golden huddle of roasted potatoes flecked with herbs, and a colorful medley of winter vegetables.

He had a much more creative hand with the AutoChef, she considered, than she ever would.

'The heart, the initials,' he began.

'Their signature.'

'Yes, but also a declaration, don't you think? Not only we did this together, but we *are* together.'

'True love.'

'Wouldn't they think so? The heart holding their initials symbolizes just that. Add the fact they don't use their victims sexually.'

'Because they're committed to each other, and that would be cheating.'

'Without the heart, what would you have concluded?'

Considering, she ate – whatever the drizzle of sauce was, it had some kick. 'I would probably have concluded team. It's possible for one killer to select, lure, overcome and torture with varied strokes. But it's more likely two, given the range of the victims. A woman's less likely to stop on the side of the road for a strange man, or open the door to one at night. Two of the LCs weren't licensed for same sex – not that they wouldn't have potentially gone off menu, but best probability: The client was male. Easier, too, for a lone woman to lure a single male with the will-you-give-me-a-hand-with-this-heavy-object ploy.'

'So your most likely conclusion would be a two-person team: one male, one female.'

'Most likely. I wouldn't have ruled out a single, but most

likely. But . . . ' She nodded as she ate. 'Without the heart I wouldn't have seen them as a couple, as romantically linked. Sex, sure, but not romantically.'

She nodded again. 'And they want to be acknowledged as that. Interesting.'

'Where's the trigger?'

She smiled now, and though they were always low on her list, sampled the vegetables. 'You know, not all criminals think like a cop.'

'The successful ones – even reformed – do.' He picked up his wine, studied her over it. 'It's unlikely they woke up one morning and decided. Well now, what do you say we take a ride out today, find ourselves someone to torture and kill – at least not without what they saw as cause. One of them may have killed in a rage or in defense of the other – the romantic angle again – or even by accident.'

'Which could have set them off,' Eve agreed. 'Or they discovered torture as a sexual stimulant by happy accident during the commission of another crime. Or one brought the other in on his/her perverted hobby.'

Roarke glanced toward the board. 'It appears they're skilled hobbyists.'

'Yeah, and that's a hitch for me. How do you get good at anything?'

'Innate ability and true interest lay a foundation. But it's practice, isn't it, that hones a skill. They didn't start with the victim currently first on your board.'

'I don't think so. You can see they've escalated, gradually. Less time between – but then a longer gap. Consistently they kept the victim alive longer until they settled on the two-day period. But the teamwork seems too smooth to have started where we have them now. And those gaps?'

'Victims not yet found or identified as such.'

'There the FBI and I are in disagreement. Their profilers think the twenty is it – or close. Twenty-one now with Kuper. I think those gaps are most likely as-yet-unfound vics. Killers like this don't de-escalate unless they're forced to stop for a period of time. They lean in my direction with the longer gaps, but they're focused on this group, this route. They have a low probability of a vic before the woman in Nashville. And they've spent too much time debating if they're serial or spree killers.'

'I doubt the terminology matters to the victims, or those who loved them.'

'Yeah. You fill in these gaps with vics – no cooling-off period. You consider the victimology – no specific type, chosen at random. You've got spree killers, sexual sadists who *can* feel, but only for each other. Most likely a man and a woman, most likely somewhat attractive, nonthreatening in appearance and demeanor. In none of the interviews or can-vasses, including my own, has anyone remembered an individual or individuals who stood out, who seemed off.'

'So they do neither.'

'Ordinary enough not to stick out. Smart enough not to

do anything that draws attention. A couple, that lowers suspicion right there. Having drinks at a bar, checking into a motel, renting a cabin. Switching vehicles regularly, so by the time we're looking for one, they're in another.'

'It's early to be frustrated, isn't it?'

'For Kuper, yeah, but when you look at the whole picture, they've had a hell of a streak. I've got a hell of a lot of data, but nothing that pins them.'

'What do you do next?'

'Keep pushing on Kuper. Why did they choose that neighborhood? Was it completely random, or was there a specific reason? We have one wit who saw the vehicle, so we push there. Dark all-terrain or van, and he was leaning toward a van. We do what we can do for Kuper, but we need to find the first. We have to work back from the first known, look at missing persons, at unsolveds, at what was deemed accidental death. Everything rays out from the first.'

'Aren't the feds doing just that?'

'They've got somebody poking, but primarily they're focused from the first known and forward. I need to reach out to local law enforcement south and west of the first known. Missing persons,' she continued. 'Runaways, accidents, unsolveds.'

'Won't that be fun?'

'Not even close.' She blew out a breath, picked up her wine. 'I'm going to run probabilities, using the current route, working back from the first known.'

'I can do that for you, and faster. You don't have any financial data searches to entertain me. The geography and navigation should.'

'It's all yours, ace. Thanks.' She cut a small bite of pork. 'This couple, they came from somewhere, that's another key. They grew up with parents or fosters, had some education, some source of income. And, given their profile, one or both of them probably has a sheet and some history of violent behavior.'

'History together?' Roarke wondered. 'That bond.'

'I don't see long-term history, unless we find the killings go back years. And I don't see them getting away with this for years before it hit the radar. They're not kids,' she continued. 'People tend to notice kids. Yeah, I saw a couple of kids hanging out around there. Why aren't they in school? What trouble are they getting into? Plus anybody skewing teens, early twenties, isn't likely to have the control needed to target a vic, have a place to hold one, wipe everything. Probably not out of their thirties, either.'

'And why is that?'

'How do you squash these impulses that long? They're in there – they just needed the right trigger. Everybody's capable of killing, given the right circumstances. Not everybody's capable of torture. Add the heart in again? Not everyone's capable of enjoying or romanticizing torture.'

She nudged her plate aside. 'Would you kill for me?'

'I would, yes, of course.'

'Jesus, don't say it without even a second's thought.'

'I don't need a second's thought. Consider who we are, Eve. We're both capable of killing, and have done so. But there's . . . criteria. Would I kill to protect you, to save your life, to save you from harm? Without hesitation. Would I kill because you said, Do me a favor, I'd like this person dead? I don't have to give it a second thought as you'd never say that, want that, ask that.'

'If I did.'

He polished off his wine. 'I think we'd have to have quite a conversation.'

'Okay.' That satisfied her. 'Would you torture someone for me?'

His brow lifted. 'We are stepping into odd territories. All right, then, I'll follow you in. To save or protect you from harm, if I believed torture – of any nature – would accomplish that, then, yes, I would. Would I – or you in the same circumstances – find that increased sexual passion, no. Deliberately causing pain is an ugly business. We've both been used physically, emotionally, and know how ugly it is.'

'That's right. Some people who've experienced abuse become abusers. So I need to look at that, too. Somebody hurt her – a parent, authority figure, spouse, partner. Now you're the one in control. You're the one who gets to deliver the pain and the fear.'

She rose, wandered to the board. 'But not for payback, not right out anyway. Because it feels good. Who knew how

114

good, how exciting it could be to cause the pain, the fear? And now that you know it, you can't stop.'

'An addiction.'

'Exactly. And again that's why it didn't start here.' She tapped the board, the image of the first victim. 'This wasn't the first taste. They knew what it was going to feel like here. The first? That was a surprise. Maybe what you'd call a revelation. I know what they are. I've got a pretty good sense of what they are already. But who, and why. I can't see it.'

He rose as well, came over to stand behind her. He laid his hands on her shoulders, brushed his lips over the top of her head. 'And it worries you because you know there'll be another.'

'New York's the biggest urban area they've been in, that we know. And when I look at the map, the route, that holds true. Here, they can pick and choose like nowhere else. That has to be exciting. And motivating.'

'So they'll want another quickly.'

'If they don't already have one, they will within another day. I'd be surprised if it took any longer. Two days to play with the victim before the kill. The last two, Kuper and the vic in New Jersey, barely a week between the grabs. Addicts always need more and quicker. It won't be long before they need another.'

'As who they are and when they started are key, I'll work up your probabilities.'

'Thanks. You put the meal on the table, I'll take care of the debris.'

'Fair enough.' He tipped her face up to his a moment, tapped the shallow dent in her chin. 'All and all – considering who we are – it's good to be home.'

When he went into his adjoining office she carted the dishes into the kitchen, stacked them in the washer. They made a good team, she thought, worked well together – the cop and the (former) criminal. The ridiculously rich man with his roots in the alleyways of Dublin, and the woman who'd squeezed out a life on a cop's salary who'd grown up in the system after the nightmare of her first eight years.

Few – including herself – would have predicted they'd match and mesh as they had. That they'd become all to each other.

She doubted the killers she sought seemed so ill-matched on the surface. People noticed such things, too. They looked right together, she believed. Looked as people expected a couple to look.

And they sure as hell worked well together.

She thought of Roarke again, and how easily she'd agreed to accept his offer of help on an official investigation.

Trust, she realized. Not just attraction, not just passion, not just a mutual goal. There had to be trust to work as a team.

With that in mind she went back to her desk to review her notes.

7

Eve read Baxter's roundup of the interviews, did a spot-check on the recordings. Nothing stood out, nothing popped – and she hadn't expected it. But it gave her a chance to evaluate Trueheart's interview techniques, his rhythm.

A good balance with Baxter's slicker style, she decided.

She made another note to team Trueheart up in interviews with other detectives, take him out of his comfort zone.

She finalized another report to Whitney and Mira with her conclusions that data and evidence indicated Kuper had been a random victim, the last known in a long-term spree by two unsubs, and not target specific.

She let Morris know they'd ID'd Earnestina. Morris reported that the victim's mother had come in, had asked when she could have her son. Eve recommended the body be turned over to the next of kin or her representative as soon as possible.

No point, she thought, just no point in prolonging the misery. Kuper's body had told them all it could.

She reached out to two more primaries, which entailed long, winding conversations, no fresh insights or information, and promises on all sides to share all data.

When Roarke came back in, she was running fresh probabilities on the New Jersey victim.

'I've generated several routes, with three being top contenders,' he told her. 'These three run too close in probability to pull one out at this point. Even those would have any number of variance.'

'Can I see them, on screen?'

He set it up. 'This brings them from southeast Texas, through Louisiana, into Arkansas, touching into Mississippi before meeting up with your first known in Tennessee. It also speculates, as you see from the highlighted points, other most probable stops in Tennessee, and across the Missouri border through Kentucky, which eliminates the gap before West Virginia, and the second point in West Virginia. Another in the western part of Maryland eliminates the gap prior to Ohio. You've two in Pennsylvania, but it seemed unusual, and the computer agreed, that they wouldn't hunt in one of that area's more rural, less populated areas, so there's yet another point there before the jog over to New Jersey, then into New York.'

'Some detours, but a fairly direct route northeast.'

'The second comes from the west. I started as far west as California, across Nevada, into Arizona, through New Mexico. Touching on Texas, then into Oklahoma, once

118

again into Arkansas, and the route remains as the first from there.'

'California. A long way, a lot of time.' A lot of potential bodies, Eve thought.

'Both, yes. It would be a southeastern route to start, curving into a northeastern direction. The last route supposes they had a purpose in Tennessee or changed directions there, initially coming from Florida, going through sections of Alabama and Georgia, potentially Mississippi again before your first known in Tennessee, and the following route would remain as the other two.'

'What's the probability range?'

'From 70.2 to 73.4. It's far too speculative for higher without more hard data.'

'Let's take the third one.' She studied it, tried to imagine it. 'Coming from the south – where it's warm and sunny, right? They'd have started out in the fall – most likely – for this timeline – but winter's coming. People do leave the warm and sunny for the cold and bitter, but if you're on a killing spree, and you've pulled it off in the warm, why not wait for spring to drive so far north?'

'New York as destination,' he reminded her.

'Yeah, I get that, they want to come take a big, bloody bite out of the apple. But, then, why not work to get here before the holidays? See it all dressed up? People do that, they come in armies to see the holiday fuss. Why leave reasonably warm for seriously cold? Given human nature, I'm going to rate this three out of the three. The second, coming from California.'

She wandered around the board, looked back on screen. 'That southern chunk, same deal, but maybe something happens. You've got to blow. Or you just start off. A longer trip than coming from the southeast, so maybe back in the summer. Probably that far back. Not thinking about winter, and off you go. But that's a lot of unfounds and/or unsolveds.'

'Pick any point along that route as a starting point,' Roarke told her. 'Arizona, New Mexico, Oklahoma. Any of those are more likely than the points north of them.'

'Yeah, that's why I like it, and I don't.' Studying, speculating, she hooked her thumbs in her pockets, drummed her fingers. 'They could've started anywhere from the far western point, and it makes logical sense on the map. Timeline.... it strikes more possible if they had their first here? What is this?'

'New Mexico.'

'Why did those map people, or state-naming people go with so many New Wherevers?'

'So speaks the New Yorker.'

'Question still holds. If they were so attached to the Mexico or the Hampshire or the York, why didn't they just stay there? Anyway, about there, or that part of Texas or Oklahoma. That gets a higher bump from me, and so does the first possibility. Up from southeast Texas, hit Louisiana, Mississippi, Arkansas. Why is S-A-S pronounced S-A-W? It should be Ar-*Kansas*. Did Kansas object?'

Oddly enough, he found the question perfectly just. 'I can't tell you.'

'It doesn't apply to this, but it's a question. Second one's highest for me.'

Again, oddly enough, he thought, it had struck the same for him. 'Why? And that's also a question.'

'It's that south-to-north deal again. Warm to cold. That's just a gut thing, but it strikes me.'

'It did the same for me,' he told her. 'But that may be as I'm used to how your mind travels.'

'Or it may be because it just seems right. We'll work on missing persons, unsolved on the other routes, but I'm going to focus my own efforts on the second.'

She reached for her coffee on her desk, realized it wasn't there. Even as she frowned Roarke handed her what was left of it.

'This is good,' she told him. 'Gives us angles to work until we get the next body.'

He ruffled her hair. 'That's positive thinking.'

'It is. I'm positive there's going to be a next body. What's despicable is knowing another DB may give us more to work with.'

She studied the map again, shook her head. 'So working back, that's the best we can do. I'm going to put this together, send it out. Peabody can start doing some searches on the first route.'

'Why don't I do the same on your least likely? If nothing else you may be able to cross it off.'

She looked at him. Even in casual clothes, he radiated

command. He'd have plenty of his own to see to. 'That's a lot of boring cop work for one night.'

'Boring enough I can get some of my own somewhat less boring work done at the same time.'

'I owe you.'

'We'll work out a payment schedule.'

'Yeah, like I don't know that currency.'

He laughed, pulled her in for a kiss. 'Which makes me the richest man in the world.'

'You already are – pretty much.'

'Not without you.' This time he kissed her forehead, tenderly. 'Not any longer.'

He meant it, she thought as she returned to her desk. And she understood the sentiment. Once, the badge had been enough for her. All for her.

Not any longer.

With the first route in Peabody's lap, another in Roarke's, Eve buckled down on the second probability. She tapped into IRCCA, refined it region by region, splitting into three searches. Missing persons, unsolved homicides and, the last, incidents that combined the two.

It took time – it always did – so while she waited for the initial results, she went back to her board, chose a victim at random.

She sat, reviewed the case file, asking herself what she might have done differently, if anything, if there were any gaps she could fill, what pattern she could begin to create.

Escalation was a clear pattern – the increase in the violence and duration of the torture, the narrowing of the time between known kills.

Standard, she thought, for spree killer profile and pathology.

From first known to last known, she noted, the time frame went from eighteen hours from last seen to TOD to forty-nine hours. The gap between first known vic TOD and second's last seen ran ten days. The gap between the victim in New Jersey and Kuper ran four days.

No more traveling, if she read them right. Settled in now. No more small towns, no more back roads. Big city time.

She shifted, looked out the window at the dark.

They'd have another one now, or soon. Before morning if the pattern continued. And that gave her two days to find them, and save a life.

Her eyes rounded with shock when the results began to come in. Too many missing persons who remained missing, she decided, and too many unsolved.

She focused in on the third search, and its lesser number.

'I may have a couple possibilities,' Roarke said as he came in. Then lifted his eyebrows as he saw the fierce look on her face as she worked. 'And I'd say you have their scent.'

'Southeastern Missouri. That little wedge that squeezes between Arkansas and Tennessee.'

'A backwater place called Cutter's Bend.'

That fierce look flicked up. 'You hit that one.'

'It just barely edged into my search. A nineteen-year-old boy, gone missing last September on his way home from the ballfield one balmy evening. He never made it home.'

'His body was found nearly a week later, dumped in a wooded area over the Tennessee border. Decomp and animals had gotten to him by then. Broken wrist, broken fingers, gashes, punctures, no sexual abuse in evidence, but evidence of binding on what was left of his wrists and ankles. Blunt force trauma, back of the head, some burn marks in evidence.

'Ten days before our first confirmed on the day he went missing. No carved heart, but decomp, animals, that's not likely anyway. And if you follow from this vic—'

'Noah Paston.'

'Yeah, follow from Paston to the first confirmed and you get Ava Enderson.'

Roarke stepped over, edged a hip down on her desk. 'I didn't turn her up.'

'Nobody has. She went missing right about the time two kids stumbled over Paston's remains. Traveling alone, from Memphis to Nashville, last seen – confirmed – having dinner at a diner about seven in the evening, about ten miles off the highway. Friendly sort, according to the waitress who served her. She said she was heading to Nashville to have a little reunion with some girlfriends, but since they weren't due till the next day, she was toying with stopping for the night, getting off fresh in the morning. How her car was acting up anyway.'

As she spoke, Eve brought the woman's ID shot up on screen. 'The waitress recommended a couple places. Enderson said she wanted quiet and rustic, something out of the way. So the waitress told her about this place, some sort of inn. Enderson looked it up on her PPC, liked the look, booked a room.'

'And, I assume, didn't make it there.'

'You assume correctly. Her car was found about two miles shy of this ... Here it is.' She highlighted it on screen. 'Sundown Inn. Broken down. Hood up, her luggage still in the trunk. The in-dash comp had been removed – expertly. They haven't found her.'

'Show me the route,' Roarke requested, then nodded as he studied it on screen. 'I see, yes. Very logical navigation from the boy, to this woman, to the first confirmed.'

Yes, she had the scent, and had to push up, pace as she followed it.

'I've got another in Kentucky that rings for me, and one in West Virginia I know in my gut is their work. That one was doing the hiking/camping thing, which baffles me. Why would anybody do that on purpose? Huddle down by a fire outdoors, sleep in a tent? But they do. His wife sent out an alarm when he didn't check in – as he checked in every morning – and didn't answer his 'link. She raved at the cops until they went out to his campsite. He registered it. Not there, and they figure he's just gone hiking as there's no sign of foul play.'

She prowled back, stared at the screen.

'Six days before they found his body, down a ravine. Animals and decomp again, and they ruled it as accidental death. But the wife raised serious hell, went to the media, got lawyers, hired a private investigator. So they flagged his file.'

Eve gestured as she sat again, split-screening the ID shot with the route. 'Jacob Fastbinder. And I believe the wife here as he was a hiking fanatic, took hiking trips at least twice a year, every year since he was about twelve. He knew the region, he was smart and prepared and he was careful. And he didn't have his pack when they found him. Locals said it could've been lost or dragged off, but that's bullshit. Didn't have his fancy hiker-guy wrist unit, either. ME can't confirm if some of the wounds were inflicted or suffered during the fall.'

'You'll talk to the wife.'

'Oh yeah. She went for burial, that's what I got from his obit. I think she might be willing to have his remains exhumed and examined by a forensic anthropologist.'

'You'll pull in DeWinter.' Roarke nodded. 'A good call.'

'I've got a couple more I want to look at harder.' She rubbed her tired eyes. 'But I know these up the count. Can't say if the kid in Missouri was the first – still doesn't feel like it, but he's theirs.'

'Now he's yours.'

She shrugged, glanced toward the AutoChef.

'You need sleep. You can't contact the wife of the hiker at this hour, or roust any of the police on these cases, not at this hour.'

He pulled her to her feet. 'Unless Peabody hits as well, you can start your route in Missouri, and move back from there if you feel the boy wasn't their first. Give your brain and your instincts a rest.'

She didn't argue only because she wanted to let it settle in, stew around in her subconscious. Noah Paston – and she'd add him to her board in the morning – hadn't been their first.

'Paston,' she said as Roarke tugged her out of the room. 'The locals did a thorough job – and when he was found over the state line, called in the feds. Small, rural-type community. People knew the kid. Liked the kid. He'd had a breakup with his girlfriend, and a push-and-shove with the guy she dumped him for, but nothing serious. And the push-and-shove partner was alibied tight, and just didn't read like a killer.'

In the bedroom she toed off her skids. 'He did okay in school, opted to do online courses instead of going to college so he could stay home and help with the family business. Garden center. And he played ball, coached Little League along with his father. People liked him, it comes through the reports.'

'Why not the first?'

'It just doesn't read for me. It's wrong place/wrong time

again. In general he drove home from the ballfield. He had a small truck. But he lent it to a friend about an hour before practice ended. And he stayed longer to work one-on-one with a kid, walked the kid home. That wasn't his usual routine, so if somebody was lying in wait for him, he wouldn't have come when they expected. He took a short cut, since he was walking, or told the kid he was going to, and he headed off in the direction of the back road that would cross a field and over that to his house. That was at dusk. Just getting dark.'

'And these two drive by, see him.'

'Yeah, could be that. Ask him if he wants a lift, ask for directions. Or the woman lures him somehow. He's an athlete, young, fast. He's got a baseball bat, but they get him. He's not an easy target, not really, but they see young, stupid, alone on a back road in the dark. He's a kid, so it's not for money. He didn't have any to speak of. A 'link, and they never found it, a good bat and glove, but nothing of real value. And they don't rape him or abuse him sexually, so it's not that.'

'Luck of the draw.'

'That's how it looks to me.' It was circling in her brain, and she wanted it to sink in. 'And the first isn't going to be like that. The first had a reason, had the fuse that lit up. I haven't found the first.'

'Why dump the body so far away – over state lines, pulling in the FBI?'

She pulled on a nightshirt. 'They were en route some-where – had a destination in mind for the night. Took him along, likely incapacitated. I have to figure they didn't think about crossing the state line, didn't consider that. Just take him a good distance, gives them more time to play.'

Still thinking, she stretched out on the bed, running an absent hand over Galahad's head when he leaped up to join her. 'Out-of-the-way places around there, like with the vic heading to Nashville. An old house, cabin, fishing shack, whatever. Clean it up when you're done, dump him far enough away from the kill site. Who'd look?'

'You.'

'Now, yeah. Plenty of hindsight now.'

'*Then,*' he corrected, and slid into bed beside her. 'You'd have considered the route, just as you are now – considered they'd need somewhere to hold him, and you'd have looked.'

'It doesn't help him now. There's one in Arkansas, low probability but I want another look. And a second in West Virginia, I think—'

'Tomorrow.' Roarke wrapped an arm around her, tugged her closer. 'Let it sit until tomorrow.'

'You just want me to pay up.'

'I had considered letting that debt ride, with considerable interest, but I'm more than willing to take payment now.'

'You're always willing.'

Eyes on his she traced her hand down his chest, his torso, his belly and found him hot and hard.

'See?' She wrapped her fingers around him. 'How do you guys live with this?'

'It's a man's burden to bear.'

'Just a few inches, and it rules the brain, the ego and can obliterate common sense.'

'"A few"?' he countered, making her laugh.

'Knew that would get you.'

'Used properly it can rule a woman's brain, her ego and obliterate her common sense.'

'I guess you're going to show me how to use it properly.'

'It would be my pleasure.'

He rolled on top of her, but first used his mouth, very properly, on hers.

She let herself sink in, found it easy – where once it had been impossible – to set murder and death aside. To take and to give without the world crowding in.

Just the two of them – or just the two of them after the cat landed on the floor with a thump of irritation – in the big bed under the sky window. Just as it had been only the two of them on the island, through long, sunny days and breezy, balmy nights.

He could take her away, with that mouth, with those skilled hands. They roamed over her now, gliding over her shape as if he'd molded it in glass.

Love, she knew – where once she hadn't believed – could be quiet and sweet, and still hold the world.

She twined around him, loose and willing, swelling his

heart with a sigh that whispered contentment, stirring his blood with the press of her fingers. And he was twined in her – heart, blood and spirit – so intricately woven together they fused into one.

'I love you,' he murmured in English, and again in Irish as her heartbeat thickened under his hand, as her pulse leaped against his lips.

She tightened around him, hard and fast. 'You are love to me. You are love.' She framed his face, eased him back just enough to meet his eyes. 'Mine,' she said, drawing his lips gently, gently back to hers.

She could drift down, down into that bottomless well of love, into the deep and the breathless. She could float even when sensations shimmered over her, through her, into her. And rise up, drenched, when shimmer turned to spark.

She took him in, took in the hot and the hard, took him with her into the deep and the breathless so they rose and fell together.

Hands clasped tight, beat meeting beat. When they broke, love spilled through them.

She curled against him, holding on to the warm, the shape, drawing in his scent. And her lips curved against his throat.

'Paid in full, pal.'

'I'll note that in the ledger, with a memo you've helped me bear my burden for yet another day.'

She snorted out a laugh as her mind began to fuzz toward sleep. 'How's the brain, the ego and all that?'

'Doing well, thanks. And yours?'

'It's good. All good. We're good.'

He stroked her back as she drifted away, felt the bed give when the cat deduced the coast was clear and jumped back up.

He thought, it was good. Very good indeed.

It wouldn't be good for Jayla Campbell. She was beyond pissed as she trudged her way across Carmine, hunched against the cold. If Mattio hadn't been such a fuckhead, she wouldn't have stormed out of the party, wouldn't be what seemed like miles from her apartment – and without a damn cab in sight.

He'd had his hand – *both* his hands on that blonde's fat ass, and they'd been rubbing crotches. No excuses this time, no 'I was only fooling around' this time, no 'But, baby, I was half stoned' this time.

They were down to the *D* done.

She should never have come out tonight away. Early workday, and she didn't know the neighborhood. She hadn't known anybody at the stupid party.

She should've listened to her roommate and stayed home. But she'd been a little pissed at Kari for saying Mattio was a cheating dickwad. She'd been a little pissed, she admitted now, because she'd known it was true.

Why the hell did he have to be so good-looking, and so good in bed?

Down to the *D* done, she reminded herself, blinking back tears and taking her lumps by texting her roomie.

On my way home – done with this crap. Wait up, okay, if you're not in bed? Get up if you are. I want wine and whine. J

She blinked at tears that came as much from anger as the loss of the cheating dickwad.

'Hey, miss! Hey, sorry!'

She heard the voice – major twang in it – and kept walking.

'Please, I'm sorry, but I'm really lost. Can you just tell me how to get to Broome? Is that right? Is Broome right?'

The twangy voice hurried up to her, and the woman owning it shivered and bit her lip. 'I'm just lost, and I'm awful nervous. If you could just tell me which way to go. It's so cold, and I can't find a taxicab.'

'Tell me about it.' Jayla sighed. 'Did you say Broome?'

'Yes, with an "e", is that right? I'm not from New York.'

'Shocked face.'

The woman smiled, then looked down. 'Oh, would you look at that?'

Instinctively Jayla looked down, bent over a little.

It hit her like a hammer. Maybe it was a hammer. Pain exploded, the world spun, going red at the edges. She tried to cry out, but only managed a moan.

Something – someone – shoved her, yanked her. She fell hard, hard enough to steal what little breath she had still in her lungs.

'I've got her, honey!' The twangy voice came as though through a tunnel, a tunnel flooded with water. 'Let's go, I've got her. Told you to let me pick 'em, Darryl. I've got a knack.'

Somebody laughed. Even as she whimpered, tried to turn over, the hammer struck again, and knocked her into the dark.

8

Eve woke to the familiar. The scent of coffee, Roarke, already dressed in one of his master-of-the-business-universe suits on the sofa in the sitting area working on his PPC as the screen, on mute, scrolled with financial data she'd never understand. And the cat sprawled over the top of the sofa like some feline potentate.

Really, it didn't get much better.

She lay still a moment, taking it all in – and still he sensed she'd waked as his gaze shifted to hers.

'Good morning.'

'It feels like one,' she decided.

She pushed up as nothing beckoned more alluringly that the scent of coffee. Since he'd gone for a pot, she walked over, poured an oversized mug, and gave herself that special glory of the first morning sip.

'How many countries and/or off-planet stations have you talked to this morning?' she wondered.

'Only Italy and Olympus. It's a slow day.'

'In your world,' she countered as it was barely six a.m. 'Shower,' she declared, and took her coffee with her.

Next to coffee, real coffee, pulsing jets and raining showers of steaming hot water equaled the finest start to any morning. There were days she didn't think twice about it – such things had become routine. And other days she remembered, with brutal clarity, the cold, the hunger, the dark spaces, the painfully bright ones.

She had a flash of the room in Dallas – red light from the sex club blinking, the frigid cold because the temperature gauge was broken, the hunger gnawing like a rat in her belly fighting with the avid fear her father would come back drunk, but not drunk enough, and hurt her again.

She'd been eight, with hunger, fear and pain her constant companions.

Why should she think of that now, on a good morning with hot water flooding all over her and the clean, faintly green scent of the shower gel rising up with the steam?

She'd dreamed, Eve realized. No, not her old nightmare, not that horrible night she'd killed Richard Troy as he'd raped her. But he'd been in there, somewhere.

Her first instinct was to dismiss it – she couldn't claim to be over the years of trauma, but she'd learned how to cope with it, to put it in its place and move on. But dismissing it gave it – him – too much power, and might subvert whatever her subconscious had worked on while she slept.

So she let her mind drift, let her thoughts play back as she stepped from the shower into the drying tube. And while the warm air blew around her, she heard music.

The cello. He'd played the cello. A requiem, Dorian Kuper had called it as he sat, wearing black tie, teasing mournful notes out of the instrument with the bow and his skilled fingers.

A requiem for all.

She'd seen the faces of the dead, sitting quietly in the audience of what had been the opera house, all dripping, glittering chandeliers and gilt. With each of the dead spotlighted in icy-blue light.

See me. Stand for me.

So many of them, she'd thought. Those known victims, the others she believed had been.

And empty seats – for those yet to be known, or worse, those yet to come.

Too many empty seats, she thought as she stepped out of the warm air, took down the robe tidily hanging on its hook.

Richard Troy had walked onstage, grinning that wild grin, a conductor's baton in his hand.

Let's liven it up! Time for a happy tune. Killing pumps you up and puts a spring in your step. You should know that, little girl.

'Fuck you back to hell,' she muttered, and heard her dream voice echo the sentiment.

That made her smile, if a little fiercely. He couldn't get to her anymore, couldn't make her quake and shake.

But the dream, or the memory of it, told her nothing she didn't already know. There were many, and there would be more.

She went back into the bedroom, noted Roarke had two covered dishes on the table.

It would be oatmeal – something else she'd resigned herself to.

When she walked over, sat beside him, he took her chin in his hand, turned her face to his for a kiss.

Another fine way to start the day. Even when oatmeal followed.

When he removed the warming lids, she saw she hadn't been wrong. But he'd added a side of bacon, a bowl of fat berries, and another bowl of the crunchy, caramelly stuff. When you added the berries and the crunchy stuff to the oatmeal, had bacon, it all went down easy enough.

'Why does stuff like oatmeal that's good for you have to be weird?'

'There are many among us who don't consider oatmeal weird at all.'

'I bet there's more of us who do,' she mumbled, and disguised it with the berries and crunch.

'It's a fine way to start a snowy day.'

'Snow?' She looked up, looked toward the window into the gray and the white.

Not the thin spit of yesterday's snow, she saw. But thick, fast white flakes.

'Shit.'

'It's lovely from here, with breakfast on the table and the fire crackling.'

'Which would be great if we could sit right here until it stops.'

'Is there anything you can't do here through the morning?'

She could probably work at home. Her equipment here – and the other equipment available to her – put what she had at Central to shame. But—

'I need Peabody,' she began.

'I can arrange transportation for her.'

He could, she thought, and would. And still *but*.

'I just got back from leave. My people need me around, as much as I can manage. And Trueheart takes his detective's exam tomorrow. Baxter's a wreck over it.'

'Being a wreck over his young aide speaks well of him. And don't claim you didn't fret about it when Peabody took hers.'

'I trained her. If she'd bombed it, I'd have kicked her ass.'

'How do you think our young Trueheart will do?'

'He'll pass. If he doesn't it means he's not ready. It means he let nerves screw him up. A cop can't let nerves screw him up, so that would be not ready. Unless he and Baxter catch a hot, I'm going to use them on my investigation. It's more hands and eyes, and it'll keep them both busy and occupied.'

'You're a good boss, Lieutenant.'

'The cops under me deserve one, so I need to be. If Trueheart makes it I'm going to request another uniform.'

'Anyone in mind?'

'A couple I'll look into, if and when.' She felt the cat start to slink down the sofa like a snake when she picked up some bacon. 'What's on your plate today?'

'A number of meetings, reviews – much of which, lucky for me, I can handle from here via 'link or holograph. I'll venture out later. I want to go by the youth shelter – work's progressing very well there. And as I've also been away, I'll want to spend time at my office.' He scooped up oatmeal happily enough. 'I'm also a good boss.'

'Of legions.'

As the cat bellied over, eyes fixed on bacon, Roarke merely turned his head, raised an eyebrow. Galahad rolled onto his back, yawned hugely.

'Why does he think he's going to get away with it?' Eve wondered. 'He never does.'

'You can't get the prize without reaching for it.'

Acknowledging the point, she reached for the prize of more coffee – and her communicator signaled.

'Hell.' She rose, went over to pick it up from the dresser. 'Dallas.'

'Dispatch, Dallas, Lieutenant Eve. See the woman at 623 Bond, apartment 902. Whittiker, Kari has reported a possible missing person. Notification of possible missings flagged at your request.'

'Right. Who's missing?'

'Campbell, Jayla, age twenty-four, mixed-race female. Last seen, 754 Carmine, apartment 615, at approximately twenty-four-thirty hours.'

'Acknowledged. I'll take it. Dallas out.'

She frowned at the comm before setting it down again. 'Probably nothing. Probably hooked up with somebody, but I had them flag any missings or possible missings over the age of sixteen. They've never gone for kids, that we know of.'

'Small blessings. Do you want me to go with you?'

'No point. I'll take it solo, just meet up with Peabody at Central. The woman hasn't been out of touch for even eight hours, so it's probably nothing.'

'And yet.'

'And yet.' She headed for the closet. 'If this turns out to be one of theirs, we've got a hell of a lot more time than anybody's had before. That's a start.'

She came out with a navy-blue crew neck sweater, brown trousers and a brown jacket. And frowned again when he gave her the Galahad/bacon raised eyebrow.

'What? What's wrong with this stuff?'

'Keep the sweater and trousers.' He rose, plucked the jacket away from her, and strolled into the closet.

'Why can't I get it right?' she demanded. 'I think I do get it right, but you like to make me think I don't get it right.'

'It's not altogether wrong. There's just a better choice.'

She yanked on a support tank, muttering about better

141

choices, wriggled into underwear, and was hooking the trousers when he came out with a jacket – a brown one, damn it.

But one that had a subtle needle-stripe of navy. The boots were navy, too, with a wider brown stripe up the sides to the ankle.

She knew she'd never seen them before.

'Waterproof, insulated,' he told her. 'Your feet will be happier.'

'How many pairs of boots do I have in there?'

'I wouldn't know.'

'You keep buying them, so you ought to know.' She tugged the sweater on, shoved at her hair when her head came out.

And he kissed her. 'One of my small pleasures. Would you deny me?'

She took the boots, sat down. Felt the warmth, the solid support the minute her feet were inside. 'Do you know how many pairs of boots I had before I met you?'

He only smiled as she rose, reached for her weapon harness – which told her he undoubtedly did.

'Two, and one pair didn't really count as they were emergency use only because they were trashed. I still caught the bad guys.'

'You did. Now you get to catch them with more comfortable and stylish feet.'

She took the jacket from him, put it on and began to stow

what she needed in various pockets. 'You know I married you for sex and coffee, not boots.'

'Isn't it nice, then, to have the bonus?'

This time she grabbed his face, kissed him. 'Yeah. I'm going to grab a few things from the office here, then I'm in the field. See you tonight.'

'I'll be here until about eleven, I'm thinking, if you've need of me. Meanwhile, take care of my cop.'

'Nearly top of my list,' she said and strode out.

'It's not, no, not nearly top.' He glanced over, saw the cat had managed to take advantage of the distraction and snag the bit of bacon still on Eve's plate. 'And that's why you continue to try, isn't it? Now and again, you hoist the prize.'

Galahad ran his tongue over his whiskers, and belched.

By the time she got downstairs her coat lay draped over the newelpost with the Peabody scarf folded neatly over it, the Mr Mira snowflake hat on that, and a fresh pair of gloves added to the mix.

She thought to stuff the hat in her pocket, thought of the thick snow, reconsidered. She'd just look at it like a good-luck charm, she decided. Until she managed to lose it like she lost every hat and every pair of gloves she'd ever owned. She wound the scarf on, and because dangling ends were – to her mind – an opponent's opportunity to strangle in any hand-to-hand, tucked them inside the coat.

Pulling the gloves on, she walked out into the wall of snow

143

where her car already sat running, heaters, she imagined, turned to blast.

Routine, she thought again. Such things had become routine. That didn't mean she took them for granted.

She imagined Summerset had given a dry, ghoulish snicker as he set out the snowflake hat, and sniffed when he'd set out the surely doomed gloves. But he'd put them out.

'So thanks,' she muttered, and drove off in her warm, ugly car.

She sent Peabody a voice mail, letting her partner know she was checking out a possible missing persons, and to plan to report to Central as usual.

'Push on the potentials I copied you on,' she added. 'Let's get a sense of the vics, and the local cops on them. If anything rings on this possible I'm checking, I'll bring you in.'

She could have Baxter and Trueheart start on the two she hadn't reviewed thoroughly, she considered. But it could wait.

She worked her way down to NoHo, forced to drive defensively on every block. Because there were snow-phobic morons on every block, she concluded. Which included pedestrians in such a hurry to get out of the snow, they didn't bother to look when they used the crosswalk.

Maxibuses inched along until she wanted to obliterate every last one of them – and she comforted herself that at least the weather held off the hyping ad blimps.

It took her twice as long as it should have to get to Bond,

and the shock of finding a parking space nearly in front of the building almost caused her to lose it to a sneaky sedan.

She hit the sirens, shocked the sneaky sedan, and slid smoothly into the space.

The sedan, obviously pissed and suspicious, remained inches away. Eve stepped out of the car, thinking: Want to take me on, pal?

She opened her coat, flashing her weapon in its harness, held up her badge. Stared.

The sedan moved along.

Another nice note to the morning, she decided, and trudged through the snow to the entrance of the building with its nicely repointed brick, snow-covered steps and curly iron rail.

A solid building, she determined, carefully rehabbed, decent security with cams and palm plates.

She started to use her master, thought better of it, and pressed for 902.

The answer was quick enough to tell her whoever was on the other end had been standing close.

'Yes.'

'Lieutenant Dallas, NYPSD. Ms Whittiker.'

'Yes. Yes. I'm buzzing you in. Please come right up. I'm waiting. Come right up.'

Eve pushed in the door at the buzz, at the *thunk* of locks deactivating. The small lobby showed the same care as the exterior with clean fake wood floors and a pair of elevators with shiny black doors.

She took one to the ninth floor, pleased when it ran smooth and nearly soundlessly. Even as she stepped out, a door down the corridor opened.

The woman wore short, stylish dreds around a carved-in-ebony face. Huge brown eyes looked exhausted and worried as she gripped her hands together.

'Are you the police?'

Eve took out her badge. 'Lieutenant Dallas. You're Kari Whittiker?'

'Yes, come inside. They said, when I contacted the police, they said Jayla hadn't been out of touch long enough to be considered missing. Even when I explained everything, they said to wait another day, to try contacting her 'link, other friends. Then they tagged me just a little while ago, and said somebody was coming.

'Did you find her? Is that why you're here?'

'No. I'm just following up.'

'You're a lieutenant.' Those tired, worried eyes sparked. 'Lieutenants don't just follow up. My father's a Marine, so's my brother. I know how rank works.'

'I'm following up as I'm checking into any reports of missing persons in connection with another case. Why don't we sit down, and you can explain to me what you explained when you called this in?'

'What other case?'

Smart and sharp, Eve thought, which might be helpful. But right now she needed data. 'Ms Whittiker, asking me questions isn't going to help locate your friend. Answering mine might.'

'Okay, you're right. I'm sorry. I didn't get any sleep.'

She gestured to a chair in a living area that said female without the frills. Warm colors, a multitude of pillows, soft throws, flowers and candles.

'When did you last see Ms Campbell?' Eve asked.

'She went out about nine last night, with Mattio. Mattio Diaz. They were going to a party, I'm not sure where. In the West Village, I think.'

'You're roommates?'

'That's right. We've lived together for nearly four years now – roomed in college, and got this place right after.'

'I'm going to assume she's stayed out all night before this, and you have another reason to be concerned.'

'Yes, yes to both.'

Kari clasped her hands together again. She wore skin pants the color of iron and a thick hip-length sweater in red – and to Eve's eye worked hard to stay calm and coherent.

'She texted me at about twelve-thirty last night, said she was on her way home because I'd been right and Mattio was a dick. She asked me to wait up if I wasn't already in bed – I wasn't. I mean I was, but I was watching a vid. So I got up, got out a bottle of wine and our stash of emergency chocolate brownies. But she didn't come home. I waited until about one, tried her 'link, but it wouldn't go through.'

'Wouldn't go through?'

'Like the charge died, or the 'link broke, or something. I couldn't even get to her v-mail. I tried again and again, but she never answered.'

'How about this Mattio?'

'Oh, I tagged that fuckhead.' Now she radiated disgust. 'I waited until nearly two in the morning because I didn't want to talk to him, but I tagged him. Still at the party, stoned – big surprise. He said she'd left – couldn't say when, didn't much care if you ask me, and had his usual line about how she'd misunderstood, and gotten jealous.'

Tears swam into her eyes but didn't blur the fire behind them.

'He's a cheat, and a loser. And I was so glad when Jayla texted me because she really sounded done this time. I can play it back for you.'

'Yeah, do that.'

Kari pulled it out of her pocket. 'I've played it over and over, as if this time I'll realize I missed something, but—'

She hit play.

Eve listened, and began to feel the burn.

It was the voice of a woman who was pissed, who was heading home because she wanted her girlfriend and a sympathetic ear. Not one who'd have decided to go back to a party or hook up with some other guy for the night.

'How would she have gotten home?'

'She'd have cabbed if she could. She doesn't like the

subway, doesn't like being underground. So if she couldn't find a cab, she'd have walked.'

'It's a long walk on a cold night.'

'She was pissed, and that would keep her going awhile. Lieutenant, I know what you're thinking. She's a grown woman. She had a fight with her boyfriend, started home, changed her mind. Maybe she ducked into a bar, or hired an LC, or ran into somebody she knew and went with him. But she wouldn't. She asked me to wait up for her. She'd never have left me worried this way. She'd have contacted me. We're friends. We're best friends. We're like sisters. I *know* her, and she wouldn't do this. Something happened to her.'

'Where does she work?'

'She works for a modeling agency – which is where she met Mattio Dickwad Diaz. He's a model. She books models with ad agencies, with designers. Frosted. She worked for Frosted. They're in the Flatiron Building here in New York. They've got agencies in Europe and Asia. She travels some-times.'

'Did she have trouble with anyone? Did anyone bother her?'

Kari grabbed one of her dreds, twisted it, untwisted it. 'She works with models, so there's a lot of drama and demand. She's good at it. There'd be somebody pissed, sure, if she rejected them, or the client turned them down when she sent them out. Nobody specific that I can think of.'

'Any guys who wanted to take Mattio's place with her?'

'Plenty. She was wasting her time with him. Take the guy across the hall.'

'Across the hall?'

'Yeah.' She dropped her hand, sighed a little. 'Luke Tripp. He's single, he's cute, he's interested. But she's had her focus on Mattio, making it work with him.'

'This neighbor ever get pushy?'

'Oh God no. I wish he would, a little, and maybe she'd take more notice.'

'How about Mattio? Did he ever get pushy, physical, any kind of abuse?'

'No physical, no. "Abuse"?' The fire flashed against the fear again. 'I think it's abusive to be a serial cheater who turns it all around so it's the fault of the person he cheated on. But that's me. He's an asshole, but he'd never hurt her that way. Or anyone. They might fight back, and hit him in his precious face.'

She asked more questions, got the clear picture of a young woman – happy and successful in her work, with an eclectic circle of friends – who'd been hung up on the wrong man for about eight months.

'Can I take a look at her room?'

'Oh, sure. Look anywhere, at anything. Can you put out a – what is it – an APB or something? Maybe she had an accident. I called the hospitals and clinics, the emergency centers. Everything I could think of, but—'

'Get me a recent photo of her,' she told Kari, to give her something to do. 'We're going to look for her.'

'You're going to look for her.' Kari grabbed Eve's hand. 'You promise?'

'I'm looking for her now, getting information from you, seeing where she lived, seeing her things. We'll double-check at the hospitals.' And the morgue, Eve thought.

'Thank you. Thank you so much. Her room's this way. I've got lots of pictures. I'll get one for you.'

'I'd like to have your 'link.'

'Mine, why?'

'I'm going to have someone in EDD – Electronics – try to narrow down the location. Where she was when she texted you.'

'You can do that?' Kari pulled it out of her pocket. 'Here, whatever you need.'

Eve used her own to contact McNab.

'Yo, Dallas.' His pretty face came on screen – the flash of silver links curving along his ear nearly blinded her. 'Snow day!'

'I need a location off a text. Can you do that without the actual 'link in your hand?'

'I'm the magic man. Tag me on it, or connect it to yours, and give me a couple mo's. She-Body,' he called out. 'Got a task for your LT going. Don't suit up yet. We were about to put on the snow gear, head out,' he told Eve.

'I'll tag you on the civilian's 'link.'

151

'Use this code,' he said, while the screen showed his movement around the apartment to the second bedroom they used as a mutual office.

She used the code he gave her, heard the signal on his end.

'Okay, what model are you using?'

'How the hell do I know?'

'Never mind, wait, let me . . . ' She saw his comp now, and the codes flashing over his screen. 'There it is, okay. Order Function/Control/Interface.'

She did as he instructed, felt the 'link vibrate lightly in her hand.

'Texts coming up. Which ones are you after?'

'That one.' She could just see Jayla's name on McNab's screen. 'The last one from Jayla Campbell.'

'"Wine and whine", nice one. Couple more mo's on this. Did you know the 'link's deactivated?'

'How?'

'I can dig into that if you want, but it's nonresponsive. This text was sent near Carmine and Sixth. Somewhere in a two-block area.'

Peabody's face pushed onto the screen. 'What's up? Do you have something hot?'

'I've got something. I'm currently on Bond, checking out a possible missing person. You head over to Carmine, talk to the people who gave a party last night.' She reeled off the address. 'Subject's name is Jayla Campbell. Get what you can.

Save me time and tag Uniform Carmichael, have him check medicals for Campbell. I'll get back to you.'

'You are looking for her,' Kari said from behind her. 'You think something really bad happened to her.'

'Whatever's happened, I'm looking for her.'

Eve got a good sense of Jayla Campbell. She liked popular music, nothing too cutting edge, nothing too nostalgic. She had a love affair going with shoes, and kept her wardrobe separated into the professional wear, the party wear and the hangout wear.

She leaned toward the conservative in sex, opted for the yearly birth-control implant – and was due for a recharge there in three months.

She liked her work, had hopes to climb the ladder to full partner, and struggled to keep steady on a healthy nutrition and exercise routine.

She had a younger sister, still in college, and parents who were going to celebrate their twenty-sixth anniversary in the fall.

She believed, according to the journal she kept on her bedroom comp, she was the woman to make Mattio a star, and to make him a good man.

Not in love with him, Eve deduced. Thinks she is, but it's not the long-haul. And there was just enough about Luke Tripp – the cute neighbor – to show Jayla was paying some attention there.

She enjoyed a varied social life, much of it work-centered,

kept a decent budget with occasional splurges – which included hair and skin care, an apparent priority.

By the time Eve left the apartment, she visualized a woman with a good work ethic, one who enjoyed interaction with people – friends and strangers alike. A dependable woman. Not one who would leave her closest friend and roommate hanging and worried.

She knocked on the door across the hall.

The man who opened the door had a compact body and an attractive face. His dark hair stuck up in wild tufts, as if he'd combed it with a rake. And his eyes, warmly blue, widened when she held up her badge.

'Luke Tripp?'

'Yeah. You're the police. Did you find her?'

'No, we haven't.'

'Ah, Jesus.' He dragged his fingers through his hair, added more tufts. 'Kari just told me about an hour ago. I've been tagging everybody I can think of, but nobody's seen her.'

'When did you last see or speak to her?'

'We got home from work at the same time yesterday, walked in together. Talked for a couple minutes, like you do. Later, about nine maybe, I was restless, so I decided I'd hit the gym. It's right around the corner. I rode down in the elevator with her and Mattio.'

He said the name in a spit of contempt.

'Don't like him much.'

'*At all*,' Luke corrected. 'He's an asshole, and he treats her like crap. She deserves better.'

'Like you?'

He let out a half laugh, then just sighed. 'I wish.'

'How about after the gym?'

'After? I . . . Oh, well, God, you're looking for where I was when she went missing.' This time he pressed his fingers to his eyes. 'Okay, anything that helps. I ran into a couple gym buddies, and we went out for a brew. I'd've been home by midnight. Do you want to come in, do you want to look around?'

'No. I'm just crossing things off the list.'

'Kari said she was upset about Mattio – big surprise – but you've got to trust me. She'd never do this to Kari, never just drop off the grid. They're family.'

No, Eve thought when she left the building, the woman she pictured had a good, solid sense of responsibility, and wouldn't do this to a friend.

Eve pulled out her 'link to coordinate with Peabody on the next step.

9

She arranged to meet Peabody at Mattio Diaz's building, on the west edge of Greenwich Village. She didn't have the same happy luck with parking, and had to settle on a price-gouging underground lot three snow-packed blocks away.

The hike convinced her Roarke had been right – as usual – about the boots.

The snow kept the traffic, pedestrian and vehicular – thinner than normal in the trendy neighborhood, and she noted several stores had opted to close, at least for the morning.

She spotted a glide-cart operator dressed for exploring Siberia, down to the goggles. A couple of indeterminate sex huddled in the steam of his grill over a bag of chestnuts that scented the air. And a gang of kids raced by with the manic energy that told her schools had taken a snow day.

She spotted Peabody – pink coat ridiculously cheerful through the thick curtain of snow – and McNab with her. He wore atomic cherry with an earflap hat of such eye-burning colors she imagined it had come from Peabody's oddly skilled hands.

They, too, huddled over a bag of chestnuts.

'Hey, Dallas!' Like the coats, Peabody's voice was ripe with cheer. 'Did you hear?'

'Hear what?'

'We're going to get six to eight inches!'

'Well, whoopee.'

'I didn't have anything cooking,' McNab began, and held out the bag to share. 'I asked Feeney, and he said to come on along.'

She shook her head at the chestnuts which then vanished into one of his half a million pockets. 'Fine. I'm going to talk to the reputed dickwad about what happened last night. I could use you to triangulate. Peabody's got the locations of the snatch and dump on Kuper. Let's see how it plays with the area where Campbell sent the text last night.'

'I can be all over that and back in no time.'

'Let's get the hell out of this damn snow.'

'It's so pretty.' Peabody turned her face up to it, let it catch on her eyelashes.

'It's also going to make it harder for us to dig up anybody who might have seen Campbell or the people I strongly suspect grabbed her. What did you get from the party people?'

'Nothing much. A couple of guys threw the party – good space for one. Neither of them even realized she was gone. Didn't know her anyway. But there was another guy there this morning – stayed over.'

'Had a threesome,' McNab put in as Eve used her master to get into the building. 'Definitely.'

'I have to say yes to that,' Peabody confirmed. 'The third guy talked with her some. He wants to get into modeling. He's got the looks. She gave him her card. And he noticed she had some words with Diaz – who'd been sexy dancing – with a lot of hands on various body parts – with a blonde. Wit says she was really steamed, and he couldn't blame her as it was pretty in-your-face. He said something to the blonde after he saw Campbell grab her coat and take off. The blonde's name is Misty Lane.'

'The hell it is.' Eve shook snow off her coat.

'Yeah, *professional* name. A model/actress/cocktail waitress. The blonde just laughed it off, and said guys like Mattio were for fun, not for keeps. He says it was after midnight, but couldn't pin it down.'

'Good enough.'

The converted-to-lofts warehouse boasted a freight elevator some people found charming. Eve considered them death traps and opted for the stairs.

'Nadine's thinking about a place like this,' Peabody said.

'Like this?'

'On her list of possibilities. Big, trendy loft space. The others are a brownstone – a la Charles and Louise. And the third's a multilevel penthouse type condo in some slick building.'

'Number three,' Eve said.

'Oh, did she decide? Last I talked to her Roarke had given her some different properties to look over, but that's as far as she'd gotten.'

'That's what she will decide.'

'Maybe, but whichever way she goes, she's after full, top-of-the-line security. That near-miss with Roebuck scared her.'

'Good. I told her not to open the damn door. Next time she won't.' Eve paused on the third floor. Despite the momentary stupidity, Nadine Furst was a friend. 'She's doing okay?'

'Yeah. She took a delayed vacation – solo this time. Just a few days. She's already back – mostly, I think, because she wants to move as soon as she can.'

And, Eve imagined, because the top on-screen crime-beat reporter couldn't stay away from the action for long.

She knew the feeling.

She buzzed at Diaz's door, and got a tinny computerized voice.

Mr Diaz has engaged the Do Not Disturb option. There was a jumble of noise, a sort of wheeze – as if the comp had asthma. **Please leave your name.**

'Cheap tech,' McNab commented. 'Bottom of the barrel.'

Cheap tech or not, it currently stood in her way. Eve took out her badge. 'Scan this,' she ordered. 'This is official police business. Inform Diaz now.'

The scanning function is currently inactivated. Please leave your name.

Eve pressed the buzzer, held it down.

The Do Not Disturb — through the speaker came the equivalent of a computer death rattle — Name leave unable to process.

Ruthlessly, Eve ignored the dying gasps, kept her finger on the buzzer.

It took more than a few of McNab's mo's, but the next sound was human.

'What the fuck!'

'NYPSD. Open the door, Mr Diaz.'

'Well, Jesus, it's barely *morning*.'

Things rattled and thunked, and the door cracked open.

Yeah, he was a looker, Eve thought, even half asleep and obviously strung-out. Unearthly green eyes, thick black lashes, chiseled cheeks covered with scruff and a tumble of dark hair streaked with red gave him the kind of polished sexy used on billboards.

'You can let us in, Mr Diaz, or we'll arrange to have this conversation at Central.'

'Central what?'

Apparently the gods had used up their quota on his face, and hadn't had much left over for brains.

'We're cops, so that would be Cop Central.'

'What the fuck!'

'The fuck will be explained in the course of the conversation.'

'Well, Jesus,' he said again, and opened the door.

He hadn't bothered with clothes – apparently the quota had included the body that matched the face on the scale.

Beside her Peabody gulped audibly.

'I was sleeping,' he said, and gave a king of the jungle stretch. 'What's the prob?'

Eve bent down, picked up a pair of fake leather pants. 'Are these yours?'

'Yeah, so?'

'Put them on.'

'Sure, if it bothers you.' He smirked. 'But naked's natural. Anybody got any coffee?'

'Gee, fresh out.'

Clothes – a shirt, a couple of thongs – his and hers, Eve supposed, and a very skimpy black dress littered the floor. Knee-high black boots, and mile-high glittery heels lumped together in another pile.

'I take it you weren't sleeping alone,' Eve said.

The smirk reappeared as he tugged on the pants. 'Don't usually.' Then he yawned, managed to look sexy doing so. 'I need a Vitasmooth.'

So saying, he sort of glided off through an opening framed in wavy glass block. Eve heard kitchen rummaging.

'Asshole,' McNab muttered, and Peabody only cleared her throat and gulped again.

He came back with a jumbo tube filled with spinach–green liquid. 'Sorry, last one.' And took three big gulps. 'Wow, head rush. Nice. So what's this about?'

'Jayla Campbell.'

'Jay-jay?' He shrugged, glided again to one of the two chairs in the big space, slumped down, drank again. 'What about her? Last I heard dancing with somebody wasn't a cop deal. She's pissed, fine. No reason to call in the cops.'

'She's missing.'

'Missing what?'

Eve strode over, slapped her hands on the arms of the chair and leaned in. 'Listen carefully.'

'Sure. You've got mag eyes. Anybody ever tell you? You could model with those eyes, your build. I've got connections.'

'Shut up and listen. Jayla Campbell left the party she attended with you last night and hasn't been seen or heard from since.'

'She's probably just sulking somewhere. She's moody.'

'We have reason to believe otherwise. You were one of the last people to see her. When did you last see or speak with her?'

'I don't know, at the party, when she got the bug up her ass about Misty. We were just dancing.' His gaze shifted toward another opening covered by a gauzy black curtain.

'And you and Misty danced back here?'

The smirk came back, as if it couldn't help itself. 'No crime there.'

162

'What time?'

'Jesus, I don't know, exactly. We partied till about two, I guess. Then we walked back here – couldn't get a damn cab – and we had a lot of sex.' He smiled now, full, showing perfect white teeth. 'Jayla said we were done so, you know, free agent. She's just sulking somewhere,' he repeated. 'Wouldn't want to go home where her bitch of a roommate would rub her nose in it, right? That one took it way wrong when I said how maybe the three of us could get it together.'

'You really are a fuckhead.'

'Hey!'

Eve shoved back. 'Consider this, I could get a warrant, come through here and turn the place inside out. That would turn up all the illegals you didn't already consume.'

'I don't use! You can't prove it.'

'Yes, I could, but you're not worth it. Listen up, dickwad, the woman you've been involved with for several months, the one who helped put that face you're so proud of out there, is missing. She may be hurt, she may be dead. Pretend to care.'

'It's not my fault she got a bug up her ass. What do you mean "dead"?'

For the first time he looked concerned. Eve merely turned, signaled to Peabody and McNab.

'What do you mean "dead"?' he repeated, as she walked out.

'Let him stew on that,' she said.

163

'He's really, really pretty,' Peabody said, 'and he's really, really a fuckhead.'

'The pretty fuckhead didn't have anything to do with Campbell going missing – other than piss her off so she was out alone. I'd give him a couple weeks in a cage for that, if I could.'

'He wouldn't last a couple,' McNab muttered.

'Exactly.'

'You were staring.' He scowled at Peabody as they trooped downstairs. 'When he was naked.'

'Well, duh. Naked. And built. If he'd been a girl, you'd have been staring.'

Eve cast her eyes to the ceiling, quickened her pace from a walk to a jog down the steps. But she could still hear them.

'I bet he bought that body.'

'He got a really sweet deal if he did. But I like yours, right down to your bony ass.'

Eve didn't have to see – thank God – to know Peabody gave that bony ass a squeeze to highlight her point.

'Total skeeze.' Apparently McNab couldn't give it up. 'And he totally hit on you, Dallas. Roarke would squash him into skeeze juice.'

'If he was worth being squashed, I'd have squashed him myself.' She stopped at the bottom of the stairs, bringing both of them up short. 'A *skeeze*,' – she kind of liked the word – 'a fuckhead, a dickwad. He's all of that and a bag of rice cakes.'

'Chips. It's a bag of chips,' Peabody told her.

'Chips are good. Rice cakes are crap. He doesn't get chips.'

'Oh.' Peabody frowned over it before she nodded. 'That makes sense.'

'And the point is he doesn't know or care where Jayla Campbell is. We don't know, either, but we do care. Forget him. We've got about a three-block hike to where I'm parked. Considering the weather, I'm going to pull in some beat droids, shoot them Jayla's ID shot, have them canvass the area between the party and her apartment, using the most likely route that would take her through where she texted her roommate.'

'I can do that.'

'Then do it,' she told Peabody. 'And you, put the locations together. The first snatch, the first dump, and the last known location of Campbell.'

She pulled out her 'link when it signaled, saw Baxter's ID, and pushed her way out into the world of snow. 'Dallas.'

'Hey. You've got a Deputy William T. Banner out of someplace called Silby's Pond, Arkansas, in here. He wants to talk to you about our spree killers. I checked, and he's legit – been with the sheriff's office there for five years. I put him in the lounge since he's pretty firm about talking to you first.'

'Silby's Pond?' She tried to remember if she knew the name, but there had been so many on the choices of routes. 'I'm on my way in from Greenwich Village. We've got another missing. Take this data, get the wheels turning.'

'Shoot it at me.'

'Jayla Campbell,' she began, and filled him in.

She drove through abominable traffic with the scent of McNab and Peabody's roasted chestnuts and the hot chocolate they helped themselves to from the backseat AutoChef.

Snow and homey scents were one thing during the holidays, she thought, but those were over. Why couldn't they be done with it all now?

By the time she pulled into her slot at Central, she felt as if she'd trekked across the Arctic Circle.

'Why are they even out there?' she demanded. 'The people, especially the people who can't drive? NY tag number Echo-Charlie-Charlie-eight-seven-three. Issue an auto ticket.'

'An "auto ticket"?' Peabody repeated as they all climbed out.

'That's what I said. Didn't you see that idiot woman? Creeping along at twelve miles an hour?'

'Um. Well, it sort of pays to be cautious when—'

'While she was slapping on lip dye with her vanity mirror down, so she's looking at herself instead of the damn road – *and* babbling on her 'link while she's at it. Could've put it on auto if she needed to admire herself instead of fucking drive, but no, she's creeping and weaving and doing her christing makeup.'

'Oh. Well. Do you really want to fine her? I always felt sort of crappy issuing autos when I worked Traffic.'

'Get over it. Slap her with driving while stupid.'

With McNab giving her butt a pat for support, Peabody issued an auto-citation while they took the elevator up.

'They don't stalk the vics,' Eve said, shifting gears. 'There's not enough time for that. It's luck of the draw. It doesn't matter who – rich, poor, young, old, male, female. If the pattern holds we've got two days to find them before they finish Jayla Campbell.'

'The weather's helping them now,' McNab commented. 'Cold, wind, snow, sleet. People spring for a cab or take public. Or stick close to home. They've just got to find a solo walker in a relatively quiet spot.'

'Right now they're two for two in New York.'

As the elevator began to stop and start floor-by-floor with cops and civilians piling in, Eve pushed out.

'Odds are they boosted this dark all-terrain or van they're using. Peabody, run a search for stolen vehicles fitting that, try New Jersey and Pennsylvania. And, yeah, it's a general type in a big area,' she said before Peabody could point it out. 'But we start, and maybe whittle it down before they decide to switch again. They may have taken it from another victim.'

She wove her way through people on the glides, moving up and up.

'McNab, get me that triangulation. They're downtown somewhere. They have to have a place to live, to take the vics. Low security – can't have cams picking them up carting in a vic. Nothing popped yet on the canvass of abandoned, so either we haven't hit there yet, or they've found somewhere private.'

When she turned into Homicide, Baxter signaled from his desk. 'Alerts on Campbell are out, Loo. The media's already doing bulletins.'

'Okay.' She saw his gaze flick up to her snowflake hat. Eve yanked it off, stuffed it in her pocket. 'What's the deal with this Arkansas badge?'

'Well, he's mannerly, but he was pretty firm he needed to talk to you.'

She pulled off her gloves, scarf. 'Still in the lounge?'

'Last I checked.'

With a nod, she shoved the gloves in one pocket, the scarf in another, and headed out still wearing her coat.

She wanted coffee like she wanted to live. She wanted to sit down in the quiet, write everything up. Update, analyze, think.

In her head a clock was ticking, and there were less than forty-eight hours left.

She paused at the door to the lounge with its lines of vending, its tiny tables and hard chairs. She spotted him quickly.

A half mile of leg stretched out under the table. Long, narrow hands worked a PPC while a vending cup of something sat neglected in front of him.

A lot of wavy hair the color of a wheat field, a long narrow face to match the hands. He either hadn't shaved recently or wore the scruff on purpose.

He wore jeans, boots that had seen a lot of miles, a flannel shirt that made her think of lumberjacks even though she wasn't entirely sure what a lumberjack was.

A black parka hung over his chair back, and a duffel bag was under the table.

He looked up when she started toward the table. Blue eyes, she noted. Not Roarke-blue, but few were. His hinted at gray, showed smudges of fatigue under them, and a cop alertness in them.

'Deputy Banner.'

'Yes, ma'am. Will Banner.' He shifted his long legs, rose. Unfolded was more like it, she thought. He was an easy six-five with a build like a beanpole.

'Lieutenant. Lieutenant Dallas.'

He took the hand she extended in one with a rough, hard palm. 'I sure do appreciate you meeting with me, Lieutenant.'

'You're a long way from home, Deputy Banner.'

'That's the God's truth. Farthest I've ever been.'

'Where's Silby's Pond?'

'We're in the Ozarks, ma'am, not—'

'*Lieutenant. Sir* if you want. *Dallas* will do.'

'Sorry. Y'all do things different here. We're in the north of Arkansas, Lieutenant, not far from the Missouri border. Prettiest country you could ask for.'

His voice was caught somewhere between drawl and twang – leaning toward the drawl.

'What brings you here?'

'I'm hunting the same two you are. The same who killed this Dorian Kuper. He's their latest. You did a search last night through IRCCA on missings and homicides in my area.'

'How do you know that?'

'I get alerted whenever there's another victim, whenever there's an official search through for more.' Though he shifted his feet his eyes stayed steady on hers. 'Lieutenant Dallas, I understand you're working with the feds, and they've given you their profiles and data and whatnot, but they don't have all of it.'

'And you do?'

'If I did, your victim would likely still be playing his cello. But I believe – I *know* I have more. If you could just spare me fifteen minutes. I understand you're busy, and you're on an active investigation, but I'm asking you for fifteen minutes. I've come a hell of a long way.'

'Let's take it in my office.'

She could all but see relief slide through him before he bent down for his duffel. 'I'm grateful.'

'We don't usually shove fellow law enforcement out the door.'

'You do hear things about New York City.'

'I bet. When did you get in?'

'That's a story.'

She imagined that easy, heading toward lazy, drawl worked well on stories.

'I didn't get the alert about your victim until into the afternoon. I talked to Special Agent Zweck, like I did with the one right before, and before that. They've been working their way to you, Lieutenant, for months now. It seemed to me with the search you started last night you're leaning that way.'

'It's an angle.'

'It's the right angle, and because I saw how it seemed you might be leaning, and – I hope you'll understand – after I did some research on you – I figured you might be open to a face-to-face with me.'

He paused just inside the bull pen, looked around. 'You sure are busy around here. Back home, there's the chief, me and two other deputies and our dispatcher.'

'How many people in Silby's Pond?'

'Right about thirty-two hundred.'

'There's more than that in this sector of this building.'

She gestured him toward her office. He stopped again inside it, studied her board as she shrugged out of her coat.

'You know there's more. Half again more maybe.'

'It hasn't been updated since I left yesterday. I'm late getting in because we have another missing person.'

'Jayla Campbell. I was reading the bulletin,' he said when she narrowed her eyes, 'when you came in. The timing's right, I see you know that, too. They've got her. They'd've started right in on her last night, too. Excited to have another. They'd've already started hurting her.'

'There's no official victim in Silby's Pond. I'd remember.'

'No, ma'am. Sir. Lieutenant. Sorry.' He scrubbed at his eyes a moment. 'I was saying how I figured you'd be willing to talk with me, so I drove up to Branson, as it'd be the best place to get a shuttle through to New York. I got the last one heading out, figured I'd hit lucky. Until they dumped us in Cleveland 'cause of the weather. So I rented a truck, and drove the rest.'

'From Cleveland, in this weather.'

'The only way to catch them is to catch up to them. I haven't managed that yet.'

'Have a seat. You want coffee?'

'All I can get. Black would be just fine, thanks.'

She got two from the AutoChef.

'Who do you think they killed in your town?'

'Melvin Little. He's what you might call a fixture around those parts. He served in the Urban Wars, and he never could get through that, if you know what I mean. He came home, to his parents, a younger brother and a sweetheart. What my own daddy tells me, is Little Mel — as he was called, being small in stature — used about any substance he could get his hands on to muffle the nightmares, the voices, the memories. I know this doesn't matter, but I want you to know him.'

'You're getting your fifteen,' she told him.

172

Nodding, Banner took a hit of caffeine. His eyes went wide and glassy. 'Sweet Baby Jesus, what is this? Is this New York coffee?'

'Not exactly. It's real coffee. I've got a connection.'

'Real coffee.' He said it like a prayer, with awe and reverence.

Remembering her first taste of Roarke's coffee, she smiled. 'Need a minute?'

'It could take days.' He smiled back, and she saw, beneath the fatigue, a great deal of charm. 'Wait till I tell the boys back home.' Then he sighed. 'Little Mel, he couldn't adjust back. They tried what they try, but he was just one of the lost. There were too many, I guess. He didn't like being indoors much, so he took to sleeping out in the hills, in the woods. You have what you call here sidewalk sleepers.'

'Yeah.'

'And they, some of them, they make a kind of home for themselves out of what they scavenge. He did that. His family took him food and supplies, but after some time, it was clear enough he wasn't coming back. Most times he was drunk or high. He never hurt anybody but himself.'

She could see Melvin Little – Banner painted him well. And she sensed more. 'What was he to you?'

'His sweetheart? That's my grandmother. She loved him, loved the boy he'd been, but she couldn't reach the man who'd come back. She married my grandfather, but she still went out to see Little Mel from time to time, take him food and fresh clothes. I got in the habit of going out to check on him every week or two.'

'So you looked out for him.'

'We did what we could. It's true he might go rifling through a car or a cabin or shed now and then if it wasn't locked up, take what caught his eye. More often in the last couple of years. Not when anyone was in them, you understand, and he never did a break-in. If it was locked, he left it be. Otherwise, he'd just go on in, poke around, take something to add to what he called his collection. Might be a fork or a doorknob, a broken clock.'

'You considered him harmless.'

'He was harmless.' Banner took a moment, another hit of coffee. 'We had a boy go missing once. The family had gone camping, and the boy wandered off. We were putting the search team together when Little Mel comes walking into the campsite with the boy riding on his shoulders. The boy said how he'd been chasing a rabbit, and he got lost, and was crying and hurt his foot. And Little Mel came along, gave him a candy bar, wrapped up his foot in a handkerchief that was, truth be told, none too clean, and said how he'd give him a ride back to his mama. And he did. He never hurt anybody.'

'What happened to him?'

'I knew when I went out to check on him something was wrong. Not that he wasn't there, but his things, they were jumbled up.' Banner paused, shaking his head. 'He took pride in his collection, and there was an organization to it. And that day, there wasn't.'

He looked up again, into Eve's eyes. 'You know how you get that pull in your belly?'

'I do.'

'I had that. I went looking for him, at his usual places. Where he liked to fish, where he'd take what he called his preambles. I didn't find him until the next day. I went back the next morning, took his nephew's son who's a friend of mine so we could cover more ground. I found him in a gully, all broken up. You'd have thought how maybe he'd slipped off the track above, taken a long, bad fall. But he was a damn mountain goat, I swear. He'd been dead three days.'

'Evidence of torture, of binding?'

'Broken bones, cuts, bruises, some burns. But ... they ruled it an accident. Burns could've come from him smoking whatever he managed to smoke, or his campfire. Breaks and cuts and bruises from the fall. We got a report a cabin had been broken into. Lock smashed. A few things taken – not really what Little Mel tended to take – and like I said, he never broke in. They found a little blood, and it was his, so it looked like he'd gone on in, just cut himself on something. Not a lot of blood. But we didn't find anything that was missing in his collection, or along the way he'd have taken if he'd gone up that ridge and taken a fall.

'It could've happened that way, he broke in, cut himself,

was maybe careless on the track and fell. You can see the logic to it, if you didn't know him. But just over a week later, a boy went missing up in Missouri.'

'Noah Paston.'

'Yes, ma'am – *Lieutenant*,' he corrected. 'You'll have to give me time to break a lifetime habit. No question he was taken. There was no accident there. And clear signs he'd been bound, cut and burned and smashed up. A young, athletic boy and poor lost Little Mel don't seem to have much in common, but they were both alone, both in what you'd call remote areas, both with cuts, burns, broken bones. I couldn't let it go.

'I can show you the list I have, the names and locations I've been putting together since last August.'

Arkansas, she thought. It fell right into her route. 'I'd be interested in that, in comparing it with my own list. Not updated,' she repeated when he glanced toward her board. 'Not just with Jayla Campbell, but with the possible victims I put together last night. Is Ava Enderson on your list?'

'She surely is.'

When she named more, he shut his eyes like a man who'd found home, nodding, just nodding until she came to Jacob Fastbinder.

'That one's a heartbreaker. Jennifer – Ms Fastbinder – she's pushed all she can push on it, but he doesn't fit the FBI's vic-timology. And like Little Mel, it reads just as easy as an accident.'

'Do you know her?'

'Never met, as such, but we've had a number of conversations and correspondence.'

'I intended to contact her today, request she allow the body to be exhumed and transported here to our forensic anthropologist.'

'If you'd let me talk to her, I think I can make that happen. I don't suppose you could have a look at Little Mel.'

'Are there remains to look at?'

'He's buried in the family cemetery, like his mama wanted.'

'Having two would give DeWinter comparisons,' Eve considered, and made the call on the spot. 'We'll take him. I need to speak with my commander, but we're going to take both of them if you can pull it off.'

'Little Mel's mama's going to take more talking to than Jennifer Fastbinder, but I can be persuasive. I'm hoping I can persuade you to let me have another cup of this coffee.'

Eve wagged a thumb at the AutoChef. 'Do you know how to work one of those?'

'They're about the same wherever you go.'

'Then help yourself. Take it back to the lounge – can you find it again?'

'I've got a good sense of direction.'

'Start persuading. I need some time here to do the same, then I'm going to set up a conference room. When are you due back in Arkansas?'

'I'm on my own time. I took leave.'

That put a hitch in things. 'Does your chief know you're here, what you're doing?'

'He does.' Banner poked at the AutoChef. 'He doesn't see this the way I do, but he's given me a lot of room. And I've got leave coming.'

'Okay. Go work on clearing the exhumations, and I'll work on getting the forensics here.'

She sat, and when he'd cleared the room, did a quick and thorough run on him before she contacted Whitney's office and asked for a window.

10

Whitney sat at his desk, the city he served spearing up through the window at his back. His big hands rested on the arms of his chair; his eyes, dark and keen, stayed on Eve's as she briefed him.

He wore command as he wore his suit – a good fit with clean lines. While she spoke, his wide, dark face remained impassive.

'And this deputy traveled here from the Ozarks on his own time and dime because the searches you ran were flagged by him.'

'Yes, sir.'

'And he did this – at the base – because he believes a war vet with PTSD, with a history of substance abuse and anti-social behavior was one of the victims of the spree killers currently being sought by this department, others, and the FBI in spite of the ruling of his own ME – and the subsequent determination of accidental death by the FBI.'

In blunt, logical terms it didn't ring the bell, but ...

'The local ME in this case is also the town doctor – a GP.

I checked, and she's only worked on a handful of murders in seventeen years. The FBI has profiled these unsubs, has cemented their victimology. So far they're not very flexible about thinking outside those lines. Deputy Banner's vic is on the route I've speculated independently, as are several others both Deputy Banner and I have on our separate lists. They didn't start with Tennessee, Commander. The Nashville vic is only the first we can determine had the carved heart. And the gaps between killings are inconsistent – until you fill them in with the names both Banner and I have added.'

'Have you spoken with Special Agent Zweck?'

'No, sir, and I don't intend to at this time.' She paused only a moment when he raised his eyebrows. 'They're not interested in this line or these victims – Banner's already been shot down there. If we find evidence they were part of this spree, I would, of course, share all data and information. I realize this is all based on speculation, Commander, but it's logical speculation. It fits. And it's a big stretch to dismiss the fact both Banner and I have hit on so many of the same names.'

He tapped a finger on the edge of his desk. 'It's a big stretch to exhume two bodies and have the remains transported here, to have our people and resources study them for the purpose of overturning CODs.'

'If either of those CODs are overturned, I have a third body. Noah Paston, age nineteen, abducted, tortured, murdered – missing the carved heart in September.'

'That would bring the tally to twenty-four,' Whitney stated.

'Paston's body wasn't cremated but buried. If we determine either Little or Fastbinder – and I lean to both – were killed by these unsubs, I believe Paston's parents would agree to have his body exhumed and tested.'

'And Jayla Campbell?'

'She's the next, but she won't be the last. It's my belief that coordinating with Banner, compiling our separate investigations will open something up, help us find her in time.'

Nearly ten hours off the forty-eight already, Eve thought.

'We have no names, no faces. They're like ghosts, Commander. That tells me they look normal, ordinary, and know how to blend and behave in a way that doesn't bring attention. I've got uniforms and droids canvassing the area between where Campbell was last seen and her apartment, using the location McNab pinpointed where she texted her roommate. She made it that far, and we don't know how much farther. Walking alone, as Kuper was, as Little was, as Fastbinder was.

'There's a mistake somewhere,' she continued. 'There always is, but nobody's found it. Not yet. Mistakes may have happened further back, where nobody's looked closely enough. We find a mistake, and maybe we're in time to save Campbell.'

He tapped his fingers on the arms of the chair, then leaned forward. 'I want to talk to Banner's superior.'

'Chief of Police Lucius Mondale. I did a quick background

on both of them. Small-town cops, sir, but solid from what I can find. I sent you that data and Mondale's contact information.'

'I'll speak with him, and let you know my position on this. Meanwhile, coordinate with Banner. Information's never wasted.'

'Yes, sir.'

'They were coming here,' he said as she stepped back.

'Yes, sir, by any route I've projected, New York is probable destination.'

Rising, he walked to his wall of glass, looked out, hands linked behind his back. 'That will be one of their mistakes. Keep this low on the media radar as long as possible.'

'Absolutely.'

'Get it done.'

'Yes, sir.'

Time, Eve thought as she hurried back to her division. The clock ticking for Campbell, and now a second clock running. How quickly could she get the remains into DeWinter's hands – and Morris's, she added. She wanted that team on this angle.

They'd miss nothing.

Was Melvin Little the first? She'd done a background there, too. The man had been barely a hundred and twenty pounds, and over seventy. But not altogether an easy target. A war vet who'd known the woods, the hills. Who'd survived in them for decades.

Working in her head, she swung back into the bull pen.

'Peabody, set up a conference room – all our data on this investigation. Where's Baxter?'

'They caught one.'

Eve switched gears, glanced around. 'Detective Carmichael, Santiago, are you on something hot?'

'Just tying one up in a bow, Lieutenant,' Santiago told her.

'Tie it fast, then work with Peabody. Is Uniform Carmichael still in the field?'

'He hasn't come in as yet. I can check in with him,' Peabody offered.

'Do that.'

She headed for the lounge, pulling out her 'link as she went. 'I need Dr Mira,' she said before the admin could do more than identify the office. 'As soon as possible. We've had another abduction, and I have new information on the unsubs she's profiled.'

'I'll relay your request, Lieutenant.'

'Now.'

Eve clicked off, left a brisk voice mail for Garnet DeWinter, and was leaving one for Morris when she walked back into the lounge.

'Wheels are in motion,' she said, holding up a hand to keep Banner in his seat. 'I need this pushed through fast. I need you to clear as much of the decks as you can for this. I'll get back to you. Progress?' she asked Banner.

'Ms Fastbinder not only agreed, she's got a judge on tap

who'll push through the order mostly, I think, because he's relieved she'll take this out of state, and out of his hair. I just finished talking to my chief. I talked Little Mel's mama into it, and he'll get it done. Mostly, I think, for the same reasons as the judge.'

'Doesn't matter why as long as it's done. My commander will be speaking with your chief.' She gave him a measured study. 'If Whitney gets the impression you're a rogue lunatic, Banner, we're not going to get very far.'

'I might be fixated on this, and there's a girl who decided I was a lunatic when I joined the police, but I'll hold up.'

She sat, studied him again. She didn't see rogue or lunatic. 'The cabin where his blood was found, where items were taken and not recovered, who lives there?'

'It's a rental type. Lots of them around. This one was shut up for a few weeks. Septic issues the owner hadn't gotten around to dealing with.'

'So, empty.'

'That's right.'

'Security.'

'A lock on the door.'

'Easy target for somebody looking to score a few easy-to-transport items. The unsubs break in, start taking what they want. Little comes along. Altercation, he's killed or incapacitated. How far from the cabin did you find him?'

'Not counting the drop? It'd be maybe a half a mile on the

back road, another quarter mile to the trail where they say he fell off. Some say jumped, but that's bullshit.'

He drew in a breath, shoved at his hair. 'Sorry, I didn't mean to use hard language.'

'The day "bullshit" is hard language in a cop shop, that's the day I turn in my badge. Which is never. Did your people look for blood in the cabin? Signs somebody cleaned it up.'

'We can handle that kind of thing. It was just a little blood. They missed it when they cleaned up, in my opinion. Used a tarp, like they've used on others. Keep the blood off the scene.'

Just how she saw it. 'Then he wasn't the first, either. He was just one of the next. We trace back from this vic, this Little Mel. And we'll find the first. We find the first, we'll find them.'

Her eyebrows shot up when he reached out, covered her hand with his. He pulled his back quickly. 'Sorry – that's probably not allowed. It's just ... I've been waiting a long time to hear somebody say that.'

'Saying it, proving it, finding them, there are a lot of steps between.'

'I've been taking some of them, best I can. I'm going to be straight with you. I've only worked two murders, and both of them were pretty clear-cut right from the start. First was the Delroy brothers, Zach and Lenny. Not bright lights, either of them, and with a taste for bad booze and homemade Jump. The two of them got revved up on both, fought over a card game, and Zach, he picked up a fireplace poker and caved Lenny's head right in. Tried to cover it up saying somebody'd busted into their place, but like I said, not a bright light.'

He shifted a bit as if looking for comfort in the hard chair. 'And the second was a woman come down from Pittsburgh with her husband for a holiday. Not much of one for her as he had a habit of beating the hell out of her for fun. He'd blackened her eye and busted open her lip before she got outside to the car, locked herself in. Then she proceeded to run him over when he came out after her.'

'Hard to blame her.'

'There's that. She said right out she wanted to make sure he was dead this time, and that's why she backed up, ran over him again. Three times. Anyway, like I said, pretty clear-cut. We don't get a lot of killings – not purposeful – in Silby's Pond.'

'You've gotten this far on this one.'

'Since Little Mel I've worked it every day. Sometimes only an hour or so, but every day. I'm hopeful now that I've got somebody like you, a real murder cop, it'll break.'

'Then let's get going. We'll move this to the conference room.'

She rose, waited while he grabbed his coat, his duffel.

'It's a hell of a place, your Cop Central,' he commented as they started out. 'Lots doing.'

'If you're interested, I can have somebody show you around.'

186

'I wouldn't say no to that.'

Someone let out a war cry, high and wild. Eve pivoted, saw two uniforms giving chase. The man they pursued charged like a bull, head down, teeth bared, his eyes lit like lanterns with whatever substance he'd smoked, swallowed or syringed. He bowled over an unfortunate civilian clerk whose legs flew out from under her, sending her and the file bag she carried flying.

'Excuse me,' Eve said, cut across the corridor as the man, long, red hair streaming back in its skinny braids, fists pumping in the air, ran like the possessed.

Her right cross barely slowed him down, but it shifted his attention enough to have him swing those pumping fists in her direction. One glanced off her shoulder, and she went with it, spinning around and coming back with a side kick to his gut.

He grunted, made a grab. She stomped hard on his instep, followed up with a knee to the balls, then tried the right cross again.

That one had him staggering back, but he grinned at her through the blood that bloomed on his mouth. She braced for the next round, but the stagger gave the uniforms time to catch up.

Eve stepped back while they grappled, considered moving in again as fists and elbows jabbed and bashed and war cries echoed. Then a third uniform leaped in from the side.

'For Christ's sake,' she said when they finally had him

down and in restraints – where he laughed like a loon. 'For Christ's sake.'

'It's Mad Fergus, Lieutenant.' One of the uniforms, his own lip bloody, managed to pant it out. 'We thought we had him, but you never know what's going to set him off.'

'Somebody see to that woman he knocked down, and get him out of here. If you can't control a prisoner, keep them away from my division. You embarrass me.'

She turned, noted that Banner was helping the civilian clerk to her feet.

'Sorry about that,' she said when he joined her again.

'You move fast. If you'd kicked me in the gut the way you did that one, I'd've been flat out and gasping like a trout on the line.'

'I guess Mad Fergus is made of sterner stuff. What does that mean?' she wondered as she rolled her stinging shoulder. 'What does "stern" have to do with it? Never mind.'

'He landed one.'

'He's not the first.' Rolling her shoulder again, she led the way to the conference room, gestured him in.

'Detectives Peabody, Santiago, Carmichael, Deputy Banner.'

After an exchange of *nice-to-meet-you*'s, Eve studied the nearly completed board. 'Are you caught up?' she asked Carmichael and Santiago.

'Peabody filled us in.' Santiago tapped Campbell's photo. 'We've got under two days to find her.'

'Then let's not waste time. Deputy, give what you have to Peabody. She'll get it up. I'm going to run through what we've talked about for the others while we get the board finished. Melvin Little,' she began.

She found herself pleasantly surprised when Mira came in. It meant pausing for more introductions, and a quick reprise.

'Rough, steep trail like that?' Carmichael studied the images Banner had brought with him as they ran on screen. 'He could've slipped off. I'm not saying he did,' she added. 'I'm saying if you ran that probability, it would come in high.'

'Yes, ma'am, it would – and did – but not if you knew Little Mel. I don't care how messed up he was, he never set a foot wrong on a trail or a track.'

'The cabin, the small amount of blood.' Mira crossed her legs, angled her head. 'If, as the ruling determined, he had injured himself while rummaging through, there should have been more blood, not just a few drops in one location.'

'Agreed,' Eve said. 'Did your sweepers run the lights?'

'Sweepers?'

'Your crime scene people.'

'Oh, yes, sir, they did. No sign there'd been blood cleaned up. And I can tell you, he wouldn't've bothered.'

'None of the stolen items were recovered?' Santiago asked.

'There wasn't much of real value taken. And not the sort of things that would raise a flag if you took them to a pawnshop or, hell, a flea market.'

Mira folded her hands as she examined the image of the victim. 'Your medical examiner ruled those burns as self-inflicted.'

'Yes, ma'am. Either accidental or when he was high.'

'I strongly disagree, and believe our own ME will also.'

'I'm right pleased to hear that.'

'Morris and DeWinter will get a shot at these remains, and the remains of the suspected victim found in West Virginia,' Eve said.

'Your locals botched this one.' Santiago looked over at Banner. 'The feebies, too. No offense.'

'Not a bit taken.'

'We speculate,' Eve began, 'they worked as a team, had a routine on Little. Had the cabin, vacant at that time, he wandered in or by, they took him, used a tarp to catch blood and fluids, transported him to the high track, dumped him off and went on their way. The lack of the carved heart? They hadn't started that flourish at this time. He was early on. Not the first, but early. So we work back from this point.'

'A lot back from there.' Carmichael frowned. 'What got them started, that's going to be key. What set them off? If they're lovers, and that's how it reads, maybe somebody – a parent, authority figure, a spouse – trying to keep them apart. Or somebody moves on one of them, and it goes south from there. The first kill, whoever, wherever, whyever, it's what sparked it.'

She looked at Mira for confirmation.

'In my opinion, yes. That's the break, the "spark", if you will.'

'I've got a few possibilities,' Banner told them. 'Mostly I've been working forward from Little Mel, and beating my head against the FBI, but I'd started working back some. I've got three that are ... well, just maybes right now.'

'Let's see them.'

He looked at the unit Peabody used. 'That's a little more advanced than what I've worked with.'

'I'll get them up. Doc code?'

'Ah, not a code so much. I filed them under MBM – Maybes Before Mel.'

'On it. I've got a cousin who lives in the Ozarks,' Peabody said as she worked. 'A little place outside of Pigeon Run.'

'I know Pigeon Run. Pretty spot.'

'It is. I haven't been there since I was about sixteen, but I remember. She and her man and their boys run a farmer's market co-op.'

'Lydia Bench and Garth Foxx?'

Surprised, Peabody glanced around. 'Well, yeah. You know them?'

'A little. My sister more. She hauls harvests down to them, and hauls stuff back at least once a month. It's a small world no matter how big it gets.'

'Let's keep the world focused on murder for now,' Eve suggested. 'Get the data up, Peabody.'

'It's coming.'

'This here's the first.' Banner nodded toward the screen as the name and ID shot scrolled on. 'Vickie Lynn Simon. A licensed companion, worked out of Tulsa mostly. Her body was found on a farm road about ten miles out of the city. Beaten and stabbed. Overkill, they called it.'

'That was closed yesterday,' Eve told him. 'You were probably on your way here. They tied a second vic to it, and tracked down the killer. It looks solid, and the second vic was killed last week. This isn't ours.'

'Then I've only got two maybes. This one, Marc Rossini, owned a restaurant in Little Rock. Beaten, stabbed, burned. Right inside the restaurant, after closing. Busted the place up, too.'

'I looked at that one,' Eve remembered. 'We can leave it as a maybe, look deeper, but it doesn't ring for me. Rossini had a gambling problem, and owed a couple hundred K. Reads like enforcement that went too far.'

'One more, then. Robert Jansen. Beaten – defensive wounds on this one. Head caved in – likely by a tire iron. Broken leg, blows to his back, face. Defensive wound on his hands, arms. His body was found off the road, in some high brush off Highway 12, some south of Bentonville. They figured he'd been dead about a week before some kid needed to pee, and his mama pulled over, took him into the brush. Likely scarred that boy for life. The animals had been at the body by then.'

'That's one of mine,' Eve said, gaze sharpening. 'I'd just started looking at this one. It fits the route. Business trip, right? Guy's on a business trip, and driving from Fort Smith to Bentonville in a rental car. Car's never turned up.'

'No, ma'am.' Banner caught Santiago's smothered laugh. 'Sir, that is. FBI dismissed this one out of hand. No signs of torture. It reads like maybe he had car trouble, or he stopped – maybe to pee or to give somebody a hand. That somebody went at him, he fought back, and got a tire iron to the back of the head and across the face for his trouble.'

'Took his vehicle, wanted the vehicle.' That was the play as Eve saw it. 'Where's their vehicle?'

'Didn't find any. I checked, and none of the towing companies picked one up. None of the local law enforcement has a report on any abandoneds in that area.'

'Could've been on foot, but I don't much like it. One could've driven each vehicle, then they'd sell one. Opportunity.' Eve began to pace. 'Get him to stop. Seasoned business traveler, why does he stop on some bumfuck road?'

'A skirt,' Santiago offered.

'Yeah, most likely. Having some trouble, honey? Why, yes, I am. Thank you so much for stopping. It's dark and scary out here. Partner moves in. Looks like a slam dunk, right? Maybe even something they've done before. Just boosting a ride, but this guy does some damage. Maybe he goes after the woman, and the partner bashes him. Maybe he's getting the best of the partner, and the woman grabs the tire iron and whales in. Oh-oh, look at that. Dead guy, or seriously hurt guy. What to do.'

'Drag him into the bushes,' Peabody finished, 'and get the hell out of there.'

'Then, look what we did, together. Wasn't that exciting? Wasn't that a *rush*?'

Oh, it played, Eve thought as it ran through her head. It played like a big, fat violin at the opera – and just as tragically.

'His blood's on them. Bashing heads will do that. The smell of it, the feel of it, the look of it, all warm and red and wet. It just gets them going.'

'Together.' Mira nodded. 'It cements their relationship, takes it to this new level. He – the victim – becomes the enemy they defeated for each other. And sex is a reward. It then becomes a goal. And it requires more. More time, experimentation. This, if this was the first, or at least one of theirs, was quick and brutal, and not necessarily pre-meditation.'

'Jansen was their happy accident,' Eve said. 'So they think, What if we planned it out, what if we set it up and did it again, knowing how it's going to make us feel? It works for me.'

'Just like that.' Banner looked around with a kind of wonder.

'No, not just like that. Santiago, Carmichael, you're going to – Where the hell is this?'

'Closest would be Monroe, Arkansas, not far from the Oklahoma border.'

'You're going there.'

'Yee-haw,' Santiago said.

'Dig into it. At some point there was a second vehicle. Find it. Peabody, do a full run on this vic, talk to his people, get a good sense of him – and pull all salient reports and files. He could be the first, it works. They didn't really mean it, but it felt so damn good. Mel Little, look at the route. He could've been the next – more planned out. Not refined yet, but more planned. Maybe we'll find another between, but not more than one. Oklahoma?'

She signaled for Peabody to bring up the map. 'If this is the first, they probably came from Oklahoma. Maybe that's their origin – it's likely, it's logical. We're going to do an IRCCA search on stolen or highjacked vehicles moving back. Maybe they started out stealing cars, using a network to strip them, chop them, sell them. Working the back roads, the small towns. This area – they'd need to be familiar with the area for that. So Oklahoma's where we start. Grab some gear,' she told Santiago and Carmichael. 'I'll get you a shuttle, and a vehicle at destination.'

'Road trip.' Carmichael pushed up, pumped a fist. 'I drive first.'

'Damn it.'

Ignoring them, Eve pulled out her 'link, wandered a few paces off. Clock's ticking on Jayla Campbell, she reminded herself. She'd use whatever resources she had to save time.

She'd thought to tag Roarke's brilliantly efficient admin, Caro, but his face slid onto her screen.

'Lieutenant.'

'Hey. I need a favor.'

'Didn't I just receive payment for one of those?'

'Let's start fresh. I need a shuttle, fast.'

'Where are we going?'

'We're not. Santiago and Carmichael are going to Arkansas. We've got a lead. I need them there as fast as possible, with a vehicle – nothing fancy – waiting for them on the other end.'

'I can do that. I'll have Caro send you the appropriate data.'

'Thanks. I can squeeze the standard fees out of the budget.'

'I prefer other methods of payment. Have you found their first victim, as hoped?'

'It looks good for it.'

'Then I'll get this ordered. Caro will pass on the docs and numbers. And I'll take my fee later.'

'Ha ha.' She clicked off. 'Shuttle in the works,' she told the room, and kept going. 'I'm going to clear the paperwork. Carmichael, Santiago, get that gear and be ready to move. Peabody, look after Banner. Mira, I could use a quick meet before you leave for the day.'

So saying, she strode out.

Banner let out a long, long breath. 'Does everything always move so fast around here? Does *she* always move so fast?'

Peabody considered, smiled. 'Pretty much.'

11

Mira poked her head in Eve's office. 'I've got about ten minutes before I have to start a session.'

'Great.' Eve swiveled around from her desk. 'We've got two days – some under that now – but you'd agree that's the pattern.'

'It's unlikely they'd shorten the time. There could be unforeseen events that would shorten it, but the torture is the thrill, and the bond. The killing is necessary, the end goal and the final release, but prolonging it sweetens that release.'

'They need a place.'

'Yes. Private.'

'I'd lean toward a private home, or a building with low security. So far the abandons and vacants haven't panned out. Not a flop – not private enough. Not a hotel, and they just don't strike as the type that can afford to rent a nice roomy brownstone. Anything like that, they'd need to pass some sort of security check first, have the damage deposit. A basement unit, maybe, in a low- to mid-level building. Or ... they snagged somebody who already had what they wanted.'

'You think there might be another victim?'

'The timing's tight, but they have to have a place. So either they set it up on their way here, hit on one pretty much right after they got here. Or they scoped somebody, along the route, in New Jersey maybe, or locked one in after they arrived. If that's how they've worked it, they took some care disposing of the body, or kept the vic alive so we can't track them through the vic.

'My question. Are they smart enough for that? Smart enough to plan that out, to case a location, a building, and grab a vic who could give them access?'

'Yes, I think so. They've had months on this spree. If, as you believe, New York was the destination, they'd plan. They've gotten better at their hobby. It's not a mission,' Mira said when Eve lifted her eyebrows at the term. 'It's not their life's work. It's entertainment for them, and that bonding.'

'People get tired of hobbies, and give them up.'

'Yes, they do, and, yes, at some point they may. Right now, it's much too exciting, and they've had success. Factor in we believe this is a couple, romantically and sexually, as well as a killing unit. Couples have ... spats, disagreements. They fall out of love. If that happens ...'

'They could turn on each other,' Eve speculated. 'Or separate. We have to hope they stick. Separating or one doing the other? That changes the pattern, and it would change the MO.'

'As long as they're bonded, as long as they love, they'll not

198

only work as a unit, they'll protect each other. If/when you find them, they're still bonded, it's possible – probable – they'll die together rather than allow themselves to be taken – and separated.'

'Yeah, I've already considered the suicide-by-cop angle. Catching them comes first, not giving them the satisfaction of going out together in a fucking carved heart is next on the list.'

She pushed up, paced. 'What's your impression of Banner?'

'Committed to this, a little wide-eyed, but solid. I suspect he's taken a lot of rejection – the FBI, other law enforcement – through his investigation. He hasn't given up, and giving up, putting it aside, would've been easier.'

Eve nodded as she moved around the room. 'He doesn't strike me as someone who'd go rogue. If he did, I'd cut him loose. Okay, thanks.'

She dropped down in the chair again, looked over at her board. 'She's in pain, and she's scared. "Why is this happening to me?" That's what keeps going through her head. She wants to see her family and friends again. She wants it to stop, just stop. If we find out anything from Arkansas, if I can work the location – because it has to be downtown – and if she's tough enough to hold on, we've got a chance of getting her out of this.'

'If there's anything else I can do, you've only to let me know.'

Eve shifted around. 'When the remains get here from the

two vics we've got coming in, it would help if you either worked it with DeWinter and Morris or reviewed their reports. The shrink angle's an angle. I don't want to miss any of them.'

'I'll make sure of it.'

Alone, Eve set up another missing-persons run looking for any individual or individuals reported missing since the previous August with a residence or business in New York.

When her 'link signaled she noted Garnet DeWinter's readout, answered.

'Dallas.'

'You might have asked.'

'Asked what?'

'If I had the time to examine and report on two sets of exhumed remains. It may be you don't fully understand what we do here, or the fact I currently have on my table bones from two subjects recently discovered buried in concrete footings after the demolition of a building.'

'How old are they?'

'Approximately one hundred and twenty years.'

'Then they can probably fucking wait. Jayla Campbell,' she snapped and turned so the 'link showed the board and Campbell's photo. 'She has maybe thirty-six hours – with luck – before the two lunatic lovers who are currently torturing her end it by slicing her across the belly from hip to hip and letting her bleed out, probably while they have hot sex.'

The insult on DeWinter's striking, sharp-featured face faded. On a sigh, she ran a hand over her sleek-for-work hair. 'You might have given me some background.'

'I'm in a little bit of a hurry considering Campbell is only the last of at least twenty-one confirmed victims. And I have four more probables, including the remains heading your way.'

'If you'd given me some background, I might have been able to use some influence to get the remains here quicker.'

'How?'

DeWinter aimed a cool look out of sharp green eyes. 'I have connections, and ways to use them. Which I'll be doing right now. I'll need a full report on this investigation, the profiling, and the previous victims.'

'I sent it to you about fifteen minutes ago.'

'Oh.' This time DeWinter huffed out a breath. 'We really need to learn how to communicate better.'

'Right. I'll get on that.'

'If you do, I will.'

Eve struggled back an impatient retort, mainly because DeWinter had a point. 'Fine. Review what I sent you. Any questions, tag me. Morris will be working with you, and Mira's going to make the time. I need to know everything I can know about the two vics. The feds don't group them in with this. I do. Prove me right.'

'I prove you right, you buy me a drink.'

'Sure, whatever. I'm pressed here.'

'So am I now. I'll get back to you.'

Eve took a moment, pressed the heels of her hands to her eyes. Thought: Coffee.

She started to rise when Peabody's pink boots clomped toward her office.

'I've got data on Jansen – our potential first vic.' Her gaze flicked to the board where Eve had already added his photo.

'Based in Columbus, Ohio. He was an efficiency expert. Businesses hired him to come in, give them advice on, well, efficiency. Where to cut expenses, where to add stuff. Age forty-three, divorced, no kids. Nobody had reported him missing for about a week because he worked independently for the most part, and had just finished a job in Fort Smith. He was on his way to Bentonville, and had a few days off in there. He'd rented a pewter Priority sedan in Fort Smith. 2060 model, Shining Silver exterior. That's apparently in the wind. A lot of traffic bumps, no criminal. Made a good living, had a good rep, spent about thirty-six weeks a year on the road, and apparently liked it. More colleagues and clients than friends – my take – and boxed a little in college. Kept in shape.'

'Put up a fight, more than expected. You see a guy in a nice car, traveling alone. You want the nice car, and don't figure to have much trouble. He gives you trouble, ends up dead. More colleagues and clients than friends,' Eve mused. 'Less likely to stop for a couple or another man. So the woman still leads my theory there. I'm betting she's got some looks. He got out of the car. If she'd been hitching, or just flagged him down, no need to get out.'

'A breakdown, or she pretends she's hurt so he gets out to help her.'

'Breakdown leads. They had to get to where they were, and it's not easy walking distance to anywhere much that I can see. Did anyone know what he might have had on him, with him?'

'Luggage – an efficient packer, as you'd expect. Two good suits, some shirts, ties, underwear, toiletries, workout gear. Two pair dress shoes, two pair running shoes. A tablet, a PPC, two 'links, some cash – he'd withdrawn eight hundred from the autobank in Fort Smith the afternoon of his departure. His immediate supervisor said they all carry a decent amount of cash for tips. Good tips, apparently, lead to more efficient service. Business credit card and two personal. None have been used since he left Fort Smith. He had a good wrist unit. I've got the make and model, and started a search. Same for his electronics.'

'Get sizes.'

'Sorry?'

'On the clothes, the shoes. If they didn't sell them, and likely within a few days along the projected route, then they used them. If they used them, we'd have a body type, a shoe size.'

'Huh. Who'd have thought of that?'

'I thought of that. Get the sizes, see if one of those colleagues or clients can zero in on descriptions of the clothes
he'd have packed. If not, try his hotels. He'd have used laun-
dry service somewhere.'

'On it. Ah, Dallas?'

'What? I need to finish updating Whitney.'

'I got a civilian liaison to show Banner around – and told
him about The Eatery, such as it is.'

'Okay, great. Go away.'

'Dallas, he doesn't have anywhere to stay – in New York.'

'There are a zillion places to stay in New York.'

Peabody's puppy-dog eyes should've warned her, but Eve
was distracted.

'Yeah, he asked if I could recommend a hotel, maybe close
to Central. He's been going for about thirty hours straight
now, and, well, he's on his own nickel. I get the impression
deputies in Silby's Pond are more underpaid even than detectives in New York.'

'Christ, Peabody.' Realization and twangs of guilt hit at
once. 'I see where you're going, and you're going to want to
do a fast U.'

'Just hear me out first, okay?' Peabody waved her hands
in the air as if to ward off any boot aimed at her nose. 'If
you put him up, he'd be right there. Anything breaks anywhere on this, he'd be right there. And I was thinking,
McNab and I could bunk over – same reason,' she said
quickly. 'And we could keep him occupied so you wouldn't

have to, if necessary. Carmichael and Santiago are already on their way west. Something could break tonight.'

'Fuck me.' Eve resisted just dropping her head to the desk, maybe banging it there a few times, because, like DeWinter, Peabody had a point.

'Set it up. You deal with Summerset.' That torture would be spared her, Eve decided. 'I don't want to hear him griping about running a halfway house for cops.'

'I'll take care of it. Ah, we're going to have to go home, get some stuff. We could haul Banner with us, but . . .'

'Oh, for – I'll take him. When I'm damn good and ready. He can catch some sleep in the crib if he needs it. Go the hell away before you have me taking in half the damn department for the night.'

Eve put her head in her hands a moment. Coffee first, she decided. Then she'd contact Roarke – text him – that's the way to let him know she was bringing cops home – one of them a complete stranger. Update Whitney, review the run on missings, then—

Her 'link signaled, and, grinding her teeth, she answered DeWinter again.

'What the fuck?'

'And hello to you, too. Both remains will be exhumed within the hour. I should have them by eighteen hundred.'

All pissiness vanished. 'That's fast. Maybe I owe you a drink for that, too.'

'I'll take it. I've arranged to start the exam this evening

205

with Morris. Dr Mira will consult via holo, if necessary, and come into my house in the morning.'

'Okay. How about I just buy you a bottle?'

'Drinks,' DeWinter said, 'and conversation, Lieutenant. It's time. I'll keep you updated.'

'I'll do the same. It's appreciated. Hell, I've got another incoming. Later.'

She clicked off, took the next. 'Commander, I'm about to send you an update.'

'Before you do, Banner is fully cleared by his chief. This is not officially part of the federal investigation, however, I want every inch of all asses covered. Make that update in full detail, Lieutenant, and copy Tibble.'

Eve nodded. Asses covered completely with their own chief in the mix. 'Yes, sir. Briefly? We may have caught a break.' She ran through quickly what she'd write in more detail on Jansen.

'To expedite I requested the transpo from Roarke. The detectives are already en route.'

'Include the request for compensation in the report.'

'He won't take it, Commander.'

'Put it in. Roarke is free to donate said transportation, but through channels. I want all appropriate paperwork.'

'Yes, sir.'

She clicked off, figured she'd have to see to the bulk of said paperwork as, in Roarke's place, it would bug the shit out of her.

She thought, yet again: Coffee, text Roarke. This time she nearly made it to the AutoChef before footsteps headed her way.

'Sorry, LT.'

She might've snarled at Baxter, but he looked pale, heavy-eyed.

'What?'

'Wanted you to know we're back, can take some of the grunt work.'

'Okay, there's plenty of it. Sit.' She got two coffees. 'What did you catch?'

'Caught and closed, open and shut. Christ.' He took the coffee, stared at it. 'You know, you think it can't get to you anymore. You've seen it all, seen as bad as it gets. But you never have. Guy's supposed to pick his kids up for his week. Divorced deal. Fourteen-year-old girl, eight-year-old boy. Guy's been out of work for a while, got pushy with the ex a few times. Nothing major, mostly verbal shit. Yelling, argu-ing. She answers the door today while the kids are getting their stuff. And he smashes her, face-first, with a sledge-hammer. Then he goes for the kids. Just goes at them. You could see how they tried to get away, how the girl used her body to cover her brother.'

Baxter stared into his coffee, shook himself, drank it. 'He pulverized that little girl, Dallas. Like she was a thing, and not his own kid. The boy, they said he might make it. Legs are smashed, one of his arms, but his sister took the worst. When the man thought he was done with them, he went back and finished the wife.'

He took a slow drink of coffee. 'Neighbors heard some of it, called it in, came running. He just walked out, walked out into the street into traffic. Driver who hit him tried to stop – she had a baby in the car. They're okay. Just shaken up. The impact knocked him into another oncoming, and that one didn't have time to try to stop.'

'He's dead.'

'I wish he wasn't.' Baxter said it viciously. 'I wish to Christ we could've peeled him off the pavement and put him in a cage, run a loop of those kids in that cage for the rest of his motherfucking life. His own kids, Dallas. His daughter's brains splattered all over the wall, the floor. For what?'

'We're never going to know the answers, Baxter, and we're never going to have seen the worst. There's always worse than that waiting to happen. And if it doesn't get to us, if we don't feel it, then it's time to turn in our papers. Where's Trueheart?'

'I told him to go home, told him to take some personal. But I know he's going to hang around the hospital awhile longer. The boy – his grandparents are there, and he's got more family, so that's something. He's got the exam tomorrow, so I told him to try to put it away, for now, focus in. Maybe we stop the next one before he kills his kids. Get his shield, and maybe the next time, we get there before the brains are all over the wall.'

'You should go home.'

'Can't do it.' He lifted his gaze to hers. 'Give me a job, will you, Loo? Any damn thing.'

'I'm running another missing-person search,' she began, explained the parameters. 'Take it down to residences and businesses downtown. Run a parallel to missings over the last two weeks.'

'Got it. Thanks.'

He got to his feet, looked at her board. 'You know some of them are never going to get out of your head. We keep doing it, knowing the job's going to put more of them in there. You have to believe it matters.'

'You can believe it because it does. These two? Time's running out on them. Let's find the fuckers.'

'I'm on it.'

When he left, Eve pulled up the call, the family, the IDs of the wife, the kids in Baxter's head. She'd have them in her head now, but it had to matter.

Considering the stream of interruptions, she managed to get the report, in painful detail, hammered out and sent to Whitney. Then, after a quick debate, decided she'd take the rest home, where interruptions would be minimized. Then realized she'd already gone past her end of tour.

She pulled what she had from her missings search, grabbed the rest of what she needed, snagged her coat.

And remembered she had to take Banner with her.

She found her bull pen still full of cops.

'Pack it in,' she ordered, then moved over to Trueheart.

'How's the kid?'

'He's out of surgery. He's going to need at least two more trips in, the doctor said, and they're keeping him in an induced coma. But they said he's going to pull through, that odds are in his favor now. And his family—'

He broke off, took a long breath. 'I mean, his grandparents and some others are with him. The doctor said, you know, young and healthy, it adds weight on his side.'

'Okay. Now put it away for tonight. Go home, study up. Don't even think about it,' she said, anticipating him. 'You don't put off your exam, or your life, for something you can't change. He's in good hands, and you did the job.'

'That's what Baxter said.'

'Then listen.' She looked around at Baxter. 'Send me what you have, and go have a beer with Trueheart, then get him home. Make sure he doesn't embarrass us tomorrow.'

'Will do. Dallas, I'd like to keep on this. While the kid's taking the exam, I can keep on this tomorrow.'

'I'll loop you in. Peabody, get what you need and make it snappy. We've got work. Where's Banner?'

He leaned back out of a cube. 'I was working on some notes and contacts. Detective Peabody said I could use this space.'

'Bring what you have. We're moving.'

She swung on her coat as she strode out, leaving him to catch up with her.

'I sure appreciate you giving me a bunk, Lieutenant. I don't want to put you out.'

'We've got plenty of bunks, and you'll pay for it, starting with a stop on the way. I'm picking a missing at random, checking out a location. They're somewhere, maybe we'll hit.'

'Can't know till you know. Ms Denning took me on the fifty-dollar tour,' he added as they squeezed into an elevator. 'The place just goes on and on. I went through your EDD, and I gotta say, I've never seen anything like it.'

'I say that every time I go in there.'

His face broke into a grin. 'Sure is colorful. The captain up there?'

'Feeney.'

'Captain Feeney, he reminds me of my uncle Bill. Smart as a Sunday suit and easy to be around as a good hound dog. He sure sets store by you, Lieutenant.'

'He trained me. Best cop I know, and I know some good cops.'

'He said how if you're on the trail of these two, you won't stop till you bag them.'

'Are you asking a question or making a statement, Banner?'

'Maybe both.'

With breathless relief, she pushed off on her level of the garage. 'Dorian Kuper,' she said. 'He wasn't the first, but he was my first on this. Played the cello, has a mother who'll never get over this. Turned out to be a friend of a friend.'

'I saw him on your board.'

'That's right. And so will I, every day until this is done. This is my ride.'

She saw surprise before he covered it, then hit the codes to unlock the doors. Surprise flickered again when he folded himself in and the seat adjusted for him.

'Sure is comfortable.'

'Gets me where I'm going.' She pulled out, did the arcing turn to the exit. Paused briefly, studying the traffic, the road conditions. 'Goddamn winter,' she muttered, and zipped out fast enough to have Banner subtly adjusting his safety harness.

'She moves, too.'

'Why do men think about cars as female?'

'It's love, I suppose. You'll excuse me for gawking,' he added as he did just that, craning his neck to get a better angle on the ad blimp currently hawking a blizzard sale as it crept along a slate-gray sky. 'I didn't see much on the way in. Preoccupied,' he explained, clearing his throat softly as Eve nosed between a Rapid Cab and a creeping Mini. 'Didn't know what to expect when I got to Cop Central.'

She cut around a corner, just beating the WALK signals and the pedestrians pushing to flood through.

'I sure didn't expect to be riding through the city with a big-city badge on the way to check out a lead.'

'I don't know if it reaches "lead" at this point. Missing's Wayne Potter, age sixty-three, twice divorced, three offspring with three more between them. Worked as a furniture mover. Last seen August eighteen.'

She cut the next corner, slapped vertical and skimmed over a slow-moving panel van.

'He'd rented a camper,' she went on, 'was allegedly going on a two-week vacation. He and the camper were last seen in the vicinity of Louisville, Kentucky. He never came back, and both he and the camper poofed.'

'Sounds like it could fit in pretty smooth.'

'It could. Or Potter, who apparently despised and was despised by both his ex-wives, had little to no relationship with his remaining family – including a brother to whom he owed about seven thousand dollars – decided to just keep going, and is currently camped somewhere thumbing his nose at New York and everyone in it.'

She considered her options, thought fuck it, and double-parked.

'Basement unit, this building.' She flipped up her On Duty light as blasting horns serenaded.

Ignoring them, Eve eased out, skirted the hood. 'You carrying, Banner?'

'My service weapon. I had to check it when I came into Central, but Detective Peabody arranged for me to get it back.'

'Be ready,' she advised as she approached the building. 'But don't get twitchy.'

'I've only had to pull it four times since I've been on the job, and never once had to fire it.'

It was hard for Eve to imagine, but she nodded. 'That's a good record to hold on to.'

She flipped back her coat, rested one hand on her weapon, took out her badge with the other.

Minimal security on the door, she noted, bars on the windows.

'Hit the buzzer.'

It didn't take long, and only an instant more for Eve to drop her weapon hand, adjust her coat back over it.

She looked down into the round freckled face of a boy she judged at around ten.

'You're not Sarri,' he accused.

'I'm not. Got a parent at home?'

'MOM!'

The shout had another kid – a girl, Eve deduced, as it wore a bright pink dress with brighter blue tights. And eyed her as suspiciously as the boy.

'You can't come in 'cause you're a stranger.' She shouted, a higher decibel than her brother, for her mother.

'I'm coming, I'm coming. For God's sake, let me – Nathan Michael Fitzsimmons, what have I told you about opening the door?'

'It's supposed to be Sarri.'

'It's not.' The woman, obviously harried, dark hair clipped messily up, fuzzy slippers covering her feet, scooped both kids behind her.

'NYPSD.' Eve held her badge up again. 'I'm sorry to disturb you.'

'What's the matter? Is Sarri—'

'No problem,' Eve said quickly. 'We're looking into a missing-persons matter. Do you know a Wayne Potter?'

'No, I'm sorry, I— Oh, wait. Sorry, step in for a second. It's freezing out there, and I'm letting the heat out.'

She shut the door behind them. 'I think that's the person who used to live here. One of the neighbors upstairs mentioned the name. We moved in last October. Mrs Harbor – upstairs – she told me he'd left one day and never came back. Left his things, his family. I was a little nervous for a while once she told me, wondering if he'd come back and try to get in. But he hasn't.'

The buzzer sounded again, and both kids shouted: Sarri!

'Thanks for your time.'

Eve edged back, let the woman open the door.

Sarri, bundled in a coat, hat, scarf, boots, gloves, all hitting every color of the spectrum was immediately covered in kids.

'That's my sister in there,' the woman said with a laugh. 'The world's favorite aunt. Sorry I couldn't help.'

Eve went back to the car through the chorus of angry horns and cursing. 'One more,' she said. 'It's on the way.'

She had better luck with parking at the skinny townhouse, with a second-level slot, but no more inside.

Another woman, this one a weeper, who reported her longtime roomer/lover had vanished one evening when going out for a pack of gum. A small shrine stood under the front window – photographs, flowers, candles, an empty bottle of wine (the last, it seemed, they'd shared) a single red sock and a pair of black gloves.

It didn't take long for Eve to work out a theory – not the alien abduction the woman currently held firm – and slightly longer to extricate herself and Banner.

'That's enough for now. Jesus.' Eve shook her head as she pulled back into traffic. 'Aliens, for God's sake.'

'I've got a cousin back home who claims he's been abducted four times.'

'I don't think Curtis Hemming's been anal probed by scientists of the planet Grum. He walked out for gum and kept walking because he wanted to get away from the lunatic who'd decided he was her soul mate. Sex is one thing, obsession's another. In any case, the unsubs aren't using either of those locations, and it's improbable they ever crossed paths with Potter or Hemming.'

'We'll refine the search, see if we can cut out some of the walk-aways.'

She shoved through a knot of traffic, swerved around a maxibus, made her way through a snaking line of cabs.

'You sure can drive, Lieutenant. You sure can drive.'

Eve glanced over. 'That's not a comment I get often,' she decided and bulled her way uptown.

12

When Eve drove through the gates Banner gave a low, through-the-teeth whistle and said, 'Holy hell.'

She glanced over, saw he'd leaned forward, eyes fixed ahead.

She'd gotten used to the mass and magnificence, she admitted, but she understood absolutely the staggering impression the house made, its windows lit against the dark sky, its silhouette both powerful and fanciful with snow – white and blue in the lights – spread at its feet.

'I saw the vid,' he told her, 'but it sure smacks you upside the head live and in person. Sort of like a castle, isn't it, right inside the city.'

'He's Irish,' Eve said, as if that explained it all.

'Biggest house I've ever seen.'

'Me too.' Mildly embarrassed, she pulled up, parked. 'Summerset – that's Roarke's ... man of everything,' she decided, 'will have your room ready. You can get settled in, and we'll take this in my home office.'

'Good enough. I want to say again, I appreciate this.'

'Rooms we've got.'

'I can sure see that.' He got out, hauled up his gear. 'Biggest house I've ever seen,' he called out against the wind, 'in the coldest place I've ever been to. It's a by-God experience.'

She led the way inside, saw – as expected – Summerset in the foyer with the cat squatting beside him. They both gave Banner the eye.

'This is Deputy Banner.'

'Yes, Detective Peabody informed me. Welcome to New York, Deputy.'

'Thank you, and thanks for the room. Will Banner,' he added, stepping forward, extending a hand.

Summerset inclined his head, shook hands while the cat sniffed suspiciously at Banner's boots.

'You'd be – what is it – Lancelot?'

'Galahad,' Eve corrected as Banner crouched, ran a hand smoothly over the cat, head to tail.

'Galahad – knew it was one of those knights. Like I said, I saw the vid. Lucky cat – two eye colors. That's a lucky cat.'

Galahad apparently agreed as he arched under Banner's hand, then rubbed along his leg.

'Deputy Banner will be in the Park Room.' At Eve's blank look, Summerset smirked. 'I'll show you up.' He gestured toward the elevator. 'May I help you with your bag?'

'I got it, thanks. Elevator, right in the house. Another first for me.'

'I'll be in my office once you've settled,' Eve told him, a little irked that the cat padded along at Banner's heels.

Unabashedly gawking again, Banner grinned back at Eve as the elevator doors closed him in with Summerset and the cat.

It all felt off, she decided. Not one snarly remark from Summerset – one smirk hardly counted – the cat going off without even giving her a glance.

It occurred to her that she wasn't just used to their usual evening ritual, she liked it. So, sulking a little, she shrugged out of her coat, very deliberately hung it on the newel post before jogging upstairs.

She headed to the bedroom first. It would take Banner some time to unpack, get his bearings, so she pulled off her jacket, considered her weapon harness, then decided to leave it on.

She was debating whether to change her boots for skids when her 'link signaled.

Santiago.

'Dallas. What have you got?'

'Carmichael's got culture shock, but she's recovering. Met up with the locals, talked to the woman and kid who stumbled on the body. We'll be meeting with the coroner in a bit. Nothing much to add, as yet, but that stretch of road, LT, where they found the body, there sure isn't much traffic along there. We were there a good half hour and didn't see one vehicle pass by. It's a damn good spot for a killing.'

'Somebody got lucky, knew the spot or knew how back roads in backwaters work.'

'One of those. The other is, Carmichael and I both agree there had to be a second vehicle. It's the middle of nowhere. Coroner report says tire iron, a good-sized one. Who hitches and hikes along carrying a big-ass tire iron?'

'Possible breakdown, vic is changing a tire, gets jumped. But then they'd have to get the tire iron from him. Second vehicle makes more sense.'

'We're backtracking the vic's movements, and we'll head on, doubling the check the locals did last summer on sitings of the rental. Nobody took tire impressions back then at the scene, or checked for blood on the road.'

'Fucking A.'

'Yeah, we said. We'll go over it tomorrow, in daylight, but it's been months.'

While Eve talked to Santiago, Roarke came in the front door. He was mildly irked himself as his last meeting had run over, and weather in Halifax was delaying a project.

He removed his coat, wondered idly where Summerset might be. He tossed his coat over Eve's, started upstairs. He went to his office first, laid down his briefcase. He had work, but for later. At the moment he wanted his wife, a quiet glass of wine. He'd kept current with the media reports, and as there'd been nothing new on her investigation, imagined they'd be hip-deep in it that evening.

After he'd changed, he thought, he'd have that wine with Eve. That would clear his head enough of business.

He heard movement in Eve's office, stepped in.

He saw a tall, leanly built man with a messy mop of corn-silk hair rocking back on the worn-down heels of scarred boots, thumbs comfortably in the pockets of faded jeans. And a stunner on his belt.

Roarke slid his own hand into his pocket, and onto the mini stunner he carried in it.

'Can I help you?' he said very coolly.

The man turned, his hand going to the butt of his own weapon. Quiet blue eyes met wild blue – and Roarke recognized cop. But kept his hand where it was.

'Deputy Banner. Will Banner. I'm waiting for the lieutenant.'

As am I, Roarke thought. 'And why is that?'

'This.' He gestured to the board with his left hand. 'You're Roarke?'

'I am.'

'Sorry to just be ... Summerset showed me in. I got in from Arkansas this morning. I sure do appreciate your hospitality.'

Banner's hand dropped from his weapon, then outstretched as he crossed to Roarke.

Roarke accepted the hand, but stayed on alert. 'You're involved in the lieutenant's investigation?'

'It's looking like it. I know you sometimes consult on

cases, but I don't know how much you're into this one. I'd be more comfortable, if you don't mind, if Lieutenant Dallas filled you in.'

'So would I.'

Roarke noted the cat slide off the sleep chair, wander over, wind through Banner's legs, then come over to do the same through his own. And back again.

'That's a good cat. I got a dog back home – he's with my folks while I'm gone. But this one here makes me think I ought to get me a cat, too. He's good company. Ah … I'm in the Park Room? It sure is nice, and I can see clear over to Central Park.'

'Would this be your first time in New York?'

'That's right. It makes my head spin a little. Um, we've got Detectives Peabody and McNab coming.'

'Do we?' Roarke said, brutally pleasant. 'If you'd wait here, I'll go find the lieutenant.'

'I'll be right here.' Banner turned back to the board. 'Right here.'

Roarke made his way to the bedroom. He wanted out of the bloody suit, and wanted a bloody explanation as to why he'd found a cop from Arkansas in his house – and apparently sleeping in one of the guest rooms.

Eve was still on the 'link when he walked in, and held up a finger to hold him off.

She might have poured gas on a fire.

'I'll get you what we get as we get it, and you do the

same. Everything, Santiago, as it comes. Time's clicking down.'

'Yes, sir.'

She ended the transmission, circled her neck. 'I've spent more time on the damn 'link today than . . . ' The frigid blast from his eyes got through. 'What?'

'I've just come across a Deputy Banner, apparently from Arkansas, apparently involved in your investigation, and apparently staying in our home.'

'Yeah, Banner, I told you. Is he already in the office?'

'He is, and you bloody well didn't tell me a bloody thing about it.'

'I did. I texted you before . . . ' Coffee, she remembered, text Roarke – and she'd been interrupted.

'I was about to,' she corrected. 'I got interrupted.' She scowled at the 'link still in her hand, shoved it in her pocket. 'I've had a million interruptions today. I meant to text you, I started to.'

'A man I've never seen before – armed, by the way – is wandering freely around the house.'

'He's a cop.'

'And what possible difference does that make?'

'Well, it's not like he's going to steal the silver, or whatever. I ran him. The commander talked to his chief. He's solid.'

'Again, what possible difference does that make?'

She threw out her hands, baffled. 'All.'

He yanked off his tie. 'Bollocks, Eve. I believe I have a

223

right to be consulted, or at the very least informed, before we're housing a complete stranger.'

'I was going to! You have people in here when you want them.'

His eyes, hot now, fixed on hers as he shrugged out of his suit coat. 'And who have I had wandering free – a stranger to you with a stunner on his belt – without your knowledge?'

'Okay, okay, you want to be pissed, be pissed. I got interrupted, and I forgot. I've been a little preoccupied with murder.'

'I won't have murder as your excuse for every shagging thing, as preoccupation with it is a matter of course. And one I've accepted fully.'

She started to snap back, then imagined it from his side. She didn't want to imagine it from his side, but it came over her too clearly. Guilty now, and defensive, she paced away.

'Two kids and their mother got smashed to pulp with a sledgehammer – by the father.'

'Ah, Christ Jesus, what a world you live in.' Roarke scrubbed his hands over his face.

'Baxter and Trueheart caught it, and Baxter came into my office, shaken up, when I was about to text you on Banner. He doesn't get shaken up easy. I'm his LT, Roarke, I had to put things aside and listen to him.'

'You did, of course.'

'Then things just kept rolling, and I forgot. So I'm sorry. Be pissed.'

'I am.' He changed his shirt for a sweater, cooling off as he did. 'You're fond of your Marriage Rules, so add this to them. If and when you've the inclination to host a complete stranger to me, you don't forget to let me know. As the next time, I might stun first, ask questions later. I'm firm on that one.'

'I suck at it, you know I do. I don't get why you keep getting pissed that I suck at it.'

'You don't, so when you do something that sucks, as you say, it's very annoying.' He continued to change while she said nothing. 'Both children?'

'It looks like the boy's going to make it. His older sister shielded him as best she could with her own body.'

'And Baxter?'

'He'll get through it. It's what we do.'

'It is, yes. It's what you do.' And for better or worse, what he often did now as well. 'And this Banner?'

'He's solid, like I said. He came here on his own nickel, hopped a shuttle when he got the alert about my searches. Then drove the rest of the way when weather dumped him in Cleveland. He's been pursuing this, mostly on his own time, since last summer because the feds and the locals don't think his vic was in the stream. I do. Anything we can get may help us find Jayla Campbell before it's too late.'

'Then we'd best get to work on it.'

'I'm sorry. I am.' Though she felt annoyance at every damn thing tangling up with the sorry. 'And I'm going to be sorrier because I forgot to tell you Peabody and McNab are coming, too.'

'Banner told me.'

'Shit.'

He crossed to her, set his hands on her shoulders. She noted, with relief (and a little more guilt) the temper had faded from his eyes. 'It's our home, and those you want are welcome here. But—'

'Not strangers with stunners.'

'Unless you give me prior notice.'

'Got it.'

'All right, then. We've left our guest cop alone in your office long enough.'

'I thought he'd take longer to settle in. He's been going since yesterday.'

'Then I imagine he could use a beer and a meal.'

'Thanks.' She cupped his face, kissed him. Gave him another as she'd decided, positions reversed, she'd probably have slapped harder than he had. 'Seriously.'

'You're welcome.' He kissed her back. 'Seriously.'

They started out together.

'Perhaps you'd fill me in,' Roarke suggested, 'as I'm apparently well behind.'

'It's a lot.'

Eve gave him a quick roundup as they moved to her office.

There Banner sat in the sleep chair, the cat comfortably on his lap. He looked half asleep, roused himself when they came in.

'Sorry. Zoning out some.'

'The lieutenant tells me you've been at this since yesterday. I expect you could use a beer.'

The wary look on his face lifted with an easy grin. 'I sure wouldn't turn one down.'

'Eve?'

'Yeah, beer's great. I'll get it. And food, I guess. Pizza work?'

Banner flashed that grin a second time. 'When doesn't it?'

'Cops. The same everywhere. Arkansas, is it?' Roarke asked Banner while Eve went into the kitchen.

'Silby's Pond. Seems a long ways from here.'

'In the Ozarks, isn't it? Lovely country there.'

'You've been?'

'Around and about. And how did you come to being with the police?'

'Circular route, I'd guess. I always figured to work the family farm, did some deputy work summers when there was time for it – and a need with tourists and such. But, well, the farm's been in the family five generations, and you've got an obligation there. But my daddy set me down one night a few years back, and he said he could see my heart wasn't in it, and you had to do what your heart was in. That was police work for me.'

'Your father sounds like a wise man. Thanks, darling,' he said as Eve brought out the beer.

'He is, and a good farmer. So's my sister and her man, so the farm's in good hands. I help out when there's time, but I wanted to be a cop. Good beer. We brew our own – family recipe. I'm going to send you some after I get home.'

'Clomp and prance,' Eve said and got a puzzled look from Banner. 'Peabody and McNab.'

'I'll see to the pizza,' Roarke said as they came in.

'Did I hear pizza?' McNab bounced in, but was smart enough to release Peabody's hand at Eve's narrowed stare.

'And beer. You'd rather a glass of wine, Peabody.'

'If it's okay.'

'One,' Eve decreed. 'Then it's coffee and it's work. Santiago checked in.'

While Roarke set up the meal, Eve filled in the others.

'What kind of bumfuck bozos don't check for blood at a crime scene?' McNab glanced over at Banner. 'Sorry.'

'It's hard to take offense. They weren't my bumfuck bozos, but close enough.'

As the others did, he helped himself to a slice. Bit in. Sat, just sat.

'This is *pizza*. Is it like the coffee?' he asked Eve.

'It's New York. Morris and DeWinter should already have the first remains. She expedited, and they were going to start tonight.'

'That's quick work.'

'Time's the issue. When they verify these two victims are part of our stream, we can pull in more resources. It's Santiago and Carmichael we need. We verify the first victim, we're closer to ID'ing the killers. The first is going to be closer to home, closer to where they knew – and were known. The first is key.'

She looked toward the board. 'But Campbell may not have time for that.' As she rose, Banner started to get to his feet. 'Sit. Eat. I want to update the board. It helps me think.'

She got to work. 'Why don't you brief the others on the two stops we made?' she said to Banner.

'The lieutenant's running searches on missings who have homes or businesses in the city here, figuring maybe they got somebody we haven't found, and are using their place for their killing room.'

'Have to be private,' Roarke speculated. 'Soundproofed. Even gagged, such matters made noise. And low security or they'd show on disc when bringing in a victim.'

'We stopped at two, eliminated them. Regular civilians living there.'

'Others to eliminate,' Eve said. 'We'll spread out tomorrow, bring in some uniforms. They've got a place, one they're comfortable in. One they could take Kuper to. One where they're working on Campbell right now.'

'Downtown,' Roarke added.

'Probability's high. Peabody, put the sector on screen.'

*

While they ate, while they worked, Jayla Campbell struggled to rise above the pain. Going under it was a kind of escape, but they always brought her back, gave more.

She'd stopped trying to understand it. It simply was.

How long she couldn't tell, not any longer. Hours, days, weeks. There was only pain and fear, and the certainty there would be more.

They'd had sex on the floor, against the wall, sometimes blessedly out of sight. Though she could hear them grunting or wailing, laughing.

They liked when she tried to scream, when she cried and begged. So she tried not to, but sometimes she couldn't stop. Just couldn't stop.

They looked so ordinary. Monsters shouldn't look so ordinary, so much like ordinary people. The woman was pretty, in a hard, slutty sort of way, and the man – good-looking, sort of gangly and . . . stupid, she thought now.

He went along with anything the woman said.

Cut here, she'd say – and he would.

They were eating now, and the smell of the Chinese take-away made her want to gag. She hadn't eaten since the party. Sometimes they dribbled water in her mouth, but they never gave her food. Sometimes the water was laced with salt, and they laughed and laughed when she choked.

Monsters shouldn't look like ordinary people.

They'd taken her clothes, but she'd gotten over the worst of that. Neither of them touched her in a sexual way – as if she cared about that now. They saved the sex for each other.

They were naked, too, as they ate, and sometimes they smeared sauce on each other and licked it off.

That, too, made her want to gag. At least she could close her eyes or turn her head. When they were involved in each other, she barely existed for them.

She wished she would stop existing for them.

They talked eagerly, avidly.

He said they were star-crossed lovers. The woman – Ella-Loo – loved when he quoted Shakespeare or talked about how they were lovers like Bonnie and Clyde.

She didn't know who Bonnie and Clyde were, but the woman did; and she'd laugh and strike poses that made the man – Darryl – moan or lick his lips.

She listened to them when she could, to every word. If she lived – and she didn't believe she would, but *if* – she would remember everything. She would tell the police everything. And she would hope with every cell in her pain-filled body, the police killed them in the bloodiest, most brutal, most horrible way possible.

She wanted to kill them with her own hands.

She wanted her mother. She wanted Kari. Sometimes when she floated away, she wanted Luke, and his shy smile.

She wanted anything and anyone who wasn't this. Anything that wasn't strapped to a table under bright lights with something round and hard between her teeth, something where she couldn't feel her own blood oozing out of her body, or the jagged pain of broken bones rubbing viciously together if she moved even an inch to try to find comfort.

There was no comfort.

'It's something different, and daring,' the woman was saying. 'We don't want to get bored, right, honey?'

'Are you bored, Ella-Loo?'

'Not with you, baby. Never! You're my hero. But just think how exciting. If we did *two*, at one time. If we kept them going longer. Oh, it makes me wet just thinking of it.'

'I like you wet.'

He stuck his hand between the woman's legs. Jayla closed her eyes.

'I'd be wetter, hotter with two. You can pick this time. Oh, yes! Get down there, baby, and get to work.'

She yelped, she laughed, she groaned. 'Fuck me hard, baby, hard! Then let's go get another one. Let's get a man. Maybe we can make them fuck each other. Let's make him rape her while we watch. Oh, oh, *Darryl*!'

'Anything you want. Anything. I love you, Ella-Loo.'

'Make me scream, Darryl. Make me scream. Then let's go get another.'

And she smiled, feral and fierce, turning her head to look at Jayla as Darryl drove and drove and drove into her until sweat dripped off his face.

She smiled her monster smile as she came.

*

In the office, Roarke listened as the room of cops worked theories, ran searches. He listened while Eve spoke to Morris on the 'link, while she consulted with Mira.

His mind worked back to the first – the one they believed was the first.

A businessman killed on the side of the road. No vehicles left behind. Battered – fought back – smashed skull.

Nothing like the others, he thought. No torture, no sense of time taken. But he trusted his wife's instincts.

The first, perhaps an accident, or a matter of impulse. The spark, possible, for all that came after.

'Someone towed it off.'

Distracted, a little annoyed, Eve glanced around. 'What?'

'You've two options on your first – on this Jansen. They had a second vehicle, and drove off separately, or they left a vehicle behind.'

'No vehicle was recovered or reported on scene.'

'And you've never heard of auto theft I'm supposing. Driving off in two, it's not impossible, of course, but then they'd have to dispose of one, and they'd not be together after the kill – when the blood would be high.'

'Wait.' She held up her hand to ward off comments, narrowed her eyes. 'When the blood would be high,' she repeated. 'If this is the first, if this started the ball rolling for them, it would be that high after the kill. Driving off separately? Cooldown period. So, less likely. But no vehicle reported or recovered.'

'Darling Eve,' he said, and had Banner glancing at her sideways, 'it's a very remote and rural area, yes?'

'So?'

'And I'll wager more than a pint there'd be a towing service or two, and beyond that – a farming sort of area? Those with tow bars handy enough. And it's: Look there, mate, at that car/truck/van on the side of the road. Out you get to have a look. It may be it's broken down—'

'Which would be a reason to boost another car, okay.'

'Some mechanical problem, that may be. Or it's been previously boosted, and time to switch out. But either way, an enterprising soul might tow it off, strip it down or alter the van and resell it. Surely even in that area, they'd have a chop shop handy enough, or someone who'd pay to have another vehicle on their land.'

When she frowned, he smiled.

'Speaking hypothetically, of course, one who once made a bit of a living boosting vehicles may have cruised along such back roads and byways for just such an opportunity.'

'Slapping a tow bar on it, hauling it off to another location.'

'And making a tidy little profit through little effort,' Roarke concluded. 'You might have your people down there put the arm on towing companies, farmers, mechanics and such.'

He looked over at Banner. 'Would you have such events in Arkansas, Will?'

'Could be. There was a guy the next county over who ran a chop shop. They picked cars off the interstate mostly, but hit the back roads, too. I never thought of it. People know people, and you hear tell.'

Eve already had her 'link out. 'Carmichael.'

'About to contact you, LT. Having some Arkansas barbecue, and have to echo Santiago. Yee-haw. The coroner—'

'Wait on that. I want you to push this angle, and now. Towing company, mechanics, garages, maybe little farms or whatever the fuck. Ability to tow away a vehicle. Let's theorize,' she began.

When she'd finished, clicked off, she looked over at Roarke. 'It's a good angle. The locals should have been all over it. You're handy.'

'I do my best.'

'Maybe it happened that way. I like the logic of it. Maybe they boosted whatever they dumped – or just dumped. Either way it could take us back to the prior step, the earlier location. It may give us names.'

She looked at the board, at Jayla. 'Coffee,' she said.

'I'm all about that,' Banner agreed. 'Dallas, I may know somebody who knows somebody around there. I'm a little pissed I didn't think of it before.'

'Spend any time boosting cars, Banner?'

'I didn't, but I can't claim not to know some who did. I may be able to help your people down there.'

'Then get on it. Peabody?'

'Sir.'

'Coffee. Lots. Now.'

While they worked the new angle, Ella-Loo, in a micro skirt taken off an LC they'd killed and whose name she'd forgotten, struggled with a bulky armchair.

She was freezing in the skirt, in fishnets, and a short, fake leather jacket – taken off yet another victim – but inside she was furnace hot.

The guy came bustling along, 'link in hand, hood of his parka thrown up. 'Yeah, yeah, I'm on my way. Jeez, it's like the South Pole out here tonight. I'm nearly there. Fire it up!'

'Hey, cutie?'

She called out, shook back her hair, saw him turn his head, give her the eye.

'Back to you,' he said into the 'link and stuffed it in his pocket. 'What's shaking, baby?'

'Could you just give me a hand, for one little minute? I can't lift this silly thing in here, and I need to get it in before my completely *ex*-boyfriend comes back.'

'Sure, no prob. Bad breakup?'

'So bad. He hit me!'

'Ah, come on.' The guy hunkered down to lift the chair. 'You're better off. I can get this if you take that side and—'

Darryl leaped in, weighted sap – Ella-Loo's idea – whacking down on the back of his head.

236

He made a sound like a balloon letting the air out, and crumpled.

'Quick, baby, quick, before somebody comes!'

It took a couple of hard hefts to get him and the old, reliable armchair in the back of the van. Ella-Loo scrambled in after, happily giving the groaning man another good whack before yanking the duct tape around his wrists.

'Let's go, baby! We got him good. I can't wait! I'm already wet. I'm already hot.'

'Save it for me,' Darryl called, zipping out to drive the short two blocks back home.

13

Jayla knew struggling only caused more pain, but she went into a frenzy of it when she heard them leave. She screamed against the gag until her throat felt burned and bloody, twisted her body, strained up with her arms with everything she had left in her.

It wasn't enough.

Fresh wounds opened on her wrists, her ankles so the thick tape binding them rubbed raw and wet. Her fight cracked the NuSkin they'd slapped on some of her wounds, so they seeped again. She tasted her own tears and hysteria until, exhausted, she went still.

Remember, she ordered herself. Remember everything in case, just in case she lived through this.

They had her strapped on some sort of board, tied and taped down. Rope around her waist, her belly. Sometimes they choked her with another until she passed out.

Plastic – she thought – under the makeshift table. She could hear it swish and crinkle under their feet when they hurt her.

A window. She could just see a window, barred, and a big brown couch where they sometimes had sex. And a screen – they watched porn and game shows on it.

An apartment. Maybe street-level, she thought because she could hear traffic when they went out or came in through the door.

A white ceiling – dingy white, be specific, Jayla – dingy white ceiling with those round lights inside it.

They never turned the lights off.

They brought in takeaway food – never deliveries, at least not when she'd been conscious. A lot of beer and jug wine. And once, at least once, she'd smelled Zoner.

She could describe them perfectly.

All she had to do was get away, and she could describe them both perfectly right down to the matching tattoos.

Little hearts with *D* and *E* inside, etched in blue and red over their own hearts.

People would be looking for her, she could comfort herself with that. She had people who cared about her, and would be looking for her.

But how would they find her?

Why hadn't she called a cab? Why hadn't she used her *head* and called a cab when she'd walked out of that stupid party? Why had she gone in the first place? Why hadn't she stayed home and watched vids with Kari?

She began to weep again, struggled again. And slid into shivering sleep.

The noise woke her. For a moment she was back in her college dorm with Kari, trying to sleep while a party went on in the next room. She tried to roll over – and the grinding pain brought her back.

They had music on – shit-kicking country music with some woman yodeling about how she was gonna hunt down her man. They sang along, top of their lungs, while they set up some sort of folding table.

The woman danced around it, rubbed her ass into the man's crotch, danced away again on a giggle.

Jayla could see the plastic on the floor now.

And the body sprawled facedown on it.

Her first reaction was a kind of crazed jubilation. She wouldn't be alone. They'd have someone else, might forget to hurt her, even for a little while.

Shame avalanched over the ugly joy, reminded her whatever they did to her, she was still human. She could still feel shame. And pity.

Together they rolled the body over, began to undress the man – no, she saw and the pity heightened. A boy. Younger than she was. Twenty, maybe twenty, and pale as glass.

He stirred a little, moaning. Darryl picked up the sap – they'd cracked at least one of her ribs with that weighted leather bag – and slapped the boy on the side of the head with it. Like you might slap a fly – absently, with a mild annoyance.

'Don't want him waking up as yet,' Darryl said. 'Need to get him situated first.'

'He's about the whitest thing I've seen outside of that snow on the ground outside.' Ella-Loo snickered as she dragged off the boy's pants.

She dumped out the contents of the pockets while Darryl finished getting him stripped down. And opened the wallet.

'Got less than twenty on him. Shit, and no wrist unit or nothing. Name's Reed Aaron Mulligan.'

Jayla repeated the name over and over in her head. She'd remember Reed Aaron Mulligan. About twenty, on the skinny side, milk-white skin and some freckles, reddish-blond hair with a sorry-looking goatee on his soft boy's face.

'Key swipe, few loose credits, nice little pocketknife. One of those – what-do-you-call-thems?'

Darryl glanced over. 'Multi-tool. Lemme see.' He took it from her, examined it. 'It is a nice one,' he said and slipped it into his own pocket.

'Boots're pretty new, and the coat, too.'

Christmas presents, Jayla imagined. From his parents. His parents would be looking for him soon.

'Too small for you,' Ella-Loo said to Darryl, and standing, tried on the coat. 'It's warm.'

'Not pretty enough for you, baby.'

'I bet we can get something for it, and the boots.' She tossed them, and his pants toward the couch, then studied Reed Aaron Mulligan with her hands on her hips.

'Pecker's nothing to write home about, but we get some

241

Erotica in him, get the wood going on him, he'll do all right.'

She turned to Jayla then, smiled that hot, feral smile. 'He's going to rape the shit out of you.'

Jayla wanted to close her eyes, just close them and go away again, but she made herself meet those hard eyes. Made herself stare back into them until Ella-Loo picked up the sap, slapped her once, twice in the crotch.

The pain burst in her center, radiated everywhere.

'There's a taste for you.' Angling her head, as if considering, she slapped each of Jayla's breasts in turn.

As Jayla's body arched and fell, Ella-Loo watched the bruises bloom.

'I never tried any sex stuff with any of them. It gets me hot.'

'Me too.'

She glanced over, saw the gleam in Darryl's eyes, the way his hand was working between his legs.

'Not yet, baby. Not yet. Let's get our new friend here situated, like you said. We're going to want to soften him up a little.'

Jayla crawled into herself, into the tight, dark space where the pain pushed around the edges. After a while, she couldn't say how long, she heard the awful, almost inhuman high-pitched sound, one she'd heard herself make.

And knew they'd begun to soften up Reed Aaron Mulligan.

*

Eve read over DeWinter's very preliminary report, again.

Too early to be conclusive – and that just burned her ass – but DeWinter believed, and Morris concurred – that a number of Melvin Little's injuries had been inflicted prior to his fall. Some as much as twenty-four to thirty-six hours prior.

She waded through the science-speak, the ass-burning probables, possibles, and pulled out the meat.

Sharp-bladed instrument nicked bone, blunt object on oldest wound, back of skull. Femur fracture due to forceful downward strike.

Maybe by a tire iron, Eve thought as she paced and read, paced and read.

Numerous bones in the right hand crushed.

Further testing to continue at oh-seven-hundred.

She took heart from Morris's postscript.

Garnet's not ready to commit, and she's correct. But he's one of yours. The local autopsy was badly botched here. This victim suffered multiple wounds – stabbing, beating, striking – at least a day prior to TOD. It would be a considerable coincidence for him to have fought with or been attacked by someone other than your unsubs.

'Coincidence is bollocks,' she muttered.

'As you've said.' Smoothly, subtly, Roarke angled himself between her and what he believed was now – another – empty coffeepot. 'You – all of you – have done all you can do tonight.'

'Santiago and Carmichael—'

'Will certainly contact you if they hit on anything. But as it's past midnight there, it's likely they'll need to pick it up in the morning.'

'What time is it here?'

'If it's past midnight there, it's past one here. It's an hour difference.'

'That drives me stupid crazy.'

'It does.' Banner dragged his hands through his hair, kept them gripped there as if it was the only way to keep his head upright. His eyes had the hazed and dazed look of a sleep-walker. 'Step across some state line and you gain an hour, lose an hour. It's confusing.'

She jabbed a finger at him in solidarity. 'See?' she said to Roarke.

'I see that our Central Time deputy needs sleep, and so do the rest of you.'

She considered feeding everybody a departmentally approved energy boost, then realized the futility. Plus she hated the way boosters made her feel. They'd all work better with a few hours down.

'Okay, we'll call it. Meet back here at oh-six-hundred.'

'I hear that. Sorry,' Banner added. 'Brain's gone soft on me. I can't remember how to get to my bunk.'

'Where'd they put you?' Peabody rubbed her eyes as she rose. 'Ah . . .'

'The Park Room,' Roarke told her.

'We know where that is, right?'

McNab nodded, got to his feet, wrapped an arm around Peabody as she leaned against him. 'Yeah, it's right down from us. We'll guide you in.'

''Preciate it.' He glanced back at the board, zeroed in on Melvin Little. 'He's got more than me now. I'm not going to forget it.'

When he followed Peabody and McNab out, Eve eyed the coffeepot.

'Absolutely not.'

'You don't get to say—'

'I do, and I'd expect you to do the same for me. Your blood must be three-quarters caffeine by now. You're vibrating with it.'

'I'm a little wired,' she admitted.

'And if there was a single stone left for you to turn over tonight, I'd get you another pot myself, and join you.'

Maybe he would, she thought, maybe he'd just tranq her and be done. But he was right. She'd turned every stone available. Maybe she'd have a different perspective on what she'd found under one in the morning.

'Towing company takes calls 24/7,' she said as he pulled her from the room. 'That's what they do. Maybe Carmichael and Santiago will hit something tonight.'

'They'll contact you if they do.'

'Once DeWinter puts her stamp on Little, and the other vic in her house, the FBI's going to angle over, or start to.'

'Does that trouble you?'

'It irks on a purely – what's it – visceral level. But the more resources the better. They've got people looking into Jayla, but their focus is north. They see New York as part of the pattern, not a destination.'

She noted when they entered the bedroom, Galahad had beaten them and was now sprawled dead center in the bed.

'The more resources the better,' she repeated, sliding her hands into her pockets, trying to pace off some of the excess energy. 'We wouldn't be this far on Little without Banner, and we wouldn't have him confirmed – and he damn well is – without DeWinter and Morris.

'And the towing angle, that's good. Wouldn't have that without your criminal perspective.'

'Always happy to help.' He turned her around, released her weapon harness.

She shrugged out of it. 'The locals didn't want that connection – the local connection. They wanted Jansen to have gotten his head caved in by some homicidal hitcher. It's all over their reports.'

'Hmm.' Roarke turned her around again, unbuckled her belt.

'As for Little, smoother if that was just his bad luck.'

He tugged her sweater over her head.

'Same with Fastbinder in West Virginia. Guy takes a wrong step, does a header into a crevice. Tragic, sure, but people aren't hammering the local law about tracking down a couple killers.'

Roarke backed her to the bed, hefted her onto the platform, nudged her to sit.

'What are you doing?'

'I'm here to help, remember.' He lifted one of her legs, pulled off her boot.

'You're working on getting me naked.'

'The reward for the help.'

'You looking for another payment?'

'I'd planned to run an account, but under the circumstances.' He pulled off the other boot.

'I am a little wired.' She boosted up her hips as he tugged her trousers down and away. 'Might as well put the caffeine to some use.'

'And if I burn it out of you, you might shut up long enough for us to both get some sleep.'

With the flat of his hand, he covered her face, gave her a gentle shove back.

And with a throaty growl, Galahad padded to the far corner of the bed, turned his back to them.

'How does he know we're not just going to sleep?'

'Animal instinct,' Roarke supposed, pulling off his own sweater before he levered over her.

'I've got some of that.' Eve yanked him down, added a quick bite to the kiss. 'Fast.' She used her teeth on his throat now. 'Fast and hard and rough.'

She was already pulsing, already pumping. And her swift, ripe greed sparked its match in him. While she struggled to undress him, he cupped a hand between her legs, sent her careening over the first keen edge.

Nothing now, nothing but need, like a fever, like a flame, burning, climbing. Mad with it, she arched up, grinding herself against him until they both shuddered.

Still arched, she locked her legs around his hips, reached up to grip the sheets as if she'd fly away without the anchor.

'Fast,' she said again, barely breathing. 'Hard. Rough.'

He drove into her, sheathed to the hilt, ripped a cry from her. And again, with the pleasure so sharp it slashed through him like a blade.

Again, and still again, with a madness that clawed up to haze his vision so she seemed suspended in smoke beneath him.

He used his hands on her, slick, quivering skin, and his mouth, while he plunged – hard, fast, rough.

She'd wanted that dark greed inside him, the animal roused, so he freed it, rode it, rode her until her strangled scream sounded in his ears, until her body shook against his. Until she seemed to melt away.

And still he rode, past reason, took more. Took all.

And with all, released.

Her ears rang with the hammering of her own heart. His knocked against her like a fist. She sensed him start to move and managed to get her limp arms around him.

'No. Just stay,' she murmured. 'Just stay awhile.'

And slept.

She woke in the dark, pulled from deep and blessedly dreamless sleep by the insistent beeping of her communicator.

Disoriented, still tangled with Roarke, she tried to push up.

'Wait. Lights on, ten percent.'

At Roarke's command, the dark lifted as he rolled away.

'My comm . . .'

'Still in your trousers.' He found them, fished the communicator out while she tried to scrub the fog of sleep away.

'Ah—'

'Block video,' he advised.

'Christ. Yes. Block video,' she ordered. 'Dallas.'

'Dispatch, Dallas, Lieutenant Eve.'

At 4:18 a.m., she learned of Reed Aaron Mulligan.

Downtown again, she thought. A full day ahead of schedule. Unless . . .

'Do you want me to wake Peabody?' Roarke asked.

'Yes. No. No, no point. It's going to be one of theirs, but that's gut, not fact. I'll talk to this Mulligan's mother first.'

'Then I'm with you. With you,' he repeated before she could object.

She was showered, dressed and pumped on coffee inside ten minutes, with Roarke barely a minute behind as he remoted a vehicle over from the garage.

Then they were out the door, into the cold, clear night, where one of his burly A-Ts waited, engine and heaters running.

'Possible missing lives with his mother on Leonard, off Broadway.'

'I heard Dispatch.' He drove fast, smooth through the gates and onto streets quiet in the predawn winter. 'This is a break-in pattern, yes?'

'If they've got him, yeah. Jayla Campbell should have had another day. Maybe something went south there, and they've dumped her body where we haven't found it yet. Or disposed of it another way. Or . . .'

'Still have her. Alive.'

'Doubtful, but I'd like to think so. And it may be this is a false alarm. The missing's twenty-one — barely.' She scanned her PPC, and the run she'd already started on him.

'A couple juvie bumps, looks like. Illegals, nothing major. Currently working as assistant manager, days, at a music store — instruments, lessons. Got some income here from a band called Thrashers.'

She dug a little deeper. 'Plays the guitar, sings. Looks like a handful of club dates — low-rent. Have to check it out, but—'

'He might have gotten lucky, might have gotten stoned and flopped with a friend.'

'Maybe. But it's their territory. Single mother, bar waitress, no sibs.' Eve put her PPC away. 'We'll hear her out.'

The Mulligans lived in a triple-decker walk-up with solid security and a reasonably clean lobby.

No graffiti on the stairway leading up to three, Eve noticed, which said something about the tenants. She'd heard a mutter of a media report on two through one of the apartment doors.

Lousy soundproofing, and someone worked the early shift.

She'd lifted her fist to rap on the door, but it swung open first.

'I heard you coming. Cops?'

'Lieutenant Dallas.' Eve held up her badge. 'And my civilian consultant. Ms Mulligan?'

'Yeah, yeah, come in. Thanks for getting here so fast. The first guy I talked to barely listened to me.'

She wore a short black skirt that showed good legs and a low-cut white top that framed good breasts. Her work clothes, Eve thought, and had only changed out her shoes for house skids, tossed a bulky cardigan over the shirt.

She radiated worry.

'Reed wouldn't not come home. I mean to say he'd let me know if he was staying out. That's our deal. I do the same for him.'

'Why don't we sit down, and you can run through it for me?'

'Oh, sorry.' She looked around as if she couldn't find her place in her own apartment. 'I can't think I'm so worried. Have a seat. I've got coffee.'

'That'd be great,' Eve said, mostly to give the woman something to do, something that would settle her. 'Just black for both of us.'

'Give me a sec.'

She moved to the rear of the room, to the jog that held a narrow, open kitchen.

She wore her flame-red hair scooped up in a bouncy tail that left her face – narrow, angular – unframed. Her run had put her at forty, but she could have lied her way to thirty-five, even with the pallor and the shadows under misty green eyes.

'I work five nights a week at The Speakeasy. It's a bar just a couple blocks over. It's a good place, not a dive. Classy, good customers. Roarke owns it – you know who I mean.'

Eve slanted Roarke a look. 'Yeah.'

'So it's a good place to work – not a lot of ass-grabbers come in. And it's close to home – Roarke owns this place, too, so it's nice. It's secure, and it's clean. Reed's a good boy. Responsible. He's got a solid day job. He wants to be a music star – that's the dream. He plays in a band, and they're starting to get some jobs. He's good. I know I'm his mom, but he's good. Anyway.'

She brought coffee on a tray with the grace and ease of a longtime waitress.

'I work four nights seven to midnight, and one night – like tonight – five to two. Reed said how he might go out late, jam with his band some. They're working on a sound, compu-boosted. He's got a knack with computers. So when I got home and he wasn't here, I wasn't worried. But when I checked the house 'link – it was blinking so I knew there were messages, I got worried.'

She picked up her own coffee, set it down again. 'The first message was from Benj – that's Reed's best friend, and one of the band. He was a little steamed. Where are you, sort of thing, why aren't you answering your 'link. You could listen.'

'That'd be good.'

Quickly, Jackie rose, flipped on the message replay.

Hey, man, wtf! We're still waiting. Answer your pocket, dude. You said you'd be here in a few. It's been a freaking hour. Tag me.

The machine flagged the message at 1:06 a.m.

And the next, again from Benj, twenty minutes later. A third from a female – ID'd as Roxie Parkingston, lead vocalist – twenty-two minutes after that.

Reed, you're scaring me now. I swear if I don't hear back from you in another half an hour, I'm tagging your mom. Don't make me tag your mom.

'She did,' Jackie confirmed. 'I was listening to the message, her last message, when she rang through. She said Reed had talked to Benj when he was on the way – walking to this basement unit Benj and a couple of the other boys share on Morton, just off Seventh. They've soundproofed it, so they practice there. It's only ten minutes away on foot. At most.

253

'Something happened,' she insisted. 'He wouldn't do this. We have a deal. All either of us have to do is say we won't be home – no explanations, no questions. But we have to let the other know. We always do. And he was on his way to Benj and the band. His dream.'

'What would he have been wearing?'

Jackie let out a long breath. 'I looked, to be sure. I got him a new coat and new boots. His birthday, Christmas. Brown Trailblazer boots – the real leather ones. It was his twenty-first birthday, and he really wanted them. And the coat, it's a Moose brand parka. Hunter green. I think he'd be wearing black pants, a black sweater. It's a band thing.'

'A girlfriend?'

'He's half seeing this girl – Maddy – and I checked with her, woke her up. She hasn't seen him for a couple days. He's got the hots for Roxie. I can see it. Hell, she can see it, but he hasn't moved on it yet. I'd know. So he's half seeing Maddy, but it's not serious, and she hasn't seen him since they grabbed a pizza the other night.'

Eve asked more questions, got a sense of a happy-go-lucky sort of guy, earning a living, helping his mother with the rent, sliding along, and dreaming of fame and fortune rocking it out for millions.

As her own closest friend did just that, Eve knew it could actually happen.

She got the contact information on the bandmates, the half-a-girlfriend, some coworkers.

'You're going to look for him, right?'

'Yes, we're going to look for him.'

'I know he's of age, but he's mostly still a boy. And he's pretty.' She pressed her lips together. 'I know there are people out there, people who prey on boys, even boys of age.'

Yes, there are, Eve thought, but she said, 'We're going to look for him.'

The minute she stepped out, she turned to Roarke. 'Your building.'

'Apparently it is.'

'Then getting the security discs shouldn't be a problem. Cam on the door. It would show him leaving.'

'I've already contacted the security company who handles this property. The system's in the basement utility. I have the codes.'

'Can you get me copies? I want to get his description out. It'll hit the morning reports. Maybe somebody saw him.'

'Five minutes,' he told her, and took the basement exit.

He was back in four, handed her the copy. 'I ran it from nineteen hundred through oh-one-hundred. Just to cover the ground.'

'That'll do it.'

She ran it through her PPC, zipping forward until she saw Reed.

'Straight up midnight, and dressed just like his mother said. Hood up. It's cold.'

She stood where she was, ran it straight through until she saw Jackie Mulligan walk to the door and key in.

'Three people out, two in between. No couples. And no reason to think they'd grabbed the kid, then bopped over here.'

'But now you're sure.'

'Yeah. You up for a walk?'

'A walk in the cold and dark? Sounds just lovely.'

'He'd walk west,' she said as they stepped outside. 'West to Seventh, turn south. 'Ten-minute walk – probably a little less as he'd be walking fast in the cold. And somewhere along the route, he ran into them. Between midnight and ten after – if he didn't detour. It's a good, narrow window.'

She scanned as they walked, looking for more security cameras, for lighted windows, for shadowy spots where LCs or dealers or muggers might lurk.

But her gut told her Reed hadn't run afoul of a mugger, or a junkie, or some random street deal. So she looked for potential stretches where someone could get a vehicle close enough to the curb to—

'Shit.' She stopped by a loading zone, checked the time. 'Right about six minutes in. Broken streetlight, right there. And glass on the sidewalk from it.'

'They broke one of the lights for cover, pulled right into the loading zone.'

'Used the woman to lure him. "Hey, honey, can you help me out a second?"' She studied the buildings, the storefronts as she spoke. 'No bars right here, and that's a damn shame. Retail, café, residential, accounting firm. Nothing that would be bustling at midnight on a ball-freezing night. But some traffic had to come by. So they had to be quick with him.'

She tipped her face up. 'Yeah, they had to be quick. And that's a mistake. Loading zones have cams. Crap cams, and a lot of them don't work at all, but we've got a shot here.'

She pulled out her communicator. 'We've got a shot,' she repeated.

14

It would take some time, but she arranged to have the feed from the loading zone cam sent to her office unit, her home unit, even her PPC just to cover every base.

And while she waited for Traffic to pull that one off, they walked the rest of the way to Benj Fribbet's basement unit, roused him and his roommates.

She watched their attitude go from pissy, to smirky, then to genuine concern.

'Come on. Nothing happened to him.' Benj, muscular, mixed-race, handsome, scratched his chest through a T-shirt where Mavis Freestone's face sent out a flirtatious, come-along-boy smile.

It wigged Eve a little to see her friend over some guy's torso.

'He's okay. You sure he's not home?'

'I wouldn't be here if he was home. When did you last see or speak to him?'

'I saw him yesterday, went by his work, just to chew a minute, and we made the plans to work here tonight – last night, I mean. I talked to him – I don't know, about midnight – few after – I guess. He was on his way here. Said he was almost here, and . . . '

'You got your 'link?'

'Yeah, yeah. I've been pissed at him.' He glanced at his roommates – one short and burly with a lot of purple hair, the other wiry with the shaved-on-one-side look and sleeve tats.

The living area boasted a sagging couch, a table covered with takeout boxes and brew bottles, and a lot of music equipment.

Benj found the 'link in the takeout rubble. Punched in, played back.

You coming or what? Roxie's here, we're all here.

Yeah, yeah, I'm on my way. Jeez, it's like the South Pole out here tonight. Nearly there. I'm nearly there. Fire it up!

Eve heard another voice, barely register.

'Hold it. Play that back, boost it.'

'Sure, but I can't get it to boost much. It's a crap 'link.'

Eve grabbed the 'link, held it against her ear.

'"Hey, cutie",' she murmured.

Then Reed's voice blasted. *Back to you.*

'That's it,' Benj said. 'You can hear how I tried to tag his 'link a couple times, I left v-mail there, and on his home 'link. And Roxie did the same.'

Ignoring him, she replayed again, listened, noted the time. Five minutes, forty-eight seconds from exiting his building to ending the transmission.

'I need this 'link.'

'It's the only one I got,' he began, then shook his head. 'Yeah, take it. Jesus, sure, take it. You really think . . . Maybe he detoured to Maddy's. They're not really sizzling, but maybe.'

'His mother contacted her, and no. Anyone else?'

'We're his crew.' He looked at his friends again. 'We're his crew, you know? We were pissed. We were all pissed he ditched us. What can we do? We can troll for him.'

She didn't see the point in it, but didn't see one in trying to stop them, either.

'That's her voice on here.' She secured the 'link in her pocket for now. '"Hey, cutie." Bitch. Right there in the loading zone. I *know* it. About halfway between his place and where he was going.'

'Wrong place, wrong time,' Roarke said, and rubbed a hand on her back.

'That's worked for them so far, but their luck's going to change. We'll get something off the damn cam, and we've got her voice on this shitty pocket 'link. We know almost to the minute when he was grabbed, and, goddamn it, they're close. They're close by.'

Legwork, she decided, and as they walked back ordered up droids and uniforms to knock on doors along that stretch of Seventh.

She'd get started on the loading zone feed, get McNab ready to boost anything they hit on there – and add more boost to the voice on the 'link.

It would be some wild luck to hit a voiceprint match, but they were due.

In the car again, she pulled out her own 'link.

'Who are you tagging at this hour?'

'Carmichael. She and Santiago can get started.'

'Eve, it's still shy of five in the morning there.'

'Why?'

'Well, the magic elephant who carries the wide dish of the planet on its massive back moves ponderously on its daily trek around the sun.'

'Oh, bite me.' But the image he'd painted made as much sense to her as the scientific one. She decided to give her detectives another thirty minutes in the rack.

'No plan. Just like the other two in New York. There couldn't have been a plan, couldn't have been a specific target. So what prompted them to go hunting last night? One, they've already killed Campbell. Ahead of schedule, or she just gave out on them unexpectedly. And they didn't get enough of a rush from it.'

'They'd dump her body quickly, wouldn't they, in that eventuality. You'll likely find her soon after the sun's up.'

'No point keeping her. Might be they went to dump her, and here comes a new one, right into their lap. But why not wait to do the dump until later? Barely midnight – it's early for a dump, less risk in another hour or two.'

'Part of the rush? That risk?'

'Yeah, maybe. Let's raise the bar a little. So maybe. Second scenario, they decided to grab the next before they finish her. They've got a place, they're where they want to be. Room for another? Got room, so why not have the next in the batter's box?'

'Or . . .'

'A duet.' She nodded. 'Two at once. We can't know for sure, not for sure, they haven't done that before along the way. We've profiled it one at a time, and it's most likely, but we can't be sure they haven't pulled a twofer.'

'With two, you could use one to terrify the other. Or you could each have your own, work in tandem.'

'A lot of ugly possibilities. Until we find Jayla Campbell's body, we're going with the scenario they took a second, purposefully. Maybe impulsively. The loading zone wasn't smart. But, if they haven't lived in an urban area, they might not be aware of the cams on those.'

'It's likely many who do and don't own a vehicle or drive aren't aware. And even many who own and do may not think of it. You have to drive onto the grid to activate the cam, and they're notorious crap.'

He gave her a half smile. 'I've lived in urban areas, and often needed a handy spot to . . . park. I should add, Lieutenant, that jamming one of those grid cams? Child's play.'

'Let's hope neither of them played the same games you did as a kid.'

Traffic thickened as they made their way uptown, with maxibuses blatting and farting along with their load of late shifts coming off, early shift going on. And the sky trams hauled more.

A few cabs zipped – most who worked the early and late shifts couldn't afford cabs. But there would be those heading out to catch a shuttle, or a high–level LC on the way home after a profitable night.

'They'd come up here sometimes,' Eve muttered. 'If you made a trip to New York, you'd do the tourist thing, wouldn't you? You want the Midtown shops, the skating at Rockefeller, the park. You'd want to see the Empire State, you'd want to join the party at Times Square.'

She shifted to him. 'You don't come all this way without the party, do you? You don't hole up inside the whole time, no matter how much fun you're having. You can do that any-where.'

'You've a point. What does it tell you?'

'Just more. They're a couple. Lovers. Mira profiles them as in love – in their sick, fucked-up way. A romantic dinner somewhere, maybe? One of the hot spots. That means the right clothes, and that means shopping. That takes money, unless they use a vic's card, and we'd be on them like rats on cheese. Souvenirs. You gotta have souvenirs.'

She rolled it over, turned it side-to-side as Roarke drove them home again.

Inside, they headed straight to her office. She smelled bacon before they made the last turn.

She might have snarled at that, but she also smelled coffee.

She walked in as Peabody handed a plate from the buffet table – already set up and loaded – to Banner.

'Hey, there you are. We figured we'd do the spread before you – you've been out already?'

Eve shrugged out of her coat, tossed it aside. 'We've got another.'

'Another? Campbell—'

'Undetermined. Mulligan, Reed Aaron, age twenty-one, snatched at midnight and change last night, heading south on Seventh between Waverly and Charles.'

'You've got a wit?' McNab asked.

'We've got a 'link trans, and potentially a cam feed. Roarke, put this on screen while I see if Traffic's come through.'

'Mulligan,' Roarke repeated, using the auxiliary to put the data on screen, 'Reed Aaron, reported missing by his mother.'

While Roarke briefed them, Eve finally connected with someone from Traffic who knew an ass from an elbow – at least in her opinion.

'Feed's coming through. I'm throwing it up. Crap,' she said seconds later when the flickering, muddy image came on. 'Can you clean this up?' she demanded of McNab.

'Some, sure. Can I?'

She frowned, realized he wanted her desk, pushed up and away.

'Bad angle, too,' she muttered. 'That's just stupid. We're not going to get a tag, angle's too high. But that's going to be enough for somebody to nail down make and model. Where are they? Where – there – somebody's getting out on the curbside. Is that somebody getting out? McNab!'

'Working on it. I can take it into the lab here or at Central, clean it up better and faster.'

'Just give me something here.'

Roarke strolled over, leaned over McNab's shoulder. The two of them began muttering in geek.

'Can't see the street-side door. Cam's just shit, but that's the woman. That's the female. Short skirt, short jacket.'

'Can't get a good read on her.' Banner strained as Eve did. 'Height, maybe. Figuring the height of the van – that's a van … maybe five-six? Hair's covered, face turned away, gloves. Can't see enough of her.'

'Is that a corner of the license plate? I think it is,' Peabody gestured. 'And that's some sort of sticker in the back window. That triangle.'

'That's better, a little better,' Eve said as the image cleared a bit more. 'Yeah, that's the woman. You can tell by the way she moves she's hunting, and she's wearing the slut stockings.'

'Fishnets,' Peabody supplied.

'Looking around, opening the back. Can you zoom in on the back, on the interior while she's got the back open?'

The image jerked, flickered again, madly for a moment, then steadied.

The woman hauled a chair halfway out the back. A big armchair, but she didn't seem to have much trouble with it. Some muscle there, Eve gauged, and a routine.

An open bag – small duffel? – on the floor. She saw a shadow move farther up.

'Pull it back! There, that's the male – getting out street side. He's in the shadows, but ... shit. Used something to break out the streetlight.'

'Slingshot maybe.'

Eve frowned at Banner. 'A slingshot?'

'That'd be my guess. We've got kids do that back home when they're bored enough. You can't see him anymore.'

'He's got to get out of sight. Slide around in front of the van, maybe slip into one of the doorways on the other side of the sidewalk. Vics are hit from behind. Peabody, I want all the security cam feed from the buildings on that side of the street.'

'On it.'

'She's looking back – a little bit of profile. Sees somebody? Yeah, yeah, see how she glances back – signaling her partner. Here it comes. Oh yeah, she pulls the hat off, shakes her hair back, so he can see her – so Mulligan can see her. Long blond hair. Probably Caucasian.'

'Jesus, Dallas, can we make her from this?'

She kept her eyes on screen as she answered Banner. 'We will make her. There's Mulligan – hunter green coat, hood up, he's blocking her from the camera, but we'll make her. Give me a hand, could you?' Eve whispered. 'I'm just not strong enough to get it inside. Aren't you sweet to stop and help? And he bends his knees, like you do, gets a grip on the chair, starts to lift it.'

It was fast, shadows and jerks, flickering and blurs, but she caught enough. The sap – some sort of sap – coming down fast and hard, and the man, the woman, shoving Mulligan inside, the woman scrambling in behind him. The door slammed shut, and in seconds, the van pulled out and away.

'They weren't there ten fucking minutes. Their luck's not going to hold, that kind of luck doesn't hold. Get that in the lab, use this one,' she ordered McNab. 'Get it as clean as you can, and send me every piece of the unsubs, every piece. I want an ID on the sticker on the back window, make and model of the vehicle.'

'Corner of the plate,' Peabody added.

'If you can do anything with it, do it.'

'I'll give you a hand with it,' Roarke told him. 'Load up a plate first. A man's got to eat,' he said to Eve.

'Fine. Would Feeney make a difference?'

'Considerable.' Roarke got a plate for himself. 'We could split up the identification and cleaning and enhancing.'

'I'm tagging him. Peabody, wake up Carmichael. I want her and Santiago working their angle now. Bring them up to speed.'

'Where do you want me? I feel like deadweight,' Banner admitted.

Eve brought up the map. 'Those are the snatch points, and the dump site. My guess is Mulligan was impulse, so their hole's close to that. I want a list of souvenir shops in that area.'

'Souvenirs?'

'Do you plan to go home without one?'

He smiled, sheepish. 'Peabody said how she could score me an NYPSD sweatshirt, and maybe a hoodie. And my mama collects snowglobes. Don't ask me why, she just likes them. I figured I'd find one before I left.'

He nodded. 'We don't see them as from here, so they'd want souvenirs.'

'And when we make them, we start showing their pictures around to the places you list. Takeout places, too, Banner, while you're at it. Deliveries would be chancy, but you can get food, any kind of food, and cart it home with you. I'm betting neither of them is much of the domestic type. And like Roarke said, a man's got to eat. Women, too.'

'I'll get started.'

'Want one more?'

'I'll take whatever you've got.'

'Pawnshops, secondhand shops. They need money for food and souvenirs, right? Electronics would be the first and easiest. But we've got a file of what Kuper and Campbell were wearing when they were taken. And I've got one now on Mulligan. If they liked the clothes and they fit, they'd keep them. But if they didn't, they'll sell them.'

'Get a plate,' she suggested. 'Work and eat.'

She went to her desk, contacted Feeney.

His hangdog face seemed a little baggier, his explosion of silver-threaded ginger hair a bit more electrified. But since he hadn't blocked video, she assumed he wasn't still in bed.

'Wait,' he said, and glugged what she knew was coffee from a bright red mug. 'What?'

'We've caught a break on the spree killers. I've got some security feed from a loading dock cam.'

'Those cams are crap.'

'Yeah, which is why I'm asking if you can give me some time on it. Roarke and McNab are already on it, at the home lab. We've got a decent image of the vehicle, some partials on the unsubs. Maybe part of a plate, and some sort of rear window sticker. We've got them taking out the latest vic.'

'The girl?'

'She's not the latest. They got one last night. Male, just turned twenty-one. No word if they dumped Campbell's body, but it's early.'

'Tell me.' He rubbed one of his baggy eyes. 'I can be there inside thirty. Put the coffee on.'

'You got it. Thanks. Peabody,' she said the minute she clicked off. 'Status.'

'Carmichael and Santiago have a couple of lines to tug. One they've got a buzz over, but they crapped out on it last night. Hitting it again this morning.'

Peabody shoveled in some eggs. 'Bubba's Body Shop, Towing and Pies.'

Eve started to speak, thought again, then shook her head. 'You're making that up.'

'Hand to God.' Peabody took a moment to lay one hand over her heart, raise the other. 'Carmichael says Bubba's wife makes the pies, and Bubba and their son run the rest. She and Santiago got a guilt vibe off the son, but they aren't giving it up.'

'They need to get the son on his own.'

'That's the plan.'

With a grunt, Eve turned back to her comp to write the report on Mulligan, and update all salient parties. She'd run a probability on Campbell's chances. Dead or alive. But she wanted to run it by Mira.

Something was going to break, and soon. She could feel it, almost hear those first cracks in the wall.

But would it be soon enough?

He'd wept while he raped her.

No, no, that wasn't right, Jayla thought. She couldn't and wouldn't call it rape. Not when they'd beaten him first, and cut him.

And her.

Not when they'd forced the sex drug into him, and held a knife to his throat unless he'd crawled on top of her. She'd tried to talk to him with her eyes. Tried to tell him to just do it, it didn't matter, she didn't blame him.

His tears had fallen on her. She wondered she didn't drown in them.

They'd put a knife to her throat, too, when forcing him to push into her wasn't enough. And Ella-Loo had pulled the gag off, told her to scream, to beg.

Beg him, beg him to stop. Scream!

So she had, though her screams were hoarse and weak, she'd screamed and begged. And all the while her eyes told the weeping boy it didn't matter. It wasn't his fault.

Once she'd believed, absolutely, rape was the worst that could happen to a woman. The ultimate violation. She knew better now. This – what they made him (Reed, she remembered. She would think of him as Reed) do to her was nothing compared to what they'd already done.

What she feared they could do. What they would do.

Everybody said rape was about power, control, and not about sex. Maybe that was true, but for Darryl and Ella-Loo, sex was part of it, too.

They pawed each other with their free hands while the boy did what they made him do. And they told each other what they'd do to each other.

And they were in such a hurry to fuck, they dragged the boy off, trussed him up again right on the floor where he fell, left him there. They raced away because Ella-Loo said she wanted the bed.

They forgot to gag her again. It took Jayla a minute to realize it, to understand the raw sounds she made were actual words.

'Can you hear me? Reed? Can you hear me?'

He kept crying, flat on his face, his hands taped behind his back, his legs bound from calves to ankles.

'I'm Jayla. Jayla Campbell.'

'I'm sorry. I'm sorry. I'm sorry.'

'It doesn't matter. It wasn't your fault. I don't care about that.' Maybe she would later, maybe she would never be able to be touched again. Maybe they'd kill her and none of it would matter anyway.

But now, this minute, she was alive. And she wasn't alone.

'Please. I'm Jayla. Can you talk to me?'

'I'm sorry.' Finally he turned his head so his swollen, blackened eyes met hers. 'They made me—'

'I know. They might've killed me, both of us, if you hadn't done it. I don't care about that. If they make you do it again, remember I don't care. Do you know what day it is? I don't know what day it is. I don't know how long I've been here.'

'I . . . I think Thursday. Or Wednesday. I can't think. I feel sick. Why are they doing this?'

'I don't know. They're the sick ones. Can you move around at all? Do you see the knives, or anything sharp?'

'I don't know. Everything hurts. I think they broke stuff. My hand . . . ' But he tried to turn. 'Who are they?'

'Darryl and Ella-Loo.' The words scraped her throat, like nails on dry wood, but she needed to speak. 'You have to remember their names. That's what they call each other. We have to try to get away. They're going to hurt you more than they already have. They like it.'

'Where are we?'

'I don't know, but an apartment, I think. Close to the street because when they open the door the traffic's right

272

outside. If you can get to the door, or a window, maybe you can get it open. Or find something sharp. They've got me tied to this table or board.'

He tried. She could hear his hisses of pain, his choked sobs and harsh breathing as he inched his way toward her.

When he managed to get to his knees, she saw his face again, gray from the effort, his eyes glazed from the pain and the remnants of what they'd forced down him.

His skin was shiny with sweat, and blood from where they'd cut him. He shivered like a man cased in ice.

'There's a knife – I see a knife on that table. If I can get over to it, maybe I can knock it down to the floor.'

'Try. Try, Reed.'

He did, scooting on his knees. She saw his hand, bone-white and badly swollen, and more blood from more slices and gouges on his back.

Pity stirred somewhere deep inside her, but heavy over it was a fierce and violent hope. If he could get to the knife . . .

He swayed, nearly went over. 'Dizzy. Need to—'

'Stop a minute. Catch your breath.'

But it was too late. He tipped to the side, tried to pull himself back. Overbalanced, he fell backward, landed on his broken hand.

His scream was thin as wire before he passed out.

15

When Feeney arrived, Eve gestured to the buffet table, and what was left.

'Still food.'

'I'll take it.' He looked at her board as he grabbed a plate. 'How long have they had this one?'

'About eight hours.'

He nodded, piled on bacon, uncovered the eggs on the warming plate, helped himself. 'Could be trying a twofer.'

'I'm hoping, as that keeps Campbell alive. I just sent in a report, and I'm going to talk to Mira about it. It could be the next escalation. One for each of them. Carmichael and Santiago may have a lead in Arkansas. But the best bet we have now is the feed from the loading dock.'

'Dallas.' Peabody held up a hand, held her comm in the other. 'We may have a little more. A café in the snatch location just opened. A beat droid's sending over their feed. Image is spotty, but we may have the male unsub on it.'

'It's cracking.' Eve turned to Feeney. 'A couple of good whacks, and it breaks.'

'Send it onto Roarke's comp lab. I'll go join the boys. Deputy,' he added with a nod to Banner. 'Looks like you had the scent all along.'

'We sure got it now.' He waited until Feeney stepped out. 'I've got the souvenir places, Lieutenant. None of them are open yet. And I've got a chunk of places that do takeaway. Just getting going on the pawnshops, but none of them are open yet, either.'

'Send me what you've got, and we'll start pushing through it.' She checked the time. 'If Mira isn't up by now, she's about to be.'

Eve started toward her desk when her 'link signaled. 'Santiago,' she said, answered. 'Give me something.'

'We cut the son out of the herd, and started working him. He's in this somewhere, LT, or knows something. But the father swooped in before we pried it out of him. They're all pretty jumpy now.'

'Get the local law into it. Pull them in, work them in whatever they have for a cop shop down there.'

'That's the thing.' Santiago's dark eyes shifted to the side, narrowed in annoyance at something – someone – off screen. 'Bubba's brother-in-law's a lawyer, and he's putting up roadblocks on this. He's also the local law's fishing buddy, and the connections are playing hell with any cooperation. It's a stall, Dallas. We can play the game, but it's going to take some time.'

'Time's the problem. How sure are you about this Bubba – and it embarrasses me to say that name out loud.'

'Guilt's oozing out of the son – name's Jimbo, and I'm sorry about that. And Bubba's getting sweaty. The mother – she's Maizie, and bakes one hell of an apple pie – we think she's clear. But Bubba and Jimbo, they're lying, Dallas. They know something, and they're lying. Any of us could get Jimbo in the box for twenty minutes, he'd fold like an accordion.'

'Is that a colorful metaphor?'

He flashed a grin. 'I'm working on them.'

'Take one for the team, Santiago.'

The grin faded fast. 'Ah hell, Dallas, Bubba's got hands like sides of beef. That's not just a colorful metaphor, it's next to literal.'

'Toughen up. Get him to take a swing at you, in front of witnesses if you can manage it. And have Carmichael stay on this Jumbo.'

'Jimbo.'

'Whatever. Keep the lawyer and the law centered on Bubba, and I'll get the son into the box. Holographically speaking.'

'I'm going to get punched in the face, and you guys are going to have all the fun.'

'Make it look good,' Eve advised, and ended transmission. Instead of Mira, she woke up APA Cher Reo.

'I had ten more minutes coming, damn it.'

'I need you to strong-arm whoever you know who can strong-arm somebody in Monroe, Arkansas. I need a search warrant for a place called Bubba's Body Shop, Towing and Pies.'

'Is this just a bad dream?'

'Fast, Reo. For the facilities, for the books, for the works. It ties in with the spree killings, and they got another last night.'

The rustling signaled Reo was pulling herself out of bed. 'Give me the data again, and give me some probable cause.'

'Bubba's about to assault one of my detectives.'

'"About to"?'

'Anytime now. If you have to wait until that happens, you could get the rest set up. The latest vic turned twenty-one the day after Christmas.'

'Don't hang that on me. Hell. Give me a few minutes. I used to sleep with a guy who knows a guy.'

Eve smiled when Reo clicked off.

'It doesn't work so different,' Banner commented. 'Where I'm from? Smaller scale, that's for sure, but it doesn't work so different from here.'

'Cops are cops. Peabody, hold the fort here. Banner, you're with me. It might be handy to have you on the interview.'

'You're going to be good cop,' Peabody warned him.

'With a little good old boy tossed in?'

Eve nodded. 'That'll work.'

She took the elevator down to the holoroom, working out the strategy in her head on the way.

'How many rooms in this place?' Banner wondered.

'I don't have a clue. I keep finding ones I'd swear weren't there before.'

'How long you lived here?'

'Three years. Three years,' she repeated with some wonder of her own. 'Jesus, how did that happen?'

'You mind me asking something?'

'Didn't you just?'

'Another something. Was Roarke really ... well, what you'd call a thief?'

Eve kept her voice mild, her face inscrutable. 'I never caught him stealing anything.'

Humor danced into Banner's eyes. 'Neither did anybody else from what I hear.'

He stepped out with her into the blank slate of the holoroom.

'I thought he'd be different.'

'Different than what?' Eve asked as she puzzled over how to program what she needed.

'Than he is. I didn't expect him to be so amiable.'

'"Amiable".' She glanced back with a half laugh.

'I figured he'd be more ... stiff, I guess. And what you'd call highfalutin. Not somebody I'd be easy having a beer with. Can I ask what you're looking to do here?'

'He's got it in here,' Eve muttered. 'He would. I want one of my interview rooms. We're going to pull Jambo into it.'

'Jimbo.'

'Right – why would anybody tolerate being called Bubba or Jimbo?'

'It's geography, I reckon.'

'We're going to haul him in once his father's busy being arrested for assaulting an officer, and the lawyer's busy trying to say Santiago incited his client and blah-blah-bullshit-bollocks. We get him in here, and if Santiago's right, and he will be, we'll crack Benjo like an egg.'

'There! I knew he'd have it programmed.'

It still took her twice as long as it would've taken Roarke, but she keyed it all in.

And the familiar dull walls, the scarred table, creaky chairs and long two-way mirror of a standard Cop Central interview room shimmered into being.

'Whoa.' Eyes wide, Banner turned a circle. 'Never did one of these officially. Just at carnivals and such. And once at a . . . never mind about that.'

Sex club, Eve deduced. 'They have those never minds in Silby's Pond?'

'They got them in Little Rock.'

'I need to check in, but when this goes down, we go fast, so I want you to play sympathetic, to a point. That good-old-boy bit, yeah, that'll work.'

She put the file she'd brought in with her on the table. 'You're going to soften him up. I'm going to scare the shit out of him, and what's in this file will finish it.'

She pulled out her 'link. 'Carmichael.'

'Working on it,' Carmichael muttered, looking away rather than into the screen. 'Santiago's just ... ouch.' She hissed through her teeth, and Dallas heard the shouting off screen. 'That's going to leave a mark. Give me five minutes to go to my partner's assistance, and I'll be back at you.'

'Fast work.'

Eve nodded at Banner. 'Faster the better. However this is set up, Banner, it's fucking serious. It's all going on record. There are three smart geeks up in the lab sweating to get us something we can use, and they will. Meanwhile, these two bozos knew something that might have led to the unsubs, might've saved lives. They knew since Jansen's body was found, and they kept it shut to cover their own asses. That doesn't sit with me.'

'Doesn't sit with me, either. It ain't right. Ain't none of it right.'

'Then give me some room, and step in when you think you can do some good.'

Gauging the time, she contacted Mira.

'Sorry it's so early, and I've only got a couple of minutes. I sent you a report.'

'I haven't read it yet. I'm just—'

'Soon as you can,' Eve interrupted. 'They grabbed another last night. Male, twenty-one. About midnight. Probability's going to go by the pattern, and give me strong odds Campbell's dead. I want your take.'

'Give me a second. They could have gone too far, too fast,

280

or her body simply gave out. We can say with absolute certainty this hasn't happened before, so, yes, the probability is high she's dead.'

'What are the chances they decided they wanted to try two at once? A dump and snatch, the same night? Maybe. But a snatch, maybe impulse, it plays, too.'

'It would be a logical escalation. It's certainly possible, but—'

'Would you read the report as soon as you can? I've got some scenarios in there, some speculation. We've got a couple of good leads working now. I have to go deal with one, but I'd like some input once you've read the report.'

'I'll go over it now, and I'll give you what I can before I go to Dr DeWinter.'

'Thanks. That's my lead,' she said as her 'link signaled an incoming. 'Later. Dallas.'

'With some regret, our sheriff arrested Bubba for assaulting a police officer. The lawyer's so pissed he hasn't noticed – as yet – I've stepped out. Santiago's bleeding and causing a serious stink. If it was real I'd tell him not to be such a drama queen. I can snag Jimbo pretty easy.'

'Do it. I'm going to use your 'link to bring you both in, on your signal. Then I'm sending you back – keep them busy as long as you can. Unless the son calls for a lawyer, we can work him on this.'

'On it. I'll send you a flag when I've got him.'

It didn't take long, and hoping she didn't screw it up, Eve

used the signal to coordinate. Carmichael's image winked in, as did the big – 'Jumbo' wasn't off – guy next to her.

He wore coveralls on a frame designed for a career as a defensive lineman. His hair, the color of bleached corn, stuck straight up from a wide, square head.

Eve figured he weighed in at an easy two-sixty, and every ounce of him was scared shitless.

'Thank you, Detective. Record on. Dallas, Lieutenant Eve and Banner, Deputy William in interview with ... your full name, sir?'

'Um. Ah.'

'Dorran,' Carmichael supplied. 'James Beauregard.'

'Have a seat, Mr Dorran.'

'I really gotta look after my ma. My pa's in trouble.'

'Detective, go ... look after Mr Dorran's ma.'

'Yes, sir. You're going to want to cooperate with Lieutenant Dallas, Jimbo. Your ma doesn't need you in trouble, too.'

She nodded at Eve, and Eve cut her image away.

'Mr Dorran—'

'Maybe you could call me Jimbo, 'cause nobody calls me "mister".'

'All right, Jimbo. Sit.'

'I don't know nothing 'bout nothing. Or about nobody neither. My pa said—'

'I'm not talking to your pa.' Voice, eyes, went frigid, and sharp with it. 'You are now talking to me. I run the

282

Homicide division for the NYPSD. You know what homicide is, Jimbo?'

'Um, yeah, sort of.'

'It's murder.'

His eyes wheeled. And, yeah, Eve thought, even holographically, she could smell the guilt pumping off of him.

'I never killed nobody. Pa neither. My uncle Buck said how we didn't have to say nothing.'

'Your uncle Buck isn't looking at being charged with accessory to murder, after the fact, obstruction of justice, and a whole fucking slew of other charges I can come up with if you don't tell me the truth.'

'I never killed nobody. And ladies don't use bad words like that.'

'Do I look like a lady?'

'You're a girl.'

'I'm a cop. I'm a murder cop, and I eat assholes like you for breakfast. I've got a prosecuting attorney chomping at the bit to have you extradited to New York and tossed in a cage.'

'I didn't do nothing!'

'Jimbo.' Banner's voice was cool water from a country stream against Eve's urban flash. 'Now, I expect you didn't mean to do anything wrong. Didn't really know you did.'

'I don't hurt people. You can ask anybody. You from Arkansas, sir?'

'Sure am. Silby's Pond.'

'I never been there, but I heard it's right nice.'

'It sure is.'

'Maybe we can arrange for you to spend some time in a cage there.' Eve slapped her hand on the file, making all two hundred and sixty pounds of Jimbo jump in his chair. 'Since this man was killed there.'

She slammed the photos of Robert Jansen, broken and battered, faceup.

Jimbo went white. 'Holy crow! Holy crow! Is he dead?'

'What do you think?'

'Holy crow. I never did that! I never hurt nobody.'

'What kind of vehicle was it,' Banner asked conversationally, 'you and your pa towed in from down along Highway 12 last August?'

'It was . . . I don't know what you're talking about.' But Jimbo twisted his big hands together, and stared at the photograph. 'Did he get himself murdered?'

'They beat him,' Eve said, voice hard. 'They burned him. They tortured him, then, when they were done, they tossed him off a ridge and left him for your goddamn holy crows. And before that, they did this.'

She shoved the dead pictures of Jansen across the table. 'Bashed his head in, dragged him into the brush to rot until somebody found him.'

'I know about that. I know about that, 'cause it was Petie West and his mama who found him. But we didn't do nothing.'

Eve dumped the rest of the photos out. 'They killed all

these people. Tortured them. Somebody's son, daughter, sister, father. You took the vehicle they left on the side of the road. How much did you get for it?'

'We . . . I ain't saying we did any such thing. But if we did, it didn't hurt anybody.'

'We could trace the damn vehicle, Jimbo. We don't know who they are.'

'You don't know who they are,' he said slowly.

'Do the right thing, Jimbo.' Banner spoke gently. 'If you don't you are hurting people. You're hurting the people they have right now.'

'They have people?'

Eve pushed Campbell's picture, Mulligan's picture over. 'They have these two people. They're torturing them. They may have already killed the woman. The longer you cover yourself, the less chance they have of getting out of this alive.'

'I gotta look after my ma.'

'They've got mothers, Jimbo,' Banner reminded him. 'How would your ma feel if somebody had you, and there was somebody who could maybe help, but he didn't?'

'My pa said if we told they'd put us in jail.'

'If you don't tell, I swear to God I'll see you both in cages, as long as I can manage it,' Eve promised. 'If you help us out, give us something that helps us find these people, save this woman, this man, I'll keep you clear of jail. And the charges currently against your father for assaulting my detective go away, too.'

'You can do that?'

'I will do that. But you come clean, and now. No more bullshit, or the deal's off. You've got ten seconds.'

'I wanna think—'

'Nine. Eight. Seven.'

'Okay, all right.' He waved his big hands in the air. 'It was just sitting on the side of the road. It didn't have no registration in it or nothing. Had fuel right enough, and the battery was charged good and proper. But the engine was finished. Somebody'd worked on it, but it wasn't going anywhere. So we towed it in. Somebody'd come around looking, we'd've given it back. Nobody did. We didn't know about the dead man till later on, and then Pa said we had to be quiet or maybe they'd think we done it. We didn't hurt nobody.'

'What kind of vehicle?'

'Quarter-ton pickup. A '52, so it was showing its age. A '52 American Bobcat, steel-gray exterior, black interior. You could see how it'd been wrecked once, and had good body-work.'

'License plates?'

'Yes'm, Oklahoma plates as I recall. Nothing inside it. No registration, like I said, nothing in the cab or the bed, in the glove compartment or nothing. Some trash here and there, that's all.'

'Where is it?'

'Where is it?'

'Where's the truck?'

'Well, after we heard about the dead man, we stripped her down, sold off the parts, and took the rest in by the piece to the recycle place. Pa said we didn't want any part of that truck, and not to say boo to a goose about it. We didn't know nothing about any of these murdered people till those New York City detectives come around, and Pa said we couldn't believe them because people were always looking for trouble and telling lies in New York City.'

He looked over at Banner. 'You hear that?'

'Well, I can say I've been here for a day or so now, and haven't found that to be true. And the people we're after, Jimbo, they're not from New York City. They're from round about where we're from.'

'I don't know how that can be. I've never known anybody could do something like this. Honest, ma'am, we never hurt anybody. We didn't know about all this. And I couldn't shut my eyes most all night thinking about it. Pa was just looking out for me and Ma, that's all. You gotta look after your own.'

The dead were hers, Eve thought. And she'd look after them.

'We may need to talk to you again,' Eve began.

'Can I talk to my ma first? She says you gotta tell the truth. She's going to be a little upset with my pa about this. She's already pretty upset he hit that detective like he did. But, well, that detective, he did get Pa riled up.'

'I bet.' Eve rose. 'I'll bring Detective Carmichael in. She'll escort you back. I'll be speaking to the sheriff.'

'So they don't put Pa in jail for hitting the detective?'

'For that, and about what we just talked about.' Again, she used Carmichael's 'link to bring her in. 'We have Mr Dorran's statement. I'll copy the record to the sheriff, and to you and Detective Santiago. I'd request that Santiago agree to drop the charges against Jimbo's father. I would also go on record as requesting no charges be filed against either Mr Dorran considering Mr James Dorran's cooperation in this matter, and the information we hope will lead to the identification and apprehension of the unsubs.'

'Yes, sir.'

'Wrap it up, Carmichael. Warrant should be through or coming for searching the towing place, any and all vehicles on it. Get it done.'

'You bet. Let's go, Jimbo.'

Carmichael took Jimbo's arm, sent Eve a quick grin. And winked out.

'Copy record, my units,' Eve ordered. 'And program end. Let's move, Banner.'

'We can trace that truck.'

'We will trace that truck. Fucking morons stripped it down and crushed it out. We might've had prints, DNA, something.' She took a breath as they rode back to her office. 'But we'll trace it, get a name. Even if they stole it, we're a step closer.'

Eve swung by the computer lab on the way, dumped the data on Feeney for a search while Banner goggled a little.

'Cutting it back to Oklahoma registration,' Feeney said and, as Roarke did, worked the screen and keyboard manually. 'Search in for American Bobcat, 2052, quarter-ton pickup.'

'Gray. A gray truck.'

'Paint's easy to change, so we'll start without it.' He grunted as the computer spit out the results. 'Got over six hundred in the first sweep.'

'If they stole it, there'd be—'

'I know how to run a search, kid.' He continued to play the comp. 'Got three stolen in our time frame, two recovered, one wrecked. Running a separate including the color.'

'Got it.' Roarke swiveled around from his station. 'The decal, back window, van in the loading dock. OBX.'

'What the hell does that mean?' Eve demanded.

'Outer Banks – North Carolina. A property owner's decal. We've narrowed the license plate. Odds on New Jersey. Highest probability on the van is a '58 or '59 RoadStar, black or navy. Give us a minute.'

At another station McNab jiggled and bopped. 'Nothing popped on facial rec, yet. I'm still trying to boost the image.'

'Initial cross-match results,' Roarke said. 'Eight-six OBX property owners with vans within our parameters.'

'Gotta do better.'

'So I will.'

'On the gray,' Feeney put in. 'We've got five matches.'

'That's workable. Names, images, locations.'

'Coming on screen. Map on screen two. We can work the route, determine the most probable.'

Eve turned her attention to the screen, watched the locations light up, backtracked from Jansen's location. 'We'll run these five. Shelley Lynn Waynes – she's right on the route if you backtrack it.'

'Bringing her up,' Feeney said.

'Age thirty-one. Married – six years – two kids. School-teacher. Her truck gets boosted, she's going to report it. Maybe lent it to a friend, a relative, but . . .'

'Low probability,' Feeney said. 'I'll tag her, suss it out, but she's whistle clean. This Bowie Nettleton's the next favorite by route. Age seventy-four, retired military. Master Sergeant, currently mayor of Three Springs, Oklahoma. Two sons, both still serving, a grandson, granddaughter, also serving. And a granddaughter in college – political science major.'

'I'm not getting a buzz, but we'll check.'

'Barlow Lee Hanks,' Eve read, eyes narrowing on the next image. 'Too old for our unsub at fifty-eight. Offspring?'

'None on record.'

'Owns his own business, mechanic, bodywork – much like the idiot Dorrans, in Lonesome, Oklahoma. Bumbo said the truck had been worked on – good work. Mechanic.'

'"Bumbo"?' Roarke repeated.

'Jimbo.' Banner shrugged. 'I guess it amounts to the same.'

Even as he spoke, Eve went with her gut. She pulled out

her 'link, tagged Santiago. 'How's the face?' she asked, studying the black and swollen right eye.

'It's had worse.'

'Get it seen to, then you and Carmichael are heading to Oklahoma. Lonesome, Oklahoma. Barlow Lee Hanks. I'd like to know who he lent his '52 American Bobcat to. Get started as soon as you can. I'll feed you details when you're en route.'

'We'll get along like little doggies.'

'Why?'

'You know, little – it's a cowboy thing. Never mind. We're wrapping this part up. The asshole keeps good records. We can track the various parts of the truck, and most are local.'

'Turn that over to the locals for now. Oklahoma takes priority. I'll get back to you.'

She pushed the 'link into her pocket. 'Thanks,' she said to the room at large.

'Data's already on your comps,' Roarke told her. 'I'll have the van narrowed down shortly.'

'Good. Let's move.'

Banner followed her out the door. 'Right in your house. You got all those juicy toys right in your house.'

'We work here, too.'

'You're telling me? Never seen such fast e-work. Might be we got something solid with this.'

'Feeney will tag the other four, but let's do a run on Barlow Lee Hanks and see what we get.'

She strode back into her office, gestured to Peabody. 'Barlow's Garage, Lonesome, Oklahoma. Basic data and financials. Make it fast. Banner, tag them up over there, see if you can get this guy on the 'link. If he's there, he's sure as hell not here. That's one. And just get a sense of him. Don't play cop. Ask him some truck question.'

'A truck question?'

'Five hundred says you've got one.'

'I'm not taking that bet.' Banner pulled out his own 'link. 'I'll take this out there.'

With a nod, Eve sat at her desk, started her run on Barlow Hanks.

One marriage, she read – with no offspring. Divorced for a dozen years. One brother, but older than he was, and the unsubs skewed younger. A nephew about the right age, she considered, so she'd do a secondary run there.

'Financials look solid, Dallas,' Peabody said, 'on the surface anyway. He's not rolling in it, but he does okay. Bought the property the place sits on about eight years ago, and he's making the payments regularly. Four full-time employees, one part-time.'

Eve nodded as she continued her own run. 'A couple minor league criminal bumps. A DUI, a bar fight, a pushy-shovy at some rodeo.'

'This isn't our guy.'

'No, but he may be connected. Better than one-in-five chance it was his truck the Dumbass Dorrans hauled off.'

She started on the nephew. Small-time rancher, sometime bronc rider. What the hell was a 'bronc'? She discovered it was some sort of horse, kept going. About the right age, she thought, with a cohab, which tipped him down the scale as she appeared to be clean and shiny on record, with solid employment.

'Could've ditched her,' Eve added. 'Taken off in his uncle's truck with his murderous partner.'

She rose to pace and think. The uncle doesn't report the truck stolen – blood's thick. Or he sold it to the nephew under the table.

But it didn't play well, not when there was nothing to indicate the nephew suddenly developed murderous tendencies.

Still.

Banner came back in. 'Hanks is definitely in Oklahoma. I just had a conversation with him about my truck – which I told him was a '52 Bobcat.'

'Good thinking.'

'Mine's running mighty rough, and I've taken it in twice to my regular, but it only smooths out for a hundred miles or so. Told him I'd heard he knew a thing or two. He agreed that he did, and had a '52 himself once upon a time, done some work on it.'

'Is that so?'

'It is so. His opinion while not a piece of cowshit, it ain't much after it hits ninety thousand miles or thereabouts. But he'd be happy to take a look at her if I want to bring her by.'

'Okay.' She turned to her board, nodded. 'Okay. We'll see what Carmichael and Santiago get out of him. It feels right. Meanwhile.'

Her desk 'link signaled. She walked over. 'What?'

'Say thank you,' Roarke requested.

'What for?'

'For Elsie and Maddox Hornesby of Bloomingdale who own a '58 Country Scout van, color Indigo, with an OBX sticker in the left rear window.'

'Why them and not the eighty-two others?'

'I culled that down to thirty-nine, then hit the Hornesbys who, from my subtle invasion of their privacy, I determined have spent eight weeks – January and February – the last three winters in the Bahamas where they own a beach house.'

'Can't report the vehicle stolen if they don't know it's stolen.'

'That would be my thought. A ... brief glance at their financials indicate they drive themselves to the Newark transpo center, use long-term parking. I've heard boosting a vehicle from long-term parking is a very handy way to acquire one.'

'I bet you have.'

He smiled at her, in just that way. 'Their contact information is on your comp.'

'You earned a thank-you. I have to move on this.'

'You're welcome.'

'Peabody,' Eve began as she cut Roarke off.

'Ahead of you. Contacting transpo security at Newark.'

Since the data was there, as promised, Eve used her desk 'link. She didn't try to figure what time it might be in the Bahamas, and didn't care.

'Maddox Hornesby.'

Eve looked at the tanned, relaxed face, the short stream of sun-streaked hair. 'Mr Hornesby, I'm Lieutenant Dallas, with the New York City Police and Security Department.'

'So I see. What can I do for you?'

'You own a Country Scout van, '58 model year.'

'That's right.' The relaxed smile faded as his eyebrows drew together. She heard a woman's voice – *'Mad! You promised no business!'*

'It's not. Is there a problem, Lieutenant?'

'Can you give me the location of your vehicle?'

'Long-term parking, Deck A, slot 45, Newark Transportation. What is this about?'

Eve turned to Peabody, who nodded.

'What is your current location?'

'I'm sitting on my deck in the Bahamas with my wife who just handed me a mimosa and thinks I'm talking to our broker. What's going on?'

'We had an incident with a vehicle that matches yours. Do you have an OBX sticker on the—'

'Left rear window, bottom corner. What kind of incident?'

'We're checking on that, Mr Hornesby, and contacting security at the transportation center. Either they or I will contact you if necessary.' She couldn't help it. 'Could you tell me what time it is there?'

'Time? It's . . . it's eight-forty-five.'

'In the morning?'

'Of course in the morning.'

Eve said, 'Huh,' fascinated and a little irritated there was no time difference.

'Did someone steal our old van?'

'We're looking into that, Mr Hornesby.'

'Mad, didn't I tell you that was bound to happen? How many times did I tell you we should take a limo to the airport?'

'All right, Elsie, all right.'

'I'm sorry, sir, but I'd like to know when you parked your vehicle.'

'January four, at eight a.m.'

'Thank you, you've been very helpful. Someone will contact you with more details.'

'Do we need to come back?'

'No, there's no need to interrupt your vacation. Thank you.'

She clicked off as the female voice began to rag on Hornesby again.

'We got the vehicle. Peabody, APB – now. If sighted, do not approach. Contact me, do not approach, follow only at a distance.'

She pushed up. 'How come the Bahamas gets to have the same time we do? It doesn't seem right.'

And setting that puzzle aside, she went for another hit of coffee.

Things were breaking.

16

Eve started a deeper run on the nephew while Peabody confirmed the all-points on the stolen van.

'Banner, Hanks has a nephew, Hanks, Curtis Monroe, age twenty-eight, rancher. Sending his contact to your PPC now. Play the good-old boy again. Confirm his whereabouts, get a feel for him. He doesn't play for me, but let's nail him down.'

'Got it. What's he drive?'

'Drive?'

'Say we had a hit-and-run in Silby's Pond, and his vehicle matches the description.'

'Okay, I got that. It's a ... '56 Toro pickup, forest-green exterior, OK plate 572 Echo-Papa-Alpha. Second vehicle, motorcycle, '60 Hawker Midnight Rider, color gunmetal, personalized OK plate: BOOM. That's Beta, Omega—'

'Got it. I'll go with the cycle.'

When he walked out, Eve rose to update her board. 'Peabody, write up where we are – all the details – send an update to Whitney, Mira, Carmichael and Santiago. Fold in Baxter and Trueheart, too. If they're clear, I want them starting on Banner's list of shops and restaurants.'

'Trueheart's got the exam today. He'd be starting in about an hour.'

'Right.' Shit. Shit, fuck, damn. 'Right. Okay, fold in Baxter. He and Banner can work the sector together with the best image McNab can pull out of the vid feed. Let Baxter know we'll be at Central with Banner within the hour.'

She studied the board as she added data, shifted data.

Hanks = truck dumped by unsubs at Jansen kill site.

That took the unsubs back to Oklahoma. And damn it, it connected them, somehow, with Hanks. Why didn't he report a theft, if there had been one? More likely he sold, under the table, or lent the truck.

Selling more likely as who lends a truck to anybody for months?

But the damn thing was still registered in his name. Wouldn't he have fixed that for a sale?

She studied the nephew's photo again. Just didn't feel right. But if there was a nephew, there might be cousins, uncles, aunts, whatever. Good buddies, or just someone he owed a major solid to.

Younger, she thought as she circled the board. Not a contemporary. Someone young enough to be his son or daughter.

Girlfriend? Maybe he went for the young ones, and she'd

sexed him into giving her the truck. Or maybe he had a girl-friend with a son or daughter who—

'Nephew Hanks is on the ranch,' Banner announced. 'Seemed like a nice guy, and upstanding come to that. Got upset about the hit-and-run, wanted to know if anybody was hurt. Cooperated straight down. I gave him the night Campbell was snatched, and he says he had a poker party that night, went till about one in the morning. Gave me a dozen names to verify, and said I could come on out and test his cycle.'

'Cross him off. We're not going to move much there until my people grill Hanks.' Not move there, she thought, but time to move in other directions. 'Wrap it up, Peabody. We're heading downtown. Banner, I'm going to hook you up with Detective Baxter. You can start canvassing those shops and restaurants on your list with the best image we have of the male unsub. You add in the couple, the age range profiled, the accent. Maybe we hit. When we get their names, faces – and we damn well will – we'll send them to you.'

'Ready when you are, Lieutenant.'

'Meet you downstairs. I'm going to go by the comp lab first.'

She found her three favorite geeks in a huddle, with one screen running face recognition, another working on enhancing the loading-dock feed.

Roarke turned to her first. 'The feed's complete rubbish.

We can push at it for hours, but we're just not going to do much better. You can't enhance what isn't there.'

'I'll take what you've got. McNab, send it to Banner, to Baxter. Might as well make the sweep and send it to all parties. Hanks is the link, and we'll pull the data out of him one way or the other. I'm going in.'

'You want my take?' Feeney asked her.

'Yeah, I do.'

'Your guy here?' He gestured to the screen and the grainy shadow of an image. 'He hasn't seen thirty yet, or if he has, he's barely had a glimpse. We figure he's about six feet, maybe six-one, lean with it. Coat adds some bulk, but not much. He wanted to be able to move fast. He's white. Low probability on mixed race from what we can figure.'

'That's more for Baxter and Banner. How about her?'

'She's clearer as she was the bait for the boy,' Roarke said, rocking on his heels now as he studied what they had of the female. 'We've calculated her height at five-five, her weight between one-twenty and one-thirty. She's got a good set of legs there. We get the hair – though it may be a wig – long and blond. Again we'd play odds on white for race, and her age? Given the body, as we don't have a clear view of the face, the analysis of her voice from what we had, most likely between twenty-five and thirty.

'I did run her voice on a dialect program as well,' he added. 'It pegs her as northwestern Oklahoma.'

'Okay, it's all more than we had, and we'll get more.' For

a moment longer she stared at the image as if she could bring it clear through sheer force of will. 'Crack's widening. Feeney, do you need a lift to Central?'

'I've got my ride. Do you want the boy?'

'I'll take him if you can spare him.'

'Take him. Tag me if you need more.' He flicked a finger salute at Roarke. 'Nice working with you.'

'And you. I'll run with this for another thirty, then I'll leave it open if you want to send more data by remote.'

'Appreciate that.' Just how much would he juggle today? she wondered – then set the idea aside as it was more than she could imagine. 'Head down, McNab. Peabody and Banner are doing the same.'

'On the way. Fun toys,' he said to Roarke, and walked out with Feeney.

Eve stuck her hands in her pockets. 'As soon as this one closes, I'll be the only cop in the house for a while.'

Roarke stepped to her, laid his hands on her shoulders. 'I like your cops.' Kissed her lightly. 'I believe I like Banner now that I've had a bit of a chance to know him. Speaking of cops, Feeney's coat's done. Summerset has it downstairs. Knowing the both of you, I assumed you wouldn't want to give it to him in company.'

'No.' Gifts were sticky enough, in her opinion. 'Anyway, you should give it to him.'

Understanding her well, Roarke gave her shoulders a squeeze. 'It was your idea, and a fine one. And he was your cop first. The two of you will survive a gift. Go on now, and mind your step out there. I definitely want a cop in my bed tonight.'

'I bet that's something you never thought you'd say.' This time she kissed him. 'Thanks for the assist. I'll keep you in the loop if you want.'

'I want.'

'Done,' she said and strode out.

He watched her go and, fingering the gray button he carried always in his pocket, turned back to the screens to do what he could in the time he had.

She jogged down, found all her cops still in a gaggle. As she grabbed her coat off the newel post, Summerset slid into view – like smoke – with a box wrapped in plain brown paper. Before she could evade, he pushed it into her hands.

'As requested.'

Not now, she wanted to say, but the box had already caught Peabody's interest.

'Whatcha got?'

'It's just a thing.' She muttered it, couldn't figure how to avoid the presentation. Get it over with, she decided, and gave Summerset the fish-eye. 'Vehicles out front?'

'Of course.'

She narrowed the fish-eye until he glided – like more smoke – away.

'Go pile in,' she told the rest. 'Feeney, give me a minute?'

Banner unfolded himself from his crouch, giving Galahad one last stroke along the way. Peabody nearly turned her head

303

in a one-eighty to keep Eve and the box in view as they went out the door.

'It's a thing,' Eve repeated, and pushed the box at Feeney. 'For you.'

His hands went directly into his pockets; his face fell into wary lines. 'Why?'

She often thought the same when it came to gifts, so only shrugged. 'Just a . . . you know,' she mumbled, and shoved it at him.

He looked puzzled, mildly embarrassed, but ripped the paper away. Wanting to keep it moving, she snagged the paper from him, balled it up, and tossed it on the closest table. Then got busy putting on her coat.

'Well, fuck me sideways.'

The stunned pleasure in his voice gave twin tugs – that mild embarrassment, and quick satisfaction. She turned back, pulling the scarf out of her pocket when he dumped the box on the floor, pulled out the coat.

'Son of a bitch!'

He grinned as he held it up. Shit-brown – she'd chosen the color as it was his usual choice of hue – the coat with its protective lining would, she saw, hit him about mid-thigh.

She'd left the design to Roarke, saw he'd gone roomy, simple, and had added the flash of captain's bars as buttons.

'You got me a goddamn magic coat.'

'Well, Roarke—'

'Son of a bitch.' Still grinning, he punched her in the

shoulder, then immediately pulled off his old shit-brown coat, dumped it on the floor.

'Bastard fits, too.' He folded it back, studied the lining with a shake of his head. 'Freaking genius is what it is.'

More comfortable discussing the body armor aspect, she relaxed a bit. 'No bulk, no weight, and it works. Deflects a full stun – I can attest. Sharps, too, though I haven't personally tested that one.'

'Son of a bitch,' he said for a third time, and met her eyes. His ears had gone faintly pink. ''Preciate it.'

'Sure.'

He bent to gather up his old coat, the box, and looked at her again. 'Really appreciate it.'

'Really sure.'

'Wait till the wife gets a load of this.' He skimmed one hand down the leather. 'Let's go get some bad guys, kid.'

'It's what we do.'

They walked out. She heard him murmur 'son of a bitch' yet again as they peeled off to their separate vehicles.

The instant she was in the car, Peabody leaned forward from the backseat she shared with McNab. 'Is that a magic coat? Did you get Feeney a magic coat? Awww!'

'What's a magic coat?' Banner demanded. 'What kind of magic?'

'It's totally frosted. See?' Peabody opened her pink coat to show off the lining. With some relief Eve let them ramble about body armor while she drove.

McNab slid up, spoke quietly near Eve's ear. 'That would've meant a lot to him, coming from you.'

He touched her shoulder lightly, then slid back. Either knowing she'd welcome a distraction or because he was greedy, he lifted his voice again.

'Who wants hot chocolate?'

And that took care of that.

She dumped Banner and McNab at Central, waited for Peabody to switch to the front seat for the trip to the lab.

On the way, she took a tag from Santiago.

'We're at the garage now, but Hanks is out on a service call. Due back in a few. We took a little poke at his head mechanic, but he's tight-lipped. We can poke at a couple of the others – the woman he's got running the service counter's got the wide eyes. She'd spill.'

'If he's not back in a few, poke. Otherwise, keep it all easy.'

'No hits on the APB?'

'Not yet. I'll let you know. Get me a name, Santiago. One name.'

'Working on it. He's rolling in now. Back at you.'

'You can feel it falling,' Peabody said, 'piece by piece.'

'There are two people it can't fall fast enough for.'

She'd do whatever she could to speed it up, she thought as she moved quickly through the warren of the lab to DeWinter's level.

Eve found the three doctors, all in lab coats. DeWinter's

was a metallic bronze that nearly matched her hair. She'd gone with ruler-straight, slicked back to leave her arresting face unframed.

Like Mira, she wore boots with scalpel-thin heels, hers in a deep green. Eve saw it matched the body-hugging dress under the lab coat.

DeWinter must have a hundred of them, Eve thought – dresses and lab coats.

Morris had chosen slate-gray over a suit of the same hue, and a single braid coiled up in poppy-red cord. And Mira had the traditional white over a suit as quietly blue as her eyes.

They made an interesting triad, Eve thought, standing around the white bones of the dead.

'Pretty clean,' Eve commented.

'The remains were in advanced decomp,' DeWinter began. 'Morris worked with what flesh there was.'

'We ran reconstructions, of course,' he told Eve, before his colleague could recount chapter and verse. 'And a number of tests you don't want to hear about. We're overruling the previous findings. The victim didn't die in a fall. There was evidence of torture.'

'A thorough autopsy, a comprehensive one, should never have concluded accidental death.' DeWinter's tone sharpened, as did the contempt in her eyes. 'There are injuries obviously caused by implements, tools – several fingers were crushed – blunt force. A hammer, most probably. If you find the weapon I could match it. I *would* match it,' she corrected.

'There was also dehydration,' Mira put in. 'We estimate the victim went at least thirty-six hours without water prior to death. If, indeed, he had suffered these injuries in a fall, he would have died instantly, not survived for more than a day.'

'Okay, that's what I needed to hear.' She looked down again, at what remained of Little Mel. Justice would come, she thought. 'What about the other one?'

'I've just started on tests, in the next room. Dr Mira and I have already concluded a visual exam, and begun preliminary testing.' He glanced at Mira.

'It's too soon to give you firm results and conclusions, but we both feel we'll have a similar story to tell you.'

Thinking it through, Eve circled the table, the remains of Melvin Little, war vet, lost soul. Harmless.

'Here's how I want to handle this. I'm going to wait until you have solid conclusions, until you put it all down, detail by minute detail, before I notify the feds. Right now, you're reassessing, testing, examining, and if we even hint where this is going, the feds might be inclined to zip in and take over after they red tape it to death. The red taping may impede us, so we'll just red tape it first.'

She glanced up, saw Morris with a slight smile, DeWinter with a more pronounced frown. 'I'd be fine with them taking it over if it would speed this up, help us find the two people who are going through what this one went through. But it won't. Objections?'

Mira folded her hands in a gesture that drew Eve's attention. 'The nature of the beast is bureaucracy, so I have to agree adding another agency to this mix would tend to slow down progress. But once conclusions are reached, conclusions that will stand in court, you must.'

'And I will. I won't hold back. This isn't about credit, the collar. It's about making sure when we get these bastards we've got everything we need to put them away for the rest of their fucked-up lives. Agreed?'

'I'd like to finish what we've started without pausing to fill out countless forms,' Morris said. 'Agreed.'

When DeWinter hesitated, frowned down at the bones, Eve tilted her head. 'You stole a dog.'

'Damn it, you'll never let that one go. Agreed, but we follow the rules, point-by-point.'

'Do that. And keep me updated. And remember this. The feds have nobody who can match the three of you. So, the ones we couldn't save help you. And I'll do whatever it takes to save the two who still can be. Together, we'll put these sick assholes away.'

'Meanwhile,' Mira began, 'I've reviewed your report. I agree it's possible they escalated to two. That both Campbell and Mulligan are alive. It's a progression. However, I can't tell you that's foregone. The longer we go without finding Campbell's body, the better the chances. I don't see them changing pattern and concealing or attempting to conceal the body, if there is one, as there's no discernable motive to do so.'

'Then I'm banking on both of them being alive, until we know different.'

When she started out, Peabody lengthened her stride to keep up. 'What are you going to tell Whitney?'

'Everything. If he tells me to bring in the feds, I bring them in. But I think he's going to see this part of it my way. They can't do any more than Mira, Morris and DeWinter on the remains – especially since they already signed off there. On the active hunt, I'll send the agent in charge everything we have. The truck, the van, the conclusions regarding those we've eliminated. I'll take whatever I can get for Campbell and Mulligan.'

'Okay. I'm all in.'

She decided to save time and contacted Whitney as she drove. He listened, said little, until she'd finished.

'Detective Peabody didn't copy the FBI on her update this morning.'

'No, sir, I gave her the list to inform. I wanted you to see the progress first.'

'Where are Santiago and Carmichael in this interview with Hanks?'

'It's going on now, sir. They haven't contacted me with results as yet.'

'Let me know when they do. Whatever those results may be, I'll inform the FBI of your progress to date. As for the ongoing lab work, they dismissed those victims from the investigation. On that, they can wait.'

310

Satisfied, Eve pulled into her slot at Central. 'Thank you, sir. Heading up to Homicide now. If I don't hear from Oklahoma in the next ten, I'll contact Carmichael.'

She got out of the car, moved fast to the elevator. 'Let's keep the momentum going. Get a couple of uniforms to coordinate with Banner. He can give them part of the list. Let's cover what we can cover. Sometimes you get lucky.'

As she stepped into the elevator, her 'link signaled.

'Give me something, Santiago.'

'How about a name, boss? Darryl Roy James.'

'Peabody.'

'Running it now, sir.'

'Who is he?'

'Hanks's woman's son. No cohab on record because he didn't want to go that route, but they've been together for about ten years. Darryl worked for him at the garage. Good mechanic, lazy asshole – or that's Hanks's opinion. Took off when he was about sixteen, landed in Texas. Did time in juvie in there – boosting rides – came back home, went to work for Hanks. In July 2057, he took off again, this time in the '52 Bobcat he stole from the garage, about six thousand in cash, tools, an antique bowie knife and so on. His mother begged Hanks not to report it, so he didn't to keep the peace.

'James did another stint in the Oklahoma State Pen. Four years for attempted robbery, armed – he had the bowie knife on him when he tried to shoplift a diamond engagement ring.'

'For the woman. True freaking love.'

'Maybe. Got busted in December of '57, got out early August of this past year. Time off, good behavior.'

'Timing works. Do they know his whereabouts?'

The elevator doors opened; a trio of uniforms started to board.

Eve snarled, laid her hand on her stunner.

They backed out again.

'He says no, and I believe him. No love lost there, LT. He took the loss on the truck and the tools for his woman, but when we said the *M* word, he spewed like a geyser. Carmichael's talking to the mother now, but it doesn't look like she knows anything much. She claims she hasn't spoken to him since midsummer, right before he got out, and it rings true. But she did say something about a woman before she got hysterical. No name, just he'd hooked up with some woman somewhere, and it was all her fault – according to the mother.'

Santiago managed an eye roll and a smirk at the same time. 'Carmichael's working it.'

'Get me her name, get all you can, then get home.'

'I'm so ready for that. Yippee-ki-freaking-yay.'

'Peabody,' Eve said as she clicked off, and stepping out this time when the doors opened and other cops piled on.

'James, Darryl Roy, age twenty-five, single, one offspring.'

Eve's head snapped around to her partner. 'Offspring?'

'He's listed as the father of a baby, Darra Louise James,

312

born in April of last year. The mother is listed as Ella-Loo Parsens, age twenty-six.'

'That's going to be her. That's got to be.' Revved, Eve jogged her way up the glides. 'How the hell are they doing all this with a baby in tow?'

'Jeez, poor baby. Not even a year old.'

Eve yanked out her 'link again, contacted Carmichael. 'Ask the mother if she knows about a baby. Does she know she's a grandmother?'

'Holy hell. I'm betting no. Hang loose a minute.'

Eve waited, pushing her way up to Homicide. When Carmichael came back on, Eve could hear the wailing from Oklahoma.

'She didn't know. I'm going to calm her down again, Dallas, but she didn't know about a kid, she doesn't know the woman's name. She only knows Darryl told her he was in love – had met his soul mate. Called her his Juliet, but he was into the Shakespeare thing, star-crossed lovers, Romeo, and all that. This was during visitation in prison.'

'Settle her down, work her some more. You and Santiago hang there until I get back to you. You may be out there a little longer.'

'Then I'm buying some damn cowboy boots.'

'If you buy pink ones, I'll hurt you, Carmichael. Work the mother. She may know more than she thinks she knows. Peabody.'

Peabody read off her PPC. 'Parsens, Ella-Loo, born Elk

City, Oklahoma. Couple of pops for possession, low-rent stuff. No marriages, no cohabs on record. Lots of short employment history, with the last one picking up in January of '58 through last August – her longest on record. A bar called Ringo's, McAlester, Oklahoma. That's where the prison is, Dallas. The Oklahoma pen.'

'Wanted to be near her man, waited for him. Close to four years – that's devoted. Go back over the employment.'

'The next is short-term. March to July, 2057, the Rope 'N Ride, Dry Creek, Oklahoma.'

'And Darryl boosted Hanks's truck, stole the cash, the tools, the knife in July, set out from there, and you bet your ass into the Rope 'N Ride in Dry Creek.'

She stepped into Homicide, held a hand up to stop anyone from asking her anything, and tagged Santiago again.

'NYPSD West,' he answered.

'Ha. Wrap it up there, asap, and head to someplace called Dry Creek.'

'Ah, man.'

'A bar called the Rope 'N Ride. Show the photos, Santiago. Get everything you can get on Ella-Loo Parsens – she worked there – and James. From there, it's Elk City and Parsens's mother.'

'Janelyn,' Peabody provided when Eve turned to her.

'Janelyn. Peabody'll send you the data. Last stop, as of now, is McAlester. Talk to the warden at the prison, and check out a bar called Ringo's where Parsens worked while James was in a cage. See who knows what. I'm going to bag these two, Santiago, and what you and Carmichael pull out of Oklahoma's going to sew them up tight.'

'Light a candle for me, LT.'

'What?'

'I lost a bet with Carmichael, and she gets to drive. The speeds you can get up to out here? She's pretty damn scary.'

'But you'll get there fast. I know when you know, Santiago. It's busting wide now.'

'We'll bang the hammer here. NYPSD West, out.'

'Peabody, get them all the data they'll need. Anybody has anything for me that can't wait, say it now,' she told the room at large. 'Otherwise, I need ten.'

She gave it five seconds, turned and went into her office. Shut the door. After tossing her coat aside, sat down and wrote everything up.

Updated her board with all the fresh data.

Sat down again, put her feet on the desk, and let herself think.

A guy walks into a bar, she thought, only there was no lame punch line to this one.

Something sparks between these two – two people, aim-less, low-rent as Peabody said. Without that meet, without that spark, maybe they just stay low-rent and aimless. But that spark lit up something vicious inside them.

They like the vicious, she concluded, it's part of what binds them together.

Eve studied the board where she now had Darryl and Ella-Loo front and center.

She's the smart one, Eve decided. As far as smarts went. He's the romantic. Gets busted for trying to cop a traditional engagement ring.

'I bet you found that stupid but touching, right, Ella-Loo? He did that on his own, a surprise for you. But you got yourself another crap job and waited for him. Three and a half years, that's love, of its kind. That's devotion. Must've gotten knocked up on a conjugal. Another tie that binds? I bet you timed that one, too.'

She rose, paced.

How the hell were they traveling, abducting, torturing and killing with a baby to deal with? Ditch the kid? Couldn't just dump it on a doorstep – why have one if you're going to toss it to fate or strangers?

She circled around that, wondered if Ella-Loo subscribed to the Stella school of motherhood. You have a kid because it may be useful or profitable, and keeps your man locked to you.

Then she let it slide away as she couldn't see how it applied, for now, to the investigation.

Wait for your man. Head east when he's sprung. In the same truck he boosted from Hanks. A truck that's showing its age now, and Darryl hasn't been able to maintain it in those three and a half years.

Does what he can when he gets out, but it gives up on that quiet road over the Arkansas border.

And that's where it really began, she thought. That's when the spark went off like a rocket.

'I know you now,' she murmured. 'We'll get more, but I know you. And I'm going to find you.'

Soon, she thought, it had to be soon, or it would be too late to save Jayla Campbell.

17

She'd lost track of time again. The pain, beyond imagining, woke her. But the ferocity of it radiating everywhere let her know she was still alive.

Jayla Campbell, she thought, fighting through the haze of pain. I'm Jayla Campbell, and I'm alive.

She turned her head, very slowly, as even that had agony raging. They hadn't hurt him again – Mulligan, Reed Mulligan. When they'd found him unconscious on the floor, they'd hauled him back onto the makeshift table. They'd treated his broken wrist with some ice, even given him some sort of meds.

He had to be strong enough, she'd heard them say, to rape her again.

They'd discussed it, giggling over some of the details. They'd ease back on hurting him – for now, and maybe up the dose of Erotica so he'd last longer.

They'd given her something that made her nauseated and weak, but she'd heard them discussing her as if she were an animal.

She stank, in Ella-Loo's opinion, and needed to be cleaned up if they were going to keep her for another day or two.

She tried to fight when Darryl hauled her up. The pain rose up in a hot flood, took her just under the surface, but she tried to fight. Tried not to weep when she heard them laughing at her.

They weren't human. The drugs, dehydration, shock had her seeing them as monsters, demons with red eyes and flicking tongues. The gag choked her screams as they dropped her into a tub of water so hot it scalded.

Someone pushed her head under; someone pulled it up again by the hair. Again and again while she swallowed water, gagged, and finally prayed for it just to end.

She woke on the table again, naked, shivering with cold and drowning in the pain.

And listened to the quiet.

'I think they're asleep.'

This time when she turned her head, Mulligan's eyes were open and on her.

'They tried to wake you up, but you wouldn't come around enough, so they went out for a while. I don't know how long. They gave me something, I kept passing out. And then I heard them laughing and having sex. Then it got quiet. I think they're asleep.'

She tried to lick her dry lips, but it was like sand against sand. 'You don't know how long?'

'I don't know. They gave me something. I just don't know.

I'm sorry. I'm sorry I couldn't get to the knife. I tried again, to get loose and get it, but I couldn't.'

She'd nearly forgotten. That moment of hope felt like weeks had passed. 'Your hand.'

'It doesn't hurt as much. If I can get loose again, I might be able to get something.'

'They're not going to hurt you, or not as much. They want you strong enough to rape me again.'

He shut his eyes. 'God. Oh God. I don't want to—'

'It doesn't matter. I told you it doesn't matter. But more, I heard them. They cleaned me up because they want to keep me alive for a couple days more, so you can rape me. They get off on it. I want to stay alive, so you have to do whatever they tell you to do to me. But I'm going to scream and try to struggle. I'm going to make them think it matters. You'll know it doesn't. They'll keep us alive as long as they get off.'

A light came into his eyes, fierce and dark against the pallor and bruising. 'I want to kill them.'

'Maybe you will.' There was a glimmer of hope in that ugly wish. 'Make them think you're weak and scared.'

'Jesus, I am weak and scared.'

'Not as much as they think. And next time you'll get the knife.'

'Next time,' he said. 'Do you have somebody? I mean, are you with somebody?'

'Not now.' She thought of Mattio. He seemed like another

lifetime. She thought of Luke, and that was a comfort. Just a little comfort.

'But there's this guy I should've paid more attention to. I wish I had. I want to have a chance to pay attention. He lives across the hall from me. Do you have somebody?'

'Not now,' he said and tried to smile. 'But there's this girl. I'm crazy for her, but I haven't had the guts to make the move. I want a chance to try.'

Tears burned at her eyes. Hope hurt. 'We're going to go on a double date, right? Deal?'

'Yeah. Deal. They're looking for us. Our friends, our family. The cops. They have to be.'

'Yeah, they're looking for us. We're going to do whatever it takes to stay alive until they find us. Double date,' she said, and closed her eyes.

When her time was up, Eve went back into the bull pen.

'I'm open.'

'Two minutes, Lieutenant.' Jenkinson pushed away from his desk, went to her. Today's neckwear sported long-eared white rabbits with orange carrots on a purple background.

'Where are you getting those?' she demanded.

'You'd be surprised how easy it is. We caught one this morning.' He ran it through briefly. A bludgeoning, the lead from a CI they only half trusted and a seedy pool hall in Chinatown.

'Snitch says the guy we want frequents that establishment,

but we go in asking about him, they're going to clam it or cover him. And we get a feeling the snitch is maybe playing both ends on this. We figure we'll go in, soft clothes, play some pool, see what's what.'

'Do it, but don't wear that tie. Do you know where to find the CI?'

'Oh yeah, he's easy to find.'

'Send a couple uniforms out, have him picked up on anything they can make stick for a few hours. Keep him inside while you play pool.'

'Nice. On it. Santiago and Carmichael still fishing in Oklahoma?'

'They've caught a few. They should be on their way back in a few hours.'

'We could use them. Got two new and open right now.'

She glanced at the main board, shoved her hand through her hair. So many. There were always so many.

'I can pull Baxter back.'

'Ah hell, Dallas, that man's like an expectant father with his boy in exam. He's better off where he is. We got it here. I figure the kid's good for it. You?'

'We'll know soon enough. Go play some pool. Peabody, I'm going to work the maps again. Jenkinson and Reineke are working a bludgeoning. Take a look at what else is new and open, see what you can put together, then pass it off to Baxter when he and Banner get back.'

'You want me to pull off our investigation?'

'Juggle, Peabody. And throw these new balls in the air. The APB on the van's out, we've got detectives looking into backgrounds and timelines out west, Baxter and our guest cop wearing out shoe leather here. We've got names, faces. I'm going to try to narrow the location. Unless you start going door-to-door in that sector, and it damn well may come to it, there's nothing we can do for Campbell and Mulligan until the next crack widens.'

She pointed to the banner over the break-room door.

NO MATTER YOUR RACE, CREED, SEXUAL ORIENTATION OR POLITICAL AFFILIATION, WE PROTECT AND SERVE. BECAUSE YOU COULD GET DEAD.

'That goes for everybody, all the time. Do what you can, pass to Baxter, and maybe he puts a bad guy away before the day's over.'

She went back to her office, scrubbed her hands over her face. Then brought the map on screen.

And began to calculate.

A half hour later, she'd refined the area of interest, considered focusing the APB there. But if she was wrong, off by even a block, it could cost lives.

Instead she boosted the search to parking garages. Maybe they kept the van off the street, at least when they weren't hunting. Having cops cruise through garages, parking lots, undergrounds might net them the vehicle.

323

And that was one step closer to Parsens and James.

She flipped to the 'link when it signaled incoming from Santiago.

'Give me something good.'

'How about a bouncing baby girl?'

'She dumped the kid on her mother.'

'Oh yeah. Mother hadn't seen or heard from her in nearly a year, and she shows up, baby in tow, last June. Spun a story about falling for some guy, thinking they were going to get married, then he took off when she got knocked up, left her flat and with two black eyes. Lots of drama.'

'Yeah, she's the smart one,' Eve mused.

'Claimed she realized how she needed family, how little Darra deserved a good start. Maybe she'd go back to school, get a good job, if they'd let them stay – that's the mother and stepfather.'

'She knows what tune to play.'

'Played it like a virtuoso. Less than two weeks in, she's gone, so are valuables and cash, and the baby's still here. Not a word since, and they're not covering, Dallas. They're both scared we're going to take the baby from them. They talked to a lawyer just last week, trying to see if they could legally adopt so the daughter can't come back and take the kid. They're nice people, doing the best they know how.

'And FYI? Ella-Loo was driving the Bobcat.'

'Did she have any friends there, anybody she might've told the truth to?'

'Carmichael's getting that data. The mother doesn't think there's anyone Ella-Loo hadn't pissed off before she left the first time around, but we'll make some contacts before we head out to the next stop.'

'Who's driving?'

His face went grim. 'Just let me warn you. Don't do bets with Carmichael. You might as well draw to an inside straight.'

'I'll keep that in mind. Just to play it safe, talk to the locals, see about getting access to their 'links in case the daughter's contacted them.'

'They already offered, but we'll breeze by the local badges, see what we can suss out.'

'Good work. Keep it moving. Tag me from the next stop.'

She'd barely clicked off when she got an incoming from Baxter.

'We got two hits, boss, bang-bang. Nothing, nothing, nothing, then two. Pawnshop and pizza joint, both on Hudson. Pawnshop between West Houston and King, pizzeria between Charlton and Vandam.'

Her attention went straight to the map. 'Fucking A.'

'After some friendly persuasion, the pawnshop ID'd James. He was in twice last week. Pizza place nailed both of them. Takeout, two visits. We're going to try this Chinese place, and there's a souvenir shop one block over.'

'Do that. I'm sending some uniforms to canvass, try some of the residences, the other businesses. If they spent time

325

walking around that area, we can narrow the field. This is good, Baxter. What did they pawn?'

'A wrist unit, sports model, and a second, dress type. Decent ones, both men's styles. A tablet – wiped clean – a keyboard, musical type, an entertainment screen, an antique vase, a silver Saint Christopher's medal. Nothing shows up on stolen.'

'Bring the tablet in. EDD will see how wiped is wiped. Send me pictures and descriptions of all. I'll check them against the vics. Did James go into the pawnshop and the pizza joint the same days?'

'First time, yeah, but about six hours apart, from what we're getting. Second time, different days.'

'Okay. Keep me in.'

'You bet. Ah, hey, I haven't heard anything from Trueheart. Have you—'

'It's too soon. Focus.'

She cut him off, went back to the map.

She recalculated, using the two hits. You go for takeaway, she thought, you go close to home. If you were driving, it didn't matter so much, but . . .

Too much time between visits on the first hits. Six hours? No, he drove to the pawnshop, possibly, but then they went back to the same area to pick up food. And back again, same area twice more.

Because it was easy and quick.

She cut six blocks north and three blocks east off her map,

let that stew while she pulled up the data Baxter sent and ran it with anything reported missing from the victims.

Tablet, she noted, wrist units – but nothing matching the pawned wrist units.

'You hit somebody in New York for this stuff.'

She shoved up, paced. None of it reported stolen – and that led her to whoever they stole it from was dead.

But not discovered. Not discovered because when the cops had a DB they checked out the DB's place of residence.

And that's where James and Parsens were living. That's what played out.

She turned back to the map. 'Getting closer, you fuckers. Getting closer every minute.'

She went to the door, shouted, 'Peabody,' then went back to the map as if she could pinpoint the location by will alone.

'Sir!'

'We're narrowing the area. Baxter and Banner have a couple hits. I'm going to have some black-and-whites cruise the target area for the van. The baby is with Parsens's mother.'

'Thank God. I had this image of her just, I don't know, tossing it out of the truck window or something.'

'She had it for a reason,' Eve said, 'and played the mother with the rehabilitating-myself-for-the-sake-of-my-tiny-baby routine, gave it a few days, stole what she could use or sell, walked out, leaving said tiny baby. That well may be dry now, but Carmichael and Santiago will pump it a little more before heading to the bar, then the prison.

'I'm heading out shortly.'

'I've got some angles for Baxter on the opens.'

'Work them,' Eve said. 'Take one, you're primary.'

'But—'

Eve cut off the protest with a look. 'We're short here, Peabody. I need you to take one, work it. Send me updates and notes, and I'll work with you. If something else pops loose on this, I'll pull you in, but right now it's steps and stages, calculations and incoming data. I'll be tagging the agent in charge soon.'

'You gotta?'

'I gotta. If I'm not here when Banner gets back, you haul him to my place. We can work there tonight if we don't have this locked.'

'Okay.' Peabody let out a breath. 'Okay, I'll take one of the opens, pass the other to Baxter when he comes in. How do I know which one?'

'You can't know, you just pick and do what you do. It's not your first round as primary.'

'Yeah, but you're always right there.'

'I'm still there, keep me in the loop, but do what you do. You've got a shield for a reason.'

Her 'link signaled. Eve glanced at it. 'That's Mira. I'm going to take this. Go, keep the balls in the air.'

'But I can tag you.'

'When you need to. Beat it.' She grabbed the 'link. 'Dallas.'

'I'm just coming in to Central. I wanted you to know that we've concluded both the victims were tortured and murdered, and it's our opinion they are two more victims of the spree killers.'

'Ella-Loo Parsens and Darryl Roy James.'

'You have them.'

'Not yet, but we have names, faces – and we have more data. I can come to you.'

'I'll come to you. Five minutes.'

She was prompt. In five minutes Eve heard the skinny-heeled boots clicking toward her office. When Mira stepped in, Eve held out a mug of the flowery tea Mira preferred.

'Oh, thank you! I can really use this.'

'Don't sit in that chair. You know what it's like.'

'Considering I've spent most of today on my feet, I'll take yours. Thanks.' She sat, took a long, slow sip. 'While not altogether careless, the conclusions reached previously on both victims are incorrect. Injuries were misinterpreted. Given the more limited experience and equipment in these cases, it's not unreasonable to understand how those conclusions were arrived at.'

'In both cases, there were people – Banner and the second vic's wife – pushing for further investigation. Those people were dismissed by the local authorities and the federal authorities.'

'Agreed, however, assessed from one angle, the victims

329

appeared to have had accidental deaths. Regardless, they were murdered. DeWinter is writing the reports, on both, in minute detail.'

'I just bet.'

'She's also requested the exhumation of Noah Paston's remains, and their transfer to her.'

'I'm going to owe her that drink.'

Mira smiled. 'And you're busy and distracted by what's happening now, so this doesn't matter.'

Eve shook her head. 'It does matter. Victims always matter, and I'm grateful you took the time to throw your weight on the pile. I'll inform Agent Zweck of your conclusions, and tell him DeWinter's report is forthcoming.'

She turned to her board, pointed at Parsens and James. 'These people will pay for the two victims you gave your time and skill to today. And for Noah Paston. They'll pay for all of them.

'They have a kid.'

'I'm sorry, what?' Stunned, Mira lowered her tea. 'The killers have a child?'

'A baby. She had it while he was doing time for getting caught trying to steal her a ring. True love.'

'This changes things.' Shifting, Mira studied the board. 'Having a child, taking a child on a killing spree across coun-try—'

'No, she dumped it on her mother before they started. From the timing, she got pregnant on a conjugal while he was inside, had the kid before he got out. She went home with it, lied about how she got knocked up, played the I'm-turning-over-a-new-leaf card, then stole what she wanted, left the kid behind. The mother hasn't heard from her since. That was back in June. James got out about six weeks later.'

'Is he aware she had his child?'

'She listed him as father on the birth certificate, which is how we knew about it. She named the girl Darra, and I figure Darryl, Darra.'

'Yes, I see.' Slowly, processing, Mira nodded. 'She had the child – the physical proof of their love – but didn't want it with them, didn't feel what a mother would feel and didn't want the child close. This is a kind of honeymoon for them.'

'Yeah, that occurred to me. I know her now. Having the kid served a purpose. It binds him to her even more, ties them together tight. It was – is – a vehicle, that's all. If she felt it would be useful, she'd go back for it, but she doesn't give the kid a single thought.'

Saying nothing, Mira nodded, sipped more tea.

Eve understood the silence perfectly.

'Stella had me because I served a purpose.' She said it flatly – it meant nothing now. 'She had to tolerate having me around because I wasn't old enough to serve the purpose she and Troy had in mind for me. She had something with Troy, then with McQueen, that this one has with James. Only Troy and McQueen were the dominants. I think Parsens runs the show here. She might not make it obvious, she might let James think he's the big, strong man, but she's calling the shots.'

'There are variables that may play in to the dominant/ submissive dynamic between them.'

Eve shook her head. 'I know her. She had the kid, dumped the kid. I'm betting she visited James in prison like clockwork. She waited for him, three and a half years. That's not a small thing.'

'They see it as love. For them it is love. Once in a lifetime.'

'Yeah, and she'll do whatever she thinks will keep him with her. He's a romantic, so when we close in, he might sacrifice himself for her. He calls her his Juliet. He's into Shakespeare.'

'And doesn't understand that story was a tragedy, not a romance. He might, yes, die trying to protect her, but with this new information I think it's unlikely they'd choose suicide. Or that she would. It's not glory they're after, or even the thrill of death. It's love, a sexual bond heightened through sadism. To love, they need to live.'

'Factoring in what we know, and what we're learning, do you think Campbell's still alive?'

Now Mira's gaze shifted to Campbell's board image. 'I think the probability of that is higher now than I would have estimated it this morning. How long that remains true . . . In any of their more urban murders, the bodies have been carelessly dumped, no attempt to conceal. I don't see why they'd change that pattern now, here in New York, so until her body is found, she's alive.'

'I figure another twenty-four, thirty-six tops. They'll get bored, want somebody fresh.'

'I won't disagree.'

Eve paced to her skinny window and back. 'If I release their names and faces to the media, odds are somebody will recognize them. But if they see their faces on screen, they'll kill and run. It's not the glory,' Eve repeated.

'Again, I won't disagree. It's a difficult call to make.'

And one she'd been wrestling with.

'I'm not releasing, unless ordered. I've held back from bringing in the feds because they may take that path. Would you throw your weight on my pile, if necessary? It's a tough call for you, too.'

'I believe they'd cut their losses, try to get out of New York, so it's not such a tough call.'

'We're narrowing the area, if that helps. Banner and Baxter got two hits already less than a block apart. It's going to zero down.'

'I'll put it in writing.' Mira finished her tea, rose. 'And I know a few people in the FBI. I'll speak to one or two with influence.'

'If that doesn't work, nothing will. It should hold them off from releasing for twenty-four anyway. And that's about all the time Campbell's got. They'd likely finish Mulligan with her, or shortly after. So if I can get another twenty-four to thirty-six, it'll have to be enough.'

'I'll push for the thirty-six.'

'Thanks. You look tired.'

'Oh, I am. I've got a few things to deal with here, then I'm going home and have Dennis rub my feet.'

'Really?'

'He does the most amazing reflexology. You look tired yourself.'

'I don't know if Roarke does reflexology.'

'I imagine he has a way. In any case, my advice is to take an hour and relax, clear your head after you're home. You'll work half the night if I'm any judge, so take an hour first. You'll be fresher for it.'

'Maybe I will.'

Mira turned toward the door, paused. 'Is the child – Darra – in good hands?'

'Santiago says the mother and stepfather seem to be good people, and want to legally adopt the kid. She's in a better place than she would be with her mother.'

'Then when you think of the child, and you will, think of that. However selfish and cold the act, the mother did the daughter a great favor. She'll be loved and tended.'

And better off than many, Eve thought when she was alone. With luck it would make a difference.

She put it aside, sat, contacted her commander to get the federal ball rolling.

18

She spoke to the commander, delighted he would contact and brief Special Agent Zweck. As she gathered up what she wanted for working at home, Baxter came to her doorway.

'Another hit at the Chinese place.'

She tossed her coat aside again. 'Let's hear it.'

'Takeout, just last night. Both of them have been in, together and separately. They call in the order.'

'We can trace it back.'

'Problem. The place overrides every four to six hours. Banner's running the 'link up to EDD, but it's old, it's crap, and even I know it's going to take time to try to pull a contact out of the hat after it's got close to a day's worth layered over it. Same with the security feed. He's taking EDD copies.'

'Have him send copies of everything to my home unit.'

'Already did. Crapped out, so far, on souvie shops, but hit at this hardware place on West Broadway.' His gaze slid toward her AutoChef, and Eve resigned herself.

'Go.' She tipped her head toward the machine.

'Gratitude.'

She eyed him as he programmed. 'Want some candy to go with it?'

He gave her a blank look. A blank *cop* look. 'You got candy in here?'

She jabbed a finger at him. 'You know something. Now you know I know you know something, and I'd grill you like a trout if I had time.'

'You doing okay, LT?' He sipped his coffee casually. 'You seem a little stressed.'

'Bite me, Baxter. Hardware store.'

'Yeah, West Broadway, right off Prince. I got this little buzz when we passed it, like you do. So we went in, and hit. James has been in, twice. Counter guy remembers – the accent stuck. James paid cash, and that helped the stick. Duct tape, cord, a roll of plastic. Friendly guy, apparently, talkative enough. Said how he and his wife just moved to the city. She really loves New York.'

'Was he on foot or in the van?'

'Counter guy didn't notice, but figured the van because he bought a jumbo roll of the plastic. Said he had other errands to run. So we hit a couple delis, nothing, but hit again at a 24/7. Got all the feed we could, but the hardware was four days ago. Everybody got the usual warning. Don't let on, don't confront, call nine-one-one.'

'Write it up, exact addresses of the hits.'

'We got her in a couple shops in SoHo.'

'Is that so?'

'We took a gander at the feed. She bought a couple pair of sexy panties, lifted a dress and the matching bras. Clerk's pretty pissed they missed catching her.'

'Sloppy, on both sides. They can't help but steal, and they'll get caught sooner or later trying to cop fancy underwear or something shiny. We don't have later, so we close in on the area. They walk, they drive, they eat, they shop.'

She shifted back to her map. 'We've got twenty-four, Baxter, I figure twenty-four at the outside before Campbell's finished. Same amount before the feds release the names and faces, and that'll finish Campbell and Mulligan for sure, and send those two fuckers running.'

'I can take Banner back out. The boy, too. He's on his way back in from the exam. But we covered all the ground, Dallas. The best we could do is cruise and hoof it, hope to spot them on the street.'

It was something she'd considered, but … 'I've got uniforms doing that. We've got other DBs who need attention. Peabody's working one, and she's got another set up for you. Work it with Trueheart.'

'It'll keep his mind off the exam results. He thinks he did okay, but said he got nervous a couple times. They're backed up – surprise. Told him results in about forty-eight.'

He slid her a look. 'Maybe you can speed that up.'

'Dead bodies, Baxter, and two I'd like to keep breathing. Let's keep focused here.'

'Right, yeah, right. He's okay with the forty-eight. It's me sweating it. I'll get moving on it.'

She wanted to get moving herself – and stop talking to every-damn-body.

She grabbed her coat again, and got the hell out before someone else interrupted her.

She'd cruise the target area. Maybe do a walk-around.

These two had murdered their way east and gotten away with it not because they were criminal geniuses, but because they'd kept moving, because it had taken time for locals to call in the feds, time to put the murders together.

But now they were . . . nesting, she thought as she wedged herself into the cop can of an elevator. Making themselves a home of sorts, getting to know the neighborhood, the city.

Out and about.

And, for now, they still felt free and clear.

Not hiding, not running, not moving on.

Yet.

She elbowed off on her level of the garage, and pulled out her signaling 'link on the way to her car.

'A big howdy from the Rope 'N Ride,' Carmichael said. 'Yee-haw.'

'You've gotta get the hell out of there soon.'

'Oh, fucking A, Dallas. Somebody just called me little lady. I'm not little, I'm not a lady. I wanted to punch him, and he was seriously cute. But I digress. Ella-Loo Parsens did her waitress thing here, and offered sexual services, for a fee, on the side. Unlicensed. But it's not the kind of place that sets much store in licenses. The seriously cute bartender told Santiago – as he wouldn't discuss such matters in front of the little lady – that bjs were her specialty.'

'Keeps her in control.'

'In my personal experience, you bet. She could be bitchy, always talked about going east. Claimed she was saving up, marking time until she could head to New York City, shake the prairie dust off her boots and live the big-city life.'

'A girl with a dream. And James?'

'Bartender's vague there, but I found another waitress – who I suspect also offers sexual favors – who remembers him.'

'Hey there, pretty little thing!'

Eve heard the drunken male voice, watched Carmichael's gaze slide over.

'Why don't you and me take a spin on the dance floor?'

'Why don't you go on out, start spinning, and I'll catch up when I'm done here?'

'Alrighty.'

'A woman could rope and ride a half dozen men, should she be so inclined, in a single visit to this establishment. Just saying,' Carmichael added.

'How many do you have spinning?'

'Lost count.' Carmichael fluttered her lashes. 'But I suspect Ella-Loo made more dispensing sexual favors than she did dispensing brews. Her coworker remembers Ella-Loo homed right in on Darryl Roy James like he was the answer to a prayer. And, in fact, warned her coworker off, got physical about it. Shoved her into a bathroom stall and threatened to slice her tits off – that's a quote – if she went near James.

'Later, said coworker walked out the back for a break – that possibly included imbibing an illegal substance – and saw the two of them banging like hammers against the recycler.'

'So, straight to sex.'

'Do not pass the bjs. Neither of them ever came back. Ella-Loo had two nights' pay coming, but they figure she made that up by stealing a case of brew from the storeroom. And the till was a few hundred short that night, according to Seriously Cute. We're going to go by, dig up her former landlord, but the word here is, she left most everything, and owed two weeks' rent.'

Eve pulled out in traffic as she listened. 'Sex and stealing, but they couldn't keep it at that. What the hell is that noise?'

'They've got a band coming in later, we're told, but they're doing Country Karaoke this afternoon – two to four. The fun never ends.'

'It's sixteen-thirty. Why don't they stop?'

'It's fifteen-thirty here, Lieutenant.'

'How can it – never mind. Check the former residence, then head to the prison. We've had some hits here. I'll send you a report. Good work.'

*

340

Eve cruised the streets, noted the pizzeria, the Chinese restaurant. Since double-parking would draw attention, she paid the freight for a lot, covered the same ground on foot, found the hardware, the 24/7, the boutique, the pawnshop, flashed the photos at other shop owners, at glide-cart operators.

They're here, she thought, scanning faces, vehicles, buildings. She only needed one of them to step outside their nest. Go out for food, a six-pack of beer.

But she saw nothing of them, and walked back to her car.

She drove home thinking Campbell and Mulligan might be trapped in one of the buildings she'd passed, and that thought clawed at her through the miserable traffic and the icy sleet that began to fall.

She wanted home and the quiet, craved it like water after a drought. Just an hour of quiet where no one talked to her, fed her data, looked to her for the answers.

She dragged herself into the warmth.

'Early *and* alone?' Summerset gave her a long, cool look out of dark eyes.

She found she didn't have the energy to take a swipe at him.

'They'll be piling in later.'

The cat padded over to bump against her leg, but she just turned to the stairs, started up without taking off her coat.

Summerset went directly to the house intercom. 'I believe the lieutenant has hit a wall. She's on her way up.'

'I'll look after her,' Roarke said.

No doubt, Summerset thought, and noted the cat had followed her up.

When she stepped into the bedroom, Roarke saw it. Exhaustion – if not physical, mental. The momentum since the morning, all the push, the rush, the progress, and she had yet to cross the finish line.

With two people's lives depending on it.

He could feel the weight she carried.

'I didn't know you were home, too.' She tossed a file bag on the sofa of the sitting area. 'And early.'

'A bit.' He adjusted his plans to finish up some work before dinner. 'How many cops in the house?'

'Just me. They'll be coming later. An hour or two, I'd say. Sorry.'

'An hour or two will do it. I was thinking a swim would be nice. Now I don't have to swim alone.'

'I really have to—'

'Decompress,' he finished. 'We'll both work better, be sharper, for the break.'

'I don't think Campbell and Mulligan are getting a break.' She heard the angry snap in her voice, held up a hand so he wouldn't snap back. 'That's wrong, just wrong, and I know better. I could feel it breaking all day, all damn day, but . . .'

Take an hour, Mira had advised her. Sometimes you had to listen.

'I could use a swim. I could use an hour with you, not talking about all this.'

'I could use the same.'

'Give me a sec.'

She stripped off her coat, her weapon harness, and after a moment's thought, sat to take off her boots. Then she stood, reached for his hand. 'Let's go.'

When they stepped into the elevator, he turned her face to his, kissed her. 'Welcome home.'

'Same to you.' Then she sighed, leaned her head on his shoulder because she could, she could do that with him without being weak.

Small, daily miracles.

'My brain's tired.'

'I know, and you've the beginnings of a headache. I can see it.'

'Is that why they're so blue? X-ray eyes?'

'Where you're concerned.'

'I don't need a blocker, just some quiet. I talked to a half a million people today, most of them at least twice. You probably did double that.'

'And won't the quiet hour be good for both of us?'

They stepped out, into and through the tropical bliss of plants and dwarf trees toward the deep blue water.

'God, that looks really good.'

'What are you doing?' he asked as she opened a case.

'Getting a suit.'

'Whatever for?'

'Look, I know I said an hour or two, and probably, but

what if cops come early? And what if one of those cops thinks, just like we did: Hey, a swim would be nice. I'm not risking naked.'

'If you want privacy . . .' He took the suit out of her hand, set it aside. 'It only takes blocking the elevator from this level, which I did.'

'Blocking the elevator.' Absently, she rubbed at the headache between her eyes. 'Why didn't I think of that? They can't get in here?'

'They could if McNab decided to bypass, which would be a bit of a challenge for him. But I believe we can trust him to respect our privacy.'

So saying, he tugged up her sweater.

She considered McNab, bypassing, then nodded. 'No, he wouldn't do that. One question,' she added as she took off her trousers, 'before the quiet.'

'I can handle one question.'

'How can it be one hour earlier in Oklahoma than it is here, and be the same time it is here in the Bahamas? Oklahoma's in the same damn country as we are, right? It's America. And the Bahamas aren't. You don't have to be a geography whiz to know the Bahamas aren't in the US and Oklahoma is. So why, for God's sake? How?'

Christ, he adored her. Just adored every inch of her as she stood there in her underwear, radiating annoyed confusion.

'Science is full of mysteries.'

'It seems like bullshit to me. Who the hell decides these

344

things?' she demanded as she stripped off the tank. 'Who made the gods of time anyway?'

'That's more than one question.'

'They're related,' she claimed and wiggled out of her panties.

Since he enjoyed her careless striptease, he waited until she'd finished, dived in, before he undressed.

She did four hard laps, then rolled over to float on her back.

'Sometimes when you're not here I do this. Just float like this and think how I'm in this big-ass pool in this big-ass house, and if that isn't enough to blow up your skirt, I've got you working upstairs or coming home soon, or better yet . . .'

She reached out, felt his fingers link with her. 'Better yet, right here. It's a really good deal for me.'

'For me as well. I'll think, Look at her, just at her, and she's mine. My one thing I wanted long before I knew to want her.'

She turned, treaded water, then slid in to twine around him. 'I really love you.'

He murmured the words back to her, in Irish, made her smile.

'They really can't get in here?'

'Locked and blocked.'

She tipped her head back. 'Then let's take each other's mind off the day. Just wipe it out before we pick it all up again.'

She took his mouth with hers, sank into him as they sank beneath the surface.

Weightless, drifting, until her feet touched bottom and they pushed off and up together.

Into air that smelled of tropical gardens where the only sound was the gentle lap of water. Cool water, warm air, and her lover's arms around her.

They sank again, mouth-to-mouth, this time with his hands gliding over her, finding her secrets so she surfaced breathless, heart thudding.

They rolled, lazy tumbles in the water – above and below – even as her pulse sprinted, as if in a race with pleasure. Slow and easy, then fast and rough. The quick changes left her weak and wanting, shuddering and eager.

She gave into it, to him, cupping his face in her hands, sinking again, sinking in bottomless love. And felt the power of her own surrender.

The water grew warmer, warmer as he guided them to the lagoon corner. Now the water churned lightly, tingling along her skin.

He loved the look of her like this, lost, and his, her hair slick with wet. Bracing her against the wall, he took himself under to explore all below the surface of that frothy water.

Her breast in his mouth, her heart leaping against his lips as her hands ran over him. And deeper, lifting her hips to find her center, feeling her come as he used his tongue to drive her.

Wet and warm, long and lean, and churning now as the

water churned. Hips rocking in invitation as he took her up again.

He glided his lips up her body, slid his hand down to where his mouth had been. And watched her fly again, her hands gripping the edges, her eyes like amber glass as she cried out.

She shuddered, went limp.

'God. God. I can't.'

'More. Just a little more. Let go. Everything. All. Let go.' Greed for her undid him. He used his hands again, used his mouth again, ravaging, ravishing. He wanted to hear her scream.

When she did, when her body arched, tight as a wire, he plunged into her, thrust after wild thrust.

'Mine.' Mad for her, mad from her, he drove into her, his mouth, his teeth at her shoulder, her throat. 'Mine. Mine.'

She cried out again, quivering. And her arms came around him, her legs banded him. 'Mine,' she said. 'Mine.'

And he let go. Everything and all.

Wrecked, they floated where they were in the quiet, bubbling water.

'I don't have a headache, that's positive.' She sighed, stroked his wet hair. 'I don't care about the Bahamas right now.'

'Then my job here is done.'

'Is it like reflexology?'

'Is what — sex? Reflexology?' He let out a half laugh as their eyes met. 'Where do these thoughts come from?'

'Mr Mira gives Mira foot rubs. Reflexology. It helps her

relax, and I wondered . . . No, wipe that out. Wipe it because it makes me wonder about them and sex, and I really don't want to.'

'Why, after I've so thoroughly . . . relaxed you, would you put that in my head?'

'Inadvertent. Apologies.' She kissed his cheek, rose. 'I've got to get back upstairs.'

'Give us a hand.' He held one up to her. 'As you've thoroughly relaxed me as well.'

They clasped forearms, and when he stood with her, she wrapped around him one more time. 'It's sleeting outside.'

'All right.'

'And we just had really terrific pool sex. It's a high point.' She stepped up and out of the pool. 'You and Mira were right. My head's clearer, and I'm going to go back to work fresher for the break.'

'Did she suggest you have sex?'

'She wasn't specific.' She grabbed a towel, tossed him one. 'But she wanted me to take an hour. Parsens — that's the female killer — had a kid with James, her partner. I'll fill you in on all of it, but he was doing a short stint in the Oklahoma State Pen, and she had a kid. She drove back to her mother's, played a tune, then left with valuables, and left the kid behind. Walked out one night, never looked back.'

Saying nothing, he turned Eve toward him, folded her in.

'It's not the same. The kid's going to be okay. The kid's better off.'

'But it brings back memories. It pokes at old wounds.'

'Some. But it helps me know Ella-Loo Parsens. It helps me think like she thinks. That's a weapon on our side. But between that and a bunch of else, I needed the break.'

'I could study up on reflexology.'

Now she laughed, began to dress. 'I'll take the sex.'

'I bet the Miras do as well.'

'Crap, you just had to, didn't you?'

'I did, yes. Now I'm after a glass of wine, and we'll have some food, as I imagine you've had little to nothing since breakfast. Your cops can fend for themselves when they get here.'

He took her hand when she'd dressed. 'Sleeting, you said?'

'Yeah.'

'I think it calls for some hearty stew.'

'That stuff with the things.'

'Of course, I was just thinking the same.'

She smirked at him when they stepped on the elevator. 'The chicken stuff with the things, the dumpling things.'

'Ah, yes. We'll see if we can manage that.'

They stopped by the bedroom first. She wanted footwear.

In the office she updated her board while he chose a white wine for the chicken and dumplings, and added a spinach salad.

She was paler than he liked, as happened too often when she pushed her own limits.

She'd started filling him in on the day when she heard the others coming.

Quiet time was over.

When they trooped in, she decided the three of them looked about as wiped as she'd been, reminding her they'd been at it nearly as long that day.

'We're putting some food together. Take thirty. Go grab a swim.'

Peabody stopped, blinked. 'Seriously?'

'Come back fresh.'

'Swim? You're saying there's really a swimming pool inside the house?'

'Not just a pool,' Peabody told Banner. 'An amazing pool, with a bubble lagoon.'

'That kicks the cow in the ass. I wouldn't mind a dip, but I didn't come with swimming gear.'

'Plenty of it down there. We can't cover a cow's ass,' McNab considered, 'but we can cover yours. Let's get wet.'

'I'm with you. Just one second. Lieutenant, I wanted you to know I contacted my chief, told him Little Mel had been murdered all along. I sent him the report on him and on Fastbinder. He's gonna talk to Little Mel's mama about it. He said . . . he said he was proud of me.'

Weariness covering him, Banner had to stop to clear his throat. 'He's a good man, a good boss, but that's not the sort of thing you hear out of him every day. I'm back on the clock, but he says I'm with you here as long as I'm useful on this.'

'I'll let you know when you stop being useful.'

His lips twitched into a smile. 'All right, then. I'll go take that dip.'

'Back in thirty,' Eve called out as the three of them got in the elevator. 'That's enough,' she said to Roarke when the doors closed, 'because as I don't see a threesome happening, there won't be any pool sex.'

He shook his head at that. 'You'll eat, and catch me up so we don't waste the thirty.'

When she sat with him, took the first spoonful of stew, it slid into her like ambrosia. She didn't know what the hell ambrosia was, but she'd bet good money the chicken and dumplings beat it.

'Ella-Loo Parsens, Darryl Roy James.'

Roarke nodded toward the updated board. 'I have that much.'

She smiled a little. 'A man walks into a bar,' she began.

She'd nearly finished, eating and briefing, when the trio came back, chattering like . . .

'What are those birds in Ireland?'

'We have more than one variety.'

'The ones in the saying.'

'Cuckoos?'

'No, but that would fit. The one is for something and another's for something else.'

'I wonder how it is I know what you're talking about. Magpies.'

'That's it.'

'We peeked into the new dojo. We didn't go in,' Peabody said quickly. 'But just wanted to see. It's mag.'

'It's an amazing house,' Banner added. 'It never stops.'

'Grab food. Roarke's about up to date.'

'What you've got smells total.' McNab sniffed.

'Chicken stew with dumplings,' Roarke told him.

'Yum! Is there enough?' Peabody wondered.

'There is.'

'I'll get it up. I remember how to work the AC in there. Least I can do,' Banner finished.

'One alcoholic beverage. Wine or beer, then it's coffee.'

'It'll be wine for you, won't it, Peabody?' Roarke rose to get her a glass. 'Ian?'

'That'll work. Maybe just wine all around. We'll all be on the same page.'

'What's the status on the electronics Banner brought up?' Eve asked.

'Feeney and I hit that, pulled Callendar in on it, too. We've got an auto running through the night.'

McNab plucked one of the crusty little rolls from the shallow bowl on the table, tossed it in the air, caught it. Bit right in.

'Problem with the 'link from the Chinese place is it's way old-school,' he said around the bread, 'and when they override it a million times, the transmissions blur together, even after you dig them out. If we knew the 'link code we were after, sure, we'd piece that with some time. Going blind, trying to find the one without knowing the code or the registered name, that's a crapshoot.'

'We'll take a look at it here as well.' Roarke brought over glasses, poured out. 'But I have to agree. It's a challenge when you know what you're after, specifically, but without knowing specifics, it's a shot in the dark.'

Banner brought out a tray with bowls of steaming stew. 'The guy at the restaurant thought he knew at least some of the order, about the approximate time. But McNab says there's a lot of layers, and a lot of people tagging up in that time frame, a lot of orders for kung pao chicken and eggrolls and that kind of thing.'

'We already cleaned up some of the security feeds.' McNab dug right in. 'That's not going to be a big. We get enough there, we figure we'll try storefront cams, see if we can catch them walking. Get a direction.'

'This here's as good as my ma's, if not better.' Banner glanced around the table as he spooned up more stew. 'And I'd appreciate it if nobody repeated that if you ever meet her. I got the impression they're likely closer to the restaurants than the hardware, because they've been there more. True enough James bought that big roll of plastic, and it's hard going finding parking there, so you wouldn't figure it's far.'

He sampled the wine cautiously, then lifted his eyebrows. 'This is nice. I was thinking, when Baxter and me were walking it, if I was after the plastic and whatnot, I'd walk, make two trips if I needed to. Y'all are more used to the traffic and all that. James would be more like me there, I think. You want to park it, much as you can.'

Eve sat back. 'Tuck the van away, only bring it out for hunting. Walk or try public transpo otherwise.'

'Driving in this city's crazy, and everybody doing it always seems more than a little pissed off. I paid what I had to pay to have the rental company come get the ride I used to get here. I'll take the bus back to the transpo station when I leave. Maybe give the subway a try.'

Eve rose, went to the board. 'Wherever they're nesting, it's highly probable it was a matter of opportunity. An empty apartment, a vacant building still can't be dismissed, or they invaded someone's home. Downtown. Trendy areas, maybe, something she'd read about or seen on screen. Can't say why at this point, but they're Lower West Side, below the West Village. North of Tribeca, west of SoHo and Greenwich Village. Nothing else fits as well.'

'You're thinking they may be holding a third person – or more,' Roarke said. 'If they saw an opportunity to force or break into a home, an apartment.'

'I've been playing with the idea, checked missing persons through the day. But they took Mulligan. That's two they've got, unless they've killed Campbell and took the time and effort to hide the body.'

'And why hide hers when they didn't hide Kuper's,' Peabody put in.

'Holding a third, or say a couple, a family?' Looking into the eyes of the killers, Eve shook her head. 'It's hard, it's messy, it's work. And if you kill them, you've got a bigger mess to deal with. Can't keep the bodies for long. Their pattern, until Mulligan, was one at a time. I figure low probability on them holding anyone else.

'But they've got a place.' She brought up the map, picked up a laser pointer, circled. 'Right in here.'

'Door-to-doors?' Peabody asked.

'I'd like to try to narrow it more, but that might be the next step. It's going to take the feds some time to read DeWinter's report, process it, figure out which ass cheek to scratch. Zweck has what we've got, and we'll see what he does with it. Maybe we pull the checking for gas leaks, something like that. I want a narrower area before we try that.'

She circled the board. 'Nothing on the van. Nothing from the extra patrols in this sector.'

'They've got to go out sometime.' McNab shrugged. 'What's the point of coming all the way to New York and staying inside?'

'They're having a real good time inside,' Eve replied.

'Eat,' she ordered. 'Then let's start squeezing the box.'

19

Her office smelled like chicken and dumplings soaked in strong black coffee – with a dash of cherry from McNab's endless fizzies.

Roarke brought in another auxiliary as she doled out assignments. Peabody to cover deep background on Darryl Roy James, Banner deep background on Ella-Loo Parsens. Roarke and McNab would continue the e-work, combing through security discs in evidence, and checking any storefront cams that may have picked up their suspects on foot.

Eve worked the maps, focused on trying to narrow the target area foot by foot.

The first interruption, a 'link tag from Special Agent Zweck, pulled her out of the groove. But by the end of it she kicked back in her chair, feet on the desk.

'I'll keep you updated,' she told him. 'You'll let me know how you want to proceed on your end.'

She picked up her coffee, and though it had gone cold during the conversation, drank it anyway.

'The feds won't sign off on Little and Fastbinder as vics of the spree killers they still refer to as unsubs.'

Banner's head came up in one fast jerk. 'What?'

'Someone's dick's in a knot over DeWinter's report — which apparently fried asses, many of which she named, specifically, before she sliced them up for the pan.'

Yeah, she definitely owed DeWinter that drink.

'The remains "in question" will be transferred to a federal facility in the morning where federal forensic specialists will examine and test.'

'That's bullshit.'

'It's bureaucracy. DeWinter's on a rampage and stomping on other dicks to get the remains of Noah Paston in her house. The boy's next of kin has signed off on it, and my money's on DeWinter. Oh yeah, I forgot.'

Eve circled a finger in the air. 'Same thing. While the feds will investigate James and Parsens, thoroughly review our reports and findings, they will not, at this time, name them as suspects. They are, officially, "persons of interest" only.'

'We've tracked them,' Peabody began.

'We've verified James and Parsens met in Oklahoma in '57. There is reasonable evidence James stole a '52 pickup matching the description of one towed away, illegally, by the Dorrans. Federal investigations will track whatever's left of that vehicle to verify or disprove it was the one James allegedly stole. We've determined Parsens bore a female child, but until DNA can be tested, the child's paternity remains a question mark for the feds.'

'Assholes,' Banner muttered.

'A sentiment I believe Zweck shares but was careful not to voice. We can't, at this time, prove without a doubt Parsens and James killed anyone or, indeed, took the route we've determined through our investigation. We haven't to their satisfaction proven either Parsens or James is, indeed, in New York. They will examine the loading dock feed, and Zweck will follow up with the hardware store, pawnshop, restaurants in the morning.'

'Stepping in our footprints,' Peabody said. 'Wasting time and resources.'

'Dicks,' Eve returned and made a tying motion with her hands. 'Here's what that means for us. We won't have the full weight of the federal resources on the investigation. We also won't have them in the way. Zweck, if I'm any judge, is going to do a lot of pushback on this. He, apparently, isn't a moron.

'It also means we've got a breather on the FBI releasing James's and Parsens's names and faces to the media. A breather, because someone may unknot his dick long enough to throw them out as POIs.'

Banner considered. 'So, nothing much changes.'

'Nothing much. Zweck's going to raise some hell – that's my take. But somebody higher on the food chain doesn't like being told they're wrong – and the mistake might, eventually in the media, make them look bad. The feds didn't listen to you, Banner, and you were right. That makes them wrong. A small-town deputy – no offense.'

'None taken.'

'Was right, and the FBI was wrong. That'll knot a lot of dicks.'

Eve nodded toward the board from where she sat. 'And if they'd done what you did, if they'd backtracked from Little Mel, tied into Jansen, maybe they'd have caught these fuckers sooner. Maybe some people would still be alive.'

'They've gotta live with that,' Banner said.

The kind of badge whose dick knotted over being wrong, Eve knew, could and did live with it. They just shifted the blame down the food chain.

'That's the maybes,' she continued, 'and that kind of maybe doesn't look good in PR and political terms. And it doesn't change a thing for us. So give me some more on James.'

Banner shoved his hand through his hair, shifted in his chair.

'He wasn't much for school, skimmed through, did some repeating, worked with a state-sponsored tutor a time or three. No extra activities, nothing over mandatory requirements. That includes sports, and that's the exception rather than the rule in small towns back where I come from.'

'Not a team player,' Eve concluded, 'not an academic.'

'Not even close. Got a weak spot for sex and women.'

'Details.'

'I got a bunch of articles here on how he had an affair with one of his teachers. He was fifteen – she was twenty-six. She did time for it.'

Eve straightened in her chair. 'Was he coerced?'

'Doesn't read that way. I'll send them to you, but it reads pretty clear he wasn't coerced, forced or pressured. Doesn't excuse the teacher, not one bit, and it's statutory rape however you slice it, but he was willing and eager. Romanced her.'

'Romance again.'

'Bought her flowers, wrote her bad poetry, gave her little gifts. Came out he'd stolen most of them. And he was also banging two other girls during the same six months – that came out when they testified. One took a slap as she was eighteen. The other was sixteen, so that's legally consensual.'

'Sex, stealing, romance. He started all of it young.'

'Had some tangles – his juvenile record's unsealed,' Banner added. 'Got a history of shoplifting and moved that up to joyriding, destruction of property, a couple minor assaults. Usual court-appointed counseling, community service. And a quick stint of rehab when he got bagged with some illegals. Can't get into any of his psych reports – they're sealed.'

Eve thought of Roarke – the quick way. Or Mira – the official way. 'We'll cut through that if necessary.' Either way.

'He showed an aptitude for mechanics – had better luck for the year they put him in trade school. Showed above-average interest and aptitude for electronics. What you get,

Lieutenant, is he's not all-over bright, but has a knack for those areas. But he's bone-lazy with it. He took off at sixteen, ended up in Texas, got popped trying to boost a car and did his time in juvie down there. We got pretty much the rest of it.'

'Get that to Mira. It'll add to the whole picture. Peabody, Parsens.'

'It's going to sound like a lot of repetition. Low-level achiever in school, no extracurriculars, with a handful of suspensions and write-ups for fighting, disruption of others, unexcused absences. Accused a male teacher of molestation. Thorough investigation there, by my eye. The teacher was completely vindicated. Solicited another – who had a recorder in his pocket, running. Sex for a passing grade was her offer. Any kind of sex he wanted. Mandatory counseling, community service assigned. Dropped out as soon as she reached legal age. No steady employment, and all employment on record is bar work. Applied for an LC license at eighteen, again at twenty-one. Both times denied.'

When she picked up her mug, frowned into it, Banner said, 'Out?'

'Yeah.'

'I'll fix you up.'

'Actually, I could do with something sweet at this point. Could you make it an orange fizzy?'

'Coming up. Keep going,' he said as he rose. 'I can hear you.'

'I dug up a couple reports, when she was a minor. She was accused of killing a dog – twice.'

Now, Eve thought. There it was. The need to shed blood, give pain.

'How young was she?'

'Thirteen the first time – they couldn't nail it down, but she'd gone a round with this other girl, over a boy. And the girl's dog ended up eating poisoned kibble. She was fifteen the next time, and it was the same sort of scenario. Only this time the dog was cut up, burned, and found hanging from a tree.'

'Bitch,' Banner muttered from the kitchen. 'I've got a soft spot for dogs. I know she's doing people, but I've got a soft spot.'

'Torturing and/or killing animals. One of the foundations of a serial killer. She'd have gone on to people eventually. With or without James, she'd have evolved to that. Any more?' Eve asked.

'We've got a few police reports with her the complainant – boyfriend at the time popping her one, other rape or molestation charges. From the photos and reports, the popping did happen, and was mutual. None of the sex charges stuck.'

'Sex as a payoff, a weapon, as currency. I've talked to Charles about this sort of thing before.'

'Charles who?' Banner asked as he came back with two fizzies.

'Former LC, current sex therapist, friend,' Eve explained.

'And if we consulted him I'd expect him to say sex was never a real pleasure for her. Always a weapon or tool. Maybe we'll find she rang that bell with James, and that's what keeps her with him. That, and the killing.'

Peabody took a big gulp of fizzy, winced, rubbed between her eyebrows. 'Cold snap. Why do I do that? She ran away a couple of times as a minor, but always came back on her own. Took off for good at eighteen. Stepfather reported stolen articles, cash, but withdrew the complaint.'

'Her mother pushed there,' Eve speculated.

'She bounced around, ended up at the Rope 'N Ride.'

'Organize it, get it to Mira. When we get these two, we're nailing them shut.'

She rose, pulled out her signaling 'link. 'Santiago, give it to me.'

'We rounded up the warden, a couple of guards, the head waitress from the place Parsens worked, her former landlord, and just to top it off, the midwife who delivered her baby. We corralled them, boss.'

'You've been out there too long.'

'Oh yeah.'

'Sum it up. You're on screen,' she said as she walked back to her office, ordered the open transmission. 'Talking to the room.'

'Yo, room. Wish I was there. According to all reports, James kept his head down and his nose clean during his incarceration. Took some classes in e-work, did well. Worked in the mechanics shop, did exceptional. He was, in fact, recommended for a job at a local garage here, but requested permission to return home after his early release, stating he and his woman wanted to go home, where their baby was being tended by family. Said permission was granted. He never reported in.'

'They took off, heading east.'

'The guards on his block said he was affable and easy. Did a lot of reading on his time in, talked about his woman, who visited him every week. They took advantage of every scheduled conjugal. According to Parsens's supervisor at the bar, she wasn't what you'd call a self-starter, didn't get along well with the other staff, and was suspected of offering sexual favors on the side. Her landlord adds to that. She brought men home, but none of them stayed above an hour, usually less. She left without notice, and owing back-rent. She drove the pickup, had it serviced a time or two – and it's believed paid for service with service.'

'No surprises there.'

'The midwife? She says definitely imbibed during pregnancy – but she could never prove it. Caterwauled – that's a quote – during delivery that, according to the source, was as easy as a cat having kittens. I can't speak to that, never having had kittens or a baby, for which I remain eternally grateful.'

'What is that *noise*?'

'It's cows, Lieutenant. Or steers. I think there's a difference, but I'm not going to ask. There are ... members of the cow/steer/cattle family in the trailer Carmichael opted to park next to. I really don't think they like it in there.'

'You should get away from there, in case they get out.'

'I'm thinking that.' Glancing over his shoulder, he walked a few paces away. 'You've been off-planet, right, LT?'

'Yeah.'

'I haven't, but I think this is something like it. Anyway, the midwife stated Parsens's labor was textbook and quick. No interest from Parsens in the kid after. The midwife was concerned enough, she went back twice a day, on her own time, to check on the baby, make sure it was clean and fed. Bottle and store-bought milk, earning said midwife's stern disapproval. Parsens said – quote – she wasn't having her tits ruined from some baby sucking them dry.

'When Parsens took off with the kid, came back without her, the midwife was worried enough to do some digging – again on her own – came up with Parsens's mother, contacted her. She ascertained the baby was there, but didn't reveal her connection to Parsens or Parsens's location, as she could've lost her license for it. But she needed to be sure the kid was alive and well. She believed Parsens capable of dumping it somewhere, or even infanticide.'

'Infanticide's a serious leap.'

'Midwife said Parsens was a lot more concerned about getting her body back in shape than the kid. Claims she saw actual hate in Parsens's eyes once when the baby was crying, and the midwife tried to get her to take care of it.'

Eve said nothing to that as the image of her mother's eyes, the hate in them when she herself had been a child, flashed into her mind.

'Mostly indifference, but that look she claims to have witnessed had her awake at night worrying. She didn't have anything to go to the authorities about, just that sick feeling.'

'Okay.'

'All over it? People tend to like James well enough. People seem not to like Parsens.'

'James does, and that's all it took. Come home, Santiago. This time I mean it.'

'*Gracias a Dios*. And when I think in Spanish I'm *verklempt*.'

She had to laugh. 'Write it up on the way, make sure Mira's copied. Report to Central at oh-eight-hundred because by *Dios* we're going to have a net around these two tomorrow.'

She clicked off, nodded as she noted Roarke and McNab had come back in. 'You catch all that?'

'Enough of it.'

'Peabody and Banner are writing summaries from their deep background. You can read them if you want, but they're mostly going to be useful in the trial phase. They further cement the pattern and profile of each, and confirm predilections, pathology, and some of the movements. I've carved off another block, eighty percent probability, using my own parameters.'

'We can maybe help you there.' McNab picked up Peabody's fizzy, took a slurp. 'We got lucky on a couple of store cams, and caught sight of James heading away from the hardware store – the roll of plastic over his shoulder, shopping bag in hand. Heading north.'

'North.' She whirled back to the map. 'If we can cut off anything south of the hardware store ... Not conclusive, but I can run two maps. How far could you track him?'

'Only half a block. The cams in that sector tend to be dicey. We could see him bopping along. I'll put it on screen. Just a half block north, head swiveling back and forth, craning up, like tourists do.'

Eve watched James bop – not a bad description for it – nearly beaning a couple of pedestrians with the roll of plastic as he did the tourist head-swivel-and-crane.

Then he zigged closer to the street, out of range of the limited cams.

'Hell. He could've gotten lucky with parking. He could've been heading toward the van. Or he could've caught a cab.'

'Maybe the van,' McNab agreed. 'Probably no on the cab. We worked that angle. He'd have more luck on corners, but we put in an official on pickups, all four corners, or anywhere within a two-block radius to start. It was a lot of checking, and we got the "it'll take time to run a search," so ...'

He glanced at Roarke.

'I looked into it.' He shrugged off Eve's narrowed look,

turned to Banner. 'Do you have any issues with me . . . circumventing the official protocol here, Deputy?'

'Not a one.'

'Well, then, we did find several pickups in that area, in that time frame. Two were single passenger fares. One was dropped off in Midtown, corner of Fifty-first and Madison.'

'I did the badge thing,' McNab said, 'contacted the cabbie directly. He doesn't remember the fare, exactly, but he says he didn't pick up anybody downtown hefting a roll of plastic.'

'The second single fare was driven to Franklin and Hudson.'

'Tribeca. I've pretty much eliminated that sector.'

'The cabbie also says she – in this case – didn't pick up any guy hauling plastic. It's not absolute, Dallas, but we lean no on flagging a cab.'

'We'll focus north. It's worth the leap. Another shot at any vacant buildings, apartments or flops in the narrowed sector. We'll do a door-to-door sweep if it comes to it, hit every street slot, parking lot, vacant lot and underground. That van's somewhere.'

'Private garage perhaps,' Roarke suggested.

'I can't see them paying that freight, but maybe. Maybe if they hit a vic with one, if they did take out somebody to make their nest who had one. We'll pull in private.'

'I can do a search for you. Residents of this sector who also rent or own garage space.'

'Good. Do that. He's got an aptitude for electronics –

according to his background.' Factor that in, she thought. 'There must be hotels, office buildings in that general area with parking. Some apartment units with parking. How hard would it be to bypass the permit, the payment, take a vehicle in and out?'

'If he's got any feel for it, and a decent jammer?' McNab nodded. 'Oh yeah, icy cake on that. We've got a couple of drones in EDD dealing with that all the time.'

'They can't help but steal, so why pay for parking? Permit parking,' she considered, 'they'd have reasonably decent cams. We'll start on that, too. Public parking lots have cams, but a lot of them are just for show. We're going to check those. After dark, after, say, nine,' she continued, pacing now. 'Anything before that's too early. Nine's too early, but it's as far as I'll cut it. We'll go by Banner's take – no need to drive in the city. Except when they're hunting. So we'll start running feeds from permit and public parking, after twenty-one hundred.'

She turned to McNab. 'Can you pull in those drones, the ones who handle this routinely?'

'I'll ask the captain, but I think yeah.'

'I'll contact Feeney. Do what you can tonight, and if we don't nail it down, we'll put the drones on it in the morning. Peabody, use the map. Start another search for any missings reported in that sector. Any DBs who worked or resided in that sector.

'Banner, use the map. Vacant buildings or units. And spread that out to recently rented. Maybe they invested some of the money they stole along the way. Focus in on basement apartments and self-contained houses. Anything you can find with a rear or side entrance. I've already started there, so you've got a jump.'

Now she turned to Roarke. 'Are you up for a drive?'

'I could be.'

'I need to cruise that sector. I want to roll through it, at night. They hunt at night. Maybe it's not the best use of my time or yours, but I can't let it go. I need to see it, feel it.'

'You'll need your boots,' he told her. 'It's still sleeting.'

'Immediate contact if anything – *anything* pops,' she said, and headed out for her boots.

'She'll want to walk it as well,' he commented. 'Are you set, Ian?' he asked McNab. 'The lieutenant wouldn't care for it overmuch, but Summerset's a good hand, and I can have him work with you while I'm in the field.'

'I've got this, but thanks.'

'Fuel up when you need to. It looks to be a long night.'

He met Eve downstairs, pulled the scarf out of her coat pocket, wound it expertly around her neck. 'It's bitter and filthy out.'

'I get that, and odds are slim they're out hunting. But—' She walked outside, into the icy sleet and wicked cold. 'It's also the perfect time to grab somebody. Most people are inside – home, a bar, whatever. It's good cover.'

Once inside the all-terrain, she frowned at the interior. 'This isn't the one from before.'

'It's another one. A bit smaller as we're not hauling people around with us. Quick,' he said as he punched it to a speed she wouldn't have attempted unless in pursuit. 'And agile.'

To demonstrate he hit vertical and flew over the gates.

'It moves. And this isn't the way you figured to spend your evening.'

'I believe we're past evening now. I enjoy working with McNab. His mind's quick, his energy infectious. And I got a Bella report if you're interested.'

She watched the streets. Plenty of cabs – few with lights on – fewer private vehicles. And a stingy scatter of pedestrians. 'McNab gave you a Bella report?'

'He's fairly mad for her. He and Peabody babysat last week so Mavis and Leonardo could have a date night. The three of them, I'm told, had a dance party. With costumes.'

'Huh.'

'She's coming up on her first birthday. Have you given that any thought?'

'No.' Panic wanted to rise. 'I don't know how to buy a birthday thing for a one-year-old. You do it.'

'We'll figure it out.'

She shifted her attention from the street to him for a heartbeat. He knew much about most, but she wasn't sure even Roarke knew what you were supposed to get for a first birthday.

'I'll ask Peabody.'

'Excellent idea.'

'There's going to be a party, isn't there? Some big, insane Mavis party. Possibly with costumes.'

'I imagine so.'

'I'm not wearing a costume, not even for Mavis. Or one of those hats. Those pointy hats.'

'There's bound to be cake.'

'I like cake. They were getting bored.'

Not Bella, Roarke thought, or her parents. The killers.

'So they wanted to mix it up.'

'I think so.' She knew them now, knew them, and it . . . 'It *feels* so. All the way here, they were on the move, had this goal – her dream of New York, and his romantic ideal to fulfill her dream. Then they got here. We assumed Kuper was their first in New York, but I'm not even close to assuming that now.'

'The tenant or owner of wherever they're – *nesting* is how you put it.'

'Yeah. They could have gone the straight rental route, but it's not pattern. Skipping out on the rent, stealing from wherever they work. I'll bet you a night in costumes when we track them back, they'll have skipped out on motels and flops, or used vacants, killed owners and tenants along their route.'

'I'm sorry, I'm still considering the bet for costumes as I don't see how I can lose.'

'Eye on the prize, pal.'

He looked at her, straight at her. 'It always is.'

'Sap.' But she laid her hand over his a moment. 'I'm going to put the map up, dash screen. Highlighting the parking areas I already earmarked. Peabody can feed us anything she gets.'

It took her some time, but since they had it, Roarke let her fight with the in-dash comp.

'Fuck me. Why can't you just say put up the damn map, and it puts up the damn map?'

As, essentially, you could, Roarke kept his thoughts to himself.

He headed down Seventh Avenue, and once south of the West Village, began to hunt with her.

'I'm not going to let them take another. It may be too late for Campbell. Her chances are razor-thin, and that goes for Mulligan because I think they might go for the double-kill.'

'A bigger thrill.'

'And that's all it's about now. All it was ever about. Let's try that lot.'

They wound through a parking garage, level by level, drove out again, cut east.

She studied every vehicle, every pedestrian.

'It's the perfect cover for them,' she said as they tried another lot. 'Everyone's bundled up, less people on the street. Even the chemi-heads and dealers take it inside or underground in weather like this.'

They gave it an hour, covering every section of every

block, driving through parking structures, into and out of lots.

'Try this one.' She gestured to a private multilevel for a run of buildings. 'We'll park, and I'll do a quick canvass on foot. You can wait for me.'

'Really?'

His *really* was another man's *fat chance*, she thought.

'You could. You won't, but you could. We'll take this last one tonight, do the foot patrol, and count on Feeney's drones in the morning.'

He doubted she knew it was going onto midnight. She had the scent, couldn't quite give it up and settle down to hunt fresh the next day.

So they'd scan another three levels of vehicles, he thought as he circumvented the permit requirement, drove smoothly in. Then they'd take a very unlovely winter's walk.

On the second level, she grabbed his arm. 'Stop! There. That van. New York plates, but the rest fits. Navy-blue, tinted windows, the right make and model. Change the plates, just an extra cover.'

She yanked out her PPC, more comfortable with that than the in-dash, ran the registered plates.

'Registered to Anthony Charles Lappans, age seven-three, East Broadway address, and that's not only not here, it's near Kuper's dump site. Keep an eye out.'

She jumped out of the all-terrain, shoved her coat back for easy access to her weapon, and approached the van.

She gestured to the sticker on the back window, circled the van, then walked back. 'I'm going to get a warrant, but you're right here, right now.'

Understanding, he got out, took out his pocket tools. After a quick glance at the lock, he selected what he wanted. He had the rear doors open in seconds.

Inside Eve studied a bulky armchair, a tool bag, a balled-up blanket, and spots and stains she'd bet her badge were dried blood.

'Close it back up, will you, and open the passenger door.'

'Dog gets the bone,' he murmured as he did as she asked.

'What?'

'You don't give up. Just keep on digging until you have the bone. Your killers are also very untidy.'

'Yeah, isn't that handy?' Her lips spread in a feral smile as she studied the litter of fast-food bags, disposable go-cups and receipts. 'I don't suppose there's a field kit in that new ride of yours?'

'There is, of course, but I think all you'll want at this point is . . . ' He took tweezers out of his kit.

Nodding, she used them to lift one of the receipts. 'From a Stop 'N Go in New Jersey. Another from a café here, on West Broad.

'Lock it back up. We've got them now. One way or the other, we've got them.'

20

She tagged Reo first, interrupting the APA's beauty sleep. Cher Reo would order the search warrant, save time.

The chain of command meant she should contact Whitney next, but her team had earned it. And briefing them first would add to the movement.

'Hey,' Peabody said when she came on screen. She blinked blurry, sleep-deprived eyes.

'I've got the van.'

'You – *what*? Holy crap, Dallas, are you kidding me?'

'They changed the plates. Do a quick run on Lappans, Anthony Charles, on East Broadway just to tie it up. Reo's getting us a warrant to search it.'

'Where are you?'

'Second level of a permit garage.' She rattled off the address. 'Get that to McNab. I want the security feed for the past five days. Have Banner start a search on the three buildings that use this garage. Vacants, missings, DBs. I'm ordering a dozen uniforms to knock on doors in these buildings.'

'Do you want us down there?'

'I want you where you are. Get the data, all of it. I'll pull you in, if we locate them, for the bust.'

'It's not about the bust – I mean being there. Me being there.'

'I know it, but I'll pull you in if and when. Work fast.'

She cut Peabody off, and woke up her commander.

She considered Mira, but she'd need the shrink after the bust. She'd want Mira once she had James and Parsens in the box.

Pacing, she ordered the uniforms, giving her own Uniform Carmichael the lead, with specific instructions. Two uniforms per door, with a story about a lead on a missing child reported seen in the building.

'They can't and won't open the door,' Roarke commented. 'Or it's highly unlikely.'

'I know it. So we can cross off any doors that open. Hostages are a possibility – other than Campbell and Mulligan – but I think that's low. They'd be compelled to hurt and use anyone they have.'

'Another possibility,' he began.

'The van's here – they're not.' If that turned out to be the case, she'd deal with the frustration of it later. 'We still have to do the door-to-doors.'

She used her comm again, ordered up sweepers for the van.

'Can you find a slot for that machine of yours, leave me

the field kit? If Reo comes through before the sweepers get here, I can start processing the van. But I want that thing out of the way. Maybe they'll decide it's a good night to pick up fresh meat, and I don't want to warn them off.'

He took a slow study of their ground, assessed it.

'Why don't I take out the elevators while I'm at it? That would limit them, if they're in the building, to the stairs. If they do come in, and from the outside, you'd hear them before they made it up on foot.'

'Good thinking.'

She'd put a couple of uniforms on the garage entrance while she and the sweepers worked. She checked the time, saw it was after midnight.

'Still time for them to hunt, but it's getting past the time frame they hit the three New York vics. The later it gets, the less chance they'll be on the move tonight. I want to get the van processed, then put under surveillance. We leave it just where it is.'

She took the field kit, circled the van again, her fingers itching to try for prints. Hearing the echo of an engine, she slipped two vehicles over, used one for cover.

From there she watched a sleet-covered sedan, an exhausted-looking woman behind the wheel, circle up as Roarke had done.

She hoped he hadn't copped the sedan's slot, but if he had, he'd handle it.

She yanked out her 'link when it signaled.

Reo, blonde hair springing in all directions, baby blues shadowed, gave Eve a smirk.

'I caught Judge Hayden watching *Any-Time Sports* on screen. He was awake and amenable. Warrant's coming through.'

'Good, quick work. Go back to bed.'

'I never got out.'

Even as the screen went blank, Eve heard the new incoming. She read the warrant – best to cross every T on this one. Satisfied, she opened her kit as Roarke strolled down to her.

'Elevator's blocked.'

'There was a four-door sedan.'

'I waited for her. The warrant?'

'We've got it.'

After switching on her recorder, she went to work on the driver's-side door first, pulled two clear prints. When she ran them for a match, got James, her lips spread in that feral smile again.

'Gotcha. Open her up, will you?'

'My pleasure.'

When she tapped her recorder, handed him her master, he waited until she'd skirted around, started on the passenger side before he took out his tools.

'Got her, too,' she told him. 'Handprint.'

She came around back, sealed up, climbed in the doors he'd opened.

'Bag's got cord, rope, duct tape, crowbar, wrenches, a hammer.'

She took out more of her own tools, tested the wrench. 'Blood on the big wrench. And the crowbar, and for the triple, the hammer.'

She tested the interior floor. 'And the carpet. We'll have the sweepers get samples, take them into the lab. They're going to match the vics. At least some of them are going to match.'

She opened the glove box. 'Flashlight, owner's manual disc, first aid kit, and this.'

With her sealed hands she held up a large knife.

'That would be a bowie knife. I'm acquainted from my own weapon collection.'

'James's former employer. The mother's boyfriend's knife.'

Processing it, she found blood, and a partial print from James, another from Parsens.

'They didn't even try to clean it. Why bother?' she supposed, 'When they're only going to use it again. Once we get them, they're never getting out.'

She put the knife back where she'd found it, took a tag from Uniform Carmichael.

'Quick, quiet, thorough,' she told him. 'Anything, anyone feels off, I get a signal. Record any door that doesn't open.'

By the time the sweepers arrived, she'd done all she could do on the van. She crossed over to Dawson, the head sweeper and, with what had gone down on New Year's Eve in mind, took a good look at his team of two.

'How's it going?' she asked him.

'Oh, well, hit some rough spots now and then, but what can you do? How about you?'

'Tonight? Good, because when we bag these bastards, we've got enough evidence to lock them in a cage for several lifetimes. I need everything processed, and everything left exactly where you found it. If we miss them tonight, they may come back for the van. We'll have it watched, but we'll want them to lead us to the vics. I don't want them spooked.'

'Full record before we touch anything.'

'I got prints, I got blood. I'll leave you to take blood samples, get them in, wrangle expedited. I didn't go as far as hair and fiber. You'll be faster there. I'd want Harvo on that end.'

He smiled a little. 'Everybody wants Harvo, but I'll make it happen.'

'Did you bring the tracker?'

He patted his own kit. 'As requested.'

'The guy's a mechanic. A good one. Make sure it doesn't show if he does a look-see. And he knows something about electronics, so—'

'We've got it, Dallas.'

'In and out, fast as you can. We're doing the door-to-doors, and I've got a couple of cops coming in in an unmarked to keep an eye on it from the first level. It's probably too late for them to come in and take a ride tonight, but there are uniforms scattered around. You're covered.'

'How many vics?'

'Twenty-four and counting – that we know of. Two more still alive, that we know of.'

'We'll sew this end up.'

Nodding, she moved off again, joined Roarke. 'I want to do some knock-on-doors. It'll go faster.'

'Then I'm with you.' But he caught her chin in his hand, his thumb brushing lightly over the shallow dent as he studied her face. 'You get so bloody pale when you push past your limit. We'll cover as many doors as you like, but if you don't have them by the end of it, or a Herculean lead, we're home after, and you'll get some sleep.'

And after that he was determined she'd take a booster – however much she disliked them – whatever it took to see her through it.

Together they covered four floors of the second building. Hit one no-answer.

But the across-the-hall stepped back out. 'I should've told you, that's the Delwickies. Nice young couple. They're away for a few days.'

Eve turned back, studied the door as if she could see through it if she concentrated enough.

'Took a winter break with some friends, down to the Florida Keys. I'm watering her plants while they're away.'

Eve let her concentration throttle back. 'You've been in their apartment in the last few days?'

'Every morning. Alice set store by her plants. Got a green

thumb, too. She's got a little orange tree in there with real fruit growing on it. It's something.'

She yawned, pushed at her mop of steel-gray hair. 'You don't want to think they'd have anything to do with taking that little girl who's missing. They're nice people. Quiet, but not, you know, creepy quiet like you hear about when the neighbor turns out to be a serial killer. He's what you call a sous chef, and at least once a week, he brings me and my husband back something from the fancy French place where he works.'

Knowing the woman had been inside the apartment every morning had been enough, but Eve let her wind out.

'Okay, thanks very much. I'm sorry to have disturbed you.'

'I've got kids, and grandkids, of my own. I'm going to keep my eye out for the little girl. Bless her heart.'

Out of all the units, the canvass netted six doors that didn't open – not counting the Delwickies as Eve considered them crossed off.

She ran them all, found two worked night shifts, and when contacted were indeed at work, on shift. Two more reportedly out of town, and on the twelfth and fifteenth floors respectively.

Low probability.

But for them, and the last two, she dragged in very unhappy supers to authorize entrance. And cleared them all.

'That's it now.' Determined, Roarke took her arm, and pulled her toward the elevators he'd released once the unmarked was in place.

'They're not in these buildings, which means you've made serious progress. You have the van, you have evidence which will put them away. You can't knock on every bloody door left in this sector, at least not tonight.'

'Could do some. The missing-girl gambit's holding.'

'Eve, if you were any paler I swear I'd be able to pass a hand through you. You need sleep, then you'll do what comes next. It's near three in the morning now. Whatever they've done to your victims tonight is done.'

She thought the same, so didn't argue, but got into the all-terrain.

'It's narrowed down more, a lot more. Compared to where we started it's like a handful of blocks. I gotta see what Banner's come up with, and Peabody. Vacants, missings, DBs.'

He let her talk it out, though her words had started to slur. He edged the heat up a bit, knowing how warm relaxed her. And when she started to droop, eased her seat back.

She was out before they reached Midtown.

She stirred when he lifted her out of the seat, muttered when he carried her to the door, then surfaced as he maneuvered to get the door open.

'What? Jesus, I went out.'

'Stay that way,' he advised and started up.

'No, put me down. God, I can't have you carrying me around in front of cops.'

'I doubt there's a single cop in our bedroom – until I get you in there.'

'I need to check in my office.'

'It's half-three, Eve. Everyone's in bed but us.'

'I need to check.'

He detoured, but didn't set her down.

'I can walk.'

'No point in it when I've got you.'

He noted the lights remained on in her office, paused in the doorway.

Peabody and McNab flopped together like puppies in the sleep chair. Banner had stretched facedown on the floor, with Galahad's limp body sprawled over his waist like a fat, furry belt.

'Christ, cops,' Roarke muttered, and gave in, set Eve on her feet.

'Take Banner,' she told Roarke, then walked over to poke Peabody's shoulder.

'Not now.' Peabody rolled over. 'We can do it in the morning.'

'Ick,' was Eve's opinion, and gave her partner a firmer poke.

'Uh-uh, in the morning.' But her eyes blinked open, stared blindly at Eve. Then cleared. 'What? You? Where?'

'Get McNab up, go to bed, and I don't want to hear about the morning.'

'Huh? Wait.' She started to sit up. McNab shifted, pulled her closer. And laid a hand directly over her left breast. 'Um.' Peabody removed his hand. 'We needed to take five.'

'Now you can have three and a half.'

'Eve, have some pity here,' Roarke insisted.

'Four. Back here, oh-seven-thirty.'

'We didn't get 'em?'

'We will. Full briefing, oh-seven-thirty, but we eliminated three buildings, and the van's being watched. Hit the rack.'

She strode out, past Banner who, awake now, sat on the floor like a man coming out of a dream.

The cat gave him a friendly head bump, then deserted him to trot after Eve.

Eve dreamed, harsh and bloody dreams, dreams where Jayla Campbell opened dead eyes to accuse her.

Where were you? I needed help. I wanted to live.

Dreams where her mother snuck in to taunt her.

I might as well have tossed you out the window like I wanted to half the time for all the good you do.

Dreams where all the known dead lay on slabs crowded into her office.

How can you sleep? they demanded. *How can you sleep?*

So, scarcely three hours after she'd closed her eyes in her own bed, she opened them again.

Roarke wrapped her closer when she started to rise. 'You've time yet.'

'They won't let me sleep. The dead won't let me sleep. How can I? They keep asking me that. How can I sleep?'

'It's you who asks it, darling Eve. Not the dead.' He hoped

to soothe her under again, stroked her back. 'Death brings knowledge, to my thinking. Of all that couldn't be known in life. So the dead know what you do, what you give.'

'I don't know. But if they know so much maybe that's why they always seem so pissed off.'

He laughed a little. 'Rest a bit more.'

'I can't. I need to get going on it again. It's today, Roarke. If we don't find them today, Campbell's dead, and probably Mulligan. I know it, like your dead know. Only hours now, or I lose both of them.'

'All right, then, we'll start.'

He gave her the shower first as he wanted to light the fire and program coffee. And something else. When she came out, he held out a glass.

She scowled at it. 'Uh-uh.'

'Have this, or no coffee for you.'

'Bollocks. And bite me.'

'It won't give that nervous edge the departmental approved does, but it will give you a slow and reasonable energy lift. I've diluted it as you'll chase it with coffee all day. You should trust me on this by now.'

The last booster he'd bargained her into taking had been okay, she remembered. 'It doesn't look like the last one.'

'It's newer. We've been selling it for a few weeks now overseas, and in Asia. Your FDA is slower to move on such things – as your FBI and all your other acronyms and initials.'

'Not the NYPSD.'

He smiled. 'That would depend on your perspective. A favor to me,' he added, held it out.

She took it, downed it, frowned. 'It tastes like . . . green grapes.'

'Which you're fond of.' Now he handed her the coffee. 'I'll grab a shower. Dress warm, will you? I checked the forecast, and we're done with the sleet, with temperatures in the single digits. A balmy eight, they're saying, for a high.'

'That's nobody's high.'

She layered a tank under a cashmere sweater in slate-gray, went with black for the jacket, the pants, the boots.

He'd probably roll his eyes, she thought, say something about trying a bit of color in that way he had, but . . .

He stepped out, a towel around his waist, tilted his head as he studied her.

'You mean business. You look strong, tough and right on into fierce. A good choice for the day.'

'Really?'

'Absolutely.'

'I'll never get it. Never. I'm going to get started. I guess we'll put on the whole breakfast bonanza when the others get up.'

'Works perfectly. I won't be long.'

'Don't you have, like, holo-meetings with Kathmandu? Is that a real place?'

He laughed again as he moved to the closet. 'It is, and I don't. I shuffled a bit. I'll give you some time if you need it, work from here this morning.'

She started out, stopped, walked back, wrapped her arms around him, squeezed. 'I forget to do that.'

He tipped her head back, kissed her. 'I see it as you remember.'

'Working on it.'

She headed straight to her office, thinking more coffee first, then diving straight in before the others crowded it. She'd have close to an hour to review, rethink and research.

But when she walked into her office, Peabody already sat at an auxiliary station, gulping coffee.

'You're early.'

Eve nodded, kept going toward the kitchen and coffee. 'You too.'

'I figured I could give the other case an hour before we started back on James and Parsens.'

The other case, Eve thought as, considering the morning, the others, went for a pot instead of a single mug.

She'd dumped that one on Peabody, and said she'd be there to help. So far, she hadn't been.

'Fill me in.'

Peabody glanced over as Eve came back in. 'You're sure?'

'Fill me in.'

'Okay. DB's a floater, surfaced at Pier 40. ME says six days in the water.'

'Who's the ME on it?'

'It's Porter. DB's, male, between twenty-five and thirty,

mixed race. He's a John Doe as his face was bashed in, then the fish – you know. And his fingers were severed.'

'By the killer, or the fish?'

'The killer. So it looks like maybe a mob hit, maybe. It sure looks like the killer didn't want the DB ID'd if and when he surfaced.'

'DNA?'

'Yeah, I've got an order in, but they're – surprise – backed up, and say at least another thirty-six. Maybe you can push them some on that.'

'I can, and will. COD?'

'Vic was stabbed, multiples, and Porter says the gut wound was COD. The finger-severing? Some ante-, some post-mortem, like maybe they were trying to get information out of him, but he died – or they were trying for a ransom deal – sending his fingers as incentive.'

'What started out, potentially, as persuasion, and finished in an attempt to blur identification.'

'Yeah, that's how it seems,' Peabody agreed. 'The time in the water – the body was weighed down with old bricks, and forensic's working on IDing those, stuffed in a jumbo recycler bag. The time in the water,' she said again, 'and the fish did the usual number on the body. The bag came unsealed, so the fish got in.'

'Tox?'

'Hasn't come in. I was leaning toward organized crime or gang, but the face-bashing – at least one blow was antemortem and broke several teeth – seems more personal. And the torture.'

'The fingers.'

'Those, yeah, that's the big one, but there were other signs of torture.'

Eve lowered her mug. 'What kind, what signs?'

'Some of the cuts and punctures were shallow, and Porter reports the vic's left foot and ankle were smashed – heavy object. Antemortem. Both knees were broken.'

'Any burns?'

'Not in his report, but the fish . . .'

Eve turned on her heel, strode to her desk and tagged Morris at home.

He didn't bother to block video – she'd never known him to. He answered, casually propped in bed, his hair loosely braided, his eyes still blurry with sleep.

'Campbell?'

'No, but possibly related. You've got a John Doe – Porter did the autopsy. Male, twenty-five to thirty, mixed race. Floater, surfaced Pier 40, been under six days. Signs of torture, Morris. Face beaten in beyond IDing, fingers severed. COD stabbing, abdomen. I need you on it, now, and I need you to push for immediate DNA. I want him ID'd yesterday.'

'I'll order the DNA now.' He tossed aside the covers. Eve caught the Grim Reaper tat on his thigh, then a solid glimpse of his very well-toned ass before he moved out of screen range. 'You'll have it within the hour. I'm on my way in.'

'Thanks.'

'I never put it together.' Peabody was on her feet. 'I never considered . . . '

'Peabody, it dropped on you less than twelve hours ago, in the middle of another prioritized investigation.'

'But I never – you thought of it in under five minutes, with just the basics I gave you.'

'And if I'd given you five minutes last night, we'd have moved on it sooner. We don't know if it's connected, but we'll know once the John Doe is ID'd.'

'They've never done anything like this – it's not the pattern. But I should've—'

'Should'ves are crap,' Eve shot back, 'and who's the LT here?'

'You are,' Peabody mumbled.

'If you want to beat yourself up,' Eve continued as Roarke came in, 'do it later. But you've got nothing to take a hit over. It's something we're going to check out. Maybe they did something like this before and nobody's found a body – or put it together, maybe it was the first time. Maybe it's not connected at all. And maybes are like should'ves. Crap. The point is, there's some correlation, and they needed a place in New York.'

'So, maybe they're using the John Doe's. Sorry about the maybe. We pursue the possibility they killed and disposed of John Doe to get his place.'

Sensing Peabody's distress, Roarke crossed over, kissed her cheek.

'I screwed up,' she said.

'Did I say you screwed up?' Eve snapped it out this time. 'You'll know when you've screwed up because my boot will be up your ass. This DB hasn't been reported missing. I've combed the missings, and nobody in his age range and race has been reported in the last week. You didn't have Morris. Porter's decent, but he's no Morris, who'd have considered this possible connection and pushed on it. We have no previous instances of disfiguration or mutilation of this sort. You're working the case, and briefed your partner and LT at the first opportunity.

'Is my boot up your ass?'

'Not exactly.'

'Then you didn't screw up. Get breakfast. For everybody. We don't have time for moping around. Move.'

'What do you want me to get — for breakfast?'

'Do I look like I give a skinny rat's ass?'

'You really don't.'

Moving fast now, Peabody went to the kitchen.

Eve narrowed her eyes at Roarke. 'And don't even think about giving me grief over that.'

'On the contrary.' He moved to her, tapped the dent in her chin. 'I was about to say well done. You gave her just what she needed. Now, why don't you tell me what this John Doe has to do with these murders?'

'Could be nothing, could be everything.' She reeled it off while she went to her desk, checked missing persons again for anyone in the range of John Doe.

'Pier 40 – it would coordinate with your map, or close enough.'

'That's right. So, possible scenario: John Doe meets Parsens and/or James, or they scope him out while they're hunting for a nest. John Doe likely lives alone, or he'd have been reported. That's playing the odds, but they're good ones. They take him down, in or near his residence. I vote for in. They have some fun with him, then do what they can to make IDing him difficult, they stuff him in a bag, add bricks. Steal those from an abandoned or a construction site, haul in the van, add bricks to the bag. Dump the body in the river, then make a nest in John Doe's place.'

'Once you ID John Doe—'

'We check out his place. What Morris finds helps determine how we check it out. Could be no more than Doe's serious bad luck, or it could be the piece we need to take these fuckers down.'

'You think the latter.'

She had the buzz, right down to her fingertips.

'Feels right.' She paced around her board, then strode to Peabody's station, began a full review. 'Feels really right. Do me a favor?'

'Of what sort?'

'Of that sort that gets McNab and Banner out of bed. When Morris gets back to me, we're going to be ready.'

21

Eve stuffed waffles in her mouth – good choice, Peabody – while she briefed a rumpled-looking McNab and Banner. Less than thirty minutes after Peabody filled her in on John Doe, she had an outline of an op working through her mind.

Maybe John Doe had lived with his wife and three kids in an uptown penthouse apartment, and nobody noticed he'd been gone for a week.

But if her hunch hit, she'd be ready.

'McNab, contact Feeney. I want eyes, ears, heat sensors ready to roll when we get an address. Peabody, you're on Carmichael and Santiago. They deserve to be in on this if it plays out the way we hope. I want them in body armor under soft clothes. We'll place them once we have a location.'

She carted her plate, polishing off the waffle as she paced around her board, studied the map on screen.

'Banner, work me some probabilities on location. Factor the van, the John Doe, and the sector I've narrowed it to. No one's approached the van since we found it, so they haven't needed it. They didn't hit any of the takeout places last night.

Maybe they risked delivery due to weather, or maybe they had enough in stock, but they'll go out soon.'

'We can figure Campbell and Mulligan are still alive,' Banner put in. 'They didn't need the van to dump bodies.'

'That's exactly right. When we move, we move on the assumption there are two civilians in distress inside. We'll have medicals standing by.'

She set her empty plate on the table. 'Anybody without magic coats uses body armor.'

'The FBI?' Peabody said.

'Will be informed – when and if we're on our way. I'll go through Zweck after I talk to Whitney.' She checked the time, again, then glanced at Roarke. 'You want in?'

'I believe that goes without saying.'

She grabbed her 'link at the first beep. 'Morris.'

'Zed, Samuel, age twenty-eight, 251 Downing, apartment 1-A.'

'Bam. Roarke.'

'I'll see to it.'

'Data being sent now,' Morris told her.

'Have you had a chance to look at him?'

'Not thoroughly, but there are similarities in some of the wounds, particularly, the COD. And here, take a look.'

'We all will. Computer, transfer 'link image on screen.'

'The water, and the fish, compromised the body. You see the damage here.'

'That'll put you off breakfast,' Banner muttered as a

close-up of pale, mottled, torn and bloodless flesh came on screen.

'I see the damage,' Eve said, stepping closer. 'And I see what looks like the side of a heart. That curve there. A fish didn't do that.'

'Agreed. I won't slap at Porter for missing it – overmuch. I might not have found it myself if I hadn't been looking for it, specifically.'

Yeah, you would, Eve thought. 'It's enough. It's what we need.'

'For what you have to do, yes. But Samuel deserves more from me. You'll have a complete, amended report before noon. I hope you have those who did this to him before that.'

'Count on it. Thanks.'

She turned. 'Roarke?'

'I've got it.' He continued to work his PPC. 'It's a twelve-unit building.'

'Tell me it has a basement unit.'

'It does. Give me a moment. Your gut remains reliable, Lieutenant. 1-A is a basement, one-bedroom unit, currently rented by Samuel Zed.'

'Suit up,' she ordered. 'Move out.'

She had Roarke drive the bigger version of the A-T while she read the rest of Zed's data.

'Peabody, Zed was employed as a line cook at the Fish House. Find out why nobody noticed he hasn't been on the line for the past several days. Mother and one sib live in Indiana, and likely don't know he's been missing. McNab?'

'On with Feeney now, Dallas. We'll have it covered.'

She turned in her seat, gave Banner a straight look. 'You warm enough, Deputy?'

'Yeah, sure.'

'That's not going to last. Roarke's going to drive by the target, and you're going to get out. I've got uniforms keeping an eye out. You'll do the same. I don't want them taking a look outside, spotting cops. So you're going to find a spot. Maybe you get something from a glide-cart or café – as long as you can keep the target in sight. You're going to look like a tourist.'

'I can do that.'

'If they come out, or one does, you follow. Don't get made, don't get close, just keep me updated.'

'I can do that, too.'

'Peabody, tell Banner what happens if you screw up.'

Peabody smiled a cheery smile. 'You find her boot up your ass.'

'You don't want to find my boot up your ass, Banner. Keep your eyes open, and that's it, until Santiago and Carmichael are in place. When they are, I'll tell you where to go.'

'I've got enough boots of my own, and I appreciate the chance to be a part of this. I've got good eyes, Lieutenant.'

She decided to count on that, and brought up the vid map Roarke had sent her of the target building and its neighbors.

'We walked right by this building last night. I walked by it on my own the day before. Right by it.'

'As you can't see through walls, walking by it was all you could do.' Roarke sent her a quick look. 'There's no time to beat yourself up,' he said, repeating her words to Peabody.

She couldn't argue, and instead contacted the uniforms to tell them Banner would be on point.

She edged forward in her seat when Roarke turned onto Downing. Quiet street – at least at this hour. On the shabbier side but trying to hold on.

Barred windows the norm for basement and street level. Apartment 1-A of number 251 had bars and privacy screens, no exterior cam. She couldn't make the locks from the drive-by.

'Drop Banner on the corner. Eyes, Banner, nothing but eyes.'

'That's a big yes, sir.'

He climbed out, hunched his shoulders against the cold, then sauntered across the street in the crosswalk.

'They might make him for a cop if they look out and look close, but they sure as hell won't mistake him for a New York cop.'

'Which is why you put him on point.'

'Which is why,' she agreed. 'And because we wouldn't be this far unless he'd stuck on Little.'

She checked the time, gauged the distance to Central and contacted Whitney.

She was still updating him when Roarke pulled into Central's garage.

'I'm in Central now, sir, and heading up to the division. I'll brief the team, coordinate with Captain Feeney. We'll be in place in under an hour. I'm looking at forty minutes. I'll contact Special Agent Zweck now to apprise him of the situation so the FBI can join us.'

'I'll contact Zweck. At the moment this is an NYPSD op.' His tone was brisk and final. 'I'll let you know if and when that changes.'

'Yes, sir, thank you.' She ended transmission as they piled into the elevator. 'Damn straight. Let's get this on, and get it on right before federal red tape trips anything up. Roarke, you can make this elevator bypass floors, go straight to my level, right?'

'An express ride? Happy to.' He pulled out his PPC, went to work.

Seconds later, Peabody said, 'Whee!' as they zipped straight up.

Eve was off and striding to Homicide the second the doors opened.

'McNab, use our single and rarely reliable wall screen in the bull pen. I don't have time to fight for a conference room.' She turned into the bull pen. 'Get the vid map up. Carmichael, Santiago, front and center.'

She hesitated a moment when she spotted Carmichael's sapphire-blue cowboy boots with jewel-colored studs running down the sides. 'Are you serious?'

'Sheepskin lined, Dallas. Warm as it gets. You said soft clothes. Santiago bought a hat.'

His lip actually curled. 'I'm not wearing it.'

'Not on an op, but on the job, five full days. He lost a bet.'

He shook his head sadly at Eve. 'I didn't learn from my mistakes, and now have to pay the price.'

'Pay it later. Target's the basement apartment, 251. We believe the two vics are still alive in there. Banner is currently on point, on location. We have four uniforms, here, here.' She used the laser pointer. 'Two with eyes on the rear exit, here. The rear exit is an escape window, backed by a short alley to Bedford.'

She highlighted it with her pointer.

'According to our expert consultant civilian who accessed the blueprints, the escape window must be released from the interior to unlock the bars, then lifted manually. To get out, you climb up and out. An unlikely exit, but our e-team will bypass the release. You'll take the rear, close off that escape route.'

'We got that,' Santiago said.

'Medicals will be on tap, Seventh and West Houston. EDD will have its van at the end of the block, east side. We're after four heat sources, two suspects, two victims. EDD will approach the building from the east, get us eyes and ears, if possible.

'We go when I say go. Body armor?'

Santiago tapped his chest. 'We're geared up.'

'You're clear to go to the location. Let Banner know when you're there. And tag me. McNab, body armor. Roarke, can you zoom in on the target door? I want to see the locks.'

'They're standard click/slide with dead bolt,' he told her. 'Middle range. Not utter crap, but nothing fancy. Might be a riot bar on the inside, but we'll know that once we have eyes in there.'

'We'll take a battering ram, in the event.'

'No cam, no alarm that I can see, and none added in during building rehab some twelve years ago. They've a Judas hole, and that's all.'

McNab came back wearing the black armor over his sweater of screaming red with shivering silver stripes to match, Eve supposed, his silver pants.

'EDD's in the garage, Lieutenant.' He pranced to her in his red-and-green plaid boots. 'And Feeney's in the van.'

'Let's move out. Roarke, you're with Feeney. Let's go save lives and kick ass.'

She ran it through, over and over on the drive, but she understood, too well, you couldn't know all the angles, all the movements, until you were in it. Having two civilians, likely restrained, certainly injured, added to the issues.

Saving lives came first.

'You're on the vics, Peabody. Once EDD verifies their location, getting to them, covering them, that's your prior-ity. I'm putting Uniform Carmichael with you. He's got the most experience. Cover the vics, cover your ass, cover each other.'

'In that order?'

'Pretty much. None of the vics we've investigated had evidence of stun marks. But we don't go in assuming they don't have stunners. We know they have stickers and tools.'

She pulled up behind the EDD van. 'He's going to be more inclined to protect her than she is him. But she's not going to go down easy. They're a lot of stupid, but they're wily. Don't forget it.'

'You, either.'

They got out. Before Eve could rap on the back of the van, Roarke opened the door, held out a hand to boost her, then Peabody, in.

'Setting up for heat sources,' he told her.

Feeney worked the equipment, McNab jiggled beside him.

'Just refining coordinates. Most of that unit's below street level.' Feeney fiddled, fooled, then rolled his shoulders.

'Got you four. Two in the northeast corner.'

'That would be the bedroom,' Roarke said, studying his PPC.

'Two more, front of the unit.'

'Living area.'

Eve hunched over Feeney's shoulder.

'Probable suspects are still in bed. Probable victims, also horizontal, about eighteen inches between them.'

And alive, she thought. Still generating heat.

She stepped out again, to use her comm, coordinate her team, and to have the van transferred.

Roarke jumped out. 'I have your eyes and ears, Lieutenant.'

She should've figured he'd wheedle his way out of the van and into the action.

'Set me up.' He handed her earbuds first, and another set for Peabody. 'We're on the move,' she said. 'Feeney, if anything moves in there, I hear about it.'

'Hey, She-Body?'

McNab leaned out the back of the van, reached out so they did the little finger tap Eve had seen them do dozens of times.

'Back in a few,' Peabody told him.

'On approach,' Eve said as they started down the block. 'Stay alert. No detectible movement inside.'

Even so, they crouched, took the last few yards at a bent jog. Weapon drawn, she went down the short steps first, sidled over to the side of the door. Peabody took the opposite side while Roarke hunkered down with the portable unit.

'Give us a few seconds here.'

Inside, Reed turned and twisted his arm from the shoulder. His broken hand throbbed so brutally with the movement he could hear the sound of it inside his head. His breath wheezed through lips so dry they bled.

He felt as if he'd been at it for days. He'd passed out from the pain a few times, but he could see, through the privacy screen, it was still daylight. Still morning, he thought.

'Jayla.' He barely recognized his own voice. 'Jayla, wake up. You have to stay awake. Come on, talk to me. It's looser, a little looser. If I can get my arm free . . .'

Her eyes fluttered open. 'I just wanna sleep now. I wanna go to sleep.'

'You can't. Look at me. Remember, remember, that's what you said to me before. They're still asleep. I'm going to get my arm out. Maybe this time I can get us out. I know I hurt you. I'm sorry.'

'It's not that. You didn't. Not you. They're going to kill me today, just like she said. She said, "We're going to kill you tomorrow," and I don't want them to. I just want to sleep, and not wake up. There are angels when you sleep.'

'No. Jayla.' He twisted harder, and the pain came in white-hot bolts. They'd cut her when they'd forced him to rape her – the second time the night before, they'd cut her to add to it all. He could see her blood on the stained plastic.

She hadn't been able to fight and cry the second time. She'd only lain there. And she hadn't heard what the bitch had said, not all of it. She hadn't said they were going to kill her tomorrow. She'd said they were going to make *him* kill her.

And that was a terror beyond the pain.

The terror rose like bile in his throat when he heard a giggle.

They were awake, and it would all start again.

'Some movement from the source closest to the front window,' Eve murmured. 'One of the vics is awake. And, wait . . . movement from the bedroom. I need to see, Roarke.'

'Nearly there.'

She stared at the screen, watched it flicker, then pop clear. A floor littered with outdoor gear. Before she could demand, Roarke began to slowly slide the eyes over.

'Hold. We've got eyes on the two civilians. Visual confirmation on Mulligan. He's awake, struggling, sluggish. Visual confirmation on Campbell, who appears to be unconscious. Both are bound. She's got blood leaking from somewhere. There's a lot of it on the floor. No visual on suspects.'

'Ears are coming,' Roarke murmured.

'If they're still in bed, we move in, cover the civilians. Uniform Carmichael, move in here now. Banner, move on the front.'

Roarke tied in audio. And Eve heard a giggle.

'Suspects are up, up and moving. Get the locks.'

'One second. No riot bar.' Roarke angled the portable aside, took out tools. 'You're low, as usual.'

'I'm high, you're high. Peabody, Carmichael, you're in behind us and cut right, get to the civilians. Banner, bring the rest in now.'

'We're clear,' Roarke told her.

'Enter in five, four, three.' She used her fingers for the last count. And they hit the door.

The crash shook the air. Shouts, a wall of noise and movement followed it.

James, naked, held a ballpeen hammer. Parsens, wearing sexy stolen underwear, a small kitchen knife. Parsens screamed, turned to flee.

'Stop! Police!'

James hurled the hammer. Eve heard it *thwack* against the wall as she dodged.

'I've got him,' Roarke said coolly. 'Why don't you take care of the woman?'

James, wild-eyed now, charged at Roarke. Knowing her man, Eve left him to it, went after Parsens.

When Eve found the bedroom door closed and locked, she just shook her head. Rearing back she kicked once, twice, nipped away from a flying bottle when the door crashed in.

'Give it up, Ella-Loo.'

'Stay away from me, or I'll kill you!' She swept another bottle from the floor, this time smashing it against the wall, then jabbing out with the jagged glass with one hand, the knife with the other.

'Are you kidding me with that? Do you not *see* the stunner in my hand?'

'I'm going to cut your face off.'

'Okay, give it a shot.'

Swinging the broken bottle over her head, swiping and jabbing with the knife, Ella-Loo leaped forward. Eve considered the stunner in that brief second, then went for the more satisfying. A left cross.

She had to pull it, a little, to avoid the knife. But not much.

She wasn't sorry when the bitch fell back onto shattered glass and, screaming, rolled over bloody.

'Yeah, how do you like it?'

A dark part of her might have enjoyed rolling the murdering bitch right back over the glass shards, and maybe the boot that stepped down on the knife caught a couple fingers under it.

The quick, shocked yip didn't hurt her feelings.

But the cop kicked the knife aside, and yanked the spitting, screaming woman up, shoved her facedown on the bed.

'You're under arrest.' She slapped on restraints as Ella-Loo shrieked for Darryl. 'That's for multiple counts of murder in the first, just for starters.'

'Darryl! Darryl! Get this bitch off me!'

Eve leaned down, covered her recorder. 'My man is infinitely more than the excuse for one you have. And he's already taken Darryl down.'

She uncovered the recorder, hauled Ella-Loo up. 'You have the right to remain silent, but go ahead, keep right on screaming. It's fucking music to my ears.'

Ella-Loo whipped her head around, snapped her teeth.

'Oooh, a biter. Now I'm scared.'

As Eve dragged her toward the door, Banner rushed in.

'You got her. You okay?'

'I'm dandy, she fell on some glass, so she'll need medical. I haven't finished reading her her rights. Why don't you take her, Deputy, and do that?'

'That would be my considerable pleasure, Lieutenant.'

'She's a biter.'

He showed his own teeth. 'I've dealt with biters in my time.'

Eve took a breath when Banner hauled Ella-Loo out, flexed her left hand a couple times, then followed.

Darryl, still naked, lay on the floor, unconscious while a uniform cuffed him. Eve glanced at Roarke.

'I'd say that was grand fun, if not for . . .'

Together they looked over at the wounded.

Medical worked on them while cops cut bindings, and Peabody soothed.

'Don't let her die.' Tears streamed down Reed's face. 'Don't let her die, please. They made me rape her. I raped her, but she stayed strong. She didn't blame me. Don't let her die. Her name's Jayla. They hurt her so bad. They wouldn't stop.'

'We know who she is.' Eve stepped over to him. 'We know who you are, Reed. Nothing that happened here is your fault. Medical is going to do everything they can for her. For you.'

McNab laid a blanket over him, stepped aside for medical. They lifted Reed onto a stretcher.

'Don't let her die.' Reed's gaze clung to Eve's. 'Her name's Jayla.'

She turned to one of the MTs, studied Jayla's gray face as she did. 'Will she make it?'

'Lost a lot of blood. We're pumping it and fluids into her now.' He shook his head. 'I can't tell you, but we're about ready to get her out of here.'

'I want to be informed of her status, and Mulligan's. I'm Lieutenant Dallas, out of Central.'

'I know who you are. Most of us do. I'll add it to the data. Bastards sure worked her over. Take them down hard, Lieutenant.'

She planned to.

'I want this scene secured,' she called out. 'I want sweepers in here. Everybody seal up, now. All records on, now. Suspects locked tight, examined and treated medically. By the book, people, every page of it.'

She walked over to Carmichael and Santiago. 'The scene's yours if you want it.'

'Then we've got it,' Santiago told her.

'Document everything, down to the last fleck of dust. Copy me, Whitney, Mira, Reo and Special Agent Zweck.'

Carmichael looked at the pool of blood on the plastic, the spatters of it, the smears of it on knives, hammers, screwdrivers, jags of glass.

'Sweat 'em hard, wring 'em dry.'

'Count on it.'

Eve stepped out into the cold, found it glorious after the stench. 'Thanks for the assist,' she said when Roarke stepped out beside her.

'Oh, no, I'll be seeing this one through. I shuffled some things, as I said, and I can get a bit of work done at Central. I'll enjoy seeing you sweat 'em hard, wring 'em dry.'

'She might not make it. I could see it in the MT's eyes. They don't think she'll make it. A few hours earlier . . . who knows.'

'Eve.'

'I know, I know. It's not on me, not on anybody but the two who did this to her. But she held out, with everything they did, she held out, held on. And now she might not make it.'

She rubbed her face hard.

'I need to contact her roommate.'

'I'll do that,' Peabody said from behind her. 'I'll make the contacts for both of them, Dallas. Maybe with friends there, with family, they'll both have a better chance. Banner and I will ride back with EDD, and I'll make the contacts.'

'All right, good. I'll brief Whitney – and get Mira in on this.' She blew out a breath that streamed away in a cloud. 'Let's get it done.'

She walked away from the nightmare of a dead man's apartment – remembered they had next of kin to notify there.

'Consider my arm wrapped around you.'

'What?'

He smiled at her. 'You'd object to such a gesture when cops can see you, but know it's there, to lean on.'

'I'm okay. We caught the bad guys.'

'Peabody knew you could do with a bit of alone with me. Use it.'

'He – Reed – he's hurt, but not as much as she is. They didn't hurt him as much because they needed him physically able to rape. He's going to make it, but . . . He might never get over what they made him do. He's just a guy, just a regular, apparently decent enough guy, and he'll have to live with this. They raped him, too. By forcing their will on him.'

'Mira, or someone like her, will help him understand that, and cope with it.'

'It takes a long time to cope. It takes a lot to cope with that. Some never get there.'

It put a hole in her belly remembering how close she'd been to never getting there.

'I don't think I would have gotten there without you. I wouldn't have gotten there, even with Mira, without you.'

'Now you've done it,' he murmured. 'Cops or no.' He wrapped one arm around her, then the other. 'You got there. We both did. And I wouldn't change a moment of the time, good or bad, we've had together since I first turned and locked eyes on you. What a jolt that was through me.' He touched his lips to her brow. 'I've never recovered.'

'Not even a minute of change?'

'Not one.'

'Because change one, change all.'

'Now you've remembered.'

'Okay.' She breathed deep, pulled back. 'No more sloppy stuff on the street.' She strode the few paces to the van, called into Feeney. 'Got their asses.'

'Now fry them up, kid.'

Roarke watched that hard grin flash on her face, and thought: There's my cop.

22

Revved and ready, Eve marched toward Homicide.

'You already know how you'll work them,' Roarke commented.

'Got a plan.' She slowed her pace when she spotted Zweck. 'May have to adjust it. Special Agent.'

'Lieutenant. We need to talk.'

'Sure. My office.' She gave Roarke a glance, led the way into the bull pen where every cop in the room gave Zweck the fish-eye.

She gestured Zweck back as Roarke wandered across the room, perhaps to admire Jenkinson's latest neckwear.

'Have a seat,' she invited, but Zweck just shook his head.

Reading him, Eve shut the door, then opted to edge down on the corner of her desk. 'Parsens and James are in custody.'

'I heard.'

'Clean op, no officers injured. The suspects are now being or have been treated by medical for minor injuries sustained during the op. Both Campbell and Mulligan were taken to

Clinton Hospital. The medicals on scene indicated Campbell's chances are rocky.'

His mouth tightened, just for an instant. 'I know who balled things up on our end.'

Recognizing barely suppressed rage when it was steaming barely a foot away, Eve only nodded.

'They're both superiors, but I intend to use your work on this, your reports and this morning's results to have them both reprimanded. They have superiors, too, and I'll go as far up the chain as it takes. My report on this morning's NYPSD operation will be delayed while I ... assess the details and make a determination.'

She nodded again. 'Okay. Understand, I want my shot at them, and Deputy Banner sure as hell deserves his, but I don't give a single cold damn who gets the media on it, or which jurisdiction locks them up for the rest of their sick, twisted lives.'

'The federal government will insist on hosting them for the rest of their sick, twisted lives, but in the meantime, take your shot. I'll make sure you have the time you need.'

'Good enough. Do you want a seat in Interview?'

'I'll observe for now.'

'Good enough. I'll set you up. Come,' she called out at the knock. Peabody poked her head in.

'Sorry to interrupt, but I thought you'd want to know the suspects have been cleared medically. Word is Whitney's on his way down, and Dr Mira is on her way.'

'Have them brought up, separate boxes. They can simmer awhile.'

Peabody flicked a glance at Zweck. 'Our boxes?'

'Yes, our boxes. Keep them separated.'

'I'll get out of your way,' Zweck said. 'Just let me know when you're ready to start on them.'

'I will.'

Peabody edged aside to let him out. 'He's not taking over?'

'Pissed at his own people, so he's flipping them the bird. He'll observe for now, give us first crack. So let's make it good. We'll switch off between you and Banner. I want to take James first, with Banner, move to Parsens, with you, back to James, probably you, back to James, Banner. But we'll see how it plays.'

'I'll set it up. Whitney,' Peabody added under her breath, but Eve had already heard his authoritative stride. 'Commander.'

'Detective. Good work. Lieutenant,' he said as he stepped into the doorway.

'Commander. I would have come to you.'

'I believe you've been and will be busier than I today.' He filled her office, a big man in a small room.

'Detective Peabody, bring them up.'

'Yes, sir.'

'I'll have a full written by end of day, Commander, but would like to start the interview process first. We have a window, provided by Special Agent Zweck to keep this in NYPSD hands.'

'One I'll widen if you need it. You brought them in, you'll close this down. Chief Tibble adds his weight to that – and his well-done.'

'Appreciated, sir.'

'APA Reo will participate at this point, but a federal prosecutor will take over. The suspects will be remanded to federal custody when we're done.'

'Understood, Commander, thoroughly.'

He smiled a little. 'Good. The media's been quiet on this because they haven't connected the dots, but this will explode, and soon. I believe the first leak started . . . ' Deliberately he consulted his wrist unit. 'About ten minutes ago.'

Which meant his hand had been on the tap.

'The NYPSD identified, located and apprehended the two individuals who cut a bloody swath across the country. Two individuals who took at least twenty-four lives since they began their murderous spree in August of last year. The feds can have their bite of the credit,' Whitney concluded, 'but they won't take the whole pie.'

'A good slice of that pie goes to Deputy Banner, sir.'

'Agreed, and the department will recognize his invaluable assistance. I have reason to believe the FBI will do the same.'

He turned when Mira and Reo came to the door.

'Jack, Eve.' Mira stepped in, then sideways to make room. 'You've been busy.'

'Heck of a morning already.' Reo, her sunny hair groomed, her eyes sharp and alert, set her briefcase on Eve's desk. 'Any way I can get coffee before we start?'

Eve edged over to the AutoChef.

'There has to be a way to widen this room,' Whitney commented. 'I can find it in the budget.'

'If it was bigger more people would come into it. Respectfully, sir,' Eve added as she programmed coffee.

Since she had time, she took it, filled in the details, outlined her basic strategy.

When she was alone in the office again, she took a deep breath. Four people in that space sucked up a lot of air. She put a file together, and went out.

'Banner, you're up first. Peabody, Observation. Tag Zweck, let him know we're starting. Where's James?'

'He's in Interview B.'

'He's first.'

Banner fell into step beside Eve. 'I appreciate the chance to sit in, Lieutenant.'

'You more than earned it.'

'Doesn't mean I can't appreciate it.'

'You get that NYPSD sweatshirt yet, Deputy?'

'I sure did.'

'Wear it proud. Here we go,' she said, and opened the door to Interview B. 'Record on. Dallas, Lieutenant Eve, Banner, Deputy William, entering interview with James, Darryl Roy, regarding cases H-52310, H-52314, H-52318 and connectings. Mr James, have you been informed of your rights?'

They'd cleaned him up, put some NuSkin on a cut above his left eyebrow, and dressed him in a prison jumpsuit. The virulent orange didn't do much for him. Nor did the purpling bruise on his jawline.

'Where's my Ella-Loo?'

'In custody, her ass in the fire, just like yours. Have you been informed of your rights?'

'I want to see her. I want to see her and make sure y'all didn't hurt her.'

Eve sat across from him, the table between them. Set the file down. 'You have the right to remain silent,' she began.

'They told me all that already. You want to bring Ella-Loo to me right now.'

'Then you've been informed of your rights?'

'I said so, didn't I?' He banged a fist on the table, restraints rattling. 'I don't say nothing about nothing until I see Ella-Loo.'

'You don't see Ella-Loo until you say something about everything.' Eve leaned back. 'Those rights you heard? That's all you get. The fact is, Darryl, I can make it so you never set eyes on her again.'

Rage rose up into his face in a red flood. 'You can't keep her from me. We're meant. We're true lifetime love.'

'You think? We'll see how "true", how "lifetime", she figures when she realizes that lifetime's going to be in an off-planet concrete cage.'

Now she leaned forward. 'You're going down and down hard, Darryl. Get that? Never going to see the true light of day again. This isn't going to be a couple years in the Oklahoma State Pen, with conjugals and visiting rooms, time to read and take classes. This is multiple, consecutive life sentences, the hardest of hard time.'

'You don't scare me. You come busting into our place—'

'Yours? Samuel Zed's.'

Darryl's look went sly. 'Sure, good old Sammy. He said how we could stay there. He had to go on a trip for a bit, and we could stay there, keep an eye on the place for him.'

'Is that so?'

'Sure is.'

'Did that trip include spending time floating in the Hudson River, without his fucking fingers?'

'Don't know what you're talking about.'

'Where'd you meet him?'

'Some bar or other.'

'What bar?'

Cocky, he smirked at her. 'Hell, honey, you've got so many of them, who knows?'

'Did Ella-Loo wag her tits at him, *honey*, lure him in?'

The red flood rose again. 'Don't you talk about my girl that way.'

'Did she promise to fuck him, so he'd bring her home? Which one of you smashed his teeth in? Which one of you cut off his fingers?'

'I don't know what you're talking about. If Zed got into trouble, got himself killed, it's not on us. We were just watching the place for him.'

'Were Jayla Campbell and Reed Mulligan watching the place, too?'

He aimed his gaze just above her head. 'I don't know who that is.'

She heard truth for the first time. He didn't even know their names. 'The two people you had tied down so you could torture them. So you and Ella-Loo could cut them and burn them and beat them because torturing and killing gets you off, you miserable fuck.'

He stretched his legs out under the table, sucked air through his teeth. 'You don't know nothing. We met up with the two of them, and they said they were into that sort of thing, that lots were here in the big city. We were all just fooling around, is all. They say different, they're liars and you can't prove otherwise.'

Eve opened the file, dumped photos of the tortured dead on the table. 'All these people, Darryl. Were all these people into it?'

'I don't know those people.' But he looked at them avidly, with hints of excitement and pride in his eyes.

Eve started to push up, increase the pressure. But in a quiet voice, Banner said, 'Melvin Little.'

'Say what?'

'Melvin Little. Right here.' Banner nudged the photo closer.

'Where you from?'

'Silby's Pond, Arkansas, same as him. He was a friend of mine.'

'I'm right sorry about your friend, but me and my Ella-Loo ain't never been to Silby's Pond.'

'You want to protect Ella-Loo, don't you, Darryl?'

'I'd do anything for her.'

With his finger he traced a heart over his chest.

'I'm not going to let anybody hurt her. I'd *die* for her.'

'I can see that.' A hint of admiration eked into Banner's tone. 'I can see the two of you are meant, just like you said. So you need to understand, we can prove what you did to my friend, and to all these others. We can prove you were in Silby's Pond, and how you and Ella-Loo met in the Rope 'N Ride back in Oklahoma.'

'"No sooner looked but they loved." That's Shakespeare, friend.'

'All right. We can prove you and Ella-Loo loved your way across country, how when you got out of prison, the two of you started east in the truck you'd stolen about four years before from Barlow Hanks.'

'Hell.' The cocky smirk came back. 'I gave Barlow cash money for that truck, and if he says different, he's a liar.'

'You crossed into Arkansas,' Banner continued in that same easy, conversational tone, 'and you killed Robert Jansen with a tire iron, took his car, and you drove on to Silby's Pond, and broke into that cabin. Then Little Mel came along.'

'Don't know those people,' Darryl said with the same stubborn stupidity. 'You saying so don't make it true.'

'We can prove all that, prove all these people died at your hands. You need to understand, Darryl, we're just giving you a chance to help yourself now and protect Ella-Loo. You don't tell us what you did, it's likely you won't see her again. It's likely they're going to put her someplace where somebody's going to hurt her 'cause you're not there to look out for her.'

Darryl leaned forward, fists clenched. 'I won't let you do that.'

Eve pushed up, out of the chair, changed the focus. 'We'll do what we want. Buy a clue, asshole. Think about it, think about Ella-Loo being in that cage where you can't get to her, can't touch her, can't help her. Think about it,' she repeated, tapping the table, the photos. 'And see if you remember any of these people when we come back. Dallas and Banner exited interview, record off.'

She stepped out. 'Not bad,' she said to Banner, 'not bad at all.'

'I wanted to reach over, take him by the throat, ram his face into the table until it was nothing but blood. I never felt that kind of violence in me before.'

'Killers can bring it out.' He'd gone a little pale, Eve noted, as he leaned back against the wall. 'Why don't you take a break?'

'I think I will. I'll come into the observation place, but I'm going to take a break first.'

She watched him go, then went back to her office, generated another set of photos before tagging Peabody on her comm. 'Heading for Parsens now.'

'I'm on the door.'

Different strategy, Eve decided, and said the same to Peabody. 'We hit her hard. No good cop.'

'Hot damn.'

'Put on your bitch face, Peabody.' Eve opened the door, noted orange didn't do much for Parsens, either. 'Record on. Dallas, Lieutenant Eve, and Peabody, Detective Delia, entering Interview with Parsens, Ella-Loo.' She fed in the case numbers, talking steadily as Ella-Loo bitched.

'You can't push me around this way! I'm all cut up. I want to go to the hospital. You molested me, you grabbed my tits. I don't want to talk to you.' And finally. 'What did you do with Darryl? I want my Darryl!'

'Have you been read your rights, Ella-Loo?'

'Fuck you and your rights. I want to go to the hospital. I want Darryl.'

'You've been medically cleared, and seeing Darryl's not going to happen. Probably ever.'

Pure shock leached color from her face. 'What do you mean "ever"? He's the husband of my heart and I got every right to see him.'

'The only rights you have are these: You have the right to remain silent.'

She continued to read out the Revised Miranda over

Ella-Loo's shouts and demands. 'Do you understand your rights and obligations?'

'I understand you're a titless bitch.'

'I can read them off again, and keep reading them off until you say, for the record, whether or not you understand them. Or we can go, leave you alone here to think about it for a few hours.'

'I understand them just fine. I want my own clothes, and I want Darryl, and I don't have to say nothing to some dyke cop.'

'We don't give much of a shit about what you want,' Peabody said, made Eve proud with the grinding, vicious tone she used. 'The only clothes you're going to be wearing from now on are what you've got and prison blues. You look like an overbaked pumpkin in orange, but I bet the women at Riker's are going to eat you right up.'

'I don't know what Riker's is, and I'm not going.'

'Just temporarily,' Eve continued. 'After a short stay I'm betting on Omega. That's off-planet. Jayla Campbell and Reed Mulligan – the two you were torturing when we met? They have a lot to say about you and Darryl.'

'They're liars. We were partying. No law against doing what you want to do in your own home. Consenting adults.'

'They consented to being bound, cut, burned, beaten, raped?'

'They're sick, that's what. Darryl and me were just going along, just experimenting. But we'd had enough and were going to make them get out of our place.'

425

'Your place?' Peabody roared it, grabbed the file, dumped the photos, found Samuel Zed. 'His place, you twisted twat. Are you so stupid you think cutting off his fingers meant we couldn't ID him? Look what you did to him.'

When Peabody shoved up, rushed around the table, pushed the photo in Parsens's face, Eve just sat back, let her ride.

Go, Peabody, she thought.

'Get away from me!' Ella-Loo shrieked it. 'Don't touch me. You're not allowed to put hands on me.'

'I'm allowed to do whatever the hell I want to sick, psychopathic sluts.'

'Are not! Darryl! Get her off me! I'll tell!'

'Tell who?' Eve wondered. 'Who's going to believe you over cops? And things happen to recordings all the time. Glitchy equipment. How about we unlock her restraints, Peabody? You can do what you did to the last one. I've got your back.'

Peabody bared her teeth; her eyes glittered. 'Let's go.'

When Eve started to rise, Ella-Loo tried to hunch into a ball. 'You can't, you can't. He attacked me, that's what happened. Darryl was just protecting me. That guy there, that guy he was trying to rape me, so Darryl protected me. It was self-defense.'

'And somehow in this self-defense, Samuel Zed lost all his fingers.'

'We . . . we were afraid. We were afraid we'd get in trouble, so we dropped him in the water.'

She kept herself hunched, shot hate-filled looks at Peabody.

'We needed a place to stay, so we went to where he lived. That's all we did. He was raping me, and Darryl stopped him. Darryl's a hero.'

'Clearly. Where were you when this alleged attempted rape occurred?' Eve asked.

'I don't know. We just got to New York City. It was dark. We were having a drink somewhere, and I just went outside for a minute, and this guy grabbed me and started tearing my clothes, and Darryl came out and stopped him.'

'Outside some bar, at night, in single-digit temperatures, some guy grabs you and tears at your clothes.'

'That's what happened. Self-defense.'

'Nobody noticed the attempted rape, the self-defense that resulted in a dead body. And somehow you still had time to dig out the dead man's identification, had time to transport said dead body – in the van you stole.'

Confusion flickered over her face. 'I – we – nobody wanted to help us. Nobody. We didn't steal nothing.'

'The van you stole,' Eve continued, 'from long-term parking at Newark Transportation. In your worry and distress – attempted rape, killing the alleged attacker, you devised a plan – not to run and leave the body, or contact the authorities, but to haul him up, bash in his face, cut off his fingers, stuff him in a bag with bricks and dump him in the Hudson.'

427

'We didn't want any trouble. We just borrowed that van. We were going to put it back.'

'Like you were going to put Robert Jansen's vehicle back?' Still snarling, Peabody shoved a new photo in Ella-Loo's face. 'After you beat him to death with a tire iron and dragged him into the brush off Highway 12 in Arkansas? Or did he try to rape you, too?'

'I don't—'

'Say you don't know what we're talking about.' Eve said it coldly, and had Ella-Loo's eyes shifting to hers. 'Just try it. Were they all self-defense and partying? I won't bother with names – you didn't know or care about names. 'From Highway 12 to Silby's Pond.'

As Eve ran through locations, Peabody grabbed each photo, pushed it in front of Ella-Loo's face.

'You're going away, and nothing's going to change that. Digest that for a while. Where you go, how long? You've maybe got a little wiggle room there. Are there more than this? That's one. And two, chapter and verse, Ella-Loo. You tell us everything you did, you and Darryl, and maybe we can make you a deal where you won't get eaten alive, where you've got some chance of getting out again. Keep up the bullshit, you're gone until you die.'

'I've got a kid!'

Now Eve rose, walked around, leaned down behind Ella-Loo. 'I know. I know you dumped her on your mother, just dumped her and walked away and haven't seen her since. Use

428

her, Ella-Loo? Use her and I'll find new ways to hurt you, ways that'll make what you and Darryl did to everyone on this table look like a picnic in a springtime meadow. That's a promise.'

Eve straightened. 'One chance, and one only. You tell us about everyone on this table. Details. And you tell us if there are any more. We have live witnesses, we have physical and forensic evidence, we have your trail, we've got everything we need to put you away. Keep lying, and we're done. You're in an off-planet hole for the rest of your life. And Darryl's in another. You'll never see each other again. Dallas and Peabody exiting Interview. Record off.'

Outside the room where Ella-Loo wept hysterically, Eve turned to Peabody. '"Twisted twat"? "Sick, psychopathic sluts"?'

'I liked the alliteration. It just came to me.'

Eve punched her shoulder, a sign of high marks. 'Scary Peabody did good.'

'I liked it. Scared myself a little, too, but I don't get the deal, Dallas. We don't need to deal on this.'

'If it plays out, you'll get it.' She went with Peabody to Observation. 'Banner, you're up. Agent Zweck, I'm going to set them up for you.'

'They both believed they could and would continue,' Mira told her. 'That they were entitled to as what they did brought them together, fulfilled their needs, enhanced what they see as their love. I don't believe she'll turn on him. She may, as she has done, insist he only protected her. But she's as devoted as he, on the basic level.'

'I don't need her to turn. It's going to be saving each other as much as themselves that locks it. Let's finish off Darryl. These two aren't going to take as long as I thought.'

With Banner she went back into the room, resumed recording, sat.

'Okay, Darryl, thinking time's up. Here's how it's going to go. Two choices now, the same two I just gave to Ella-Loo.'

'I want to see her. You have to let me see her. We swore we'd never be parted again.'

'No, I don't have to let you see her. But . . . ' She paused, as if thinking. 'I will if you choose wisely. Now, she's already told me some of it because she's looking out for herself, and for you, but this is only going to work if both of you cooperate.'

'What'd she say?'

'She loves you, Darryl, anybody can see that.'

'We're two people, but inside one heart.'

'Right. I know that's why you carved the heart with your initials into the people you killed for each other. Now, I can't tell you what she said or I'd be influencing your statement. I can only say she explained some of it to me. Like how you borrowed the van you've been using from long-term parking in Newark.'

'That's right. We just borrowed it. Nobody was using it.'

430

'And she told me about Samuel Zed. The man whose apartment you've been living in. You have to tell us what you did to him, Darryl. If you lie, that's it. It's over. The prosecuting attorney, she's pushing this hard. It's going to be what I told you before. Off-planet, forever, for both of you. The place they'll put her, Darryl, if this goes to trial in New York? If our PA takes it?'

Eve shook her head.

'The other inmates, the guards? They're going to look at a beautiful woman like Ella-Loo, somebody like her, and they're going to hurt her. They're going to do terrible things to her. I know you don't want that. I know you want to protect her. She told me how you protect her, always.'

'I do! And I will.'

'Then protect her now, Darryl, and I can work this with the State of New York, I can try to keep the two of you together. You're going in, that's something I can't do anything about. But if you give me what I need, I'll go to bat for both of you with the PA.'

'If I could just see her—'

'When we're done, I'll fix it so you see her.'

'Promise?'

'On the record, I promise when we're done, you'll see each other.'

'And we'll be together after?'

'As long as I'm in charge, you'll be together. But you have to tell us everything, on the record. If you lie, it's done.

431

We're going to start with Zed, the one you dumped in the river.'

'Okay. You gotta understand. It's all about love. Our love is bigger than anything else in the world. Ella-Loo really wanted to come to New York. It was her dream. And we needed a place to stay, a place to have our life here. She was talking up this guy, this guy here.' He tapped the picture. 'In the bar, and she got him to say where he lived, how he lived by himself and all that. It was meant, you see. It was like fate. After a while, she said how she'd like to see his place, and they went. Just a couple blocks away. And she made sure the door stayed unlocked.'

'Okay,' Eve prompted. 'That's good. Then what happened?'

'When I went in after them, he had his hands all over her. It just brought on the fury. We didn't mean to kill him so quick. It happened fast. We were going to keep him around, see how it all went, but he had his hands on her, so I hurt him more than I meant.'

'But you still kept him alive for a bit, right?'

'For a little while, yeah. He had to tell us some stuff so I could go on into his computer and send off an email to where he worked. Said he had a family emergency and had to be away for a while. Then we had to get rid of him, and we talked it over, and we took his fingers off, 'cause of the prints.'

'Was he still alive when you cut off his fingers? Remember, if you lie, I can't keep you and Ella-Loo together.'

432

Darryl wet his lips. 'Might be he was still alive for some of it. And when we beat up his face some, but he was dead pretty quick. Then I went out, and got some bricks from this place I saw where we were maybe going to stay. But it was too cold in there for Ella-Loo, so that's why we needed a real place.'

'If you're going to start a life together, you need a place.'

'And you wanted Zed's.'

'It was fate. Just like me and Ella-Loo finding each other. So we loaded him into a bag with the bricks, tied it up, and took him out to the river.'

'That's good, Darryl. Telling the truth's going to help. But I think you left something out. Something you and Ella-Loo did, together? After you killed Zed, before you dumped his body. Did you use his bed for it?'

He grinned now, wide. 'We couldn't wait for the bed. We've got such a powerful need for each other, and we were all keyed up from killing him so fast. The floor's a featherbed when you're in love.'

'So you ... made love,' Banner said, 'on the floor by the body?'

'Then we got the bag and the bricks.'

Sensing Banner's rage, Eve squeezed his wrist under the table. 'Okay, Darryl, we're on track now. Let's go back to the beginning. You can't leave anything out, or I can't protect Ella-Loo. Was Jansen, on Highway 12, the first person you killed together?'

'That guy in Arkansas? We didn't set out to kill him. We just needed a car as the truck was finished. Ella-Loo got him to stop, but then he started to fight me, and she had to hit him with the tire iron, and he fell hard. It was pure accident that time, that's the truth. We had to give him another whack or two, just to be sure, then we dragged him off into the brush, and we wiped down the truck real good, loaded our things into the car. Ella-Loo was all keyed up, you know. The blood and all. And we pulled off a ways down the road, and when we made love . . .'

His face lit up, all but glowed. 'It was like riding a shooting star. We knew nobody'd ever felt what we did. It wasn't the same when we did it again the next day, and we knew to reach up to heaven again that way, what we needed to do. It's what we had to do to fulfill ourselves and our destiny. What it was, was our true love right.'

'So the next time, you looked for someone.'

'Well, the next time, he kind of found us. We were just borrowing this cabin, over near Silby's Pond, and this guy, he comes in and he asks what we're doing, and says we shouldn't oughta be in there, 'cause we broke the lock. Just this pissant guy, talking a little crazy. So I hit him with the poker from the fireplace, then we thought maybe if we kept him around, took our time with it, we'd ride that shooting star longer. And we did. Lord knows, we rode that star.'

'Details, Darryl, and they need to match with Ella-Loo's.'

*

For the next two hours, he took them through every horrific detail of the bloody route across country.

Twice she sent Banner out for the sweet soft drinks James requested – and to give him a short break from the interview.

When it was done, she looked at the two-way glass, nodded.

'That's it, Darryl, that's all of it?'

'I swear to God, it is. If I left anything out it's 'cause I don't remember or got mixed up is all. You're going to fix it now so Ella-Loo and me can be together, so I can see nothing bad happens to her.'

'The deal's good as long as I'm in charge.'

On cue, Zweck stepped in with two agents he'd contacted. 'Darryl Roy James, you're under arrest for the murder of twenty-nine human beings, for the abduction, forcible imprisonment and torture of same. For the abduction, forcible imprisonment and torture of Jayla Campbell and Reed Mulligan, the attempted murder of Jayla Campbell and the rape of both Campbell and Mulligan.'

'I don't understand. I thought I was already under arrest.'

'By the NYPSD,' Eve said as she rose.

'You are now charged with federal crimes, and the FBI hereby takes jurisdiction of all matters pertaining. You're in federal custody, and will be transported to a federal facility.'

'With Ella-Loo?'

'Not a chance in hell.'

'But you promised!' Darryl rounded on Eve. 'You said!'

'As long as I was in charge.' She shrugged. 'Now I'm not. We're done.' She walked to Zweck, murmured something. He nodded.

'Hold him here,' Zweck ordered.

Eve walked out with Zweck and Banner while Darryl shouted for Ella-Loo.

'Peabody and I will wrap her up. Banner, you don't have to hear all this again.'

'I'm in it till it's done. I'm just going to contact my boss. I want to talk to him, then I'll be back to watch.'

'Same play?' Zweck asked as Banner walked off.

'Same play. Do me a solid, Zweck. Vendings hate me. Get a Pepsi.'

When she started to pull out credits, he shook his head. 'On me. I owe you more than a tube.'

'I'll take it.' And she drank deep, not deep enough to wash the sickness out, but deep.

Then she went in to do it all over again, hear it all over again, with Ella-Loo.

Epilogue

By the time it was done, she wanted a week's long shower, she wanted to sleep for a year.

Ella-Loo's recounting didn't vary by much. It might not have been as romantic as Darryl's, might not have included rides on shooting stars, but she rolled it all out.

Some was fear — fear for herself at the idea of being in a place where someone could do to her what she had done to others. And some was her sick and terrible need for the man who'd flipped that murderous switch inside her.

In the end, with Ella-Loo fighting the restraints, cursing Eve, screaming at the federal officers who hauled her up and out, Eve kept her promise.

They pulled Darryl out of his interview room at the same time.

And they saw each other.

'Darryl, Darryl, help me. Don't let them hurt me.'

He fought like a madman, screaming for her. 'Ella-Loo! I love you, Ella-Loo! I'll find you. They won't keep us apart.'

'I love you, Darryl! I'll wait for you. I'll wait forever!'

The feds pulled them off in opposite directions, with the corridor echoing with their desperate declarations of love.

Zweck held out a hand for Eve's. 'Lieutenant, anytime you need anything from me. Anything, anytime, you've got it.'

'Appreciate it. I'd like to know where they end up.'

'Worlds apart, Lieutenant. That much I can promise.'

When he walked off, Eve pressed her fingers to her eyes. When she dropped her hands, she looked straight at Roarke.

'You're still here?'

'I've come and gone a few times, but yes.' When he laid his hands on her shoulders, she gestured him into interview. Shut the door.

Then let herself lean, let herself be held.

'You always think, this is the worst. It can't be worse than this. You have to think it, or you can't do the job. You have to think it even knowing there's going to be worse. So far, this is the worst. Hearing them tell it, how they enjoyed it, how they needed it, how they got off on it – and that was how they defined love.'

'You abdicated to the FBI, did the work and handed the result to them. That's love. For the victims, for justice, for the job. And this is love.'

He drew her in again, laid his lips on hers. A long kiss, gentle and kind that brought the sting of tears to her eyes.

'I know it. Helps to hear it, but I know it. Need to pull it together.'

438

'I want to take you home.'

'Not yet. I need to contact Kuper's mother, tell her we got them.'

'Of course. Yes.'

'Maybe help her close a door. And I want to check on Campbell.'

'She's alive. Both Mira and Whitney have been checking. She's quite a fighter.' He drew her back, rubbed her shoulders. 'She's alive, and her chances are good now. She's not clear, but her chances are good. And she's not alone. She has friends and family with her, as does the boy. Mulligan.'

'Good, okay, good. That's a bright spot in this muck. And I've got another. You should come with me. You could use it, too.'

'I like bright spots.'

She started to open the door, looked back at him. 'Whatever came before, whatever comes after, I know what love is because of you.'

He took her free hand. 'Whatever came before, whatever comes after, it's you who've shown me love changes everything. Lifts everything. Gives everything.'

'We're going to have dinner tonight, just the two of us. No cops but me, no work. Like a date, okay?'

'Want a date, do you?'

It surprised her more than him. 'I really do.'

'Then it's more than okay.'

Steady again, she went out with him, and into Homicide.

'Wait for it,' she murmured to Roarke, and moved to Baxter's desk.

'Hell of a bust, LT.'

'One for the books. Listen, I know you've been anxious about Trueheart's results, but I've been kind of tied up with this pair of sadistic spree killers in love.'

'I got that. He's handling it. We've been busy, just closed the one we caught yesterday. I tried to find out, but it's going to take another twenty-four.'

'Huh. So you actually think I'd let two of my men sweat it for forty-eight? You figure I can't juggle in a contact, put a little weight on it?'

'You did? Hey, thanks, Dallas. Can I—'

He stopped when he caught the look on her face. 'Ah, shit.'

'Look, Baxter, it's a tough exam, and plenty don't cut it through on the first try.'

'Yeah, yeah, hell. I'd like to be the one to tell him. I can cushion it.'

'I thought you should. Figured you should be the one to tell Trueheart we're going to have a new detective in the division. He's getting his gold shield.'

'I'll— What?'

'What kind of cop doesn't know when he's being strung?'

'He passed.'

'He passed flying, Baxter. Be proud.'

'Holy shit. Holy shit.'

She saw the look in his eye when he surged up. 'Try to kiss me, Detective, you won't wake up for a week.'

'I gotta kiss somebody. Peabody.'

'What?'

Exhausted, she glanced over a second before he hauled her out of her chair, tipped her back smooth, and laid a healthy lip-lock on her.

'Hey, hey,' she finally managed as he swept her straight again.

'Trueheart!' he called. 'Front and center.'

'We catch one?' Trueheart hurried over, earnest and shiny in his uniform.

'Not this time. Congratulations, Detective.'

'I passed?' Trueheart's throat worked. 'I passed?'

'Flying, I hear.' He shook Trueheart's hand, then embraced him. 'Good work, partner.'

'I passed,' he said again, almost like a prayer, and shut his eyes.

When he opened them again, he looked straight at Eve. He exchanged another manly backslap with Baxter while the other cops in the room applauded. Then he stepped over to Eve.

'I wouldn't be here if it wasn't for you.'

'I dropped you in, you made the grade. Congratulations, Detective.'

He shook her hand, then wrapped his arms around her.

Because he was young, and it was a moment, Eve let him.

'Don't hug your LT,' she advised.

'Yes, sir. No, sir.' He broke away, laughing.

'The Blue Line,' Baxter announced. 'After shift. Every-damn-body. I'm buying. We're going to celebrate my boy here.'

Applause turned to cheers at the prospect of free drinks.

'I've got—'

Roarke squeezed Eve's shoulder to stop her from declining.

'Nothing either of us would rather do,' he finished.

He ran his hand down her back as cops got up to slap Trueheart's back, shake his hand, rag on him a bit.

'I told you no more cops tonight,' Eve reminded him. 'You don't have to do this.'

'His lieutenant should raise a glass to him, and I'd like to do the same myself. We've room for a few more cops in our bright spot. I've some things to see to. I'll find you, end of shift.'

Yeah, he would, she thought, watching him go. They'd raise a glass to a good, young cop. Maybe another to a hard job, well done. Then they'd have a date.

It wasn't a bad way to end a long day.

Read an extract from

BROTHERHOOD IN DEATH

The new J.D. Robb thriller

out February 2016

Prologue

Loyalty to the dead had him traveling to SoHo in icy rain rather than heading home. At home he could have put up his feet – tired today, he admitted. He'd have enjoyed a cozy fire, a good book and a small glass of whiskey while waiting for his wife to get home.

Instead, he sat in the back of a cab that smelled faintly of overripe peppers and someone's musky perfume, as it skated along the nasty street toward what he feared would be an ugly confrontation.

He disliked ugly confrontations, wondered sometimes about people who, by all appearances, enjoyed them. Those who knew him would say he had a talent for evading or diffusing them.

But this time, he expected to go head-to-head with his cousin Edward. A pity, really, he thought as he watched the ice-tipped rain strike the cab windows. It hissed as it struck, like angry snakes.

Once, he and Edward had been close as brothers. Once they'd shared adventures and secrets and ambition – lofty ones, of course. But time and divergent paths had separated them long ago.

He barely knew the man Edward had become, and understood him not at all. And sadly for him, liked Edward even less.

Regardless, they had shared the same paternal grandparents, their fathers were brothers. They were family. He hoped to use those blood ties, those shared experiences to bring their opposing views to some reasonable middle ground.

Then again, the man Edward had become rarely stood on middle ground. No, Edward staked a claim on his own ground and refused to move even an inch in any direction.

Otherwise, Edward would hardly have engaged a realtor to sell their grandparents' lovely old brownstone.

Why, he wouldn't even have known about the realtor, about the appointment made for a walk-through and assessment of the house if Edward's assistant to his assistant – or whatever title the girl owned – hadn't slipped up and mentioned it when he'd tried to contact Edward, arrange for a powwow.

He didn't have much of a temper – anger took such effort – but he was angry now. Angry enough he knew he could and would create a stink and a scene in front of the real estate person.

He had a half share of the property (as Edward had taken to calling it), and it couldn't be sold without his written consent.

He wouldn't give it; he wouldn't go against his grandfather's express wishes.

For a moment, in back of the cab, he was transported to his grandfather's study, with all its warmth and rich colors, its bookcases full of books smelling of leather binding, wonderful old photos, and fascinating memorabilia.

He could feel the frailty of his grandfather's hand, once so big and strong, in his. Hear the waver of a voice that used to boom like cannonfire.

It's more than a house, more than a home. Though that's a precious thing. It has a history, has earned its place in the world. It's earned a legacy. I'm trusting you, you and Edward, to honor that history, and continue that legacy.

He would, he told himself as the cab finally pulled to the curb. At best, he would remind Edward of those wishes, that responsibility. At worst, he would find a way to buy out his cousin's interest.

If it was only property, only money, then money Edward would have.

He overtipped the driver – purposely because the weather was truly horrible. It might have been the generosity that prompted the driver to roll down the window and call out that he'd left his briefcase in the back of the cab.

'Thank you!' He hurried back to retrieve it. 'So much on my mind.'

Gripping the briefcase, he navigated the ice rink of a sidewalk, walked through the little iron gate, and down the walkway – shoveled and treated as he personally paid a neighborhood boy to see to it.

He climbed the short flight of steps as he had as a toddler, a young boy, a young man, and now an older one.

He might forget things – like his briefcase – but he remembered the passcode for the main door. Laid his palm on the plate, used his swipe card.

He opened the heavy front door, felt the change like a fresh stab in his heart.

No scent of the fresh flowers his grandmother would have arranged herself on the entrance table. No old dog to lumber into the foyer to greet him. Some of the furniture sat in other homes now – specific bequests – as some of the art graced other walls.

He was glad of that, as that was legacy, too.

Despite the fact he also paid a housekeeper – the daughter of his grandparents' longtime employee, Frankie – to tend the place once a week, he scented the disuse as well as lemon oil.

'Long enough,' he muttered to himself as he set his briefcase down. 'It's been empty long enough now.'

He heard the sound of voices, and for a moment wondered if they, too, were just memories. Then he remembered his purpose – Edward and the realtor. They were, he imagined, discussing square footage and location and market value.

And neither thinking, as he was, of family dinners around the big table, of blackberry tarts filched from the kitchen, of proudly presenting the woman he loved to his grandparents in the living room on a sunny Saturday afternoon.

He forced himself to push through the mists of time, start back toward the voices. Sentiment wouldn't sway Edward, he knew. If another reminder of a promise made to a man they'd both loved didn't do so, perhaps the reminder of the legalities would.

Failing all, there was money.

Still, he didn't want to sneak up on them like a thief so called out his cousin's name.

The voices stilled, annoying him. Did they think they could hide from him? He continued back, clinging to the annoyance as a kind of weapon. And turning into the room he'd thought of in the cab, he saw Edward sitting in their grandfather's desk chair.

His cousin's eyes were wide – even the one swollen with a darkening bruise. Blood trickled in a thin line from the corner of his mouth, stained his teeth as he started to speak.

Annoyance forgotten in shock and concern, he stepped forward quickly.

'Edward.'

Pain erupted, a flash of fire bursting in the back of his head. Helpless to stop his own fall, he pitched forward. Seconds before his temple struck the old oak floor and turned everything black, he heard Edward scream.

1

After a long, tedious day – the first half spent in court, the second half with paperwork, Lieutenant Eve Dallas prepared to shut it all down.

At the moment all she wanted out of life was a quiet evening with her husband, her cat, and a glass – or two – of wine. Maybe a vid, she thought as she grabbed her coat, if Roarke hadn't brought too much work home.

Tonight – do the happy-time boogie – she was bringing home none of her own.

She could extend that wish list, she decided as she dug out the scarf her partner had made her for Christmas. Maybe a swim, and pool sex. She figured no matter how many deals Roarke needed to wheel, he could always be talked into pool sex.

She found the silly snowflake cap in another pocket of her long leather coat. Since the sky was heaving down ice, she tugged it on. She'd sent her partner home, had a couple of detectives out in the cold, working a hot. They'd contact her if they needed her.

She reminded herself she had another detective, newly minted, whose induction ceremony was slated for the next morning.

But right now, on a particularly ugly January evening, she had nothing on her plate.

Spaghetti and meatballs, she decided. *That's* what she wanted on her plate. Maybe she'd beat Roarke home, and actually put that together for both of them. With wine, a couple candles. Right down in the pool area – no, she corrected as she started out. Maybe at the dining room table, like grown-ups, with a fire going.

She could program a couple of salads, use a couple of his half a zillion fancy plates.

And while the ice snapped and crackled outside, they'd—

'Eve.'

She turned, spotted Mira – the department's shrink and top profiler – all but leaping off a glide and rushing toward her, pale blue coat flying open over her deep pink suit.

'You're still here. Thank God.'

'Just leaving. What's the deal? What's wrong?'

'I'm not sure. I . . . Dennis—'

Instinctively Eve reached up to touch the snowflake hat, one Dennis Mira had snugged down on her head in his kind way on a snowy day in the last weeks of 2060.

'Is he hurt?'

'I don't think so.' The normally unflappable Mira linked her fingers together to keep them still. 'He wasn't clear, he was upset. His cousin – he said his cousin's hurt, and now is missing. He asked for you, specifically. I'm sorry to spring this on you, but—'

'Don't worry about it. Is he home – at your place?' She had already turned away, called for the elevator.

'No, he's at his grandparents' – what was their home – in SoHo.'

'You're with me.' She steered Mira into the elevator, crowded with cops going off shift. 'I'll make sure you both get home. Who's his cousin?'

'Ah, Edward. Edward Mira. Former Senator Edward Mira.'

'Didn't vote for him.'

'Neither did I. I need a moment to gather my thoughts, and I want to let him know we're coming.'

As Mira took out her 'link, Eve organized her own thoughts.

She didn't know or care much about politics, but she had a vague image of Senator Edward Mira. She'd never have put the bombastic, hard-line senator – sharp black eyebrows, close-cropped black hair, hard and handsome face – on the same family tree as the sweet, slightly fuddled Dennis Mira.

But family made strange bedfellows.

Or was that politics?

Didn't matter.

The Eve Dallas series

Eve and Roarke are back in
Brotherhood in Death
out February 2016